THE
SPY COAST

www.penguin.co.uk

BY TESS GERRITSEN

RIZZOLI & ISLES THRILLERS

The Surgeon

The Apprentice

The Sinner

Body Double

Vanish

The Mephisto Club

Keeping the Dead

The Killing Place

The Silent Girl

Last to Die

Die Again

I Know a Secret

Listen to Me

STAND-ALONE THRILLERS

Girl Missing

Harvest

Life Support

The Bone Garden

Playing with Fire

The Shape of Night

THE
SPY COAST

TESS GERRITSEN

bantam

TRANSWORLD PUBLISHERS
Penguin Random House, One Embassy Gardens,
8 Viaduct Gardens, London SW11 7BW
www.penguin.co.uk

Transworld is part of the Penguin Random House group of companies
whose addresses can be found at global.penguinrandomhouse.com

Penguin
Random House
UK

First published in Great Britain in 2024 by Bantam
an imprint of Transworld Publishers

A CIP catalogue record for this book
is available from the British Library.

ISBNs
9780857505194 hb
9780857505200 tpb

Printed and bound in Great Britain by Clays Ltd, Elcograf S.p.A.

The authorized representative in the EEA is Penguin Random House Ireland,
Morrison Chambers, 32 Nassau Street, Dublin D02 YH68.

Penguin Random House is committed to a sustainable
future for our business, our readers and our planet. This book is made
from Forest Stewardship Council® certified paper.

To Will

CHAPTER 1
DIANA

Paris, ten days ago

She used to be the golden girl. *How things have changed,* she thought, staring in the mirror. Her hair, once artfully streaked with sun-kissed highlights, was now what could only be described as dead-mouse brown. It was the most unobtrusive shade of hair color she could find on the shelves at the Monoprix, where she'd gone shopping after a neighbor mentioned that a man had been asking about her. That was the first clue that something might be amiss, that someone was asking about her, although there could have been a completely innocent explanation. He might have been an admirer, or a man trying to make a delivery, but she did not want to be caught unprepared, so she'd headed across town to a Monoprix in the third arrondissement, a neighborhood where no one knew her, and she'd bought hair color and eyeglasses. These were items she should always have kept on hand, but over the years she'd grown complacent. Careless.

She studied herself as a brunette and decided that the new hair color was not enough. She picked up scissors and began to cut, ravaging her €300 hairstyle by L'Atelier Blanc. Every snip of the scissors was like another slash to the fabric of her new life, a life she'd so carefully curated. As handful after handful of freshly cut hair slithered onto the bathroom tiles, she kept snipping, her regret soon turning to rage. Everything she'd planned, everything she'd risked, was now all for nothing, but that was the way of the world. No matter how clever you think you are, there is always someone cleverer, and that was her mistake: not considering the possibility that she could be outsmarted. For too many years, *she* had been the smartest person in the room, the one who was always two steps ahead and could outmaneuver anyone else on the team. The secret to success was to not let the rules get in your way, an approach that others didn't always appreciate. Yes, mistakes were occasionally made. Yes, blood was sometimes unnecessarily spilled. She'd made enemies along the way, and some of her colleagues now despised her, but thanks to her efforts, the mission was always accomplished. That's what had made her the golden girl.

Until now. *Snip.*

She studied her reflection, this time with a cool and critical eye. In the ten minutes it had taken her to chop off her prized locks, she had gone through all the stages of grief for her lost life. Denial, anger, depression. Now she'd reached the stage of acceptance, and she was ready to move on, to shed the carcass of the old Diana and breathe into existence a new Diana. No longer the golden girl but someone seasoned by experience into tempered steel. She would survive this too.

She swept all her fallen hair into a trash bag and threw in the empty box of hair dye as well. She had no time to sterilize the place, so she'd leave behind traces galore of her presence here, but that could not be helped. She only hoped that the Paris police would rely on their typical sexist instincts to assume that the woman who'd lived in this apartment, the woman who was now missing, had been abducted. A victim, not a perpetrator.

She put on glasses and tousled her newly cropped hair into a messy swirl. It was merely a light disguise, but it should be enough to throw off any neighbors she might encounter on the way out. She tied off the trash bag and carried it out of the bathroom and into the bedroom, where she retrieved her go bag. What a shame she'd have to abandon all her beautiful shoes and dresses, but she needed to travel light, and leaving behind a closetful of designer fashions would make her disappearance look all the more involuntary. So would leaving behind the art she'd collected over the years, after her bank accounts had bloomed: the antique Chinese vases, the Chagall painting, the two-thousand-year-old Roman bust. She'd miss them all, but sacrifices had to be made if she was to survive.

Carrying her go bag and the trash bag with the hair clippings, she walked out of her bedroom and into the living room. There she gave another sigh of regret. Unsightly blood spatters stained her leather sofa and arced across the wall where the Chagall hung, like an abstract extension of the painting itself. Crumpled beneath the Chagall was the source of that blood. The man had been the first attacker through her door, so he was also the first one she'd dispatched. He was just your typical manly man whose hours at the gym had paid off in bulging biceps but not in brains. This was not how he'd expected the day would end for him, and he'd died with a look of surprise on his face, probably never expecting it would be a woman to take him down.

He must have been badly informed about his target.

She heard a whisper of a breath behind her and turned to look at the second man. He lay at the edge of her precious Persian carpet, his blood seeping into the intricate pattern of vines and tulips. To her surprise, he was still alive.

She walked over to him and nudged his shoulder with her shoe.

His eyes flickered open. He stared up at her and fumbled for his weapon, but she'd already kicked it out of his reach, and all he could do was flap his hand on the floor like a dying fish splashing in its own blood.

"*Qui t'a envoyé?*" she asked.

His hand flapped more frantically. The bullet she'd fired into his neck must have damaged his spine, and his movements were spastic, his arm jerking robotically. Maybe he didn't understand French. She repeated her question, this time in Russian: *Who sent you?*

She didn't see any glint of comprehension in his eyes. Either he was fading too fast for his brain to function, or he did not understand, both of which made this worrisome. She could deal with the Russians, but if someone else had sent these men, that would present a problem.

"Who is trying to kill me?" she asked, this time in English. "Tell me, and I'll let you live."

His arm stopped flopping. He had fallen still, but she saw comprehension in his eyes. He'd understood the question. He also understood that it really didn't matter if he told her the truth; either way, he was a dead man.

She heard men's voices in the hallway outside her apartment. Had they sent others as backup? She'd delayed too long, and there was no time left to interrogate this one. She aimed her suppressor and fired two bullets into his head. *Nighty night.*

It took her only seconds to scramble out the window and onto the fire escape. Her last glimpse of her apartment was bittersweet. Here she'd found a measure of happiness and enjoyed the well-earned fruits of her labors. Now the place was a slaughterhouse, with the blood of two nameless men polluting her walls.

She dropped down from the fire escape into the alley below. At 11:00 p.m., the streets of Paris were still lively, and she easily slipped in among the pedestrians strolling down the busy avenue. She heard a police siren in the distance, moving closer, but did not quicken her pace. It was too soon; the sirens had nothing to do with her.

Five blocks away, she tossed the trash bag into a restaurant dumpster and kept walking, the go bag slung over her shoulder. It held what she needed for the moment, and she was not without other resources. She had more than enough to start over.

But first, she had to find out who wanted her dead. Unfortunately, it was a multiple-choice question. She had assumed it was the Russians, but now she wasn't sure. When you piss off multiple factions, you end up with multiple enemies, each with his or her own talent for mayhem. The question was, how had her name been leaked? And why, after sixteen years, were they coming after her?

If they knew her name, then they must know about the others as well. The past, it seemed, was about to catch up with them all.

So much for a comfortable retirement. It was time to go back to work.

CHAPTER 2
MAGGIE

Purity, Maine, now

Something has died here.

I stand in my field, staring down at the evidence of slaughter in the snow. The killer dragged the victim through fresh powder, and even though snow continues to fall in a silent tumble of flakes, it has not yet covered the killer's tracks, or the grooves carved by the dead carcass as it was pulled toward the woods. I see a smear of blood and scattered feathers and clumps of black down trembling in the wind. It's what's left of one of my favorite Araucanas, which I prized for her reliable production of pretty blue eggs. Although death is merely a pinpoint in the larger circle of life, and I have seen it many times before, this particular loss hits me hard and I sigh, sending my breath swirling into the cold.

I glance through the chicken fence at what's left of my flock, which is now down to three dozen chickens, barely two-thirds of the original fifty chicks I nurtured last spring. It's been only two hours since I opened their coop door and released them for the day, and in that brief window of time, the predator moved in. I have one last rooster, the only one who's survived repeated eagle attacks and raccoon depredations, and he now struts the enclosure, all his tail feathers intact, looking unalarmed by the loss of yet another of his harem. What a useless cock.

So many of them are.

As I rise back to my feet, a flicker of movement catches my eye, and I stare at the woods looming beyond the chicken fence. The trees are mostly oak and maple, with a few sorry spruces struggling in the shade of their overpowering neighbors. Almost hidden in the underbrush is a pair of eyes, and they are watching me. For a moment we simply stare at each other, two enemies facing off across a snowy battlefield.

Slowly I move away from my mobile henhouse. I make no sudden movements, utter no sound.

My enemy watches me the whole time.

Frozen grass crunches beneath my boots as I ease toward my Kubota RTV. Quietly I swing open the door and reach in for my rifle, which is tucked in behind the seats. It is always kept loaded, so I don't need to waste time scooping up ammo and sliding in bullets. I swing the barrel around, toward the trees, and take aim.

My shot cracks, loud as thunder. Startled crows rise from the trees and frantically flap into the sky, and my squawking chickens make a panicked dash for the safety of their henhouse. I lower the rifle and squint at the trees, scanning the underbrush.

Nothing moves.

I drive my RTV across the field to the edge of the woods and climb out. The underbrush is thick with brambles, and the snow hides a layer of dead leaves and dried twigs. Every step I take sets off an explosive snap. I have not yet spotted any blood, but I'm certain I will find it because you always know—somehow you can feel it in your bones—when your bullet hits its mark. At last I see the proof that my aim was true: a blood-spattered bed of leaves. The mangled carcass of my Araucana hen lies abandoned where the killer dropped it.

I wade deeper through the underbrush, pushing aside branches that snag my trousers and claw at my face. I know it is here somewhere, if not dead, then gravely injured. It has managed to flee farther than I expected, but I keep pushing ahead, the steam from my breath spiraling away. Once I could have sprinted through these woods, even with a heavy rucksack on my back, but I am not the woman I once was. My joints have been worn down by punishing use and the inexorable passage of time, and a hard landing from a parachute drop left me with a surgically pinned ankle that aches whenever the temperature drops or the barometer falls. My ankle is aching now. Aging is a cruel process. It has stiffened my knees, lacquered my once-black hair with silver, and deepened the grooves in my face. But my vision is still sharp, and I haven't lost my ability to read the landscape, to interpret the clues in the snow. I crouch down over a paw print and note the speckle of blood on the leaves.

The animal is suffering. That is my fault.

I haul myself back to my feet. My knees and hips protest, unlike the days when I could launch myself out of a cramped sports car and take off at a sprint. I tramp through a patch of blackberry bushes and emerge into a clearing, and there I finally locate my nemesis, lying motionless in the snow. A female. She looks healthy and well nourished, and her thick fur is a lustrous red. Her mouth hangs open, revealing razor teeth and jaws powerful enough to slice into a chicken's throat and snap its neck. My bullet hit her squarely in the chest, and I am surprised she made it this far before she collapsed. I prod the body with my boot, just to confirm she's dead. While this particular problem has been solved, taking the fox's life gives me no sense of satisfaction. When I heave out a breath, my sigh is the sound of regret.

At sixty years old, I have amassed more than my share of them.

The fur is too valuable to abandon here in the woods, so I grab the fox by its tail. She's been eating well, dining on my chickens, and she's so heavy I have to half drag her out of the woods, her body carving a trench through dead leaves and snow. I lift her up and roll her into the bed of my Kubota, and the carcass lands with a sad thump. While I have no use for the pelt, I know someone who'll be delighted to have it.

I climb into the Kubota and drive across the field, to my neighbor's house.

*

Luther Yount likes his coffee burned, and I can smell it from his driveway as I climb out of the RTV. From here, I can see across the snow-covered field to my own farmhouse, which stands on a knoll beyond a colonnade of handsome sugar maples. Mine is not a grand house, but it's solid enough, built in 1830, according to the real estate agent who sold it to me. I know her information is correct, because I tracked down the original deed for Blackberry Farm. I believe only what I can confirm for myself. My home has unobstructed views in every direction, and if someone is approaching, I will see them, especially on a clear winter morning, when the landscape is stark and white.

I hear the lowing of a cow and the squawk of chickens. A set of small boot prints track through the snow, heading from Luther's cabin toward the barn. His fourteen-year-old granddaughter, Callie, must be in there, tending to her animals, as she does every morning.

I thump up the porch steps and knock. Luther opens the door, and I inhale the skunky scent of coffee that's been left too long on the stove. He fills the doorway, a white-bearded Santa in a red plaid shirt and suspenders, and he's wheezing from the woodsmoke and the perpetually dusty state of his cabin.

"Why, good morning, Miss Maggie," he says.

"Good morning. I've brought a gift for you and Callie."

"What's the occasion?"

"No occasion. I just thought you'd find some use for it. It's in the Kubota."

He doesn't bother to pull on a coat, instead stepping outside in his wool shirt and blue jeans and bog boots. He follows me to the RTV and gives a murmur of admiration as he looks down at the dead fox and then strokes its fur.

"She's a real beaut. So that's the gunshot I heard this morning. You take her down with one bullet?"

"She still managed to run fifty yards into the woods."

"She's probably the same one who took out two of Callie's hens. Good job."

"Still, it's a shame. The fox was just trying to make a living."

"Aren't we all?"

"I thought you could use the pelt."

"You sure you don't want to keep it? It's a nice one."

"And you'll know exactly what to do with it."

He reaches into the truck bed and hauls out the carcass. The effort makes him wheeze more loudly. "Come on in," he says, cradling the dead animal like a grandchild. "I just poured myself some coffee."

"Um, thanks. But no."

"Then at least let me send you home with some fresh milk."

That I definitely welcome. The milk from Callie's grass-fed Jersey cow is unlike anything I'd tasted before I moved to Maine, rich and sweet enough to be worth the risk of drinking it unpasteurized. I follow him into his home, where he drops the fox carcass on a bench. The poorly insulated cabin is only marginally warmer inside than it is outside, even with the heat from the woodstove, so I leave my coat on, but Luther seems perfectly comfortable in just his shirt and jeans. I don't want his coffee, but he sets two mugs on the kitchen table anyway. It would be rude to refuse the invitation.

I sit down.

Luther slides a pitcher of cream to me. He knows the way I like my coffee—or at least the only way I can tolerate his coffee—and he also knows I can't resist the cream from Callie's cow. In the two years since I moved onto the adjoining property, he's no doubt gleaned a number of details about me. He knows that I turn off my lights every night around 10:00 p.m., that I'm up early to feed and water my chickens. He knows I'm a novice at tapping maple trees, that I mostly keep to myself, and that I don't throw loud parties. And today he's learned I'm a decent shot. There's still a lot about me that he doesn't know, things I've never told him. Things I will never tell him. I'm grateful he's not the kind of man who asks too many questions. I value a neighbor who's discreet.

I do know a great deal about Luther Yount, though. It's not hard to pick up the essence of the man just by looking around his home. His bookshelves are handmade, as is the rough-hewn kitchen table, and bundles of dried thyme and oregano, both cut from his home garden, hang from the overhead beam. He also has books—lots and lots of books, about a confoundingly wide range of subjects, from particle physics to animal husbandry. Some of the textbooks bear his name as author, evidence of Luther Yount's previous incarnation as a professor of mechanical engineering, before he resigned from the faculty of MIT. Before he left behind academics and the city of Boston, and perhaps a few personal demons as well, to remake himself as this disheveled but happy farmer. I know all this about him not because he's told me, but because I delved thoroughly into his background, as I did with all my nearby neighbors, before I bought Blackberry Farm.

Luther passed inspection. That's why I feel perfectly at ease sitting at his kitchen table and sipping his coffee.

Boots thump onto the porch, and the door swings open, admitting a blast of cold air along with fourteen-year-old Callie. Luther is home-schooling her, and as a result, Callie is charmingly feral in ways that make her both wiser yet more naive than other girls her age. Like her grandfather, she's serenely disheveled, her barn coat streaked with dirt and stray chicken feathers trapped in her brown hair. She carries in two baskets of freshly collected eggs, which she sets down on the kitchen counter. Her face is so flushed from the cold that her cheeks look as if they've been slapped.

"Hey, Maggie!" she says as she hangs up her coat.

"Look what she brought us," Luther says.

Callie looks at the dead fox lying on the bench and runs her hand across the fur. She shows no hesitation, no squeamishness. She's been living with Luther for most of her life, ever since her mother died of a heroin overdose in Boston, and life on this farm has taught her to be unsurprised by death.

"Ooh. It still feels warm," she says.

"I brought it straight over," I say. "Thought you and your grandpa could make something nice with it."

She beams at me in delight. "The fur's so beautiful. Thank you, Maggie! Do you think there's enough to make a hat?"

"I'd say so," says Luther.

"Do you know how to make one, Grandpa?"

"We'll look it up, figure it out together. Can't let something that pretty go to waste, eh?"

"I'd like to see how you do it, Luther," I say.

"Want to see how I skin it too?"

"No, I already know how to do that."

"Do you?" He laughs. "You always manage to surprise me, Miss Maggie."

Callie sets the egg baskets in the sink. With the tap running, she begins spot-cleaning the eggs with a rag so they'll look pristine in their cartons. At the local co-op, they'll sell for seven bucks a dozen, which is a bargain for free-range organic eggs, considering the labor and feed and the perpetual battles with bobcats and foxes and raccoons. Not that Luther and Callie depend on egg sales for their livelihood, because Luther has a sizable investment account. It's another little detail about him that I managed to unearth. These are Callie's chickens and Callie's earnings, and she is already a fine businesswoman. I've never met a fourteen-year-old who can so efficiently slaughter and gut an old layer hen.

"It's sad you had to shoot her, but I've lost too many of my hens too," Callie says.

"Some other predator will just move in," Luther says. "Way of the world."

Callie looks at me. "How many did you lose?"

"Half a dozen just this past week. The fox took one of my Araucanas this morning."

"Maybe I should get some Araucanas. Customers seem to like those blue eggs. I could probably charge more for them."

Luther grunts. "Blue eggs, brown eggs. They all taste the same."

"Well, I should probably get going," I say, and stand up.

"So soon?" says Callie. "You hardly got a chance to visit."

It's a rare fourteen-year-old who craves conversations with a woman my age, but Callie is an unusual girl. She is so at ease in the company of adults that I sometimes forget how young she is.

"When your grandpa gets around to sewing that fox hat, I'll be back," I say.

"And I'll make chicken and dumplings for dinner."

"Then I'll most certainly be back."

Luther gulps down the rest of his coffee and rises to his feet as well. "Wait, let me get that milk I promised you." He opens the refrigerator, setting off the musical clink of glass milk bottles on the shelves inside. "If it weren't for these blasted health regulations, we could sell our milk off the farm stand. Just sit back and collect the money."

Money that he doesn't need. Some people like to flaunt their wealth, but Luther seems embarrassed by his. Or maybe it's a tactic for self-preservation, hiding what others might want to take from you. He takes out four glass bottles of milk, each topped by a thick layer of cream, and sets them in a paper bag. "Next time someone drops by your house, Maggie, let 'em have a taste of this. Then you send 'em straight over here to buy more. A strictly private sale, of course. Keep the state of Maine out of our hair."

I'm already at the door with my prized milk when I register what he's just said to me. I turn back to him. "What do you mean, *next* time?"

"Didn't someone come by to see you yesterday?"

"No."

"Humph." He looks at Callie. "Maybe you heard wrong."

"Heard what wrong?" I ask.

"There was a lady at the post office," says Callie. "I was picking up our mail when I heard her ask the postmaster how to get to Blackberry Farm. She told him she was a friend of yours."

"What did she look like? Young, old? What color was her hair?"

My rapid-fire questions seem to take Callie aback. "Um, she was young, I guess. And really pretty. I didn't see her hair because she was wearing a hat. And a nice down jacket. A blue one."

"You didn't tell her how to find my place, did you?"

"No, but Greg at the PO told her. Is something wrong?"

I don't know the answer. I stand there by their open door, holding my bag of milk bottles, the cold air sweeping in past me. "I wasn't expecting anyone. I don't like surprises, that's all," I say, and walk out of their cabin.

Is something wrong?

The question still unsettles me when I later drive into town to pick up supplies. Who is asking for directions to my farm? The query could be perfectly innocent, asked by someone in search of the previous owner, unaware that the woman passed away three years ago at age eighty-eight. She was, by all accounts, legendary for her sharp wit and her bad temper. My kind of woman. That *would* be the logical reason for a visitor to ask about Blackberry Farm, because there's no reason for anyone to come looking for me here. In the two years I've lived in Purity, Maine, nobody has.

I want to keep it that way.

In town, I make my usual rounds: to the feedstore, the post office, the grocery store. These are all places where I easily blend in with other silver-haired women, all of us bundled up in our winter jackets and scarves. Like them, I seldom draw a glance of interest. Old age confers anonymity, which makes it the most effective disguise of all.

In the village grocery store, I go unnoticed as I wheel my cart up and down the narrow aisles, picking up oatmeal and flour, potatoes and onions. Eggs, at least, I will never have to buy. The liquor selection in this little town is pitiful, but they do carry two different brands of single-malt scotch, and even though neither is particularly to my taste, I buy a bottle anyway. I am trying to preserve my supply of thirty-year Longmorn, and I do not know when I'll be able to find another source for it. Any whisky is better than no whisky.

As I stand in line waiting to pay for the groceries, I could be mistaken for just another farmer or housewife or retired teacher. For years, I taught myself not to stand out, not to draw attention, and now it comes effortlessly, which is both sad and also a relief. Sometimes I miss the days when I was noticed, the days when I wore short skirts and spike heels and could feel men's gazes on my body.

The checkout clerk rings me up, then does a double take when she sees my tab. "That'll be, um—wow. Two hundred ten dollars." She looks up at me, as if expecting me to dispute it, but I don't. It's because of the whisky. It's not even my favorite, but some things in life count as necessities.

I pay the bill and carry the bags outside. I'm loading them into my pickup when I glimpse Ben Diamond, wearing his usual black leather jacket. He's walking into the Marigold, the café across the street. If anyone in this town has his fingers to the wind, it's Ben. He might know who's been asking about me.

I cross the street and follow Ben into the Marigold.

I immediately spot him sitting with Declan Rose in a corner booth. As usual, both men sit facing the entrance, a habit they cannot shake, even in retirement. Declan looks like the history professor he used to be, with his tweed jacket and his handsome lion's mane of hair. At sixty-eight, his once-black hair is half-silver, but it's still as thick as it was when I met him, nearly four decades ago. Unlike the professorial Declan, Ben Diamond looks vaguely menacing, with his shaved head and black leather jacket. It takes innate command presence to pull off a look like that at age seventy-three, but Ben still has it. As I walk toward their booth, they both look up.

"Ah, Maggie! Join us," says Declan.

"Haven't seen you in a while. What've you been up to?" Ben asks.

I slide into their booth. "I had a fox problem to deal with."

"I'm guessing the fox is now deceased."

"As of this morning." I look up as the waitress passes by. "Coffee, please, Janine."

"Menu?" she asks.

"Not today, thanks."

Ben is studying me. Reading faces is a talent of his, and he must sense there's a purpose to my joining them today. I wait until Janine is out of earshot before I ask the men my question.

"Who's been looking for me?"

"Is someone looking for you?" Declan says.

"There was a woman, someone new in town. I heard she was in the post office yesterday, asking how to find Blackberry Farm."

The men glance at each other, then at me.

"News to me, Maggie," says Ben.

Janine brings my coffee. It's weak, but at least it's not burned like Luther's. We wait until she walks away before we speak again. It's just force of habit for us. The reason the men always choose this booth is because it feels like a safely isolated outpost, far from inquisitive ears.

"Are you worried about this?" Declan asks.

"I don't know if I should be."

"Did she ask for you by name? Or just the farm's name?"

"Only the farm. It may mean nothing. How would she know I'm the one who lives there?"

"They can find out anything if they really want to."

We pause as two customers get up from their table and walk past us, toward the cashier. The silence gives me a chance to consider Declan's words. *If they really want to.* That's what I count on these days, that I'm not worth the trouble to track down. There are always bigger fish to fry, and I'm just a small fish. Or maybe a medium-size fish. Why go to the effort of tracking down a woman who doesn't want to be found? Over the sixteen years since my retirement, I've slowly let down my guard. Now I'm so accustomed to being a small-town chicken farmer that I've started to believe that's all I am. The way Ben's just a retired salesman for hotel supplies, and Declan's just a retired history professor. We know the truth, but we keep each other's secrets, because we each have our own to guard.

There's safety in mutual blackmail.

"We'll put our ears to the ground," says Ben. "Find out who this woman is."

"I'd appreciate it, thank you." I put down two dollars for the coffee.

Declan says, "Are you coming to tonight's book group? It's been two months since you last attended. We miss you."

"Which book are you discussing?"

"*The Travels of Ibn Battutah.* Ingrid chose it," says Ben.

"I've already read that one."

"Then you can give us the CliffsNotes," says Declan, "because Ben and I haven't done our homework. We're meeting at Ingrid and Lloyd's house tonight. Six o'clock, martinis. With a few of those under our belts, maybe we can skip over discussing the book and get straight to the local gossip instead. Can we count you in?"

"I'll think about it."

"That's no kind of answer," Ben growls. He's trying to bully me into attending. I've always wondered how well that gangster persona worked for him when he was in the field. He's certainly never scared me.

"Okay, I'll be there," I say.

"And I'll make sure your favorite vodka's on ice," says Declan.

"Belvedere."

Declan laughs. "Really, Mags. Do you think I'd forget that detail?"

Of course he knows my preferred vodka. Inside Declan's handsome head of hair is a brain for details and a talent for foreign languages that's allowed him to master seven. I gave up at three.

Back in my truck, I drive home across back roads that are bumpy with frost heaves, through a black-and-white landscape of bare trees and snow-covered fields. This is not where I saw myself landing at the end of my life. I grew up in a place of dust and heat and blindingly bright summers, and my first winter in Maine was a challenge. I learned how to split firewood and drive on ice and thaw frozen pipes, and I learned that one is never too old to adapt. When I was young and imagined the setting for a perfect retirement, I dreamed it would be a hilltop villa in Koh Samui, or a tree house on the Osa Peninsula, where I would be serenaded by birds and howler monkeys. These were places I knew and loved, places that, in the end, I could not flee to.

Because that's where they would expect me to be. Being predictable is always the first mistake.

An alarm beeps on my phone.

I glance down at the screen, and what I see makes me hit the brakes. I pull off to the side of the road and stare at the images. It's the video feed from my security system. Someone has just entered my house.

I could call the local police to respond, but they'd certainly ask questions, which I may not want to answer. Purity's police department is manned by only six full-time officers, and up till now, I haven't had any reason to interact with them. I want to keep it that way, even if it means I have to deal with this on my own.

I pull back onto the road.

My pulse has kicked into a quick gallop by the time I drive past the colonnade of sugar maple trees and pull up in front of my farmhouse. For a moment, I remain in my truck as I eye the porch. Nothing looks out of the ordinary. The front door is closed, and my snow shovel is where I left it, leaning against the stack of firewood. The intruder wants to lull me into believing everything is fine.

So that's how I will play it.

I climb out of the truck and carry the sack of potatoes and the chicken feed up to the porch. There I drop them, letting them land with a loud thump. As I pull out my house keys, every nerve feels exquisitely fine tuned, magnifying every sensation. The rustle of the tree branches, the kiss of the cold wind on my cheek.

I notice that the filament on my doorjamb has been broken.

It's such a primitive tactic in this electronic age of home surveillance, but digital systems can fail, or they can be hacked. Over the last few months I have grown careless, not always bothering to press that filament, as fine as a spiderweb, into place, but what I heard in Luther's house this morning made me resume this precaution.

I unlock the door and nudge it open with my boot, and the mudroom comes into view. My shoes are lined up under the bench, my coats hanging on the hooks. The floor is grainy with tracked-in sand and dirt.

So far, everything looks normal. To my left is the living room. I glance through the doorway and see the sofa, the wing chairs, the stacked firewood by the hearth. No intruder in sight.

I turn right and step into the kitchen, avoiding the floorboard that invariably creaks. I see my coffee cup and breakfast dishes in the sink, grapefruit rinds in the compost bucket. Spilled granules of sugar sparkle on the table. All is as I left it, except for one thing: the scent of an unfamiliar shampoo.

That troublesome floorboard creaks behind me. I turn and face the intruder.

She is young and lithe, and she moves with the easy grace of an athlete. Early thirties, with straight black hair and blunt bangs, dark eyes, Slavic cheekbones. She seems remarkably unruffled, despite the fact the barrel of my Walther, which I've been carrying ever since my conversation with Callie this morning, is now pointed at her chest.

"Hello, Maggie Bird," she says.

"I don't believe we've met."

"Why did you choose that particular name?"

"Why not?"

"Let me guess. Bird, as in 'free as a bird'?"

"A girl can dream."

She pulls out a chair. Sits down at my kitchen table and casually brushes aside the sugar granules I spilled at breakfast, seeming not to care that I'm one trigger-pull from blowing her away. "There's really no need for that," she says, nodding at my Walther.

"I'll decide that. Right now, I'm looking at someone who entered my house, uninvited. I have no idea who you are, or why you're here."

"Please, call me Bianca."

"Real or alias?"

"Does it matter?"

"The police will need a name for the corpse."

"Oh, please. I'm here because we have a problem. And we could use your help."

I regard her for a moment, taking in the relaxed shoulders and the long lean legs, now lazily crossed. She's not even looking at me; instead, she's casually picking at a hangnail.

I sit down across from her and set my Walther on the table.

She glances at the gun. "Yes, I can understand why you might feel the need for that. You have a reputation for not trusting people."

"I have a reputation?"

"That's why they sent me. They thought you'd consider a woman to be less threatening."

"If you know anything at all about me, then you also know I'm no longer in the game. I'm a chicken farmer. I like being a chicken farmer."

There's not even a twitch of a smile on her lips. She has no sense of humor but is all business, a woman on a mission. The Agency has clearly stepped up its recruiting game since I worked for them.

"I don't know why they sent you," I say. "But now that you've seen me, you know I'm no longer in my prime, and I'm also rusty. I'm not interested in doing any more work for them."

"There'd be a paycheck for you."

"I have all the money I need."

"It could be substantial."

I frown. "Really? That doesn't sound like my cheap Uncle Sam."

"This assignment will have special significance for you."

"Still not interested." I rise from the chair, and even though getting up that quickly makes my knee twinge, I'm too proud to let her hear me groan or see me grimace. "I'll walk you out now. Tell them that the next time they send someone to talk to me, have that person knock on my door, like any normal visitor would."

"Diana Ward has dropped off the radar."

I go still. For a moment I just stare at her, trying to read her face, but all I see is cool perfection and an utterly expressionless face.

"Alive or dead?" I ask.

"We don't know."

"Last seen where?"

"Physically? Bangkok, a week ago. Since then, she's vanished, and her cell phone has gone silent."

"She's been retired for years. Left the Agency soon after I did. Why do you care where she is now?"

"We're concerned about her well-being. Actually, we're concerned about everyone who was involved with Operation Cyrano."

I can't hide my reaction to hearing those two words. I feel the shock of it reverberate through my bones, as powerful as a concussion blast. "Why is this coming up now?"

"There was a recent breach of the Agency's automated information services. That unauthorized access set off an alert, but the only file the intruder accessed was the one for Operation Cyrano."

"That op was sixteen years ago."

"And the information remains classified, for the safety of everyone involved. But now, I'm afraid your names may have been leaked, and that's why we're tracking you all down, to check on your welfare. To see if you're in need of help. I must say, I never expected you to end up in a place like *this*." She looks around at my pine table, at the hanging rack of cast-iron pans. Outside it's started to snow, and fat flakes swirl beyond the window, the kind of snow that's a delight to walk in. Bianca doesn't look like a woman who delights in snowflakes.

"As you can see, I'm settled in here, and I have a new name," I tell her. "I'm perfectly safe."

"But Diana may be in trouble."

"Diana in trouble?" I laugh. "Yeah, that's a given. But she's a survivor, and she's perfectly capable of looking out for herself. Now, if that's all you came to ask, it's time for you to leave." I go to the front door and yank it open. Despite the cold air rushing in, I hold it open, waiting for my unwanted visitor to walk out.

Bianca finally steps onto the porch, then turns to look at me. "Help us find her, Maggie. You must know where she's gone. You worked together."

"Sixteen years ago."

"Still, you probably know her better than anyone."

"Yeah, you're right. I probably do. That's why I don't give a fuck what happens to her," I say, and I close the door in her face.

CHAPTER 3
JO

Some men just need a good stabbing, thought Jo Thibodeau as she watched the paramedics load Jimmy Kiely's stretcher into the ambulance. He'd almost certainly survive his wounds, and depending on one's point of view, that was either a good thing or a bad thing. A good thing, because his wife, Megan, wouldn't have to face a murder charge. A bad thing, because it meant Jimmy would be back to make Megan's miserable life even more miserable, forcing Jo and her officers to intervene once again in this couple's never-ending drama. Even in a town as small as Purity, there was always drama, sometimes behind closed doors where no one else could hear the sobs or the fists thudding into flesh. Sometimes those private dramas spilled out into the open, and neighbors who'd seen the black eyes and perpetually closed drapes would nod and say to each other: *We knew this would happen someday.*

Tonight it did happen, and a dozen of those neighbors now stood in the parking lot of the Whale Spout pub, listening to Jimmy yell threats from the back of the ambulance, shouts that were loud enough to be heard over the music that was blaring from the bar.

"Just you wait, bitch! Wait till I get home!"

Too bad the knife had missed Jimmy's lungs.

"You're gonna be sorry! Just you wait!"

Lights flashing, the ambulance drove away, and Jo let out a sigh, exhaling a cloud of steam in the frigid air. The crowd in the bar's parking lot made no move to disperse because this was the most exciting thing that had happened in Purity since Fernald Hobbs suffered a stroke behind the wheel of his pickup and rolled straight through the boatyard and into the harbor. Even though it was fifteen degrees tonight and starting to snow again, they stood staring as though mesmerized by the rack lights of the two patrol cars. When you grow up in Maine, fifteen degrees is a balmy night for February.

"Please go home, folks!" Jo called out. "There's nothing to see here."

"He had it coming, Jo!" Dorothy French yelled.

"That's for a jury to decide. Now please, head on home before you all get frostbite. The bar's closed for the night."

With the town's only winter drinking establishment shut down for the evening, maybe the rest of the night would be quiet. Unless someone took the road too fast and skidded into a snowbank, or someone's toddler unlocked a door and wandered out of the house. For a cop, cold weather complicated everything from accidents to lost kids. Throw in a bad case of cabin fever, a couple with pent-up rage and too much to drink, and you got—

Well, you got what happened here tonight at the Whale Spout.

She walked into the bar and stamped the snow off her boots. After coming in straight from the cold, it felt like a hothouse inside, the heat cranked up to at least seventy-five. What a waste of energy. Jo looked at the bar, where she'd worked for a few summers pouring wine and shaking cocktails for the hordes from away, sunburned tourists who'd said her little seaside village was *quaint* and asked what folks did here in the winter. *Well, this is what we do here,* she thought. *We gain weight and drink too much and get on each other's nerves.* She inhaled the yeasty scent of beer and thought how good a frosty glass of Sea Dog ale would taste right now, but that would have to wait. She unzipped her jacket, peeled off her gloves and wool cap, and focused on the reason she was here: the young woman slumped at a table in the corner, with an officer standing guard beside her.

Megan Kiely had certainly seen better days. In high school, she'd been one of the most popular girls in school, a spirited redhead with a laugh you could hear from the other end of the cross-country field. Her hair was still red, and she still had a killer figure, but at only thirty-two years old, she'd had the laughter sucked right out of her, leaving behind this sad husk of a woman.

"Hey, Megan," said Jo, loud enough to be heard over the thumping music.

Megan looked up and said, listlessly: "Hey, Jo."

Jo said to her officer, "Mike, you want to give us some space? And shut off that god-awful music, will you?"

She waited for Mike to go behind the bar and turn off the speakers. Blessed silence, at last. As she sat down at the table across from Megan, she felt something sticky on the table surface, and looked down to see there was blood smeared on the heel of her hand. It had to be the asshole's blood, because Megan didn't appear to have any open wounds, only a swollen right eye, which was going to turn into one hell of a shiner by tomorrow.

"So. Shall we talk about it?" Jo asked.

"No."

"You know we have to."

"Yeah." Megan sighed. "I know."

Jo reached for a paper napkin from the dispenser and wiped the blood off her hand. "What happened?"

"He hit me."

"Where?"

"My face."

"I mean, where did it happen?"

"At home. I don't even remember what set him off. Oh yeah, it's 'cause I was late getting back from my mom's house. He punched me and I walked out. Came here, thinking I'd just wait it out till he calmed down. But he followed me. Barreled right in and came at me while I was sitting at the counter. I guess I just—just reacted. Grabbed a steak knife as I was backing away. I don't remember doing it. I just know he started screaming and there was blood, and somehow, I was holding the knife."

Jo looked at Mike, who said: "It's been bagged. And we got half a dozen witnesses who saw her do it." He shrugged. "Straightforward."

Except it wasn't. The part about a wife stabbing her husband might be straightforward enough, but what came before that was a sad and convoluted tale about a woman who'd fallen in love too young, married too young. Gotten trapped too young.

"I'm going to jail, aren't I?" whispered Megan.

"For tonight, yes. Till your lawyer can sort things out in the morning."

"And then?"

"There are extenuating circumstances. I know it, and most folks in town know it."

Megan nodded and gave a sad laugh. "I'm kind of looking forward to jail. It'd be like a little vacation, you know? I could sleep nice and sound and not have to worry that Jimmy might—"

"Megan, it doesn't have to be this way."

"But it is." She looked at Jo. "It just is."

"Then *change* it. Tell Jimmy to fuck off."

Megan's mouth tilted up in a half smile. "Yeah, that's just what you *would* say. Same old Jo Thibodeau, not afraid of anything. You haven't changed a whit since high school." She shook her head. "What're *you* still doing in this town, anyway? You could've gotten out. You could be living anywhere. Someplace warm, like Florida."

"Don't like the heat."

"The point is, you *could* be somewhere else."

"Yeah, I could. So could you."

"You didn't end up with the wrong man."

"You can always change that."

"You make it sound so easy. You don't understand how hard that is."

"No." Jo sighed. "I guess I don't." The same way Jo didn't understand how Megan had allowed herself to be sweet-talked into the arms of a Jimmy Kiely. But then, men like Jimmy usually steered clear of Jo, because she had a reputation. All the boys in town knew that if you ever punched Jo Thibodeau, she'd punch back, and twice as hard.

Jo stood up and helped Megan to her feet. "You need to have that eye looked at. Mike'll take you to the hospital first. We can worry about booking you later."

"And then I can sleep," said Megan. Tonight she probably *would* get a decent night's rest, since she'd be the jail's only occupant. This time of year, Purity's cells were almost always empty. For Jo, that was the upside of winter. No drunk summer tourists roaring across the harbor in speedboats, no petty thefts committed by bored teenagers home from school. When the nights grew long and snow started to fall, the town of Purity seemed to go into hibernation, becoming a sleepier, less troublesome version of itself.

It was that sleepy version of Purity she saw as she drove down Main Street later that evening, the storefronts already dark at 7:00 p.m., the deserted sidewalks gleaming with ice under the streetlamps. An enchanted village, slumbering on a winter's night. While it looked like a place frozen in time, Jo had seen far too many changes in her thirty-two years. What used to be the old antique store that sold mismatched chinaware and faded postcards was now a gift shop that sold fancily packaged jams, jellies, and candies. The old soda fountain where her dad used to drink Coke floats had become a wine store, which had become the Fine Grind, where they sold so many versions of coffee that you needed an Italian dictionary to figure out what you were ordering. At least the hardware store was still in business, but the eighty-three-year-old proprietor was keen to retire, and one day, that store would stop selling hammers and screwdrivers and would hawk T-shirts instead. While these brick buildings were 150 years old, an ever-changing parade of businesses and proprietors continually cycled through them because the one thing you could count on in life, even in a small town, was change.

She thought about what Megan had said to her: *What're you still doing in this town, anyway? You could've gotten out.* It was true, Jo *could* have gotten out of Purity, but she knew she'd never leave because she didn't *want* to. This was where she had grown up, where her father and grandfather and his grandfather had grown up, 250 years of Thibodeaus with their roots sunk deep into the stony soil. It was now her responsibility to protect this town, these 29.5 square miles stretching from Penobscot Bay to Mount Cameron in the west. Within its borders was the harbor and boatyard, farmland and forest, a lake, numerous ponds both named and unnamed, and three thousand year-round residents, most of whom lived along the coast within scent of the sea.

On this winter night, though, it was too cold to smell the ocean, even when Jo drove down to the landing and parked at the docks. She lowered her car window, listening for trouble, but all she heard was the splash of water against the seawall. The town's two windjammers, *Amelie* and *Samuel Day*, were covered in white shrink-wrap for the winter, and they looked like ghost ships, swaying at their moorings. Come summer, those two schooners would head out every afternoon, weather permitting, packed from bow to stern with paying passengers. *The catch of the day*, the locals called them, and while folks in town were happy to take their money, the locals were *not* happy about the traffic and chaos that tourists brought to town.

Problems that Jo was expected to solve.

She drove away from the landing, away from the sea, and continued on her rounds. First she drove west toward Lake Cameron, where the seasonal cottages were now closed down and ripe for break-ins. She turned north, taking the road past the massive oak tree where the Parker boys smashed their Honda two years ago, leaving their parents childless and devastated, then circled back east toward the coast, past the farmhouse where George Olsen shot his wife, and then himself. New people were renting that house now, a young couple from Boston trying out the rustic life. Jo assumed they knew about the Olsens' murder-suicide. Or maybe not. Maybe Betty Jones, the property manager, had cannily left that information off the rental information sheet. It was just the sort of thing Betty would do.

On US Route 1, the coastal road that led back to the village, Jo drove past the curve where a bicyclist fell and fractured his skull last summer, past the cove where a teenage girl drowned. When you live your whole life in one town, you know all the places where tragedy has occurred, because bad memories are as permanent as gravestones.

Her evening circuit complete, she headed back to the Purity Police Department and pulled into the parking stall labeled "Chief of Police." As of five months ago, that was what she was. The acting chief, anyway, until the town's select board could get their act together and decide who should replace Glen Cooney, who'd died at age sixty-four with his boots on, literally, when he'd been hit by a passing car while writing a traffic ticket. Jo had been the first responder to the scene, and she still had nightmarish flashbacks to that image of Glen sprawled in the roadside grass where he'd been thrown, his right hip twisted backward, his foot pointing in the wrong direction. He was the one who'd hired her ten years ago, but only reluctantly, because he'd doubted a twenty-two-year-old woman could wrestle a summer drunk into handcuffs. Then one night he'd watched her do it, and after that, Glen and Jo were good.

Now she was the one who had to deal with PD shift schedules and sick days and the perennially inadequate budget. Did a town of three thousand people really *need* six full-time officers? *Well, Madame Board President, we* could *do with fewer if you'd all stop having accidents and getting into fistfights and breaking into cars. Oh, and come July, could we close off Route 1 and halt the annual invasion of summer tourists? I'm sure they'd be happy to take their dollars to some other town.*

She walked into the building and headed to the desk where Glen Cooney used to sit, a desk that was now hers. She could still see him sitting here as he did every morning, with his cup of black coffee and his breakfast sandwich, his back ramrod straight, his gray hair neatly combed with the part on the left. He was a decent man, like most of the men in Jo's life, not brilliant but reliable, which was what really counted in the long run. Now that Jo had to deal with the sticky situations that Glen used to handle—the officer with the drinking problem, the church organist with kleptomania—she'd sit in this chair and wonder: *What would Glen do?*

She sat down at his desk, woke up the computer, and got to work writing the report on Jimmy Kiely's stabbing. If the evening stayed quiet, she could also draw up next month's shift schedules, and maybe work on her speech for next week's high school Career Day. Then there was the weekend to plan. The weather forecast was for clear skies on Saturday, cold and sparkling, which would make it a good day to pack up her tent and drive to Bald Mountain with her dog, Lucy. She looked forward to a night with no phone calls, no distractions, just her and her dog camping in the snow under a starlit sky.

Her radio crackled on.

CHAPTER 4
MAGGIE

When I pull up in front of Lloyd and Ingrid's handsome white colonial, I see that Ben Diamond's black Subaru is parked across the street and Declan's blue Volvo is down near the corner, which tells me the gang's all here. Surveying vehicles on the street, taking note of who has arrived and who has not, is still second nature for me. Old habits die hard.

Lloyd answers the door. "Ah, we were wondering when you'd turn up," he says as I walk into the house, bearing my contribution to the evening's potluck.

"It smells delicious in here," I say, handing him my dish. "What have you been cooking?"

"It's my first attempt at porchetta. But first, martinis! Declan already has your Belvedere on ice."

I hang up my coat and walk into the living room, where a fire—a real wood fire, not a gas insert—crackles in the hearth. The scent of curry and garlic wafts in from the kitchen, and on the coffee table, Lloyd has laid out an extravagant tray of antipasti: salami and mortadella, olives and cheeses. In this household, Lloyd does all the cooking, and judging by his waistline, he also does most of the eating. The others stand around the fireplace with martinis in hand. We may have dubbed these meetings our "book club" evenings, but what we've really come for are the martinis.

And the gossip. Gossip was the currency of our former lives, before we found our way to this quiet corner of Maine. Ben Diamond was the first to plant a flag here, nine years ago. He'd retired early to take care of his ailing wife, and his search for the perfect town pointed him here, to the village of Purity. It had everything he required: a bookstore, a decent town library, a coffee shop that served espresso, and no nearby nuclear targets.

A year after Ben moved here, his wife died, but he stayed on in Purity. A few years later he recruited Ingrid and Lloyd, and then Declan, to retire here as well. I have no doubt there are others like us quietly living out their retirements throughout Maine, a state that's long been used by the Agency as a convenient location for safe houses. While these colleagues haven't revealed themselves to me, Ben surely knows who they are. Ben knows everything.

Declan places a martini in my hand. The glass is so cold it hurts to hold it, which is just the way I like them.

"We hear you had an unexpected visitor today," says Ingrid.

I look at Declan, who was the only person I told about the visit. He gives an apologetic shrug. "You certainly didn't waste any time spreading the news," I say.

"I felt they needed to know. When an outsider shows up in our little town, it causes ripples."

"Tell us about her," says Ingrid.

I take a sip of that oh-so-cold, oh-so-smooth martini. "She said her name was Bianca."

Now they all move in close to join the conversation. The whole time, they were waiting, listening. They're always listening for any useful pearls of information that might drop.

"Bianca. The name doesn't ring any bells," says Ingrid. The others shake their heads as well.

"A new face," I tell them. "Early thirties. Five foot seven, around a hundred and thirty pounds. Black hair, brown eyes."

"Any regional accent?"

"Unplaceable to my ear. Perhaps a hint of England, RP. Received Pronunciation. Maybe she lived there for a few years."

They're all nodding, absorbing this info. These four don't need to take notes; it's now permanently recorded in their gray matter.

"What is she doing here?" asks Ingrid, readjusting her scarf. In a town where a clean shirt and blue jeans is considered dressy attire, Ingrid has never relinquished her sense of style. Her silver hair is elegantly coiled and fastened with a pewter butterfly clip, and a silk scarf is perfectly knotted at her throat. She may look like a Park Avenue matron, but her blandly pleasant expression disguises a cipher-cracking genius.

"She came about some old business I was involved in," I say, wishing now that I had never confided in Declan. "Nothing particularly interesting."

"Yet it was important enough for her to come all this way to see you. How long ago was this, um, *business*?"

"Years ago." I turn and shoot Declan a dark look. He looks right back, his gaze unflinching. "Old history," I add.

"Why are they asking you about it now?"

"Oh, you know how it is with this new generation," says her husband, Lloyd. "They don't have a decent grasp of operational history. They need us to fill them in."

Ingrid's not about to let go of the subject. Unlike Lloyd, she senses there's more to Bianca's visit than I've told them. "What did she want from you?"

I take another sip of my martini as I consider my next words. "There was a woman I worked with, years ago. She's dropped out of sight, and they want my help finding her."

Lloyd snorts. "First they tell us we've gotten too old for the business. Then they come to us, looking for help, when they realize they don't know what they're doing. Let them learn on the job, the way we did." He taps his head. "It's still all there. Every little detail, if they'd just bother to ask us."

Ben seems troubled by the conversation. At seventy-three, he's the oldest among us, and the unofficial mayor of our tight little circle. "I don't like the sound of this," he says.

"Which part of it?" asks Lloyd.

"She shows up here unannounced and asks you for assistance. That's out of bounds. This village is our personal DMZ. It's the reason we live here, to be left alone."

"Well, I certainly didn't *invite* her," I say.

"Bianca. Bianca . . ." Ingrid is searching her prodigious memory for the name. "Which desk does she work?"

"She didn't say. If I were to guess, East Asia? Only because the woman she's searching for was last spotted in Bangkok."

"An alias?" suggests Declan.

"Or she's such a new recruit we haven't heard of her," says Ingrid.

I think about the woman I met in my kitchen. Her utter confidence. The distinct whiff of lethality. "This isn't someone green. She's field tested."

"Then I shall have to ask my friends at HQS. See if they know about her."

"Also ask headquarters if they plan to send any other visitors," adds Ben.

Lloyd is back at the bar, shaking himself another martini. "What say we get on with the program? Declan's brought his famous goat curry. And I've spent all morning singeing the bristles off a pork belly, so I hope you'll give my porchetta the proper respect."

This is supposed to be a book club meeting, but no one has even mentioned the title we're supposed to discuss. Ibn Battutah and his adventures in the medieval world will have to wait until our bellies are filled and gossip is exchanged. We all move into the dining room, where the table is soon laid out with Declan's always excellent curry, Ben's Persian rice, Lloyd's pork, and my Thai larb, recipes we gathered during our years of working in far-flung places. Living abroad changes your palate; chili addiction is a real thing.

I look around the table at our circle of lived-in faces, at hair that's gray, or going gray, or—in the case of Ben—gone entirely. There's more than a century's worth of experience accumulated in these brains, but time moves on. Young people move in, and we are expendable. So we putter along in our quiet little village, talking about books we've read and dishes we've cooked and where to find the best online source for cassia bark and Sichuan peppercorns. I suppose there are far worse ever-afters.

My cell phone rings.

I'm not expecting any calls, and it's unusual for anyone to be calling me at all, because I've shared my cell number with so few people. I glance down at my phone and see Luther Yount's name on caller ID. He's probably calling to thank me again for the fox pelt I gave him this morning.

"Hello, Luther," I answer, aware that my dinner companions have stopped talking and are listening in. It's a habit we can't seem to break, listening in.

"What's happening over there?" Luther asks.

"I'm having dinner at a friend's house."

"Okay, good. I'm glad you're all right."

"Why wouldn't I be? What's going on?"

"There's some disturbance at your house right now. I heard sirens and thought maybe you had a fire or something. I just came out on my porch, and I can see police cars in your driveway. Soon as Callie gets on her boots, we're going over to take a look."

"No, don't. Both of you stay away. I'm coming home right now."
I hang up and look at four faces staring at me. "I need to leave.
Something's happening at my house."

Declan sets down his napkin. "I'll come with you."

"No, please. Stay and finish dinner. I can deal with this."

Nevertheless, Declan walks me to the front door. He's always had
a streak of old-world civility about him. Perhaps it comes from being
the son of a diplomat, or from being raised in Swiss boarding schools,
a childhood so different from my own hardscrabble beginnings. My
childhood taught me that I should never rely on a man for help; Declan
grew up believing that assisting a woman in need was his duty.

"Really, Maggie, I don't mind coming with you," he says. "If there's
any trouble brewing, you shouldn't be facing it alone."

"I certainly won't be, not with police cars in my driveway. But
thank you."

As I drive away, he's still standing on the front porch, watching.
It's almost a relief when he finally drops out of view, and I can focus
on what could possibly be going on at my house. Could I have left the
stove on? Did someone try to break in? Whatever it is, I prefer to deal
with this on my own.

When I turn onto my private road, I see blue lights flashing through
the trees. Two police cruisers. Luther did not exaggerate; it would take
something serious to bring both of Purity's patrol cars to my house.
I pull up behind one of the cruisers and step out into the strobe-like
flashes of rack lights. At once my attention is drawn to the reason why
the police are here.

There's a body lying in my driveway. The glare of the cruiser lights
illuminates the woman's face, a face I recognize. Bianca lies flat on her
back, her face looking up at the sky, her arms splayed out at her sides,
as though crucified. She wears the same clothes she wore this afternoon,
when she stood in my kitchen: slim black pants, a formfitting blue

jacket, lace-up boots. Punched into her forehead are two bullet holes. Double tap. An execution.

Three uniformed cops stand staring at me, two men and a woman. They're all young and far more accustomed to handing out traffic tickets or assisting lost tourists. Murder is not supposed to happen in our village of Purity, and on the rare occasions when it does, the police usually know whom to arrest. The husband. The boyfriend. This situation has rattled them, and they're looking at me as if I have all the answers.

"Do you live here, ma'am?" the female cop asks. She's a sturdy blonde with her hair tied back in a no-nonsense ponytail. Despite her youth, she has an air of authority, and she is obviously the senior officer of this trio. Authoritative, but still polite enough to call me *ma'am* in the respectful tone one uses for a grandmother.

"Yes. I'm Maggie Bird. I own this farm. And your name is?"

"Jo Thibodeau, Purity PD. As you can see—"

"There's a dead woman in my driveway."

She pauses, obviously taken aback by my blunt assessment. Perhaps she was expecting more drama from me—a scream, a gasp, something more than what I'm providing—but drama is not in my nature. Instead, I calmly assess the situation. I look at Bianca's hands, noting that both are bruised and black, her fingers bent and twisted at grotesque angles.

"Where have you been tonight?" Thibodeau asks.

I refocus on the cop. "I was having dinner with friends in town, and my neighbor called. He lives in that house over there." I point to Luther's cabin. "He said there were police cars in my driveway, so I came right home." I look down at the body again. "Who found her?"

Thibodeau frowns. I'm not behaving like the shocked grandmother she assumed I'd be. "A FedEx driver. He was here to drop off a package. His last delivery of the day."

I glance at my porch, but there's no package there. I've been waiting for new heating lamps for the batch of chicks I ordered for the spring, and now it seems my delivery has been inconveniently delayed.

"Do you know who this woman is, ma'am?" the cop asks.

Ma'am again. It's starting to annoy me. "She told me her name was Bianca."

"So you know her."

"Not really."

"Do you know her last name?"

"She never gave me one. I met her for the first time this afternoon, when she dropped by my house."

"Why was she visiting?"

The truth is too complicated for a small-town cop to digest. "She came to buy fresh eggs. That's the one and only time I spoke to her."

There is a silence. Perhaps I could have come up with a better answer, but a martini plus a few glasses of wine have dulled my edge. Any explanation closer to the truth would only invite more questions.

I quickly ask one of my own. "How did the body get here?"

No answer.

I look down at multiple tire tracks left by my pickup truck, by the FedEx truck, and by the two police cruisers. A confusing jumble of crisscrossing tread marks. "Did you find any vehicle nearby?" I ask.

"No, ma'am."

I bend down for a closer look at the body, and she snaps: "Back away! We need to leave her exactly as she is, for the state police."

I obey her and take a step back, but I've already seen enough. The evidence is clear from the smashed hands, the dislocated fingers. Before she was dispatched with two bullets to the head, Bianca was tortured. For information? As a statement? And why did the killer choose to dump the body in my driveway? If he or she is sending me a message, I don't know what it means.

"What time did you leave home tonight?" Thibodeau asks.

"It was around six o'clock, and there was certainly no body lying here then."

"That's three hours ago. Can anyone confirm where you've been for the last three hours?"

I'm irritated by these questions, even though I know it's her job to ask them. I also know she can't really consider me a suspect because I don't look like someone who'd torture a woman, fire two bullets into her head, and leave the body displayed in my own driveway. Not only is it unlikely, but it's illogical.

"You can talk to Lloyd and Ingrid Slocum," I tell her. "They live at 651 Chestnut Street. They were the hosts of our book group tonight, and they'll confirm I was there."

Thibodeau jots down the names in a notebook and slips it back in her pocket. Ingrid and Lloyd will of course confirm the boring truth: that we met tonight for a potluck dinner and copious wine and a spirited discussion of *The Travels of Ibn Battutah*. It's exactly the sort of evening that we retired folks are believed to indulge in. I doubt the police will ask what we are all retired *from*, because when you are over the hill, what you did in your previous life is of little interest to most people.

"I noticed you have security cameras on your property," Thibodeau says.

I'm not surprised that she looked for them; there's scarcely a neighborhood in America that's not being surveilled by someone's Ring or Wyze or Blink outdoor camera. Still, I had hoped to review the recordings myself before sharing them with the police.

"I do," I admit.

"We'll need to see the footage. And we need to take a look inside your house."

"Inside? Why?"

"There's a dead woman in your driveway, and we don't know who or where the killer is. I want to make sure he isn't hiding inside your house." She pauses. "I'm just concerned for your safety."

It's a reasonable request, which any woman who lives alone would ordinarily welcome. I nod and pull out my house keys.

Thibodeau and one of her male officers follow me up the porch steps, to my front door. It is still securely locked, with no sign it has been breached. They're right behind me when I step inside and flip on the lights. Everything is as I left it three hours ago. I don't know what they expect to see as I lead them into the kitchen—perhaps the murder weapon, conveniently left out in the open, or some helpfully incriminating blood spatters, marking the room where I tortured and shot Bianca. All they see is my old farmhouse kitchen, my cast-iron pans hanging on the rack, a few dirty dishes in the sink.

I walk them through the living room, which I've furnished in the style of sensible Yankee thrift. The sofa, upholstered in gray wool, was purchased at a discount furniture store in Bangor. The birchwood coffee table, pine end tables, and spindle-back rocking chair were yard sale finds, lugged home with the help of Declan, who's always ready to lend a hand loading up my pickup truck. There is nothing flashy here, nothing to make a cop take notice. *Ordinary* is what my house says to anyone who visits. *Ordinary* is quiet and unobtrusive and safe.

I lead them up the creaking stairs to the second floor. It's an old house with an old heating system, and the bedrooms are cold, sweater-and-wool-socks cold. Tonight, I will have to feed a few extra logs into the woodstove to cut the chill. While I resent their invasion of my privacy, anything less than my full cooperation will lead to a search warrant and a deep dive into my past, and that I can't afford, so I take them on the grand tour. Bedrooms, bathrooms, closets.

No killer hiding anywhere.

We end up in my bedroom. Through the window, I can look down at the two patrol cars parked in the driveway. My house is now a crime scene. This is not the way to keep a low profile.

"Okay, ma'am, everything looks all clear. You should be fine," Thibodeau says. She thinks she's done me a favor, confirming that the old biddy is safe. "Now if you could show us your security footage."

It's not a request but a command. While I'm loath to share any footage before I've reviewed it myself, there's no way to fend her off. We go downstairs to the desktop computer in the kitchen. It's the same computer I use to keep track of my farming business: chicks ordered, eggs sold, feed purchased. There's nothing sensitive on it, nothing worth hiding, and even my password to sign on is ridiculously simple: BlackberryFarm431#. I make no attempt to conceal from them what I type.

The home screen is a photo of one of my old prize roosters, Sir Galahad, who is now sadly deceased after a run-in with a bald eagle. The avian symbol of our country is also the bane of my flock. My security system allows me ready access from all my devices, and here it could get tricky, having two cops standing behind me as I type in another password, this one a complex series of numbers and symbols, to access the security system. My fingers move so fast that I'm sure their view of the password is hopelessly blurred.

My security home page appears. On the screen are sixteen different video inputs from cameras mounted at various vantage points on the house, as well as on the barn.

"Holy cow," murmurs the male cop. "This is some fancy setup you've got." He probably expected a one-camera feed, all that most people need and can manage. Instead they're staring at 4K high-def feeds from every point of entry.

"I left home around six," I say. "So let's start then."

I wind back the video to 5:50 p.m. It's dark by then, and the cameras have switched to IR feed. At 5:58, there I am, stepping out my front door. I lock the dead bolt, go down the porch steps, and climb into my pickup.

"And there I go," I say as my truck drives away. "Just as I said."

Thibodeau merely nods. At least now I'm off her list of suspects, if I was ever on it. The video continues past 6:05. 6:10. Nothing happens.

"What time did the FedEx man call it in?" I ask.

"7:36."

I dial up the feed to twice the speed. There's no sense sitting here for the next hour, watching while nothing happens. And nothing does happen—until 7:05 p.m.

A vehicle appears, a dark SUV, and my audio feed picks up the sound of the engine. Its headlights are off, and only the engine lights glow in the darkness. The fact the driver killed his lights tells me he knows my house has surveillance cameras. So does the fact he obscured his license plates, both the front and the rear. The car pulls to a stop at my front porch. The driver's door swings open, but no dome light goes on; he has disabled it.

I feel both cops lean in right behind me, their breath in my hair. My own heart is thudding as I watch a figure step out of the car. Hooded. Masked. In all-black clothes, loose fitting and shapeless. My cameras are the best on the market, but they cannot see through fabric. The figure goes to the rear of the SUV, pops open the hatch, reaches in for the body. There's no sound, not even the faintest grunt, as he or she drags the body out and lets it drop to the ground. I know how much strength it takes to move a limp body, and this person makes it seem effortless.

It has to be a man.

Now he does something that makes little sense. He leans over and rolls the body onto its back. Why position it face up? To make the souvenir he's left behind all the more upsetting? He probably assumes I am the one who'll discover the body, that I'll drive home tonight and there she'll be, sightless eyes looking straight up at me. He couldn't have predicted that some poor FedEx driver would show up first.

No, this surprise was meant specifically for me. And I have no idea why.

With the body now positioned, the killer climbs back in his SUV and drives away, beyond the view of my cameras. Headed someplace where his license plates can be uncovered, his hood and mask stripped off. Once again, he'll be just an ordinary man driving an ordinary SUV through town.

"What the hell was that?" Thibodeau looks at me.

"I have no idea," I say. And I really don't. All I know is, this was not a random location to dispose of a body. Whoever did it knew their actions would be captured on camera, so he took care to hide any identifiable clues. "But it proves I told you the truth," I say. "I left my house around six, when I said I did. If you need confirmation, you can speak to Lloyd and Ingrid. You can also call Ben Diamond and Declan Rose. They were at the book club tonight too. They'll all tell you I was with them this evening."

"Yes, ma'am. I'll be talking to them."

"Now, I suppose you want this video file?"

"The state police certainly will."

"Then I'll make copies for you."

The two cops are about to leave the kitchen when Thibodeau stops and looks back at me. "Do you feel safe here?"

"In my own house? Yes."

"Even after what happened right outside?"

"I can't imagine it had anything to do with me."

She regards me for a moment. In the brightly lit kitchen, I can finally read her name tag: *Officer Jo Thibodeau.* There are unsettling similarities between us, in her no-nonsense questions, in her easy command of the situation. At her age, I was equally sure of myself, but experience has taught me the dangers of overconfidence.

"Why do you think he dumped the body here?" she asks.

"I don't know."

"Did you recognize the vehicle?"

"It's a dark SUV. Half the people in this town drive one like it."

"You haven't lived in Purity very long, have you, Ms. Bird?"

"I bought this farm two years ago."

"And where were you living before that?"

45

"The last home I owned was in Reston, Virginia. But I've lived in a lot of different places."

"For work?"

"Yes."

"What kind of job?"

"I was an import analyst. I worked for a customs brokerage, handling export logistics for foreign companies." Here's the point in my CV when most people's eyes glaze over, revealing they really don't care to hear more. Her focus only seems to sharpen.

"And what brought you to Purity?"

"It's in the name, isn't it? I wanted a place with clean water, clean air. A place where I can take a walk in the woods. Why are you asking all this?"

"I'm wondering why you seem so calm about this. Why having a dead body in your driveway doesn't seem to rattle you. It would freak out most people."

"At my age, Officer, nothing much freaks me out anymore."

One side of her mouth twitches up. She has a finely tuned bullshit meter, and it's telling her I'm not giving her the whole story, but she's not going to get much more from me tonight.

"The state police will be talking to you," she says.

"Tell them not to come by until the morning. It's late and I'm exhausted."

And I *am* exhausted, but after the two cops leave my house, I do not go up to my bedroom. Through the kitchen window, I watch the activity in my driveway. I wonder if Officer Thibodeau realizes how many lies I told her tonight.

I can't imagine it had anything to do with me.

That's the biggest lie of all. Of course this has to do with me. What I don't know is what message the body in my driveway was meant to convey. Is it to terrify me? Or is it a gift, the same way a cat brings you a dead mouse? A way to tell me: *We took care of your little problem. You're welcome.* I have two options to choose from, each one leading in a very different direction.

I set my silent alarm. If any door, any window is cracked open just a millimeter, I will know about it. I head into my study, where my copy of *The Travels of Ibn Battutah* happens to be lying on the desk. It is a fascinating account of a young man's travels in the 1300s, from Morocco to Central Asia to China. Was it merely a coincidence that I happened to choose it for light reading, or was it an omen? The very night our book group discusses this same medieval travelogue is the night someone sets a match to my carefully rebuilt life, threatening to burn it down. I cross to the bookshelf, feel for the latch on the side, and release it. The entire bottom shelf swings out to reveal a niche, a bit of clever carpentry that I owe to Declan's newfound skills as a woodworker. Retirees, after all, need hobbies. Inside the niche is where I store my go bag. Over the years I have pared down the contents to the basics, just enough to skip town and hunker down elsewhere for a few weeks. Passports, credit cards, multiple bundles of cash in different currencies, and a few tools of the trade. Tools I hoped I'd never need again.

Life is full of surprises.

I pull out the bag and carry it upstairs to my bedroom. I want it right beside me. If I need to run, I don't want to be scrambling for it in the dark.

But tonight, I should be safe. There are too many cops in the driveway, too much attention focused on my house. For once, I'm happy to be the one who's being served and protected by local law enforcement. Nevertheless, I place my Walther on top of the nightstand before I turn off the lamp. The bedroom curtains can't block out the lights from the investigators' cars outside; even through thick fabric, I see the flash of rack lights.

My cell phone dings with a text message. It's Luther.

Everything OK?

I tap out the answer: There's a dead woman in my driveway.

Oh Lord!

They'll probably be talking to you next.

We didn't see anything.

Too bad.

My phone rings. It's not Luther, but Declan Rose calling. I answer it.

"I hear you need an alibi," he says.

"The police have already called you?"

"Five minutes ago. A charming Purity PD officer named Jo Thibodeau asked if you were at our little book club tonight. I told her you were. I assume the truth serves you well?"

"This time, yes."

"Are you safe there, Maggie?"

"I don't know." I watch the flashing lights through the curtains and think of how no situation is ever perfectly clear. There's always something obscuring the view, veiling the truth. I think of the go bag next to my bed and how easy it would be to drop out, skip town, even skip the country. But this is my home now, and I've spent two years building this life, settling into its rhythms. I'm tired of moving, tired of searching for a landing spot. This is it. This is where the wandering stops.

"I can come right over," Declan says. "Spend the night on your sofa."

"Why?"

"Keep you company? Play guard dog?"

I laugh. "You truly are a gentleman, Declan, but there are so many cops in my driveway right now, I definitely don't need a guard dog."

"Well then, call if you need me. For anything."

"I will."

I hang up and lie in the semidarkness, watching the lights flicker through the curtains. A dead woman lies in my driveway, the woman who asked me to help find Diana Ward. It has been sixteen years since I last saw Diana, sixteen years since I walked away from the career I loved. Those years have not been kind to me; I can see that when I look in the mirror. I wonder what Diana looks like now.

I close my eyes and picture an older Diana, her hair going gray, her skin starting to sag. Suddenly her image disintegrates, as evanescent as a reflection on water, and another image blooms in my mind. It's the face I see every night when I close my eyes, the face I will always see.

Danny's.

CHAPTER 5

Bangkok, twenty-four years ago

We meet by chance. At least it seems as if it's by chance, the sort of friendly encounter that I would normally shy away from because I am by nature skeptical of people's seemingly innocent motives. I acquired that skepticism as a child, growing up with a father who almost never told the truth, a father whose trips into town to *meet a client* were, nine times out of ten, visits instead to the Tinhorn Bar on Main Street. That's where I'd usually find him in the evening, six drinks in and raising a ruckus. There were occasions when he actually *did* meet a client, when he *did* tell the truth, and that one-out-of-ten occurrence was what always confused me. If he lied all the time, at least I'd have some measure of certainty in life. It's the *possibility* of a better outcome that screws with your mind, that breeds hope, which ultimately leads to disappointment. I was like a diamond miner who keeps pounding at rocks, searching for the gemstone in a pile of rubble. You know there's got to be one in there somewhere, and you're willing to waste your life looking for it.

Until one day, you're not. One day you say fuck it, and you pack your things and drive away, the way my mother did years before. So yes, I question everything. It's what makes me good at my job.

This afternoon, I am on vacation and hungry for spicy noodle soup. On vacation, everything feels different. The world seems almost benign, and people seem to actually mean it when they smile. That's no excuse, but it explains my carelessness this afternoon. The sky just opened up with monsoon-force rains, and everyone is scrambling for cover under the Wang Lang street market's hopelessly inadequate awnings. I cannot quite squeeze in under the edge of the awning, and the back of my jeans quickly becomes drenched, but it is a warm rain, a welcome break in the unremitting heat of Bangkok. I left my hotel and caught the ferry across the river, just for a bowl of this particular vendor's soup, which I discovered on a previous assignment in Thailand. My colleagues have already flown home, but I plan to stay four extra nights, just to enjoy Bangkok. I will sleep as long as I want to, and I'll eat what I want to, all on the government's dime. And what I want to eat this afternoon is spicy beef noodle soup.

The vendor hands me a bowl, its steam fragrant with star anise and cinnamon. It costs only sixty baht. Two dollars, which is not even worth the effort of charging Uncle Sam for this meal.

I carry the bowl to the only available table and settle onto a low plastic stool. It feels like I'm sitting at the children's table, but I'm fortunate to find any perch that's out of the rain. As I slurp up my first mouthful of noodles, I'm only peripherally aware of the man who'd been waiting in line behind me at the vendor's cart. Then I hear him ask: "What did that lady get? Can you give me the same thing?"

I glance up and see him pointing at my bowl. The Thai woman running the cart doesn't understand what he's saying. He asks her again, sounding a little helpless. A British accent. I'm not good at accents, but I know his is not posh. He's younger than I am, I think, or maybe it's just the vibe he gives off. Wide eyed. Eager. Someone who's delighted by every new experience. He has shaggy blond hair that hasn't seen a barber in months. His faded blue backpack has one strap repaired with duct tape, and there's a folded map of Thailand poking out from a pocket.

He's wearing cargo shorts and hiking sandals, and his nut-brown tan tells me he's been in the tropics for a while. His T-shirt has Thai words that translate, roughly, to *Stupid Tourist*. I wonder if he has any idea.

He shells out his sixty baht, collects his bowl of soup, and scans the area for a free table, but there are none. For a moment he stands holding his bowl, looking lost. The rain pounds on the awning, and a river of water streams the flooded street, muddying his sandals. There is an empty stool at my table. I could choose to duck my head and keep eating, pretending he isn't there. Seconds pass as I weigh my choice.

"You can sit here," I offer.

The rain is so loud he doesn't hear me.

"Hello?" I call out.

He turns and sees me gesturing toward the empty stool. Grinning, he sets his bowl on the table and folds up his impossibly long legs to settle onto the stool.

"Didn't fancy eating this while on my feet. Thanks!"

"I see you ordered the same soup," I say.

"Yours looked so good I thought I'd follow your example. Since you seem to know what you're doing." He bends over his bowl, slurps up some broth, and sighs. "Oh God."

"Really good, isn't it?"

He concentrates on the flavors. "Star anise. Cinnamon. Galangal. Fish sauce and . . ." He coughs and his face suddenly flushes bright red. "Chilis."

"Bird's-eye. Not the hottest chilis, but hot enough."

He's red and sweating from the chilis, but he keeps on eating, perhaps out of pride because I'm watching him, or because he really does enjoy it, despite the burn. I understand that. Pain is a powerful spice, the other face of pleasure. Some of us crave it, just enough of it, to remind us we're alive.

"There's something else in here I can't identify," he says, putting down his spoon. "Something earthy. Metallic . . ."

"Beef blood."

He looks up at me, startled, and I see that his eyes are a brilliant green. With that tangled mane of blond hair, he makes me think of a Viking, lost in the wrong century, on the wrong continent. "Seriously?"

"Absolutely." I wonder if I've freaked him out, if he'll push the bowl away in disgust.

Instead, he laughs. "That's brilliant! It explains the color. The richness." He lifts the bowl to his lips and drains the rest of the soup. I'm witnessing pleasure at its most primal and unabashed.

That's when the vision pops into my head. An image of the two of us lying in bed, our limbs entwined, our bodies slick with sweat.

"Do you always try to deconstruct every meal?" I ask.

"It's annoying, isn't it?"

"It just seems so analytical. You wouldn't happen to be a chemist, would you?"

"A doctor, actually. I suppose it's in my nature to dissect things, even bowls of noodle soup."

"A medical doctor?"

He must hear the skepticism in my voice because he laughs. I see by the creases around his eyes that he's not as young as I thought, but close to my age. "I know, I don't much look like one at the moment."

"The old backpack threw me off."

He looks down at the duct-tape repair. "This backpack has been through a lot, and I'm too sentimental to toss it. It's been with me through five years of charity work, in half a dozen refugee camps."

"Where?"

"I've been in Kenya and Sudan, mostly. Treating everything from gunshot wounds to malaria."

"So are you in Thailand for work?"

"No, I'm just a tourist. I have to go home to London in a few weeks, and I've never had a chance to explore Asia. I'm trying to pack in as much of the world as I can, while I can, before I have to put on a tie."

"You don't sound happy about that prospect."

"I'm not, but . . ." He sighs. "It's time for me to start earning a living."

"Why?"

"Now *that's* a question no one ever asks."

"And is there an answer?"

"My mum needs help."

That answer I wasn't expecting. "You sound like a very nice son."

"She's on her own now, having trouble keeping up with the bills." He shrugs. "You do what you have to do, but . . ." He looks at the steaming food carts, at the vendors with their tables piled high with herbs and neon-red chilis. "I'm going to miss living out of my backpack."

"Did you by chance happen to buy that T-shirt in Bangkok?"

He looks down at his shirt. "Got it off a vendor's cart."

"Did anyone tell you what it says?"

"The lady who sold it to me says this means 'happy tourist.'"

I decide not to tell him the truth, after all. He really *is* a happy tourist, unlike some of the sour-faced foreigners I see on the terrace of my hotel. The ones who are perpetually dissatisfied and always annoyed by some small detail that doesn't meet their standards.

"Where do you travel next?" I ask.

"I don't know. I've got three more weeks of freedom before I have to fly back. Tell me where I should go."

"I'm not sure I know the answer."

"You seem like someone who knows her way around the world. All the ace spots that other tourists haven't found yet."

The rain has stopped, but water continues to drip from the awning, splattering the pavement right behind him. I think of all the secret places I *do* know, places I can't tell him about because of what goes on there in the service of our national security. Places with aching beauty and terrible history.

"Try Chiang Mai," I say. "Most tourists seem to love it."

"Do you?"

"It's pretty. Not so damn hot. And you'll almost certainly like the food."

"Where do *you* go on holiday?"

"I like to go to places I've never been to."

"Like where?"

I take a swig from my water bottle and look him in the eye. "Madagascar."

He bursts out laughing. "Somehow I knew you'd say that! Everyone talks about going to Madagascar, like it's their dream destination, but I don't know anyone who's actually managed to make it."

Now I'm laughing, too, because it's true. Something always gets in the way. Another assignment, another crisis. It's the aspirational destination on everyone's bucket list.

"You're American?" he asks.

"Born and raised."

"It sounds like you travel quite a bit. For work?"

"It's one of the perks of the job."

"What do you do?"

I take another swig of water, a pause to cue up my backstory. "I'm an import analyst for Europa Global Logistics."

"Europa? As in Jupiter's moon?"

"Very good. Most people don't know that."

"What does your company do?"

"We're a customs brokerage. We handle global logistics for import and export companies. Everything from farm equipment to fashion."

Most likely he doesn't care a whit about any of this. At this point, most people's eyes glaze over and their questions stop. For those who are curious enough to actually search for Europa Global Logistics online, they'll find a nicely designed website with enough details to convince them it is a real company, staffed by real people. And they'll see my name and photo: "Margaret Porter, import analyst specializing in textiles and clothing."

"Do you enjoy the work?" he asks.

"It gives me the chance to see the world."

"But do you enjoy it?"

"Why do you sound doubtful?"

"It's just . . ." He looks away, at the market stalls. At the vendors and grocers and trinket sellers. "These people, they make their living selling things you can touch and eat and smell. It just feels so *honest*."

"And my job doesn't?"

He winces. "I'm sorry. I've just never felt a connection to the corporate world, which is probably why there's nothing in my bank account. And why my mum keeps telling me to get out of charity work."

"You could always go back to it someday. That's one thing that doesn't change in this world. There'll always be wars and refugee camps."

"True. Too bloody true."

We don't talk for a moment. Our little table is an island of somber silence in the noise and bustle of the market. The sun is shining now, the rain almost forgotten except for the steam rising from puddles on the hot pavement.

He rises to his feet, groaning as he stretches to his full height. It must have been uncomfortable for a man his size to have sat so long on that tiny stool. "I think I need to head back to my hotel and take another look at the map," he says.

"Where are you staying?"

"It's just a little mom-and-pop hotel, a few streets up. It's clean and friendly. Perfect for a man on a budget." He pulls on his backpack. The now-soaked tourist map of Bangkok droops from the outside pocket. "Thank you for the company. And for the advice on where to go next. It was a pleasure, um—"

"Maggie."

"Maggie." He reaches down to shake my hand. It's such an old-fashioned gesture, but at that instant, from this ragged Viking of a man, it strikes me as utterly charming. "And I'm Danny Gallagher. If you're ever in London and need a splinter removed or your appendix whipped out, I'm your man."

As he turns to leave, I'm teetering on the edge of Should I, or shouldn't I? I have four free nights in Bangkok before I'm scheduled to fly home. I'm on vacation with no obligations, no firm plans, and it's been such a long time since I've slept with a man. He's already walking away, and I'm just about to call out to him when he suddenly stops. Turns back.

"Would you like to meet up for a drink later?" he asks. When I don't answer right away, he flushes. "Sorry, that was forward of me, wasn't it? It's just that I really enjoyed talking to you, and—"

"Yes," I say.

*

"Do you ever come to London?" Danny asks.

We're lying in my hotel room, the sweat from our frantic lovemaking cooling under the hiss of air from the AC vent. It was either his place or mine, and hooking up in a budget hotel held no appeal for me, so here we are in the Oriental, a favorite haunt for those of us on the government's dime. It's too expensive for my personal pocketbook, but if Uncle Sam's paying for it, why not? I could see that Danny was dazzled when we walked into the lobby, his head tilted back to gape at the ornate ceiling. He was still gaping when we stepped off the elevator and were greeted by the floor steward, but the instant we walked into my room, his attention was all on me, just as mine was all on him. No words, only sighs and gasps as we peeled off each other's sweat-dampened clothes, as we kissed our way to the bed. We didn't need words; our bodies knew what to do, and I wouldn't hear anything he said anyway, not through the sound of our frenzied breaths and the blood roaring through my ears. Somehow he knows all the right places to touch me and how to feed the hunger I've ignored, the hunger I've instead channeled into my work. There's always another report I need to bang out, another asset to cultivate, a fresh source to develop. When you vow that your colleagues are off limits (and most of them are unlikable anyway), you have to grab your pleasure where you can find it.

And I've found mine in Danny Gallagher, who I now know is thirty-three years old, born in Leicester, educated in London. He is indeed a few years younger than I am, but I feel older than him in other ways too. Or maybe I'm just less innocent, more attuned to the many shades of gray in the world where the divide between good and evil, friend and enemy, is a movable line.

"I make it to London, sometimes," I say.

"Next time you come, will you call me?"

"It might not be for a while. And by then, it'll probably feel weird to call you."

"Why?"

"You may not even remember me."

"I'll definitely remember you."

"Or you'll be seeing someone else. I'll show up in London and you'll think, 'Why the hell did I ever invite her?' That's how these things go."

"Were you always such an optimist?"

I laugh and turn on my side to look at him. "Hey, we're in Bangkok. We're in lust. Let's just enjoy this."

"Does what happen in Bangkok have to stay in Bangkok?"

"Danny, you hardly know me."

"Not for lack of interest." Now he rolls onto his side, and we lie face to face on the bed. "So tell me more." He runs his hand down my thigh, and his fingers stop at my scar. "For instance, tell me how you got this."

"It's nothing, really. During college, I worked part time as a waitress in a bar. This fistfight broke out, bottles got smashed. I got hit by flying glass."

"A bar fight? I wouldn't have guessed that."

Nor would he have guessed the real story behind my scar: that I was hit by exploding shrapnel in Karachi.

"So you worked in a bar."

"It wasn't the worst job I've ever had."

"Where was this?"

So far I've avoided sharing specific details with him—at least, none that are not well-rehearsed fabrications. I will never see this man again, so there's no reason to start telling the truth now, but postcoital intimacy still envelops us, and a bit of the truth slips out.

"Georgetown." Where I actually did live for a time, even if I never worked in a bar.

"Isn't that near Washington, DC?"

"Yes."

"I've always wanted to see the White House. Is it worth the trip?"

"No."

He caresses my hip. "Seeing you again would be worth a trip. If you don't come to London, we could meet up somewhere else."

"I'm not sure that's such a good idea."

His hand goes still. He rolls onto his back and groans. "Oh God. You're married, aren't you?"

That would be an easy way to cut the line and toss him back into the sea. A fictional husband is a convenient excuse, one I've used with other lovers, but it would make me look sordid in his eyes. Suddenly, it seems important that Danny not see me that way.

He sits up on the side of the bed, his back turned to me. The city glow through the window falls on his shoulders, burnishing his skin like polished copper. When I reach out to touch him, he doesn't react.

"Danny?" I say.

"I should go back to my own hotel."

"Let's go out to dinner. I know a really good restaurant where—"

"Why?"

"To eat?"

"This didn't mean anything to you, did it?"

He thinks there's some meaning to a sweaty grope with a stranger in a foreign bed. It makes me feel sorry for him. For his innocence, for the inevitable and painful awakening to come. It also makes me want to keep him here, at least for a little while longer.

"I'm not married," I say.

He turns to look at me, but his face is backlit by the window's glow, and I can't read his expression. "Is that true?"

"Why would I lie to you?"

"When you said this wouldn't be a good idea, seeing each other again, I just assumed . . ."

"I said it because I know how these things peter out. When you meet someone in a foreign city, it seems new and exciting. Then you bring it home and you realize—"

"'Bring it home.' Like a souvenir?"

"It's what happens." My words of wisdom sound more like resignation, and I suppose that's exactly what it is. I do know how these things turn out. I know how *this* will turn out. It doesn't mean I can't enjoy pleasure wherever I can snag it.

"Stay," I say. "Have dinner with me." I stroke his naked back and feel his skin ripple with goose bumps. "We both have to eat anyway, so why not do it together?"

"It must be a lonely life," he says quietly.

My hand falls still on his back. This is not what I expected from this man. I'd wanted some hot and heavy sex and a few laughs, but I didn't think he'd hold up a mirror to my life. He has, and I don't like what I see.

"It can be lonely," I admit. "That's why I really would like you to stay."

"For dinner."

"And more. If you're in the mood."

He shakes his head. Lets out a weary laugh. "Sure. Why not?"

Why not? It's not the last time we'll say those two words to each other.

It should have been.

CHAPTER 6
JO

Purity, Maine, now

Jo had known other men like Maine State Police Detective Robert Alfond, and she knew, from almost the moment he stepped out of his SUV, that theirs would not be a cordial relationship. He paused at the edge of the crime scene, his face lit by the rack lights, a large man made even larger by his puffer jacket. He wore no hat or scarf, and Jo wondered how long he would last, proudly bareheaded in the cold. She stood only a few paces away, had raised her hand in greeting, but he walked straight past her and headed toward her officer. All right, then, so that's how this would go. Jo Thibodeau, invisible woman. He'd seen her, of course, but had probably thought, *Blondie, not important* and turned his attention to the man he assumed was in charge.

Her officer immediately pointed Alfond in her direction. *Thank you, Mike.*

"Jo Thibodeau," she said, stepping forward to introduce herself. "I've taken over as acting chief since Glen Cooney passed."

"Detective Alfond," he said.

"Yes, I know. I attended your lecture on interrogation at the academy." A lecture in which he'd paced the room like the captain of a ship, broad stanced and self-important. She nodded at the crime scene tape strung up around the body. "We've secured the scene, searched the house, and done preliminary interviews. The homeowner's a sixty-year-old woman who lives alone. She wasn't here when the body was dumped."

"That's what she says?"

"Yes, sir."

"And you know this is true?"

"I've interviewed witnesses who corroborate her whereabouts tonight, plus I confirmed it myself."

"How?"

"If you take a look at the house, you'll see she's got cameras mounted all over the place. I've viewed the surveillance video, and it shows the body being dumped. A black SUV, a male driver."

"Officer Thibodeau," he said, "you *do* understand the protocol for death investigations?"

"Yes, sir."

"And you understand your role?"

"We notify the attorney general's office and the state police CID. We secure and protect the scene, conduct a cursory search of the premises, and record pertinent information from witnesses. That's what we've done, as per Maine Administrative Code Section 201, regarding death investigations."

He stared at her for a moment, the way one stares at a dog who's suddenly started to talk. So Blondie had a mouth on her. Maybe Jo *had* jumped the gun by viewing the surveillance tapes herself, before the state's CID did. Maybe she *should* have just strung up her pretty crime scene tape and stood back to wait for the big boys to take over, but Jo had never been a patient woman. It was something she had to work on.

A new pair of headlights made them turn as another vehicle pulled up behind Detective Alfond's. Out stepped the ME, Dr. Wass, yet another large man. Maine seemed to breed large men the way it produced boulders, but unlike Alfond, whose largeness was proportionate, Dr. Wass was built like a bowling ball, struggling against the force of gravity not to roll backward down the sloping driveway.

"Why, it's Jo Thibodeau," Wass called out to her.

"Hey, Dr. Wass." They had last spoken during Glen Cooney's accident investigation, when she was still badly shaken by her mentor's death, and he had treated her then with fatherly kindness. Even now, with a dead body lying nearby, and with hours of work ahead of him, Dr. Wass was thoughtful enough to first reconnect with her.

"So you're doing Glen's job now?"

"I'm trying to." She sighed. "I miss him. He was a good man."

"Indeed, he was. How has it been so far? Walking in Glen's boots?"

"There are . . . challenges." *Like dealing with jerks like Detective Alfond,* she thought. "But I'm getting the hang of it."

"I'm sure you'll do just fine, Jo." Wass turned to Alfond. "So, Bob, what do we have?"

As the men walked toward the body, Jo wanted to join them, but the look Alfond shot her made it clear she was not welcome in their huddle. Was it because she'd cited the Maine Administrative Code to him, or was it because she was at least a decade younger than him, and a woman? She could hear him repeating to Dr. Wass what she had learned, as if *he* were the one who'd interviewed Maggie Bird and viewed the surveillance video and called Declan Rose and the Slocums to confirm Bird's whereabouts. As if *he* were the one who'd walked room by room through the farmhouse, prepared to confront a killer. Dr. Wass nodded, taking in the information, not knowing it was all the fruit of *her* labors.

What would Glen do about this?

Oh, she knew exactly what Glen Cooney would do. He'd shrug it off, the way you shrug off a muddy slicker, and he'd just walk away, because according to the Maine state code, this investigation was now Alfond's show, and there was no sense getting upset about things that were not under her control. He'd tell her she'd done her job, and now it was time to move on. Yes, that's what Glen would do.

So she left Alfond and Dr. Wass and headed toward her cruiser, where she stopped and looked back at the farmhouse. The bedroom windows were now dark and the curtains were closed, but Jo wouldn't be surprised if the woman was watching them at this moment because, judging by all her security cameras, Maggie Bird was a watchful woman. An odd woman, whom Jo could not get a handle on. She thought of how unruffled she'd seemed about the body in her driveway, and she wondered if that was simply due to the shock of the moment and her true reaction was simply delayed. Perhaps the trauma would hit her tomorrow, and that's when she'd feel the terror that most people would feel when there's a murder victim on their premises.

Or maybe the woman really was as unflappable as she seemed.

She glanced at Alfond and Dr. Wass, who were still crouched over the body, conferring over the wounds. *Let them focus on the dead woman,* Jo thought. She was going to focus on the one who was very much alive.

*

A girl and a cow were walking across the snow-covered field. Squinting against the morning light, Jo could see it wasn't a large cow, just a docile-looking Jersey, but the girl was petite and the animal out-weighed her by at least seven hundred pounds, and the sight of them so close together made Jo nervous. She wasn't afraid of dogs or snakes or screaming-fast ski runs down double black diamond slopes, but when she was ten years old, she was chased by a bull, and that gave her a healthy respect for large livestock. Jo watched warily as the girl and cow headed toward the barn, neither one leading the other, just ambling together like companions on a stroll. When the girl stopped to wave at Jo, the cow stopped, too, like a dog trained to heel.

Jo waved back. She'd heard that Luther Yount's granddaughter was homeschooled, which explained why the girl was out there with her cow this morning, and not sitting in a classroom. It probably also explained why the girl had never come to Jo's attention. Unlike the kids at the local high school, who regularly got each other into mischief, a bovine companion was far less likely to lead a girl into a life of crime. Jo watched the pair until they'd vanished into the barn, then turned to Luther Yount's cabin and climbed the porch steps.

Before she could knock, Yount opened the door. Jo was not a small woman, but suddenly coming face to face with this bearded wild man gave her a start.

"Mr. Yount?" she said. "I'm Jo Thibodeau, Purity PD."

"This about what happened next door?"

"Yes, it is."

"I talked to some detective last night. Robert something or other."

"That would be Detective Alfond from the Maine State Police. They've assumed control of the investigation."

"Told him I didn't know anything was wrong until I saw all your flashy lights next door."

"I have some questions about your neighbor. May I come in?"

There was a pause. "I guess so," he finally said.

She was unaware of any prior issues between Yount and the police, and she wondered about his reluctance to allow her into his cabin. Inside, she saw nothing particularly suspicious. Much of the furniture looked homemade, and the stacks of cartons filled with eggs told her they must keep a substantial flock of chickens in their barn. In the corner was an old Vermont Castings woodstove, where water simmered in a cast-iron pot, releasing precious wisps of humidity into the bone-dry air. A cobweb hung from the ceiling, and Jo looked up to see its resident spider dangling from one gossamer thread. Judging by the general dust and clutter in this cabin, Jo doubted that Luther Yount was much bothered by spiders. The only detail that surprised her was what she saw on his bookshelves, which were crammed with scientific and agricultural textbooks. There was more to this disheveled man in overalls than met the eye.

They sat down at the table, where she saw a half-empty cup of black coffee. She would have liked a cup of coffee, too, but he did not offer her one. "Your neighbor, Maggie Bird," she said. "How long have you known her?"

"Since she moved in next door, 'bout two years ago. Bought Blackberry Farm from old Lillian's estate. That Lillian could get real cantankerous, especially when Callie's goats got into her garden, but Maggie, she's a fine neighbor."

"How so?"

"Friendly. Quiet. Minds her own business." *Unlike you,* his gaze seemed to say. If there was anything criminal about Maggie Bird, Jo had a feeling this man would not say a word about it, just on principle. "Why're you asking about Maggie?"

"A body was found in her driveway last night."

"Yes, I know. Could've been dumped in anyone's driveway."

"But it was left in hers. And her reaction to it, well, it wasn't what you'd expect."

"What would you expect?"

"She was strangely calm about it."

"She's a calm woman. Never seen her get worked up about anything. That's just Maggie."

The door thudded shut as Yount's granddaughter came into the cabin. "What's just Maggie?" the girl asked.

"Callie, this is Officer Thibodeau," said Yount.

"Acting Chief Thibodeau," Jo corrected him.

"She's asking about Maggie."

"Why?" said Callie.

"They're just routine questions," said Jo, but she knew Yount didn't believe that, and his doubt had been picked up by the girl, who was frowning at her. Callie was wearing a stained barn coat, her Muck boots had tracked in dirt, and bits of straw were woven into her hair. Jo wondered if maybe Child and Family Services should be called about the situation, because a girl this young should be in school, not laboring as a farmhand.

"Is Maggie in trouble?" Callie asked.

"No, dear, she's not," said Luther.

As far as I know, thought Jo.

"Is it 'cause of the fox?" asked Callie.

"What fox?"

"She shot a fox and gave us the carcass," said Luther. "It was killing her chickens. Callie's too. Perfectly legal kill."

"I'm not here about a fox, Mr. Yount. I'm just trying to get a sense of your neighbor. You seem to think well of her."

"We need help, she's always right here, ready to pitch in. Callie's goats got out of their pen one day, and there was Maggie, running around in the field, helping us chase 'em down. You shoulda seen that. It was quite a show."

"And she gives me books," said Callie. "Things she says will expand my mind." She went to the bookshelves, pulled out a volume, and placed it on the table in front of Jo. It was a world atlas. "She says it'll help me decide where I'm gonna travel someday. I told her I want to see Paris, and she said that's a very good choice."

"Okay, so she's a good neighbor," said Jo. "What else do you know about her?"

There was a silence. Yount and his granddaughter looked at each other, as if the other might have the answers.

"She's a good shot," said Yount. "Took down that fox straightaway."

Jo considered this detail. A sixty-year-old woman who knew how to handle a gun wasn't all that unusual in rural Maine, but Maggie Bird was a recent arrival in the state, so she'd acquired her skill with guns elsewhere. "You're from away, too, aren't you, Mr. Yount?" Jo said.

At the sudden change in topic, Yount's face abruptly became unreadable. "I am," he said.

"My grandpa fixed up this cabin all by himself," said Callie.

"And you moved here from?"

"Boston," Callie answered cheerfully. "He was a professor at MIT."

"Did you know Maggie Bird before you moved here?" Jo asked.

"We did not," said Yount. "We met her for the first time when she moved in, and we couldn't ask for a better neighbor. I don't know what all these questions are about, but I don't have anything bad to say about her."

"Neither do I," said Callie.

Jo looked back and forth at the man and his granddaughter, and she knew she might as well give up now. If they had any dirt on their neighbor, they were not going to share it with the police.

Back outside in the driveway, Jo paused beside her vehicle and looked toward Blackberry Farm. The view was partially obscured by the row of sugar maples on the private road that led up to Maggie Bird's residence, but from here she could see the farmhouse and a white SUV parked at the bottom of the road. The state police investigators had spent all morning on the property, and a bright-yellow strip of leftover police tape fluttered on the snow, but the official vehicles had since departed. Who did that white SUV belong to?

She drove away from Luther Yount's residence and turned onto the road leading to Blackberry Farm. She paused by the SUV just long enough to note that it had Maine plates and was unnaturally clean for this time of year, when most vehicles were coated in grit and dust from the sanded roads. Two people were standing in the driveway, and they waved as Jo got out of her patrol car and walked toward them. An older couple, both in puffy coats that made them look like jumbo snowmen.

"Chief Joanna Thibodeau, I presume?" the woman called out. "We spoke to you last night, on the phone. Ingrid and Lloyd Slocum. We had Maggie at our house for dinner."

"You do know this is a crime scene?"

"Of course. That's why we're here."

"Excuse me?"

"The crime scene tape is down, so we assumed we could come take a look for ourselves. Maggie shared her security footage, and we wanted to confirm a few details."

"Such as the relative lack of blood," said Lloyd, pointing to the one red splotch in the snow.

"These tread marks," Ingrid said, pointing to the snow. "I think these are Goodyears. I'll have to go online and confirm the specific tire model."

"She was killed elsewhere, wasn't she?" said Lloyd. "And her body was dumped here later. What was her state of rigor mortis?"

"Jesus," said Jo. "Are you two retired cops or something?"

"Oh no," said Ingrid. "We're just amateurs. Enthusiastic mystery buffs."

"More like vampires."

"Do we look like vampires?"

"You think crime scenes are entertainment?"

"Absolutely not. We take this *very* seriously. Maggie's our friend, and she's not happy that her driveway was used as a body dump."

"I need to speak with her."

"Oh, she's not here. She and Declan are over at the Harbourtown Inn, talking to the manager."

"The *Harbourtown*? How did they find out—"

"Where Bianca was staying? Elementary. There are only three hotels in the area that are open this time of year. Lloyd happens to know the cook at the Harbourtown, and he said the woman was a guest there."

71

"They now serve a decent breakfast, by the way," said Lloyd. "After I gave them my recipe for shirred eggs."

Jo took a breath to quell her temper. "What are they doing at the inn?"

"Trying to find out when and where Bianca was abducted. Her rental car hasn't been located yet, so—"

"How do you know *that*?"

"The state police were all over the hotel parking lot this morning, but they didn't tow any vehicles away. Have they found it yet?"

Jo's mouth tightened. "I don't know. The state police have assumed control of the case."

"Oh." Ingrid gave a sympathetic shake of the head. "That's got to hurt."

What really hurts, thought Jo, *is the fact these people, these civilians, seem to know as much as I do. This isn't right.*

What was *really* not right was the fact she, the acting police chief of Purity, had been sidelined from the investigation of a murder that had happened in her own hometown.

"I want you people off this property," Jo said.

Ingrid's chin snapped up, and even though she was no taller than Jo, and her hair was half-silver, it was obvious from the woman's gaze she was not to be trifled with. "We have Maggie's permission to be here."

"It's a crime scene. You could be contaminating it."

"We know better than that."

Lloyd placed a calming hand on his wife's shoulder. "Ingrid, dear, we're finished here anyway."

A moment passed as the two women exchanged stares, taking the measure of each other. Then Ingrid gave a curt nod. "We'll go. If you need any assistance in the future, you have our phone number."

If I need their assistance? Who did they think they were?

Jo waited for them to leave, then climbed into her vehicle and sat staring at Blackberry Farm. *You and your friends are a puzzle, Maggie Bird,* she thought. Not that she suspected the woman of being responsible for the dead body in her driveway, but the whole situation was, for want of a better word, *odd*. While the town of Purity had its share of petty crime, murder was a rare event here, and it usually involved people with obvious motives, people whose names she knew, sometimes people she'd known all her life. That was the advantage of being a cop in your own hometown; you knew in which houses trouble was brewing. But in the past few years, newcomers had started moving in, people from away who probably believed the village of Purity, Maine, would be their refuge from big-city prices and traffic and crime. Jo had yet to take the full measure of these newcomers, and they of her, and until that happened, there would be more conversations like this one with the Slocums, with doubt and mistrust clouding the air.

With all these new arrivals, the town was changing too fast. Jo wasn't sure she liked the changes, but she could not stop them, and she also knew that without fresh blood, villages shriveled and died. She would just have to do what she'd always done: keep her eyes open, her ear to the ground.

Someone knew why a body had ended up in this driveway, and that someone was bound to talk.

CHAPTER 7
DIANA

Bangkok, now

The cadaverous face staring at her from the internet café computer looked nothing like the man she'd known almost two decades ago, and she could not mask her surprise at his drastically changed appearance. *"Gavin?"* she said into the headset microphone.

The corpse on the screen responded with a resigned sigh. "As you can see, the years haven't been kind."

"They haven't been kind to either of us."

"Don't even try to be charitable, Diana. Your effort shows."

He knew her too well, which was unfortunate. Karma, she was starting to realize, was not just an abstract concept. She glanced around at the crowded internet café. Even at midnight, it was packed shoulder to shoulder with tourists typing on keyboards. The air conditioner could not keep up with all these warm bodies, and the room smelled like sweat and coconut oil. The other patrons were all focused on their own screens; no one was paying attention to her conversation.

"I have a . . . situation," she said quietly.

"What do you want from me?"

"A bolt-hole. Just for a few weeks, until I can figure out what's going on."

"What is going on?"

"Two men came after me in Paris. They showed up at my apartment, and I took them down first. It could be blowback from Malta. And if it is, then I'm not the only one who needs to watch their back."

On the screen, Gavin's face remained impassive. He'd practiced that poker face for ages; perhaps the expressionless mask had settled into permanence. Or was it illness that kept his face so immobile? She could see a green oxygen tank behind his shoulder, but he was not in a hospital room, judging by the carved decorative panel in the wall behind him.

"The Agency is asking about Malta," he said.

"What? When?"

"They reached out to me last week. It seems Operation Cyrano is back on their radar. They're reviewing what happened in Malta, and they asked me what I remember about how it went down."

"After all this time? Why?"

"I assume some new information has come to their attention. They'll probably be talking to you as well."

Only if they can find me. "Have you spoken to Maggie?" she asked.

"I probably should. I never told her the whole story, Diana. Maybe I should. Maybe it's time she learned everything."

"What would be the point now?"

"If they're coming after you because of Malta, then we're all in trouble. Maggie, most of all. Do you know who sent those men after you?"

"I assumed it was Moscow."

"Well, you may want to consider other possibilities."

She frowned. "What do you mean? What have you heard?"

"Hardwicke."

She stared at him. "That's impossible."

"The Agency doesn't think so."

She let out a shocked breath. Glanced around at the room of tourists tapping at keyboards, staring at screens. She lowered her voice. "I need time to figure this out, Gavin. If you could give me a place to hide until—"

"I can't."

"Can't? Or won't?"

"Take your pick, Diana."

His cold-blooded rejection was not what she'd expected, but it was not surprising either. After Malta, they had parted on bad terms, and she'd never been one to inspire loyalty from her colleagues. She'd never seen the need.

Until now.

"You don't need my help," he said. "You're a survivor. It's what you excel at."

"You could be on the hit list too."

"I can look out for myself, thank you. And so can Maggie, I'm sure."

Even though her eyes were on the screen, a prickling on the back of her neck made her turn and glance at the other patrons. That's when she spotted the man: brown hair, a ratty T-shirt, tan cargo pants. He could be mistaken for any other Western tourist in Bangkok, except for his reaction to her gaze. Instantly he looked away and refocused on his computer. Had he been watching her because he saw a juicy prospect for a one-night stand, or was there another reason for his interest?

She looked at Gavin. "At least do this much for me. Find out *why* the Agency's asking about Malta."

"Ask them yourself. Just pick up the phone."

"I'm not sure that's safe."

The first hint of emotion flickered in his eyes. Alarm. "You don't think the *Agency's* behind this?"

"After Paris, I don't trust anyone. Someone wants me dead, and if it's connected to Operation Cyrano, it means our names have leaked out. Yours. Mine. Maggie's."

She glanced sideways and caught the man in the cargo pants watching her again. A detail she needed to attend to, now. "I've got to go," she said, and logged out.

She walked out of the internet café and was not surprised when, a few seconds later, the man in the cargo pants followed her. She strolled at a leisurely pace, playing the part of just another tourist, but every so often she stopped to look in a shop window and survey the reflection of the street around her. Out of the corner of her eye, she saw the man pause whenever she did, always maintaining his distance, but clearly tailing her.

Time to bring this tiresome game to an end.

Despite the late hour, there were still too many witnesses on this main street, so she turned the corner onto a quieter side street.

So did he.

Here there were fewer people, and he could no longer hide the fact he was in pursuit. He did it brazenly now, out in the open, his attention clearly fixed on her. Either he was new to this, or he considered her such an easy takedown that he could afford to be careless. She spied an alley off to her right. Narrow, unlit, littered with crates.

She turned down the alley and ducked into a doorway. In darkness, she waited as his footsteps followed her and moved closer. So close now, she could hear the rustle of his polyester trouser legs.

He never saw her attack coming.

In an instant she was behind him, his hair yanked back to bare his throat, her knife pressed to his carotid. "Who are you?" she said.

"I just—I wanted to—"

"Who are you?"

"Dave. Dave Barrett." He sucked in a panicked gasp. "Please, I was only trying to—"

"Who sent you?"

"Nobody!"

"The Agency? Moscow?"

"What? No, I—"

"Tell me or I fuck up your face good."

Panicked, he grabbed her knife wrist and tried to twist away. It was a clumsy move that got him nowhere, but it succeeded in thoroughly pissing her off and leaving her no choice. Her instincts kicked in, and what happened next was both efficient and brutal. She slid her knife down to his chest and thrust the tip of the blade up under his sternum, aiming it directly into his heart. His whole body jerked in surprise. Even though the blade had shocked his heart into a standstill, a few seconds of consciousness remained. He was aware that he was dying. Aware that this dark alley was the last thing he would ever see.

"Who sent you?" she asked one last time.

"No one," he whispered.

His head slowly sagged back, and she let his limp body drop to the ground.

A quick glance around told her there were no witnesses nearby, no one else in the alley. She flicked on her flashlight and swiftly searched his body. In the pockets of his cargo pants she found a passport, a wallet, loose change, but no weapons. Not even a pocketknife. She opened the passport and saw his name really was David Barrett, age twenty-three, from Saint Louis, Missouri.

She'd killed a fucking tourist.

When you kill an innocent, you create ten new enemies, one of her instructors at the Farm had said, but years in the field had taught her that sometimes it couldn't be helped. And this man wasn't entirely innocent. He'd clearly been stalking her, with either robbery or sex on his mind. Just your common, everyday predator.

"My mistake," she murmured.

She wiped her blade on his shirt, gathered up everything she'd touched, everything that might have her fingerprints. She'd dispose of it all in the river. As for his body, she'd let the police draw their own inevitably wrong conclusions.

Only when she was back on the main road, walking past late-night food carts and noisy bars, did her breathing steady, her pulse slow to normal. As unnecessary as that incident in the alley had been, it had told her one useful piece of information: her pursuers did not know where she was. Anyone intent on killing her could have done so in that alley, while she was distracted by Dave the Tourist.

For the moment, she was safe.

She'd learned something else tonight, too, something she'd suspected, and that Gavin had now confirmed. The Agency had reopened the file on Operation Cyrano. They were asking questions, seeking more information from those who were most deeply involved. She knew the file had not yet been declassified, because as one of the key operatives, she would have been notified of such a change. Had someone in the Agency leaked their names? What other details had been leaked? Either Gavin didn't know the answers, or he hadn't been entirely forthcoming with her.

There could be far more damage to come, operational details that should never see the light of day. Details that no one else knew. *When you kill an innocent, you create ten new enemies.* She already had enough enemies; she didn't need more.

At last she reached the Chao Phraya River, and into the black water she tossed the passport and wallet of Dave the Tourist. *That's what you get for stalking the wrong woman,* she thought. Underestimating Diana was his fatal mistake.

He wasn't the first man to do it, and he wouldn't be the last.

CHAPTER 8
JO

Purity, Maine

Jo had watched only one autopsy in her career, and it was years ago, while she was training to be a police officer at the Maine Criminal Justice Academy. As the shortest member of the class, she'd had to stand on tiptoe to look over a classmate's shoulder. Then Dr. Wass sliced open the abdomen, releasing the smell of entrails, and the male student in Jo's line of sight abruptly fainted.

After that, Jo had a fine view of the pathologist's knife.

As everyone else in the class focused on the anatomical details of dissection—how many lobes the lung consisted of and where the spleen sat in relation to the liver—Jo found herself thinking instead about the decedent himself, and what his last moments had been like. The man was old, ancient really, his face and arms mottled with age spots, like brown lichen on a venerable tree trunk. He'd been found dead in bed at his nursing home, which shocked his family because the evening before, he'd been alert and lively. Four other residents in the building had also passed away over the past month, all of them unexpectedly, and the family insisted that something was not right in the establishment.

Perhaps an angel of death, disguised as a nurse, was making the rounds, armed with a syringe of insulin. Murders like that happened, didn't they?

Staring down at the man, Jo thought about what it would be like for him, relegated to a nursing home in his final years, staring at the same four walls day after day. Did he long to once again feel the kiss of snow on his face and hear the crunch of leaves under his feet, knowing that he would never experience those things again? And then in the night, here comes the nurse with a syringe to end his ordeal. Was that an act of mercy, or was it murder? Jo didn't know. She knew only that the morgue was an unseemly place to end up, being gutted under bright lights with a dozen students staring down at your most intimate parts.

A look of pity must have crossed her face because Dr. Wass asked: "You doing all right?"

It took her a few seconds to realize he was talking to her. As she met his gaze across the table, she felt her classmates watching the interaction. Was his question directed at her because she was the only woman, a way to single her out as somehow weaker? In which case she should nip that notion in the bud with a shrug, even a laugh.

Instead, she said: "He had a hard life. It's sad to think he died this way."

"Why do you say he had a hard life?"

She pointed. "He's missing the tip of his index finger. And see all the scars on his hands? He worked with sharp tools. Maybe a sawmill, or a meatpacking plant."

Although Dr. Wass did not respond to her comments, he did study her for a moment, as if committing her face to memory. As if knowing this would not be the last time they'd speak.

Years later, when they met again over poor Glen Cooney's body, lying at the side of the road, he remembered her name. And yesterday, when she'd asked if she could view the postmortem of the woman in

Maggie Bird's driveway, even though she was not officially part of the investigative team, he'd immediately said yes.

They now had a name for the woman: Bianca Miskova. That, at least, was the name she'd used when she'd checked in at the Harbourtown Inn, and when the inn's proprietor had looked at the woman's Colorado driver's license, she'd seen nothing to make her doubt it was authentic. The Mastercard had worked, approving the charge of $195, which Jo found outrageously high, considering it was low season, but visitors to Purity didn't have much choice in winter accommodations. When the woman had checked out, around noon on the day of her death, she'd left her room in pristine shape. Where she'd gone next, and with whom she'd met, remained a mystery, as was the current location of her vehicle.

The morgue door swung open, and Detective Alfond walked in, tying a protective gown over his clothes. He halted just a few steps into the room and frowned at Jo, as if he'd mistakenly walked into a ladies' restroom.

"I asked Chief Thibodeau to join us," Dr. Wass told him. "Never hurts to have another pair of eyes."

Alfond didn't say a word as he moved to the foot of the table. He didn't need to; Jo was just a small-town cop, destined to write tickets and respond to break-ins and intercede between wrangling spouses. In this room, she was merely a tourist, here to watch the big boys work and keep her mouth shut.

So she did as Dr. Wass peeled back the drape, revealing the woman's body. She was a prime physical specimen by any measure, with a gymnast's slim hips and muscular thighs. Jo had already viewed the body at the scene, where she'd noted the grotesquely deformed fingers and fractured hands and the bullet wounds to the skull, but the glare of the morgue lights made these horrors seem bloodlessly plastic. Artificial. She looked at Bianca's half-open eyes, and as she'd done with the old man from the nursing home, she wondered about this woman's last moments. They'd surely been excruciating, and the fatal bullets would have come as a relief after the wrenching back of her fingers, the cracking of her joints. This must have happened someplace remote, where her screams wouldn't be heard. It would not be hard for the killer to find such a location, considering Purity's miles of rural roads and dense forests. Dr. Wass snapped apart ribs and lifted the breastbone. As he reached into the chest and pulled out the glistening heart and lungs, Jo kept staring instead at the woman's ruined hands. Was this punishment or interrogation?

What was he after? What did he want you to tell him?

The buzz of the wall intercom made her look up.

"Yes?" Dr. Wass called out.

His secretary said, over the speaker: "I've got the governor's office on the line."

"I'll call back later. I'm in the middle of an autopsy."

"That's why she's calling. You need to halt the procedure."

"What?" Dr. Wass yanked off his gloves and went to pick up the wall phone. "What is this all about?"

Jo could hear only Dr. Wass's side of the conversation:

I'm about to open the cranium . . . this makes no sense . . . did they explain why?

Jo looked at Alfond. He seemed just as bewildered as she was.

Wass hung up and turned to them. "Well, this beats all. They want me to bag up the body and have it ready for transfer."

"Transferred? Where?" Alfond snapped.

"Boston. Some other agency's assuming control of the remains. It's like they don't trust a Podunk pathologist in Maine to do the job."

"What the hell is going on?"

Dr. Wass looked at the body, which was now hollowed out, with most of its organs removed. What remained was little more than a shell of bone and muscle. "I have no idea."

CHAPTER 9
MAGGIE

"Grandpa says we need to watch over you now," says Callie as we stand in her kitchen, spot-cleaning the twelve dozen eggs we collected from both our flocks this afternoon. They are a pretty jumble of brown and white and aqua blue, the blue ones from my Araucanas. Today we've mingled our eggs, and tomorrow Luther will take the cartons to the co-op. It is a peaceful, zen-inducing task, wetting the dish towel, rubbing off the bits of dirt and manure, arranging the eggs in the cartons with an artful balance of colors. This is exactly what I need to be doing, after the disturbing events last night. Today, the situation seems no clearer. We know only that Bianca checked in as a guest at the Harbourtown Inn and was last seen by the desk clerk at noon yesterday, when she checked out. By the time the state police searched her room this morning, housekeeping had already cleaned it, so I doubt they unearthed much of value.

The situation has left me feeling shaken, off balance, so I am glad to be standing in Luther's kitchen, mindlessly cleaning eggs.

"Grandpa says you can stay with us, if you want," Callie says. "You can sleep in my room."

"Then where would you sleep?"

"Up in the loft."

I glance up at the cobweb-draped loft, which is scarcely larger than a crawl space, and I laugh. "Oh, Callie! There's no way I'd kick you out of your own room and make you sleep up there."

"It's not so bad. I sleep in the hayloft whenever the goats are about to have their babies." She delicately sets a blue egg in a carton. "I kinda wish you *would* stay with us."

"Why?"

"It'd be fun. Like having a mom."

I watch her pick up another egg and turn it over, searching for any smudges. Sometimes Callie seems older than her years, but at this moment she seems far younger, and so much more vulnerable. She makes me think of another girl I once knew who was not much older than Callie. A girl who was just as vulnerable and even more needy. A girl whose fate still weighs on my conscience.

"Do you remember your mom?" I ask her.

"Just a little. Grandpa says I was only three when she died. He says the city's no place for a little girl, so we moved here."

"Your grandpa's a wise man."

"Why did you move here?"

It's a question I didn't expect, and one I don't want to answer. Not truthfully, anyway.

"It was just time for me to retire. I came to Maine to visit friends and found out Blackberry Farm was for sale. And it came with *great* neighbors." I give her ponytail a playful tug, and she giggles.

"Grandpa didn't like old Lillian very much 'cause she used to yell at him all the time. He's glad you moved in."

"I'm glad I did too."

We fall silent for a moment and focus on cleaning the eggs, filling the cartons.

"Grandpa's not seeing anyone," she says. "I mean, not any women. In case you were wondering."

I suppress a laugh. This girl is shameless, and I love her for it. "He has his hands full with you, sweetie. I'm sure that's enough to handle."

The door opens, and Luther himself stomps into the house carrying two sacks bulging with groceries. As he unloads carrots and potatoes and ground meat, he says, "Ran into Bonnie from the co-op. She says the eggs are all sold out, and she asked when I'm bringing over some more."

"Working on it now, Grandpa." Callie closes a carton and adds it to the stack in the plastic crate. "At least twelve dozen, I'd say. That's eighty-four dollars."

"They'll be sold out in a day. Especially with Maggie's blue ones in there." He looks at me. "Your chickens need to lay 'em faster."

"I'll talk to the girls," I say with a smile and then snap the last carton shut. "Thank you for hauling them over to the co-op, Luther."

"You two keep track of how to divvy up the money?"

"I did," says Callie. Of course she did. While I've been distracted by the murder, the girl's been paying attention to business. There's not much money involved, with only about twenty dollars' worth of eggs from my flock, but I won't insult Callie by telling her to keep my share of the proceeds. Charity is not something she'd appreciate.

"I'd better get home," I say, and pull my coat off the wall hook.

"Won't you stay for dinner?" Callie asks.

I think about that wistful comment she made earlier, about what it would be like to have a mother, and I'm sorry I can't play that role for her tonight. Perhaps another night.

"I have friends coming to my house, so I have to start cooking. But I'm still looking forward to the chicken and dumplings you promised me."

Callie grins. "Just tell me when. I'll kill one of the roosters, just for you."

*

"The Agency won't admit Bianca was one of ours, and that's worrisome," says Ben.

He and Declan are sitting in my kitchen, the last scraps of our dinner still spread out across the table. I served them lamb stew, a dish I fall back on whenever I'm in need of comfort. It's one of the reasons I could never be a vegetarian; I would miss this stew too much. The three of us have polished off the first bottle of cabernet, and we're well into the second. I refill all our glasses. It's a point of pride for me, that I can match the men, drink for drink.

"It's been twenty-four hours," I say. "What *do* we know?"

"The state police still haven't confirmed her identity," says Declan.

And Declan's sources are reliable. He is the consummate networker, and in just the six years he's been living in Purity, he's already cultivated friends in the state police, the local fire department, and the medical examiner's office. It's what we've all been trained to do, cultivating assets the way you grow a garden, nurturing and watering them until it's time for the harvest. Declan is a true master at it. It may be due to his Irish good looks, or because of his boyhood spent in a succession of boarding schools, where making friends quickly was a necessary survival skill.

I turn to Ben. "What *do* your sources in the Agency say?"

He takes a thoughtful sip of wine and sets down the glass. "They're not talking."

"What?"

"That in itself tells us something. It's possible their access isn't deep enough to find the answers, or they have answers but they're not at liberty to disclose the truth to me. If your mysterious Bianca *was* one of ours, no one's admitting it."

I fall silent, mulling over what we know about Bianca, a woman who carried a fake ID in her pocket, and whose fingerprints appear on no databases. A woman who stood in this kitchen a day and a half ago and told me that Diana Ward had vanished. I didn't care about Diana then, I don't care about her now, and whatever misfortune she's met can probably be laid at her own feet.

But Bianca is dead, I've been dragged into a murder investigation, and somehow the mess is all tied to Diana. It always seems to be.

"Tell me about Bianca's ID," I say.

"She had a Colorado driver's license, issued to a Bianca Miskova," says Declan. "Age thirty-three. Black hair, brown eyes, five foot seven, a hundred thirty pounds. Does that sound about right?"

"Yes."

"It's all fake."

"How good a fake?"

"As good as anything our people churn out."

"So she could've been one of ours."

"Or she could have played for another team. Which most likely means the SVR." Russian foreign intelligence. They certainly are not amateurs when it comes to inserting sleepers and providing excellent fake documents.

"Then who killed her?" I ask. "Did they? Or did we?"

My question is met with silence. Neither Ben nor Declan has an answer. I don't, either, at least nothing that makes sense.

Declan says: "Maggie, we need to know more about the reason Bianca sought you out. You said she was looking for your former colleague."

"And I couldn't help her. It's been years since I saw this colleague, and I have no idea where she is now."

"How many years?"

"Sixteen."

"Isn't that when you left the Agency?"

I nod. "And she's one of the reasons I resigned."

"One of the reasons?"

"The main reason."

"Who was this colleague?" asks Ben. "You never told us her name."

I don't answer right away. Instead, I pick up the empty stew bowls and carry them to the sink. There I stand with my back turned to them, looking at my reflection in the kitchen window. It's dark outside, and except for the faint glow from Luther's cabin, the landscape is black. The remoteness and the privacy of this property is why I chose it, but this is the downside. I am all alone out here, just a woman and her chickens.

I turn to the men. "Her name is Diana Ward."

Either her name is unfamiliar to them, or they're too skillful at masking their reactions. Most likely they didn't know Diana. We're the old guard, after all, and Diana would still have been in middle school when we got our first assignments out in the field. Also, they worked on different accounts from mine, Declan in Eastern Europe, Ben in the Middle East. They probably never laid eyes on Diana.

"And she's now gone missing?" Ben says.

"Bianca wanted my help locating her. I told her I have no idea where Diana is."

"Is that true?"

I glance back and forth at the two men. "Don't you believe me?"

Ben laughs. "How long have we known each other, Maggie?"

"Thirty-eight years? Since the Farm."

"That's longer than I knew my wife, and when Evelyn died, there was *still* a hell of a lot she didn't know about me. Things I never told her. Things I lied about."

"I'm not lying to you about this."

"But you never gave us the whole story either."

"Sharing isn't in our job description."

"You're not on the job now. You're among friends. We can't help you if you're holding anything back."

I return to the table and sit down. We've known each other so long, the three of us. Thirty-eight years ago, I was the baby of this trio, recruited straight out of college, but I was already sure of myself. Too sure. I'd grown up tinkering with old tractors and herding sheep while living with an alcoholic father on a farm with a killer mortgage. I managed to escape New Mexico by bullshitting my way through a college interview, and I ended up with a full scholarship at Georgetown University, where everyone around me seemed brilliant. Top grades and stratospheric SAT scores weren't enough to stand out in that crowd, but I believed I had a spark of something special. A knack for survival, for worming my way out of any situation.

The CIA training camp knocked that notion out of my head. I may have managed to check all the right recruitment boxes, but after the Farm, I was no longer under the illusion that I was special, because my fellow recruits were just as special, or they wouldn't have made it in the door.

"The truth is, I really *don't* know where Diana is," I say. "And to be perfectly honest, I don't give a shit if she's alive or dead."

"Do I sense a wee bit of bitterness there?" says Declan.

"Yep."

"What'd she do to you?"

I pause, searching for words to describe how Diana lit the tinder that destroyed my career. My life.

"She turned me into a traitor," I say.

The truth is far more complicated, but when you live in a world of mirrors, the truth is always distorted. Too often, it's what we *choose* to see while ignoring all the inconvenient bits, the nagging details that distort our view. We crave clarity, and so we lie to ourselves.

And what I've told myself these last sixteen years is that Diana Ward destroyed me, when in truth, I did it to myself.

CHAPTER 10

Twenty-four years ago

Why not? is what makes me hunt online for cheap fares to London, six months after meeting Danny Gallagher. *Why not?* is what I'm thinking as I pack my suitcase, as I ride the taxi from my apartment in Reston to the airport. I have not seen Danny Gallagher since Bangkok, a hookup that ended up lasting the full four days of my vacation there. Together we wandered through temples, gorged on street food, drifted through the khlongs aboard long-tail boats. And we had sex, of course, the frantic, heedless sort of fucking that's possible only when you think you'll never see this person again.

And yet here I am, on a night flight to London, because in those six months since Bangkok, I haven't stopped thinking about him. All the postcards he sent kept him fresh in my mind. There was the elephant card from Chiang Mai, the sunrise-over-the-temple card from Siem Reap, the monkey-cave card from Kuala Lumpur, each with a pithy message about what new foods he'd sampled, which new wonder he'd seen. Reading them made me wistful for the days when I saw the world as a happy playground, not a war zone. Then his postcards started coming from London, with touristy images of the Tower and the crown jewels and London Bridge. Even though it's the age of email, he continued mailing those postcards because it had become a silly ritual between us, and every few weeks, I'd find another one in my mailbox.

Then a month went by, and nothing arrived. That's when I realized I'd become attached to that ritual. I found myself checking and rechecking the empty slot, wondering if this meant it was over between us, if he'd met someone else or had grown weary of our one-sided correspondence. Or if, God forbid, something had happened to him.

That's when I finally pulled up the email address he'd given me on the day we parted. I had made no move to contact him, but after eight weeks of silence, my resolve at last broke.

> I'm heading to London in a few weeks, for business.
> Do you want to have dinner?

I clicked send. I imagined him scrolling through his emails. He would see mine and wonder why, after all these months, I was finally reaching out to him. Would he open it, or would he just scroll past?

I was about to close the laptop when I heard the ding of his email land in my inbox.

Three weeks later, I'm flying over the Atlantic. I've always been good at sleeping on planes, even in the most turbulent weather, but on this flight, I'm wide awake, wondering if this is a mistake. If I'll take one look at him and see a different Danny, not the lover burnished by the warm glow of memories, but a Danny with bad teeth and receding hair. I took no photos of him in Bangkok, nor did he take any of me. We are both bound to be disappointed.

Now it all feels doomed. I check in to my London hotel, take a shower, and collapse onto the bed, but still, I cannot sleep, thinking about the night ahead. I'm meeting him at a restaurant at eight o'clock. Neutral ground. It's what I insisted on for our reunion. I don't want him to show up at my hotel, nor do I want to be knocking at the door of his apartment, because both places present difficulties when it comes to a graceful escape. I am always about having a planned escape route, whether it's from a firefight or a romantic evening, and a restaurant is a safe place to meet. I've already built in my excuse: *Sorry we can't see more of each other, but I'm staying in the city for only a few nights.*

He has booked us a table at a place called Ballade in Mayfair. I'm unfamiliar with the restaurant, but it's been a year and a half since I was last in London, where new restaurants pop up like mushrooms after a rain. A glance online at the menu—and the prices—tells me this is not a jeans-and-jacket establishment. This is a place that calls for a dress and heels, which I happen to have with me because "Be prepared" is a motto for more than just Boy Scouts.

At 6:30 p.m., I'm out of bed and getting dressed, zipping myself into my evening battle armor of blue silk. My shoes are sculpturally elegant, even if the heels are only two inches, a height suitable for navigating—or running—on cobblestoned streets. Despite the makeup I've applied, I still see shadows under my eyes and exhaustion in my face, but there's nothing I can do about that. Disaster or not, here I come.

I take the tube from Covent Garden to Green Park, joining other revelers for a night on the town. They look so young, my fellow commuters, especially when I see my own reflection in the window. I'm only thirty-six, but I've already collected a lifetime's worth of unhappy tales. I wonder if tonight I'll add another one to my trove. *Flew all the way to London to meet a prince who turned out to be a frog.* At Green Park, I step off the tube and join the separating stream of passengers heading to the Jubilee line. On the platform, I see girls in miniskirts, boys in jackets with football logos, all of them thirsty for their next drink. I am stone-cold sober. I never drink before an operation, and that's what this feels like. Operation Danny.

It's only dinner and maybe sex. And after that?

I know how to disappear. It's my specialty.

It's a short ride on the Jubilee line to Bond Street, and I emerge from the station into what feels like a carnival of noise and light. It's just a normal Saturday night in London, but in my sleep-deprived state, it's all too loud, too bustling. Too much.

The sign for Ballade is understated, and I almost walk right past the restaurant. There are no windows, nothing to indicate what sort of business lies beyond the wall of blond wood. The door is massive and embellished with polished nickel, a door worthy of a fortress. As I haul it open, I feel as if I'm storming a castle.

From the bustling street, I step into a cocoon of quiet elegance. A hostess with perfect skin, with hair clipped in a geometric pageboy, magically materializes to greet me. Over her shoulder I see a dining room with white table linens and sparkling stemware and beautiful people. No blue jeans in sight.

"Reservation under Danny Gallagher," I tell the hostess.

She doesn't even glance at the reservations list; in a restaurant this exclusive, she knows which tables are spoken for and by whom. "I'm afraid Dr. Gallagher hasn't arrived yet. He called to say he was running late. Allow me to show you to your table."

I follow her into the dining room, where she seats me at a two-top near the kitchen. Not the best table in the house, but it affords me a good vantage point from which to view the other diners, and it's a location I'd instinctively seek anyway. A glass of champagne is delivered to my table, unasked for. It's that kind of establishment, where older men dine with women two decades younger, where no one raises their voice or deigns to glance at the prices on the menu. I sip champagne, glance at my watch.

Danny is ten minutes late.

My mind goes straight to the worst that can happen. He's had an accident. He's been mugged. He's had cold feet, and I'll be picking up the tab. A career of anticipating the worst has made me a pessimist, and even though the champagne gives me a pleasant buzz and I'm sitting in an exquisite dining room, I am uneasy.

Until Danny walks into the room.

This isn't the raggedy Danny I remember from that crowded Bangkok street market where we sat at a plastic table, gorging on beef noodle soup. This Danny has neatly trimmed hair and he wears a crisp oxford shirt and a suit jacket, and instead of a well-worn backpack, he has a leather doctor's satchel slung over his shoulder. He leans over, gives me an oddly shy peck on the cheek, and sits down in the chair across from me. Despite four steamy nights in Bangkok, we are still strangers to each other. I have to readjust my mental image of him to accommodate this updated version, but all the changes are merely superficial. He wears a suit and tie now, but it's the same smile that I remember.

I lean close and murmur: "My God, Danny. This restaurant is something. I'm afraid dinner is going to cost you—"

"An arm, a leg, and a month's salary. I know. But you're here, and I want to celebrate." He glances around the room. "It's my first time here. I've heard it's impossible to book a table."

"How did you manage it?"

"One of the dishwashers is my patient, and he slipped me into the book." His voice drops to a whisper. "Now let's pretend we actually belong here."

At that I have to laugh, because this does feel like a masquerade, two vagabonds dressed up in costume. Danny makes me feel like a younger, freer version of myself, before I was forced to grow up. Before my eyes were opened to all the dark places in the world.

"You wearing a suit. I never pictured that," I say.

"I was worried you never pictured me at all, after Bangkok."

"How could I not? All those postcards."

He winces. "Too much?"

"No, it was sweet. No one sends postcards anymore. Then I didn't hear from you for months, and I realized how much I missed getting them."

"I thought you might be tired of hearing from me." He looks straight at me, and his green eyes reflect the glow of the candle flickering on the table. "It's not as if we ever planned to see each other again. When you emailed me, I was surprised."

"So was I," I admit.

The server brings the menus as well as another glass of champagne. Danny takes a sip, and the champagne leaves a glistening splash on his lip. I have a sudden, vivid memory of those lips on my breast, of his teeth on my nipple, and I remember his broad hands grasping my hips as he thrust into me. Shaken by the flood of images, I open the menu. There are no prices, and I cast a worried glance across the table at Danny.

"Does yours have prices?" I whisper.

"You're worried I can't afford this, aren't you?"

"Let's not be silly. Why don't we go Dutch?"

"Relax. I have a steady job, now. I can pay this off in installments."

Laughing, I settle back in my chair. I can drink most men under the table, but tonight, jet lag and an empty stomach have given that one glass of champagne a powerful punch, and the alcohol fizzes through my bloodstream. I see everything in soft focus, the whispering dining room, the linen tablecloths. And Danny. Not the sunburned and rumpled Danny in Bangkok, but a clean-cut and equally tempting version of him. I sip my champagne, adding more fuel to the fire even as I try to keep up my end of the conversation.

"Tell me about the new job," I say.

"It's been an adjustment."

"You don't sound thrilled about it."

He shrugs. "It's bread-and-butter medicine. But I have regular hours now, a decent paycheck."

"And no gunshot wounds or malaria to treat. Do you miss that?"

"I miss the challenge. Making do in a crisis with only the bare necessities. But my mum's happy to have me back in the country. I didn't realize how hard it's been for her since my father died. I needed to come home." He smiles at me. "She's looking forward to meeting you."

I pause midsip, the glass at my lips. *His mum.* This is not what I bargained for. "You told her about me?"

"Shouldn't I have?"

"We're hardly at the meet-your-mum stage."

"She's not scary or anything, I promise. Well, maybe she is, a bit." He pauses. "But not in a serial killer kind of way."

Now he has me laughing again, in a way I haven't in months. I'm so focused on Danny that I'm not aware of the commotion on the other side of the dining room until a wineglass shatters on the floor and a woman starts screaming. We both turn to look.

A man has slumped forward in his chair, and he clutches his throat with both hands. Even from across the room I can see terror in his face as he frantically struggles to draw in a breath.

In an instant, Danny is out of his chair, and he scrambles across the room. As everyone else gapes, Danny leans in behind the distressed man and wraps his arms around his waist. There's no hesitation, no awkward hunt for the right position; Danny goes straight to work, pulling his fists up against the man's abdomen. Three times. Five times. He yanks so hard the chair scrapes, slams down.

The man is going limp.

Danny strikes the man's back, battering him like a drum, then grabs him around the waist and repeats the abdominal thrusts. Again and again.

The man's head tips forward.

Danny drags the now-unconscious man from his chair and lowers him onto the floor. "Maggie!" he yells. "I need my bag!"

I grab his leather satchel from the back of his chair and dart across the room, past an audience of people frozen in their chairs. As Danny rummages through the satchel for his medical instruments, I can't take my eyes off the unconscious man's face. He's in his sixties, silver haired and bullnecked, a man who's surely enjoyed a lifetime of fine meals, only to have this one kill him. His finely tailored jacket tells me he can well afford a restaurant like Ballade, but his wealth can't save him now. His blood is starved of oxygen, his chest motionless. I kneel down to feel for a carotid pulse. It's still there, but irregular.

A woman behind me gasps, "What are you *doing*?"

Danny has pulled a scalpel from his medical bag.

I know what he's about to do. He has no choice because an ambulance won't get here in time to save this man. I grab linen napkins from the table and lean over the man's neck, ready to sponge away any blood. In the right hands, a cricothyrotomy is a simple procedure, but in the wrong hands, it can be a disaster. I have seen it performed only once, in a muddy field, on a man whose throat had been crushed by shrapnel. It was a last-ditch effort to save his life, performed by a frightened colleague who'd never done one before, whose shaking scalpel nicked a carotid and unleashed a bloody torrent.

But Danny knows what he's doing. He quickly finds his landmarks, presses his scalpel to the neck, and slices into the cricothyroid membrane.

The woman behind me screams, "You cut his throat!"

I press a wadded napkin to the neck, soaking up blood as it dribbles from the wound. The trachea is now open and air hisses out of the incision, but the man has such a thick neck that when he draws in a breath, the soft tissues collapse over the wound, sealing it off. We need to keep the wound open.

A server stands nearby, watching wide eyed. I jump up and snatch the ballpoint pen from his pocket. In seconds I've unscrewed it, and I hand the hollow end to Danny.

He glances at me in surprise, then thrusts the pen into the wound, opening the incision. Air rushes in and out, and the man's blue-tinged lips slowly begin to turn pink. Only then do we hear the wail of the approaching ambulance.

By the time the medics wheel the man out of the dining room, he's moving his arms, starting to look around in confusion, and very much alive. Shaken, Danny and I return to our table. I notice his shirt is spattered with blood, and when I look down at myself, I realize my silk dress is stained as well. Although he'd worked with cool efficiency, he now looks shaken, as if it has only just occurred to him how badly everything could have turned out. His scalpel could have slipped, and the room could now be awash in blood. We do not say a word, just sit in stunned silence. The whole restaurant has gone quiet as well, and the table where the man collapsed is now empty, the guests gone and their meals abandoned.

Danny asks me, quietly: "How did you know?"

"Know what?"

"What to do, what I'd need. The napkins. The pen as a cannula." He frowns at me. "It's as if you've done this before."

I think of that day I knelt in the muddy field as we tried to save our colleague's life. I remember that first slice into his neck, and the powerful spurts of arterial blood, and how his eyes glazed over in death. "I watched it done once," I say.

"Where?"

"On television. It was some medical drama."

"Television?"

"Yes."

He stares at me, as if he can't decide if he believes this or not. If he doesn't believe me now, what other doubts will he compile about me? How many before he realizes that the woman sitting across from him is just an illusion?

"Dr. Gallagher?"

We both look up to see a server standing at our table. My first wild thought is that he's about to toss us out of the restaurant because of our bloodstained clothes. Instead, he places a business card face down in front of Danny.

"One of the other diners is covering the cost of your meal tonight. He says to feel free to order whatever you wish, including from our wine list."

"Seriously?" Danny glances at me with a look of surprise. "Which table is he sitting at?"

"He would prefer to speak to you in private, if you'll call that number tomorrow. Please, have a lovely meal. And thank you." He nods at me as well. "Both of you."

I glance around the dining room, wondering which patron has so generously gifted us with this meal, but no one is looking our way. Whoever he is, he's chosen to remain anonymous for now.

"What's on the business card?" I ask.

Danny frowns at the card, then hands it to me.

Printed on the front is *Galen Medical Concierge* and a phone number. I flip it over and see that someone has scrawled a short message.

We're hiring. Let's talk.

"Are you going to call?" I ask, handing back the card.

"Maybe. I'll think about it." He slips the card into his pocket. "But tonight, I'd rather think about us, and . . ."

"And?"

He focuses on me. "And what happens next."

CHAPTER 11

Now

Declan rises from my kitchen table and opens the cabinet where I keep my treasure. Not the everyday single-malt scotch that I buy at the local grocery store, but the precious stuff. He's been in my house often enough to know where I stash it, and now out it comes, my bottle of thirty-year-old Longmorn. He pushes aside the empty wine bottles on the table and sets down the whisky with a *thunk*, a signal that the conversation is about to get serious. His lips are tight with determination as he pours whisky into three glasses and slides one glass toward me. I don't touch mine right away, instead simply watching as Ben and Declan lift their own glasses and take the first sips. A taste for good whisky is something I acquired late in life, and I'm annoyed to watch so much of my stash going down the throats of others, even if they're my closest friends.

"So did he take that job with the medical concierge?" Ben asks.

"The offer was too tempting to resist. The salary, the perks. It came with a corporate-owned apartment, in the best part of London. Most important, though, his mother desperately needed his help paying off her mortgage, and by taking the job, he was able to make her last few years comfortable. So yes, he took the job. Reluctantly."

"Why reluctantly?"

"Because of what the Galen clinic represented to him. Medical concierges are for the privileged few. For people who are wealthy enough to buy their way out of the system that everyone else has to use. They snap their fingers, and a doctor will magically appear, with whatever pills they happen to need."

"I'd sign up for that," says Ben.

"Not at the prices Galen charged." I finally pick up my glass and take a sip. With the sting on my tongue comes memories of London. Of the first time I tasted the Longmorn, with Danny.

"So he went to work for Galen," says Declan. "How does that tie in with Diana Ward?"

"That's what brought Diana into our lives. It's why Danny came to her attention. The Galen clinic led to Diana. Which led to every fucking thing that went wrong."

"Now tell us about Diana Ward. How and where did she come into the picture?"

I set down my glass, my tongue still tingling from the whisky. "Istanbul. It all started in Istanbul."

CHAPTER 12

Istanbul, eighteen years ago

Someone is watching me. Someone is always watching me, whether it's the curious children on the street or the insistent carpet sellers or perhaps agents from Millî İstihbarat Teşkilatı, otherwise known as the MIT, Turkey's National Intelligence Agency, although there's no reason to consider me a person of interest. I'm just another American businessperson, commuting on foot to my office near Taksim Square. Still, I have to assume they are watching, so every morning when I wake up in my Istanbul apartment, I mentally prepare myself for another day of playing hide-and-seek. I don't believe my apartment is bugged or my landline is tapped, but I proceed as if they are. The old lady who sweeps out the coffee shop across the alley seems to keep tabs on my comings and goings, but that could be because she's just the neighborhood busybody. Or is she getting paid by the MIT to watch me? Turkish intelligence likes to keep an eye on all resident foreigners, and when I step out of my apartment and walk through busy Taksim Square, there's an excellent chance someone is tailing me, so I do my best to look relaxed, even bored.

This morning, I'm yawning as I walk, but it's a genuine yawn, the consequence of yet another late night out on the town, barhopping and chatting up new friends. By night, I'm a social butterfly. By day

I'm just a worker bee, doing what I do five days a week. I reach the old four-story building that houses Europa Global Logistics and climb two flights of creaking wooden stairs to our offices. The placard on the door is understated, specifically designed *not* to impress. It sends the message to the public—*we don't really want your business*—and to discourage them further, there's a security keypad requiring visitors to punch in a code just to walk in the door.

I enter my six-digit code and step inside.

The front office is furnished with two desks, and it looks like what it's purported to be, the outpost of an international firm that specializes in import-and-export logistics. One desk is covered with file folders containing US customs forms, ISF paperwork, bills for trucking and shipping, and books filled with compliance regulations for countries around the world. The second desk, labeled with my nameplate, "Margaret Porter," is piled high with fabric swatches in a rainbow of colors: lustrous silks from Thailand, brocades from Belgium, richly detailed weavings from Turkey. Behind my desk is a clothing rack crowded with sample dresses from Istanbul designers, bound for New York. My focus is on fashion and textiles, and if I'm thrown into a room with genuine import/export businessmen, I know enough about the subject to more than hold my own.

I walk through the front office to the inner door, punch in another security code, and step into the room where the real business of Europa Global Logistics is done. I fire up the coffeepot, then sit down to read the latest cables from HQS, sent to us via secure link from the US consulate. There've been no earth-shattering local developments in the last twenty-four hours, but my colleague Gavin and I have various tasks bubbling on multiple burners, whether it's an asset we're trying to develop or a new source I'd like to approach, pending HQS approval. I tap out a report listing the reasons why I'm proposing this source, and I ask for additional background information before I make the initial bump.

I hear Gavin, whose desk is in the adjoining office, arrive. He greets me with his usual air salute and goes straight to the coffeepot. We're each doing our own thing; we usually do, sitting at our separate desks, typing our individual reports and cables. Gavin manages global sales of "agricultural equipment," which requires him to make occasional treks out to the hinterlands, visiting rural areas along the Turkish/Syrian border. Sometimes I travel with him, ostensibly to visit textile and carpet factories. Gavin is fifteen years older than I am, and after thirty years in the field, he desperately wants to retire. He would, if he didn't have a hefty mortgage to pay off at home and two kids attending private universities—he will probably have to keep working until he keels over. We've been stationed together in Istanbul for three and a half years now, have had no major flare-ups, and we usually don't get on each other's nerves.

In our line of work, that qualifies as a dream partnership.

I check on the latest details for tonight's fashion show, which will feature Istanbul's up-and-coming designers. It will be attended by journalists, exporters, buyers, and many of the city's most glamorous women. I will be there, as well. It's where someone in my fake line of work is expected to show up.

Next I confirm my flight reservations for the short vacation I plan to take in three days. Every chance I get, I jet off to London to visit Danny, and just thinking about seeing him again makes my mood lift. We don't see each other nearly often enough, and the result is, six years later, we still can't get enough of each other. It's true; absence does make the heart grow fonder. It also makes the loins burn hotter. It's an arrangement that works for us—or for me, anyway. Prolonged togetherness would require too much honesty between us, and I'm not ready to make *that* commitment. What I can give him is the occasional rendezvous in London or Paris or Lisbon, and then back we both go, to our separate lives, which are busy enough as it is.

"You all set for tonight?"

I look up at Gavin, who's standing in front of my desk, sipping coffee. He looks tired this morning, his brown hair standing up like dandelion fluff, the bags under his eyes more pronounced than usual. Money troubles are weighing him down, and I feel sorry for him. Sorry that he's still out here battling in the trenches, when he really wants to be retired in Thailand, sipping a beer by the river.

"I hear it's going to be a full house tonight," I say. "Eight designers, a live band, cocktails afterward. Should be quite a performance."

"And the other performance?" He doesn't need to say more; we both know what he's talking about.

I nod. "That's on too."

*

While I've never been a fan of jazz, it seems that the Turks are crazy about it, judging by the wild applause they give to the band. It is indeed a full house tonight, with every seat in the theater taken, and dozens more people standing at the back. I'm pleased by the crowd, not because I have any stake in the night's success, but because this same crowd will shortly be streaming out the doors and spilling onto the street, a tidal wave of people in which a particular face can easily be lost. I wait until everyone's on their feet and shuffling toward the aisles in a noisy exodus toward the street exit; then I head in a different direction, toward the backstage stairs. I already know the floor plan of this building, and I take those stairs to the first-floor hallway, stride past the green room where the models are stripping off clothes and makeup. There's a performers' restroom at the end of the hall. I slip inside, change into blue jeans and a dark jacket, and tie on a headscarf. Then I push out the stage door exit, into the alley.

I can hear the voices of the dispersing audience echoing from the street at the front of the theater. I head down the alley in the opposite direction and around the corner, onto a parallel street. With the headscarf concealing my hair, I could be just another Turkish woman heading home after an evening out with friends. It's merely a light disguise, but it should be enough to throw off anyone who tries to follow me. I'm not going far, only a zigzag through back streets until I reach my destination: the nondescript black Toyota sedan, parked exactly where I was told I'd find it.

I slide in behind the wheel, glance around to confirm there's no one in sight, and drive away. Unless MIT was anticipating my move and is poised to follow me in another vehicle, I'm in the clear, but I continue my usual precautionary moves. Turn right, check for headlights behind me. Turn right again. Check again. I zigzag my way to tonight's meeting point, and when I reach it, I stop only long enough to let the man, who's now waiting in the shadow of a doorway, climb into the passenger seat.

Then I pull away from the curb and off we drive.

"Any problems?" I ask Doku.

"No."

"You're certain MIT didn't follow you?"

"I did not see anyone."

"How long do we have?"

"As long as you need me. I have no other engagements tonight, except with maybe a bottle of vodka." Which is Doku's companion of choice.

I allow myself to relax just a little, because I sense he is relaxed. Or is that overconfidence? I catch a whiff of alcohol on his breath, and suddenly I'm on edge again. He's already started the night's binge. This is not good.

"Anything urgent to share?" I ask. My gaze darts again to the rearview mirror. I see nothing to alarm me.

"There has been a split in the leadership," he says. "Murat is sick of the emirate. He thinks they are useless, and he wants to return home, to the fight. He's bringing a shipment of weapons with him."

"You have details? When, which route into Chechnya?"

"It happens on the fourteenth. The usual route through Georgia, into the mountains."

"Where did he get these weapons?"

"They arrived two weeks ago, aboard a ship from Tunis."

"Who paid for it?"

"I've heard rumors. They say it was funded through a London source, but who knows where it really comes from? Money is not like water. It moves uphill instead. It flows from people who have too much of it, to people who have even more of it." He laughs bitterly. "Never to people like me."

And Doku desperately needs the money, not only to pay for his own sad pleasures, but also to support his widowed sister and her six-year-old daughter, who have recently fled to Istanbul. Doku has dangerous friends, so his sister and niece live in a different neighborhood, for their own safety. Like too many other refugees in the city, they live on the edge, crammed into a crumbling apartment building with others who are equally as desperate.

"What kind of arms are in the shipment?" I ask.

"Not the usual rubbish with missing parts. No, there are MANPADS. FIM-92 Stingers, Russian Iglas. Cluster bombs and white phosphorus. Millions of dollars' worth."

Since the end of the Cold War, a bounty of secondhand weaponry has been unleashed onto the black market. That's what will soon head to Chechnya with Murat. The ultimate destination of these weapons matters little to the dealers who trade them; if there's a healthy profit to be made, they'll sell bazookas or baby milk.

"I'm not the only one who knows about this," says Doku. "Surely the Russians know, too, and they do not play nicely. They pit us against the emirate, to weaken the resistance." He sighs, and it is a sound of resignation. "I do not think Murat will reach Chechnya alive. And his weapons will find a new home, at a new price. South America, perhaps."

The sadness in his voice is emblematic of how hopeless all these different conflicts are, how hopeless his world has become. Doku does not wish death to Murat, yet here he is betraying him, because he sees that in the long run, none of it matters. Murat is doomed anyway, and Doku might as well profit from Murat's inevitable fate.

I pull over to the curb and park. It's a quiet neighborhood, and I have a clear view in all directions. By the glow of the streetlamp, I study Doku's face. He looks more and more dissolute every time we meet, his face more bloated, his eyes puffier. I know he loves Istanbul; he tells me this again and again, and even though he hates the Russians, hates what they are doing in his native Chechnya, he does not hate them enough to give up his life here and his booze, to return to the mountains and fight.

So he needs money, enough to support his sister and niece, to stay in this city where all manner of delights are within his reach, and he's willing to betray a few secrets for it. Up till now, he hasn't given us anything major, anything we don't already suspect. I'm well aware of the split in the Chechen Emirate fighters, some of whom slipped across the border to fight alongside ISIS in Syria, while others chose to stay focused on their fight against Russia. What Doku provides us is merely confirmation, and I have yet to press him for anything more valuable. He needs to be encouraged to dig deeper, ferret out more details. It is perilous work, and neither of us is under the illusion this is a gentleman's game. He keeps dangerous company, and those opposing him are even more dangerous.

I hand him what he has come for, a stack of US dollars, and watch as he counts them. Although this seems hardly different from a transaction with a prostitute, the truth is, I've come to rather like Doku. I think the real reason he fled the war in Chechnya is that he is at heart not a warrior but a wounded soul. He has the eyes of a beaten dog, and whenever our gazes meet, he cannot hold mine but looks away, as if I'll pull out a stick and start to thrash him if he stares at me too long. He is pitiable and faithless, but he's not dangerous. Not unless he's backed into a corner.

"Find out the dates," I tell him. "The specific route he'll take through the mountains. And I want to know where this money is coming from. You said it was funneled through London."

"We have sympathizers there, you know."

"Yes, I know." People outraged by what is happening to Muslims in Chechnya. Or perhaps they're merely interested in keeping the conflict there alive for their own profit. In war lies opportunity.

He finishes counting the money. Satisfied it's what we agreed to, he slips it into his pocket. "There is one more thing I wish to ask of you."

So now the money is not enough. It's how these relationships usually go. Assets get dissatisfied or their families want more, or they begin to feel fate closing in.

"If something happens to me," he says quietly, "I want you to take care of my sister Asma and my niece."

A chill crawls up my spine and I look at him. Has he had a premonition? Is there something he hasn't told me? He is staring straight ahead, his expression unreadable in the gloom of the car. "Why are you asking me this?"

"Will you take care of them? Promise me."

"Yes, of course I will, but nothing will happen to you. Not if you're careful."

He gives a soft laugh. "Even you do not believe that."

I glance around at the street and see no one else. It's safe to leave him here. "Go home, Doku. Everything will look better in the morning."

"Not here. Take me to the club."

"I can't drop you off there. There'll be too many eyes."

"Then leave me a few blocks away from the club. No one will see us."

"It's late. You should go to bed."

"I should." He pats the pocket that holds the cash. "But someone very much needs a drink."

I don't like this, but I cannot talk him out of it. He insists I drive him to his club, a popular bar facing the Bosporus, and a gathering place for the thousands of Chechens who now live in Istanbul. He seems to spend every other night there, and will probably drink away half his money by morning.

A few blocks away from the club, I pull to the side of the road. "This is as close as I want to get."

"I have to walk the rest of the way?"

"It's a nice night. You can use the exercise."

With a sigh, he steps out. He doesn't even glance back at me as he heads toward the Bosporus. Once again, we are strangers, bound together only by envelopes of cash and a Starbucks gift card, with which he buys coffee to signal when he wants to meet me. I pull out a notebook. Before I forget, I quickly jot down the details of what he's just told me about Murat, about the Stingers and the Iglas. It's midnight, I'm tired, and I still need to write a summary and send off the cable, but for a moment I just sit in the car, mulling over what Doku told me. More arms are headed to Chechnya, which means more widows and orphans in the world. There are already enough widows and orphans, on every side, for every cause.

I start the car and drive toward the Bosporus, in the same direction that Doku walked only minutes earlier. Just as I reach the intersecting road that fronts the seaside, a black BMW roars past. It's traveling in the direction of Doku's nightclub. In that instant, I know that something is about to happen. Something involving Doku.

In the distance, a voice shrieks. A woman's.

I freeze, torn between wanting to rush to Doku's aid and needing to stay away, stay unseen. I drive around the corner. Two blocks ahead, a crowd has gathered on the street in front of the nightclub. More people are screaming. Slowly I drive toward the club, scanning the crowd. I'm just a curious rubbernecker, wanting to see what's happened. The BMW that raced past earlier is nowhere in sight. The hit was quick, and away they went. Two men stand shouting into their cell phones, frantically gesticulating as they try to summon help. A few people turn and look at my car as I drive past, perhaps worried that I'm here to shed even more blood, but all they see behind the wheel is a woman in a black headscarf, and they look away again. I should not be doing this. I should not be exposing myself to all these eyes, but I need to know if Doku is alive.

He is not.

He lies on his back on the sidewalk, legs splayed apart, a black river of blood streaming across the pavement. The crowd blocks my view of his face, but I know it's him because I glimpse the fake Rolex watch on his wrist. He was proud of that watch, even though he knew it was, like so many other things in life, a counterfeit. We are all pretending to be something we are not, and some of us are better at it than others.

I don't need proof of death; the volume of blood on the sidewalk tells me Doku's wounds are fatal. I keep driving, which is what I should have done to begin with. Drive past, drive on.

If something happens to me, I want you to take care of my sister Asma and my niece.

His sister.

If Doku was the target, then his sister could be next. Not because she knows anything, but because her death would be a powerful warning to any and all potential informants that you are not the only one who will suffer.

Asma's apartment is in Gazi Mahallesi, one of the poorest neighborhoods in Istanbul and a thirty-minute drive away. I have never met her, and she does not know about me—at least that's what Doku said. Now, as I navigate the eternally snarled Istanbul traffic, I debate what to say and how much to reveal. Meeting her face to face is a mistake, I know it is, but there's no time to make other arrangements. I'll spirit Asma and her little girl out of the building, out of the city, and then I'll think of what to do next. Gavin will have my head on a plate for this, and maybe our mother ship will want its pound of flesh from me as well, but I can still hear Doku's voice in my head. *Promise me.*

He knew. Somehow he knew he was going to die.

Get them out. Get them out.

I don't know how good her English is, or her Turkish. Will I be able to explain that her brother is dead, that she needs to flee? I consider just calling the police, anonymously telling them the woman's in danger, but that will lead to questions I can't answer. They'll probably ignore me anyway.

I have to do this myself. I promised him.

I am still three blocks away when I notice the fiery red glow. *No, it can't be. Please, let it be a different building.*

Then I round the corner onto her street and slam to a stop. Her apartment building is engulfed, flames clawing the sky. Doku told me Asma lives on the sixth floor, in a building with an elevator that never works, a building that forces her to climb six floors with her groceries. I look up, counting the stories, and realize no one on the sixth floor could possibly survive that blaze.

If they were even alive when it was started.

A policeman shouts at me to move. I call out in Turkish: "What happened? What about the people—have they been rescued?"

He shakes his head, waves me on. I hear sirens screaming, the fire trucks arriving too late to make a difference. Just as I arrived too late.

The policeman orders me to keep moving. I have no choice, so I drive on, drive past. Once again, I must leave behind the dead.

CHAPTER 13

"It's as you suspected." Gavin hands me the ballistics report. It's been two days since Doku's murder, and only now has this report leaked from Turkish intelligence. I focus on the details of the two bullets that were recovered from Doku's body. Both appear to be standard AK-47 rounds, and based on the medical examiner's report, either bullet would have proved fatal. No casings were found at the scene, because none were ejected—not from this particular weapon. I know what that means.

"You didn't hear any gunshots?" Gavin asks.

"No."

"You're certain?"

"I saw the car speed past, and then I heard screaming, but there were no gunshots. If these were fired from a standard AK-47, they would have been loud enough for everyone to hear." I look up from the report. "They used a Groza. Which means the killer must have been in bad-breath distance of him."

"Shit." Gavin leans back in his chair and rubs his eyes. I am standing in front of his desk. Outside, Istanbul traffic is as chaotic as ever, but inside this office we are in a private bubble, just the two of us, quietly dealing with a crisis. The Groza is not a weapon you find on the open market. Developed by the Special Design Bureau in the Tula Arms Plant, it is a double-barreled derringer-type pistol that is chambered for a 7.62x39 cartridge, and it produces a noiseless, flameless shot. It kills in silence, which makes it perfect for its intended use as an assassination tool, and it was developed specifically for Russian Special Forces. It is not the first time we've seen the lethal results of a Groza; in just the last year, two Chechens were murdered in Istanbul, both presumably by the Russians.

"They didn't tail us there," I say.

"You're sure no one was at the pickup point? Followed you from there?"

"No, Gavin. The hit man must have already been at the nightclub, waiting for him. The booze, that was his weak point. And that club. He couldn't stay away from that fucking club. Sooner or later, he was going to walk into one of their bullets."

"And the car you saw?"

"It must have been the killer's escape vehicle. He was probably stationed outside the club, watching for Doku to show up. Saw him, moved in for the kill, signaled the driver to come get him. By the time anyone in that crowd noticed Doku was on the ground and bleeding, the kill team would have been blocks away."

"Could anyone place you there, at the scene?"

"Absolutely not. I drove past and kept driving," I say, even as I scour my memory of that night because *absolutely* is a dangerous word. It leaves no room for doubt, or for any truths we prefer not to see. I think of the street where I picked up Doku. Had there been someone watching as he stepped into my car? Was it possible another car was poised nearby to follow us as we pulled away, a car that managed to stay with us, all the while unseen, as I wove through the maze of back streets?

No, I am not so careless as to let that happen. I am certain this was not my mistake. Except somehow it *feels* like I am responsible because it happened on the night we met, and he was killed only blocks away from where I'd dropped him off. It happened because I did not protest vociferously enough when he insisted on going to the club. I should have said no. I should have dropped him off elsewhere, but hindsight doesn't change the fact Doku was his own man who made his own choices, and I was powerless to alter his behavior. Ours was a delicate dance, both of us needing something from the other. It wasn't friendship but mutual opportunism that had brought us together.

Yet I truly do mourn his death, because he was not a bad man, merely a weak one. Now we're left with no good source inside the Turkish wing of the Chechen resistance, and those who remain are being eliminated, one by one, by the Russians.

"I'll write up the cable before I leave for London," I tell Gavin.

"The mother ship's not going to take this news well, but I don't see any way we can sugarcoat this. It looks like a screwup, Maggie."

What he's really saying is, it *is* a screwup, and it's mine, all mine. Even though he's the senior officer in Istanbul, he's absolving himself of all responsibility, and I can't blame him for wanting to cover his ass. He's got bills to pay and kids to put through college, and he can't let anything mess up his pension.

I return to my desk feeling like I've just been tossed off the lifeboat. Okay, then. At least he's letting me write the cable so I can slant it in the best way possible. The possibility of assassination hangs over every Chechen fighter living in Istanbul. The Russians took out Doku; that was purely between him and them.

Except that Doku was also our asset, and I grieve his loss. I grieve, too, for the loss of Asma and her daughter. They were the true innocents in all this, just collateral damage, lost in the churn of perpetual conflict.

*

I think about Asma and her little girl the next morning as I fly to London. The photo of their charred bodies lying in the Istanbul morgue has been seared into my memory, like too many other images that will always haunt me, of other victims, other children. To fight the enemy, you have to know the enemy's handiwork, and that knowledge has worn me down, polluted my view of the world. I look around my Turkish Airlines cabin, and instead of seeing fellow passengers sipping wine, I think of the broken bodies from Lockerbie. As I ride the taxi to Danny's apartment, I look out at the streets of London and imagine the bomb craters of Grozny.

I used to be able to shut it all out, but the nightmares are catching up with me.

Danny's still at work in the clinic when I arrive at his building, so I punch in the code on his security keypad and let myself in. He's just moved into this flat, and I marvel at the sparkling-new kitchen with its granite countertops. His living room windows look over the building's private garden, and the place still smells like fresh paint. It doesn't feel like a *Danny* sort of place; certainly, it's nothing like his first apartment in Brixton, on a lively street with pubs and curry houses, so different from this exclusive enclave in Knightsbridge. I walk through the living room, where framed photos are displayed. One is of Danny and me in Barcelona, just a pair of happy tourists in love. The other photo is of his late mother, who passed away of a stroke three years ago. I did not know Julia Gallagher well, but during our brief acquaintance, she decided I was the right woman for her son. "You're the only one he ever talks about," she told me, "the only one, I think, who will make him happy." In that way, she gave her blessing to our union, but she did not know it was based on lies.

I hate to think of what she'd say if she knew that almost nothing I told her about myself was true.

In a bathroom agleam with marble, I unpack my toiletries and strip off my clothes to take a shower. I catch a glimpse of myself in the mirror, and am bothered by how tired and washed out I appear after my flight. There's no holding back the passage of time, and I see it in the deepening crow's-feet, in the crease between my eyebrows and the wisps of gray at my temples. When I was twenty-five, I thought I'd never have to look at this version of my face. I had romantic notions of dying in action before wrinkles ever set in, but here I am, looking every bit my forty-two years of age. Living hard doesn't mean dying early; sometimes it just means those hard years end up on your face.

Maybe this is the right time for a change. I could resign from the Agency and slip into Danny's world instead. The murder of Doku has shaken me more than I want to admit, because I was probably the last person he spoke to, and I think of him dying just steps from his favorite nightclub. I may be only peripherally involved in that war, but I am still one of its combatants.

"Maggie? Are you here?" It's Danny.

I don't bother to pull on even a towel, instead stepping stark naked out of the bathroom. Laughing, he pulls me against him and joyfully lifts me off my feet. It's been four months since we were last in each other's arms, but it seems as if no time has passed at all, so well do our bodies fit together, like interlocking puzzle pieces rejoined. We never promised to be faithful to each other, but in the years since we met, I haven't been tempted by anyone else. After four months of starvation, I'm ready to devour him.

"Missed me?" he whispers.

"You have no idea."

"Oh, yes I do."

He pulls off his own clothes as we kiss our way into his bedroom. Through a haze of lust I watch his shirt fall to the floor, watch him kick away his trousers as we stumble toward the bed. His hair now has threads of gray, but he's still the same Danny I met in Bangkok, the same man who's never lost his hunger for life, and for me. By the time we fall onto his bed, I am already so aroused that his first few thrusts hurtle me over the cliff.

With a cry, I tumble back to earth. Feel my heart slow, my breaths deepen. *Sweet Danny, how I missed you.*

We coil ourselves around each other and watch the shadows grow as we listen to the distant rumble of evening traffic. I count how many days and nights we have together before I have to return to Istanbul, and my joy dims. Every reunion is a seesaw between delight and sadness, because they're always temporary. This time, the sadness feels much deeper. This time, I don't want to leave.

"And here I was planning to take you out to dinner first," he says. "Coax you into bed the properly romantic way. Then you pop out looking irresistible and ruin all my plans. Shameless wench."

"I wouldn't want to be predictable."

"Not in a million years." A pause. Then, softer: "I missed you, Maggie. When do we stop doing this?"

"Making love?"

"No. This back-and-forth nonsense. Me here, you in Istanbul, or wherever it is you'll be working next. Why does being with you always have to involve a trip through bloody Heathrow?"

"My job—"

"There are jobs in London."

"With lots of red tape for Americans."

"That won't be a problem if we're married."

I fall still. Never before have we brought up the subject of marriage. For the past six years, we've juggled our lives with no thought of anything permanent, no thought beyond our next vacation, our next adventure together. "Danny Gallagher, are you proposing to me?"

He laughs. "In my own inimitably clumsy way, yes, I am. I know it's not something you wanted to hear from me, but it's what I had to say."

"Why?"

"Because I hate it when you go away. I hate it when I don't wake up next to you in the morning. And I hate the thought it's going to be like this for the rest of our lives."

I'm so stunned I don't say anything. After a painfully long silence, he sits up on the side of the bed, his back turned to me as though to protect himself from all the ways I hurt him, ways I never realized. I reach out to touch him, and his muscles tense at my contact.

"I'm sorry," I whisper. "I didn't know that it's been so hard for you."

"But not for you?" He looks at me. "It doesn't bother you that we go months without seeing each other? That we don't have what other couples have? A home together, a *proper* home, with a cat. Maybe even a kid."

"Oh, Danny."

"No, it's okay. I know it's not what you want."

"I didn't say that."

"You don't need to. I understand." He rises to his feet and starts to get dressed. In the deepening gloom, his white shirt flutters like a ghost. "You love your job. You love having no anchor to drag you down. But, Maggie, I *want* an anchor. I want to tie my life to someone else, the way my mum and dad did. I wish you'd seen them together, because you would know what I'm talking about. They were never rich, always in debt, but they had each other." He finishes buttoning his shirt and sits down on the bed, defeat drooping his shoulders. "I can't keep this up, Maggie. The way things are now."

The sound of laughter filters in from the street, a sound that's jarring and obscene in the painful silence.

"Are you sure I'm the one, Danny?" I ask.

"Yes."

"But you hardly know me. We see each other only a few times a year."

"Then let's live together so we *will* know each other. You could move here. Or I can move to Istanbul."

"You'd give up your job at Galen?"

"I can be a doctor anywhere. Bodies are bodies."

"You'd give up all this for me? The paycheck, this apartment?"

"Maggie, I used to live in a tent treating refugees, and I was perfectly happy. This apartment isn't mine, anyway. It belongs to Galen. I wouldn't miss it, and I certainly wouldn't miss the pompous prats who expect me to jump at their every sniffle. I'll happily walk away from the job if that's what I need to do for us to be together."

I hear bitterness in his voice. He's weary of his work, just as I'm weary of mine. What a fine pair we are, both of us yearning to escape the boxes we've shut ourselves into. I think about what it would be like to settle into this apartment as his wife, to give up all the deceptions, large and small, that I've had to live with, and for once be exactly who I claim to be: Danny Gallagher's wife. I imagine myself wandering the British Museum to my heart's content, or strolling alongside the Thames without worrying who is following me.

He sighs. "It was a crazy idea. I shouldn't have put you on the—"

"Yes," I say.

He turns and stares at me. "What?"

"I'll move to London, and let's do it. Let's get married."

And just like that, it's agreed upon. It seems like a spur-of-the-moment decision, but it isn't, not really. It's the culmination of so many things. Doku's assassination. That glimpse of my own tired face in the mirror. The sad acceptance that in the grand scheme of the world, my work makes little difference. Wars will still be fought, empires will still fall, and all the bits and pieces of information I glean from my sources, all those cables I write, will simply get funneled into a government machine that chews them up and turns them into compost, like Doku's body. But unlike the false friendships I've been trained to cultivate, Danny is real. What we share is real.

"Do you mean it?" he asks. "Really?"

"Yes. Yes, yes, yes!"

He wraps his arms around me in a long strangling hug. I feel his tears against my cheek, and now I'm crying, too, crying from happiness. Something I have not done in a long, long time.

This is where I belong. With Danny.

*

By the time I board the flight back to Istanbul a week later, I've already composed the resignation letter in my head. Resigning is not as simple as merely sending a letter to headquarters. There will be debriefings and a handover of all the assets I've cultivated in Istanbul over the past three years. Last month was my twenty-first anniversary with the Agency, so I will be eligible for a pension when I turn fifty-five. This is a logical time to resign, a point when many government employees choose to walk away and start the next phase in life. My new phase will be in London, as a doctor's wife.

I'm already saying goodbye to Istanbul in my mind as I ride the taxi from the airport to my apartment in Taksim. I've said goodbye to other cities before, other postings, but this farewell is especially bitter-sweet because I love Istanbul: the energy, the history, the people and their kindness. But I am leaving it for something better, for Danny, and that's where the sweetness comes in. I promise myself I'll bring him here on vacation. I will take him to my favorite kofta restaurant off İstiklal Avenue, ply him with glasses of sweet raki, and watch his face as he samples savory *iskander* and *pide* and tender skewers of lamb.

It's almost midnight when the taxi drops me off in front of my building. The coffee bar across the street is dark, and the nosy neighbor lady is nowhere in sight. My week out of town has shaken up her schedule, too, and for once I can let myself into the building without feeling the old lady's eyes on my back. The stairway is dark, and I hit the first-floor switch, lighting up the stairs only long enough for me to climb to the second floor. Just as I'm inserting the key into my door, the stair timer switches off the light, and I'm left standing in darkness. To hell with this electricity-saving crap; at heart I'm an American power hog. I wheel my suitcase into the apartment, fumble for the wall switch, and freeze.

Something is not right.

It's so dark I can't make out even the silhouettes of my furniture, but somehow, even in the pitch blackness, I sense I am not alone. I smell the scent of an unfamiliar shampoo, hear the faint hiss of an exhaled breath. Someone else is in my apartment. Frantically I scan the darkness, but I cannot see anyone. I can only smell them. Hear them.

"There's no reason for alarm, Maggie," says a familiar voice. "It's just us."

"*Gavin?* What the fuck are you doing here?"

"We can't be seen talking to you."

We? At last I find the wall switch and I flick it on, to see Gavin sitting in my armchair. He looks stiff and ill at ease, unlike the blonde woman who's standing by the bookcase. She is young, only in her late twenties, with platinum hair that looks like silver against her black turtleneck. I have never seen this woman before, and even though this is my first glimpse of her, already I don't like her because she's standing uninvited in my apartment. I don't like the way she looks at me, as if I'm merely a specimen to be sliced open and dissected.

I turn to Gavin. "Who the fuck is *she?*"

"Maggie, I know this is unexpected. I'm sorry it had to be sprung on you this way, but we don't know if you're being surveilled."

"You broke into my apartment. You scared the shit out of me."

"It was necessary," the woman says. "No one can know I'm here." Calmly she approaches me. She's at least a decade younger than I am, but she moves with the quiet confidence of someone who's in control of the situation, and that disturbs me. It means that I am not the one in control.

"I'll ask again. Who are you?" I say.

"Diana Ward."

"Real name? Or cover?"

"It doesn't really matter. This is not about me. It's about you."

I look at Gavin. "Do you know what she's talking about?"

He sighs. "Unfortunately, yes."

"Tell me about Danny Gallagher," Diana says.

The shift of subject is so abrupt it makes my head snap back to her. "What?"

"Danny Gallagher. The man you regularly visit in London. The man you've repeatedly met up with over the last six years. Barcelona, Rome, Paris, among other places."

"HQS knows all about Danny. I informed them when I first started seeing him." It's what we're expected to do when we enter a romantic liaison. Honey traps are everywhere, and falling in love with the wrong person can endanger assets and operations. "They had no objections to my seeing him. And I did my own background check on him as well. He is who he says he is."

"Yes, born in Leicester, the only child of Frank Gallagher, a pub keeper, and his wife, Julia, both now deceased. Worked for five years as a medical doctor with Crisis International, now practices in London. On the surface he appears perfectly innocent, which is why Dr. Gallagher initially raised no red flags at HQS."

"So why are you asking about him now?"

"Because your asset Doku is dead, a probable Russian assassination."

"Yes, that's what I assumed as well."

"You were his case officer. You were within a hundred yards of him when he was taken out. That made us wonder if *you* were the weak link. So HQS asked me to take a closer look at you, and who you associate with."

"Wait. Are you accusing *me* of working for the Russians?"

"Not you, necessarily. But maybe someone close to you."

"*Danny?*" I laugh. "Oh, you really are off in Siberia. You have no idea who Danny is."

She looks me straight in the eye. "Do you?"

CHAPTER 14

For a moment—just a moment—those two words rattle me. Then I think of the man I've come to love, the man I plan to spend the rest of my life with, and the ground beneath my feet once again asserts itself and becomes rock steady. "You said you confirmed his name *is* Danny Gallagher, that he *was* born in Leicester to the parents he told me about. What am I missing here?"

"It's the work he does."

"He's a medical doctor. I confirmed that too. I've seen him in action, treating a patient. Saving his life, in fact."

"Yes, let's talk about his patients."

I hear the ominous tone of her voice. Here is where everything will fall apart for me. Here is where the truth has been lurking, just out of my view.

She sets a laptop on my coffee table, spins it around to show me the photograph on the screen. It's an image of Danny, dressed in black tie and standing with a group of equally well-dressed people. Beside him is a dark-eyed beauty wearing a glimmering red dress with a plunging neckline. She is beaming at Danny. On his other side are two men in their fifties, both holding champagne flutes. No one is looking at the camera, which tells me this was a candid shot, the subjects unaware they were being photographed.

"This was taken seven months ago," Diana says. "At a private reception in Lausanne. This *is* Dr. Gallagher, is it not?"

"Yes," I murmur, my throat so dry I cannot even swallow. "Who are these people?" I ask, but what I really want to know is, *Who is that woman?*

"The taller man on the right is Phillip Hardwicke, age fifty-two, British. The dark-haired woman is his mistress, Silvia Moretti, age twenty-six. Italian."

So she's with another man, not Danny. Thank God, not with Danny. I'm so relieved by that information that I don't immediately feel the impact of what Diana says next.

"And the heavyset man is Simon Potoyev. I think you're familiar with that name."

I look at Diana. "Potoyev?"

"Worth about two billion dollars, although he's squirreled so much of it away in foreign bank accounts, we really have no idea how much he has."

It's all starting to make terrible sense, why she's telling me this. The Russians killed Doku, and seven months ago, there was Danny, sipping champagne with a Russian oligarch. I'm certain there's no connection, but I know what it *looks* like.

"What does Dr. Gallagher know about your work here in Istanbul?"

"I told him I work as an import analyst for Europa."

"Does he know the real nature of your work?"

"No."

"Did you ever talk about your asset? Mention Doku by name?"

"*No.* I'm not fucking clueless."

"Yet here's your boyfriend, hanging out with a Russian oligarch. Did he ever tell you about *that*?"

"He mentioned he'd been to Switzerland, for work. He's sometimes asked to accompany his patients when they travel."

"What has he told you about his patients?"

"Nothing. He's discreet. The clinic he works for is strict about patient confidentiality."

"That would be the Galen Medical Concierge group."

"Yes. If you have the money, you can buy round-the-clock access to the best medical care in London. For a little extra, they'll provide doctors to accompany you abroad, anywhere in the world."

"Sounds like a plum job."

"Their clients demand the best, and they pay for it."

"In this case, is it the *doctor* these clients are really paying for?"

I look at Gavin, then back at Diana. "What are you implying?"

"Maybe your initial meeting with Dr. Gallagher in Bangkok wasn't an accident, but a dangle, and you were reeled in. Maybe *you're* the prize."

Up till now I've been able to listen while standing on my feet. Now my legs go wobbly, like two candles melting beneath me, and I sink onto the sofa. If I really was taken in by Danny, what did that say about my judgment? What other mistakes have I made? Frantically I rewind my memory back to that steamy day in Bangkok when we met. The Wang Lang food market, the little plastic stools on which we sat. I fast-forward to the years that have passed since we met, to our hungry couplings in London, Spain, Portugal. To my most recent visit with him. Did I ever tell him anything that would have been useful to the enemy? Drop any hints about the assets I was handling, the operations I was involved in?

No, I'm not that careless. And I *know* Danny; I know him heart and soul.

I meet her gaze head on. "Danny Gallagher is exactly who he appears to be. Not a Russian asset. He's a doctor, and a very good one. Why would the Russians recruit him?"

"Because of who he can reel in."

"Meaning me."

"It's a possibility we had to consider."

"And what did you decide? Am I compromised?"

She studies me for a moment, then shrugs. "To our knowledge, your cover is still intact, and there's nothing to indicate that Europa has been exposed. If they knew you were one of ours, by now they would have killed you. Or tried to turn you."

"They've done neither."

Diana eyes me, trying to decide if I'm lying. Maybe I've already been turned. Maybe I'm already a traitor. I stare back, hoping she can read the truth in my eyes.

"If you really thought I was working for Moscow, you wouldn't be here," I say. "You wouldn't be telling me any of this."

She glances at Gavin, who gives an almost imperceptible nod. When she looks at me again, there's a faint smile on her lips. It's a warning that the real purpose of this visit is about to be revealed.

"Your relationship with Danny Gallagher," she says, "opens up a valuable opportunity for us. The fact he's a doctor places him in close proximity to just the people we need intel on. Starting with that man." She points to the photo on the laptop.

"Potoyev?"

"No. Phillip Hardwicke."

I frown. "You said he's English."

"He's also every Russian oligarch's best friend. They have to move their money out of Russia, hundreds of millions of pounds every year. Hardwicke helps them transform those funds into UK assets. Restaurants, hotels, skyscrapers. They're owned by consortiums or off-shore businesses with respectable-sounding British names, but they're really owned and controlled by Russians. And people who grease the machine, like Hardwicke, take a fat cut and line their own pockets."

"The London laundromat."

She nods. "The corruption goes all the way up to the highest levels, which is why it can't be touched. There's too much money and too many powerful names involved. British authorities can't or won't shut it down, and those who have tried to bring down Hardwicke . . ." She shakes her head. "It did not turn out well for them."

"What happened to them?"

Diana types on her laptop, and a new photo appears, this one of a middle-aged man with a blandly pleasant face and a tailored suit. He looks like a banker, which it turns out he was.

"Frederick Westfield, Bank of London," says Gavin. "Diana's just briefed me on these cases. Five months ago, Westfield's body was found in his burned-out Jaguar in Saint Albans. The bones of both his hands and his feet were pulverized premortem, and there was smoke in his lungs. It was clear from the autopsy that he was tortured but still alive when his car was set on fire. The authorities ruled the death accidental. Surprise, surprise."

Diana clicks to the next photo, of another distinguished-looking man in a suit. "Colin Chapman, HSBC," says Gavin. "Ten-story fall from his office, ruled a suicide." Another tap on the keyboard, another photo, this one of a smiling woman in her forties with an expertly tied silk scarf. "Angela McFaul, an accountant working for the Hardwicke Organization. She was found shot to death at home with two bullets in her head. Police called it a botched burglary, yet nothing was stolen. All three of these people had one thing in common—they had inside knowledge of Phillip Hardwicke's financial details. And they were sharing those details with British intelligence."

Diana clicks the keyboard, and a final image appears. It's Hardwicke himself, this time facing the camera with a penetrating gaze. A posed photo. Even though it's just a picture, I feel as if he can see me from that laptop screen.

"This is the man we're dealing with. Hardwicke would have personally ordered each of these assassinations, and judging by our personality assessment of him, he would have considered it just a part of doing business."

"Tell me more about this assessment."

"You'll get the full report. Let's just say he scores at the top for aggression and narcissism. Combined with high intelligence, it makes him especially dangerous. His school records from Eton reveal a ruthlessness that scared even his teachers. This is a man who needs to be in control, who always gets what he wants, whatever the cost to everyone else."

I cannot stop staring at Hardwicke's photo. So far I've heard about three people who were murdered at his command. How many others are there that we don't know about?

"What's our stake in all this?" I ask. "If the Brits aren't going to deal with it themselves, why should we?"

"Because those laundered rubles are buying more than restaurants and real estate. The money's also going into the most profitable business of all."

"Arms," I say.

Diana nods. We both know that war is a business like any other, and like any business, it requires a healthy and continuous supply chain.

"What does this have to do with Danny? He's not a money person. He's just a doctor."

"And that's where we see opportunity. We know that Phillip Hardwicke has a seizure disorder, something he's had since he was a young man. The seizures are not well controlled, which is why he has a medical doctor travel with him whenever he leaves London. We know that Dr. Gallagher has been with him on a number of these trips, so he has uncommonly intimate access to Hardwicke. And *you* have intimate access to Dr. Gallagher. It's the best situation we could hope for."

"You want me to *use* Danny for access?" I shake my head. "You're asking too much of me."

"What were you planning to do if I hadn't told you about this?"

"I *was* planning to marry him."

"We're not asking you to change those plans. We're just asking you to keep your eyes and ears open. Pass us any intel you learn about

Phillip Hardwicke, and about any oligarchs in his circle. It's not too much to ask of you. It's not a betrayal. It's just doing your part as a good American."

"And when I've given you what you want? What happens then?"

"You can ride off into the sunset with your husband and live happily ever after. As long as you keep it to yourself, he'll never know a thing. But *you'll* know you made the world a safer place."

"And that's all?"

"That's all. Find out who Hardwicke associates with, where his money's coming from. And if you can, find out about Galen's other patients. There are probably a few Russian oligarchs among them. Give us their names, their medical conditions, anything that could point us to Achilles' heels we can exploit in the future."

"I'd need Danny's help to penetrate the clinic's database."

"No. He can't know about it. *No* one can know about it. This stays in our tight little circle."

I look at Gavin and he nods. "It has to be this way."

"What about HQS? They're aware of this plan, aren't they?"

"Only a select few."

I frown. "You don't trust the mother ship?"

Diana and Gavin exchange glances. "It may be wiser not to," says Diana, "because they'll want to bring in British intelligence. We can't risk that."

"You don't trust the Brits."

"Think about it, Maggie. Two bankers and an accountant are dead. We don't know if someone in British intelligence exposed them. We have to do this quietly." She pauses. "Your life may depend on it."

CHAPTER 15

Now

The Longmorn is now gone. Ben and Declan and I have managed to drink the rest of the bottle, and I have no idea if I will be able to buy any more. I pick up my glass and savor the precious few drops that remain. They taste all the sweeter because they are the last.

"Jesus, Maggie," says Ben. "Why haven't you told us all this before?"

"It's still classified. I *couldn't* talk about it." I set down the empty glass, and the thud of it against the table makes both Ben and Declan flinch. "I didn't *want* to talk about it," I add softly. Despite all the whisky we've drunk, we're on edge because we know something has changed in our little village. Something evil has followed me here from my old life, something that threatens to poison our sanctuary.

"Diana talked me into the operation by questioning my loyalty. She made me wonder if meeting Danny in Bangkok *wasn't* an accident. Maybe the Russians used him to reel me in, hoping they could later turn me. In Diana's eyes, I *could* be working for the other side, and I wouldn't be the first person to fall for a honey trap."

I watch Declan's and Ben's faces for clues if they believe me. Decades ago, the three of us forged bonds as trainees at the Farm, and I still consider these men my closest friends, even though months, even years, sometimes went by when we didn't see each other. On the occasions when we did meet up, usually in some bar or restaurant in a foreign capital, it was the old days that we'd talk about, the days when we still believed we could change the world. What we didn't talk about, couldn't talk about, were the details of our various operations. There's always some secret corner of your life that you cannot share with anyone. Treason would certainly be one of those secrets.

Ben snorts. "The very idea's absurd, that you could be turned." He looks at Declan, then back at me. "If we can't trust each other, who can we trust?"

"That's a pretty thing to say, Ben, but you know better. We all do. We shouldn't trust each other. We can't afford to, not in our business, and I don't even trust myself. What if I *had* been lured into a fake love affair, what would that say about my judgment? What other mistakes might I have made, what other lives lost because I was so blind I couldn't recognize the enemy?" I lurch out of my chair and carry my empty whisky glass to the sink. There I stand, surveying the darkness. It seems I'm always surveying the darkness, looking for an enemy who sometimes is far too close to home. "She made me question my own feelings. That's why I don't give a fuck if Diana Ward is alive or dead. Everything that went wrong started with her."

Declan says, calmly: "It sounds like she was just doing her job, Maggie. Warning you about the man you were involved with."

"In *love* with," I say.

"In love?"

"Yes." I turn to look at the two men sitting at my table. I've never shared this information with them before. They know only that I left the Agency sixteen years ago, that until Declan reached out to me, inviting me to join them in Maine, I'd spent years wandering the wilderness, searching for a place to put down roots. That I, like them, have memories that I've redacted, memories I've never shared. "I loved Danny Gallagher. And there was Diana, standing in my apartment in Istanbul, telling me that he wasn't just my lover; he was also an opportunity. Telling me I had to make a choice. Did I choose my country, or did I choose a man who might be working for the enemy? The job demanded that I use him, betray his trust. She said any loyal American would know what to do. So I chose. As painful as it was, I did what I had to do."

"You left him?" Declan asks.

"No. I married him."

The men stare at me, both of them silent. I find I can't look at them, so I turn back to the window, but I can feel their gazes boring into my back, like hot laser points. They are two of my oldest friends, and even they did not know I was married, or that the man whose bed I once shared still haunts me. He is the reason I am now without a partner, or even a lover, because in my mind, Danny is still my husband and always will be.

"And then what happened?" Declan asks.

I don't answer him. I just keep staring at the darkness beyond my kitchen window.

"Maggie?" Declan has moved behind me so quietly that I did not hear his approach, and he rests his hand on my shoulder. He is not a man inclined to physical displays of affection, and his touch startles me. Despite our long friendship, this is perhaps the most intimate contact Declan and I have had, and it brings back the memory of Danny's touch, Danny's embrace.

I flinch, not because Declan repels me, but because the memories are too painful. "I'm tired. If you don't mind, I'd like to go to bed now."

"Of course," says Ben, and he rises to his feet. "We'll check in with you in the morning. Come on, Declan. Let's go."

As soon as they walk out the door, I fasten the dead bolts and arm the security system. I linger in the foyer, listening to the sound of their car driving away. I hear the familiar noises of my house: the hum of the refrigerator in the kitchen, the ticking of the clock in my living room. *Fortress secure,* I think.

Alone as always, I walk upstairs to my bedroom.

But I'm not really alone. Danny is with me. He's always with me.

I peel off my flannel shirt and hang it in the closet, where it keeps company with all my other practical shirts. There are only two dresses hanging there, neither of which I've worn in months. I touch one of them, a linen sheath embroidered with tiny roses. It makes me think of another dress I wore once, a dress I've lost track of during my many moves around the world. The dress I wore on the day I became Mrs. Danny Gallagher.

CHAPTER 16

London, seventeen years ago

Danny and I are married on a cool, crisp day in November. I wear a flower crown of baby's breath and a calf-length dress printed with little rosebuds, and I carry a bouquet of red roses to match the pattern on my dress. We both wanted a small wedding because he is uncomfortable with pomp and ceremony, and I want to draw as little attention to myself as possible, so we've chosen as our venue the back garden of a small country inn in Essex. Danny's best man is his mate from college, Georgie, a goofy and refreshingly ordinary fellow who handles logistics for a charity that drills wells in African villages. He's a bleeding-heart idealist who would probably be appalled if he learned that I work for the CIA. My maid of honor is Josie, who is supposedly my college friend from Georgetown. In truth, she works for the Agency under nonofficial cover, and she's flown in just to play this role. She's been thoroughly briefed about my real childhood, my family, and my college years, and if anyone went to the effort of digging into her past, they'd learn that Josie really is a Georgetown graduate.

I've told Danny that most of my friends are scattered around the world and unable to attend, so the other guests are his. Many of them are his colleagues at Galen Medical Concierge, and their foreign-language skills reflect Galen's international clientele. The nurses include one who's fluent in Russian and Ukrainian (Natalia), another in Arabic (Amina), and one in French (Helene). Also in attendance are Drs. Leeds and Chand, as well as office manager Lottie Mason, who—unbeknownst to her—is scheduled to have an unfortunate accident in a few weeks. Not fatal, Diana promised me, but serious enough to take poor Lottie out of commission for a month, leaving a sudden opening in office staff that will need to be remedied.

I, of course, will volunteer to step in.

I know everyone here and they know me, or they think they do. I'm Maggie, the woman whom Danny met in Bangkok, the woman he's been in love with for years. The woman who was by his side when he sliced open the throat of a choking man at the Ballade restaurant and was quick thinking enough to hand him part of a ballpoint pen as a cannula.

Yes, they've all marveled over the story.

Although they're not part of the wedding party, Diana and Gavin are nearby, posing as American tourists staying at the inn. They're almost unrecognizable as they dine at one of the tables, Diana in a brown wig, Gavin sporting a handsome beard. Just a pair of curious Yanks enjoying the spectacle of a wedding in their inn's back garden. They are hoping to glimpse Phillip Hardwicke, but he does not show up at the ceremony. Instead, Hardwicke will personally host and pay for our wedding dinner, to be held at one of the restaurants owned by the Hardwicke Organization. It's a wildly extravagant gift that Danny wanted to decline, but I told him we had to accept it, because turning down a gift from Hardwicke would be insulting.

And this will give me the chance to finally meet the man.

The restaurant is La Mer, in Knightsbridge. This evening it's closed to the public and reserved only for our wedding party. At 7:35 p.m., Danny and I—now Mrs. Gallagher—step into La Mer, and we're greeted with cheers and raised glasses of champagne. This bridal dinner feels like a Kabuki play that almost everyone here believes is real—everyone except me and my fake maid of honor, Josie, who skillfully regales the other guests with made-up tales from our college years. Neither Danny nor his friends and colleagues have any inkling of whom they've allowed into their circle. I sip champagne, smile my fake smile, and watch the door for the arrival of Phillip Hardwicke.

At 7:55, the door opens, and in walks the reason for this performance. I have read Hardwicke's dossier and viewed dozens of his photos, but they did not prepare me for the sheer magnetism of the man. He's tall and as powerfully built as a panther, and at fifty-two, he still has a full head of wheat-colored hair, but it's his eyes that capture my attention. They're a chilling shade of blue, like sea ice, and even when he takes my hand and smiles at me, I don't see warmth in those eyes.

"Brilliant to finally meet you, Maggie. Danny's a lucky lad."

"I'm so glad to meet you, too, Mr. Hardwicke," I say. "Thank you for this amazing, lovely dinner." I glance around the dining room, at tables set with crisp linens and glittering glassware. "It's so generous of you."

"The best deserves the best." He smiles at Danny, but it's a coolly businesslike smile. For Hardwicke, this dinner is merely transactional. He's as the dossier described him, a man who does nothing without expecting something in return, and what he expects is the finest medical care he can buy.

I pull my gaze away from Hardwicke to focus on the stunning woman who's walked in with him. I recognize her from the photo taken in Lausanne. This is Hardwicke's mistress, Silvia Moretti, and in person she's even more striking, with dark Mediterranean features and hair as glossy as black silk. Every curve of her figure is emphasized by a skintight bandage dress. Hardwicke's hand casually rests on her hip, indicating that she is his claimed property. While her lips form a smile, her eyes are fixedly neutral; it's impossible to read either satisfaction or dissatisfaction in that beautiful face.

Hardwicke shoots an irritated look at the two burly men who have accompanied him into the restaurant. They're his security detail, and one of the men keeps glancing at the door, as though waiting for someone else to enter.

And finally she does.

Hardwicke's daughter, Bella, is just a teenager, but at fifteen years old, she already knows how to exude ennui. The fact she doesn't want to be here is evident from her glower, and the fact she hangs just inside the door, as if waiting for an excuse to escape. Unlike Silvia, Bella is not a beauty, and she's made little effort to improve the features she does have. Her ginger hair flops around her face like a poodle's fringe, and her slouch emphasizes her round dumpling shoulders. Her pink peplum shift is clearly a designer dress, but it hugs her abundant curves in all the wrong ways. While her father commands attention, Bella lurks in the background, tugging at her bra strap.

"Bella," Hardwicke snaps. "Come say hello to Dr. Gallagher's new bride."

She moves toward me and holds out a limp hand. Her eyes are a pale green and almost lashless, like some aquatic creature peering at me through aquarium glass. To her, I'm just another business acquaintance her father has dragged her along to meet. I know from reading Hardwicke's dossier that she's his only child from his marriage to Lady Camilla Lindsey, a union that ended in divorce eight years ago. Camilla, who now lives in Argentina with her polo-mad second husband, Antonio, was described as a "great society beauty." What a shame she did not pass on those genes to her daughter, who must surely be aware that she suffers in comparison to her glamorous mother. According to the dossier, Bella attends an exclusive girls' boarding school in Brighton, where, judging by her demeanor, she'd prefer to be, rather than spending this weekend with her father.

I hear the *thunk* of a dead bolt. Hardwicke's men have just locked the restaurant door, shutting out anyone who might try to walk in, and they station themselves at the entrance so no one can leave without their approval. We are locked inside for the evening, trapped by Hardwicke's obsessive need for control. No wonder Bella looks unhappy tonight; when she's with her father, she must feel like a prisoner.

I certainly do.

This is supposed to be my wedding dinner, but as I sit next to Danny at a table set with fine china and a forest of wineglasses, I feel as if everything tonight is out of my hands. Hardwicke has preordered the wines, of course. His credit card, his choice. Uniformed servers emerge from the kitchen with bottles of Domaine Chanson chardonnay, and they efficiently circle the table, filling glasses. When a server reaches Bella's glass, he pauses and casts a questioning look at Hardwicke.

"Come on, Daddy," says Bella. "Mum lets me."

"Your mum's not here now."

"It's not as if I don't drink wine when I'm with *her*."

Hardwicke scowls. "All right, half a glass. That's all."

The server pours, then moves toward the two-top where the security team is seated.

"Not for them," snaps Hardwicke. "They're on duty."

Poor guards.

Hardwicke raises his glass. "A toast to the bride and groom!" He sits directly across from me, with Silvia on his left and Bella on his right, and I cannot avoid his gaze. I've read his dossier, and I know what he's done. I know what he is. My fate rests on his *not* knowing who I am.

Our guests hoist their glasses into the air as well, and Danny gives my knee an affectionate squeeze. I smile and take a sip of wine. I'm sure it must be an excellent vintage, but I scarcely taste it because my throat feels as if it's closing over. I see Josie, my fake maid of honor, laughing at the other end of the table, embracing her role. I hear Dr. Leeds oohing over the lovely chardonnay. I feel trapped in this tableau, a figure in a painting from which I cannot claw my way out.

"I hear you two met in Bangkok," Hardwicke says. He's looking at me with such intensity that I scarcely register the server placing the amuse-bouche on my plate. Sherried lobster on a petite corn cake.

"Maggie's such a seasoned traveler, she knew just which food cart to go to," says Danny, smiling at me. "There I was, cluelessly lumbering through the street market. I saw what she was having, ordered the same thing, and sat down at her table. It was love at first sight."

"What a fortunate accident," says Hardwicke. "The right place, the right time. How is it you know Bangkok so well, Maggie?"

I feel my pulse accelerate. "My work sometimes took me there."

"You were in fashion imports, I've heard. Based in Istanbul."

What else does he know about me? I glance down the table at fake-Josie. She suddenly looks alert. If Hardwicke knows who I really am, he's bound to know that she's a fraud as well, which would put us both in a precarious position.

"You're in fashion?" pipes up Bella. For the first time she actually appears interested in me. "Are you a designer?"

"No, but I worked with lots of designers. I helped them export their fashions around the world and handled some of the most beautiful dresses you'll ever lay eyes on. Oh, and the fabrics!"

"God, I'd love a job like that."

"The dress you're wearing, Bella. Is it Italian?"

Her eyes widen. "You can tell?"

It was actually an educated guess, aided by the fact her father's mistress happens to be Italian. And it really is a pretty dress, even though it's the wrong dress for that body. The talk of fashion clearly bores Hardwicke, and he waves to the server, motioning to his now-empty glass. Bella has stepped into the conversation just in time to deflect it from a potentially dangerous direction, and for this I'm grateful.

The starters arrive, nicely puffed up little mushroom soufflés, which are a testament to a kitchen that's up to the daunting challenge of serving hot soufflés to a party of twenty-eight. Now the next wine appears, a Domaine Leroy pinot noir. The server pours a splash into Hardwicke's glass. He swirls, sniffs, and sips. "Fine," is all he says, and the server whisks around our table, filling glasses.

Once again, the server pauses at Bella's glass.

"That's enough for her," says Hardwicke.

"Daddy!"

"You've had half a glass already."

"*Hardly* half a glass. Mum thinks—"

"I don't care what she thinks."

"No, and you never did." Bella looks at Silvia, who remains coolly impassive. "I don't know how *she* puts up with it either."

"*Her* name is Silvia."

Bella pushes to her feet. "Honestly, how *do* you keep all their names straight?" She stalks off to the restroom.

There's a long silence. Silvia calmly sips her wine and says, "The girl misses her mother. You should let her go back to Argentina."

"You think Camilla wants her back?" He snorts and, to my discomfort, refocuses on me. "Apologies for the drama. With a fifteen-year-old around, there's always drama. I'd like to hear more about you, Maggie. The American who chucked her glamorous, globe-trotting career to be Mrs. Gallagher."

Danny slings his arm around me. "It was true love, of course."

Hardwicke raises an eyebrow. I don't think he believes in true love, or anything that's not transactional. "And what will you do, now that you're in London? Become a lady of leisure?"

Danny laughs at the idea. "I have never seen this lady at leisure."

"You'll be looking for a new job, then? What are your unique skills?"

I can't help but sense a trap in that question. He's probing for information, waiting for me to slip up.

"For one, she'd make a damn fine medical assistant," says Danny. "I've seen her perform under fire."

"Ah yes, I heard about the choking man in Ballade and the ball-point pen. Very clever. So the sight of blood doesn't bother you?"

"I was raised on a sheep farm in New Mexico," I tell him. "Our lambs were always getting attacked by predators." I look at my husband. "And I'd love to work with Danny in the clinic, even if it's just filing charts."

"Really? Filing charts would make you happy?" Hardwicke's gaze seems to send tentacles into my brain, probing all the secret crevices. I feel pinned to my chair, exposed to his dissection.

The servers arrive with the main course. The perfect time for me to flee the table.

"Excuse me," I say, and rise from my chair.

I retreat to the ladies' room and shut myself into one of the two stalls. I don't need to pee; I just need to give myself a moment to regain my equilibrium. I have looked into the eyes of terrorists before, have witnessed the bloody results of their work, but I've never felt so personally threatened the way I did facing Hardwicke across the table. I think of his banker, burned alive in his Jaguar. I think of Hardwicke's accountant, shot to death in her bedroom. They were murdered because someone had betrayed them. Someone with the inside information that they were informants.

Diana is right. We cannot share anything with the Brits. If I'm to stay alive, we have to keep this inside our own circle.

It's time to go back to the table and face him.

I unlatch the stall door. Just as I step out, something clatters to the floor and I hear "Oh, crap" as a blue pill rolls out from beneath the other stall door.

I pick up the pill. It's round, with the symbol of a butterfly stamped on one side. The stall opens and Bella lunges out. Her gaze goes straight to the pill in my hand.

"It's nothing," she says. "Just my prescription for nerves."

I look at the plastic baggie she's holding. It contains a half dozen more of the blue pills, and it is definitely not a prescription bottle. She reaches out for the errant pill, but I don't give it to her.

"It's dirty," I say.

"That's all right."

"It's been on the bathroom floor. You really don't want to—"

"Please."

At last, I hand it to her, and she slips it into the baggie with the other blue pills, seemingly unconcerned about the microbes that lurk in a room where people piss and crap.

"I won't say a word about it to anyone," I tell her.

She doesn't believe me. I can see it in the way her lips tighten, in her quick, nervous glance at the door. "My father—"

"Is a control freak."

"You noticed?"

"It's hard not to. The preordained menu. The security detail, locking us all into the restaurant."

"Oh, *them.*" She snorts. "That's just Keith and Victor. They're clueless. I sneak out of the house all the time, and they have no idea I'm doing it."

Teenagers. They run rings around us all.

"Look, Bella, I don't want to get you in any trouble, but you have to be careful with those." I nod at the pills. "Those are Mollys."

"How did you know?"

"I just do. They can have some pretty scary side effects."

"They make me feel happy. They make me feel like everything's okay when I know it isn't."

I reach out and touch her arm. She feels hot, almost feverish, as if her unhappiness is a furnace burning inside her. "Bella, I had a shitty dad, too, so I understand. But you'll grow up and get away, just like I did."

That brings a twitch of a smile. She shoves the baggie of pills into her purse, zips it closed. "You really won't tell anyone?"

"Not a soul."

"Even Dr. Gallagher? Because if he finds out, he'll think he has to tell my dad."

"I won't tell even Danny." I raise my hand. "Scout's honor."

She looks puzzled by the phrase, but she understands the meaning: that her secret is safe with me. "Dr. Gallagher's a nice man. I'm glad you married him," she says, and she walks out of the ladies' room.

I take my time washing and drying my hands. I don't want it to be too obvious that Bella and I had a moment together, that we made a connection. But we did. Now I know a bit more about Phillip Hardwicke and his family. I know his daughter resents him. I know he does not wield as much control as he thinks he does.

That could come in useful.

CHAPTER 17

I am sleeping with the enemy. If I'm to survive, that is how I must think of my new husband.

But Danny doesn't seem like the enemy as we lie in bed together in our little seaside hotel on the Turkish coast. While other newlyweds might head to Spain or Italy, we are spending the week in the pretty coastal village of Gümüşlük. Not many foreign tourists come here, which is why I chose it for our honeymoon. Here we can wander among deserted ancient ruins and swim in turquoise water and dine on grilled sea bream, washed down with good Turkish wine. Here we can be alone.

Or as alone as we're allowed to be.

I roll onto my side and study my slumbering husband. Morning light filters in through the window blinds, painting his naked chest in slats of gold. It is a modest hotel, one that Turkish couples on a budget might choose. The sheets are rough cotton, and some of the tiles on the floor are chipped, but it is clean, the proprietor is friendly, and our windows look out over the water. We could have stayed instead at the Pera Palace Hotel or at one of the luxury resorts in Bodrum with their marble floors and uniformed staff and twenty-four-hour masseuses, but this is the Turkey I want Danny to see. It's what a bride would do, bring her new husband to a romantic village on the Aegean to drink wine and make love and pretend that what we share is real.

This morning, as I admire his tanned shoulders and the new freckles that have appeared there, like a sprinkling of nutmeg, it *feels* real, but there's always the risk that if I'm careless with my secrets, they could reach Hardwicke. Even in our most intimate moments, I am on guard, and I have to assume the walls themselves have ears.

Danny's eyes flicker open, and he smiles at me. "How long have you been awake?"

"Oh, forever. I just enjoy watching you."

"Did I snore again?"

"Yes, but it's a cute snore. Like a cat purring." I run my hand down his chest, his belly. He's almost as lean as the day we met, but after seven years, there's no denying that time has left its mark on us. There are new silver hairs on our heads and deeper lines engraved on our faces. *Till death do us part,* we vowed, but will we actually grow old together? Will we have the chance?

"Are you hungry?" I ask.

"Always." He slings an arm over me and rolls me onto my back. "But breakfast can wait."

*

The waiter seats us at the edge of the terrace, at a table closest to the sea. The Turks are hopeless romantics, and our waiter knows we were just married, so he fusses over us like a kindly uncle. He fetches honey for our yogurt and adds extra olives and triangles of feta to our breakfast-relish tray because he's noticed that Danny has a hearty appetite. We've gotten up late this morning, and the terrace is half-empty. Although no one's sitting at the tables next to ours, I automatically glance around for anyone who might be listening, for any faces that have appeared on my radar in the past five days. I have to assume that Danny and I are not alone, even on our honeymoon. Either Hardwicke's people or my people could be tracking our moves, perhaps even monitoring our conversations, and every morning while Danny showers, I do a quick sweep of the hotel room, searching for listening devices. So far, I have not found any, but that doesn't mean they aren't there.

Surveying the terrace, I see the older British couple who arrived two days ago, a Turkish family with three children, and a pair of Dutch honeymooners. Real honeymooners. I feel a twinge of envy watching as they hold hands and lean over the table to kiss. No hidden motives for their marriage, but a true union. What I had hoped Danny and I would have, until Diana's visit changed everything.

I refocus on my husband and am unsettled to see him intently watching me. Is it a trick of the sunlight, or were his eyes always so green?

"What are you thinking, darling?" I ask.

"That we should've booked another week here. Or a month. Or why not the whole bloody year? I could live here very happily."

"You wouldn't get bored?"

"In paradise?" He looks at the sea. "Sometimes I think we should chuck away our old lives, Mags. Grab our backpacks and leave everything behind. Just you and me, citizens of the world. Find work wherever we can, wherever we're needed. We could do some real good for humanity, the way Georgie does, digging wells in little villages."

"Go back to charity work?"

"Why not? This time we could do it together." He looks at me with such naked longing that I believe him, believe he really does want to escape the job he feels trapped in, and he wants me to come along. Then, just as quickly, reason seems to reassert control, and the impulse has passed. He sighs and shakes his head. "But that's everyone's fantasy, isn't it? To run away."

"What are you running *from*, Danny?"

"Nothing. I was just rambling."

"No, really. Tell me what's bothering you."

He looks off at the fishing boats rocking at their moorings. "It's not what I imagined myself doing, working for an outfit like Galen. Instead of being out in the trenches saving lives, I'm just handing out pills to the privileged. Pills to wake up, pills to fall asleep, pills to make them happy."

"Are your patients really that hard to deal with?"

"Some of them are. Most of them are. I guess it comes with their inflated bank accounts."

"Like Phillip Hardwicke?"

At the mention of Hardwicke's name, his eyes are back on me. "You didn't take to him, did you?"

"I didn't like the way he spoke to his daughter. If he's taking happy pills, they're not working."

"In his case, he actually *needs* the pills I give him."

"For what?"

"Epilepsy. It's a consequence of an old head injury he sustained as a young man. Any time of day or night, he could collapse with a grand mal seizure. I've been working with a neurologist to titrate the various medications, but he still has the occasional episode. It's why he takes me along when he travels, to be sure there's someone to help if his seizure doesn't stop."

"So that's why he's taking you to Cyprus next month."

"I'd rather not go."

"Not fly on his private jet and stay in a nice hotel?"

"It's still work, Maggie. I'd rather be home with you. Please, let's not talk about him." He puts down his napkin. "Let's take a drive and find a nice beach."

We pack up snorkels and lunch and head up the coast. A dirt road takes us down a sliver of a peninsula to a tiny cove where there's no one else in sight. It's a place where one could easily disappear, I realize, as we walk through scrub and thorns toward the water. A place where a man could dispose of his new bride without anyone around to see it. How twisted the world now seems, that such a thought even occurs to me. That the man I love is also a man I must be careful of.

We set our beach bags and towels on the ground and strip to our bathing suits. The sand is coarse here, more like gravel, and I hobble gingerly down to the water's edge. There I pause to pull on my mask and flippers. Danny's the first to plunge in, and I watch him stroke away through the crystalline water.

I jump in and follow him, swimming toward the spot where I see his flippers splashing. Just as I reach him, he pops up, treading water. "Maggie, take a look below!"

"What's down there?"

"Come on. You'll see." He shoves the snorkel back in his mouth and dives.

I dive too.

The water's only about eight feet deep here, shallow enough to drop to the seabed with only a few kicks. He points at the shelf of bleached coral, long dead and clearly ancient, judging by what's embedded within it: an amphora. I imagine it tumbling off a boat thousands of years ago. Tossed away, perhaps, or dropped in a moment of carelessness, to land on the seabed. As centuries passed, as cities on land rose and then crumbled, underwater, the coral kept patiently growing, engulfing this timeworn bit of litter.

Danny touches my shoulder, and I meet his gaze through my mask. He's smiling, excited by the find. We both kick to the surface, where we bob, treading water, and he pulls the snorkel from his mouth.

"That was amazing!" I say.

"Maggie—"

"I wonder what else we'll find down there?"

"I love you."

I laugh. "Isn't that why you married me?"

"I just want us to remember this. Remember this moment always. Let's promise each other."

We are alone out here, where no one else can hear us. The only sound is the splash of water lapping against us, and if ever there is a time to tell the truth, it is now. Every second that I don't respond only compounds my sense of guilt, for the secrets I'm keeping from him. I want to be honest, but I can't, because it's not in my nature to trust anyone. My childhood taught me there will be consequences if I do.

He glances at the shore. Another couple has just arrived in the cove, and they're now spreading a blanket on the beach. We are no longer alone. The moment to speak the truth has passed.

"Let's have lunch," I say. And I swim away, back to the beach.

CHAPTER 18

Now

I'm thinking of that honeymoon week on the seaside as I drive my Kubota RTV across the field, water buckets sloshing behind me. It is fourteen degrees this morning, and in a few hours, there'll be a layer of ice covering the floor of the Kubota's bed, where the water has splashed. It seems like forever since I last wore a bathing suit and sandals, since I last soaked up the sun on a beach. Instead of a bathing suit, I'm now wearing a wool sweater and a down coat and Muck boots. I park the Kubota outside the chicken run and switch off the current to the solar-powered electric fence. I leave the chickens shut inside the henhouse as I haul feed and the first bucket of water into their enclosure. Farmwork is mostly drudgery, but the daily rhythm of it soothes me: the slosh of water filling the buckets, and the clatter of feed pouring out of the sacks. When I stay busy, I have little time to reflect on what I'd prefer to forget, but this morning, I can't seem to shut out the memories. I tip water into the trough, and the splash makes me think of swimming in the Aegean. I pour feed, and it makes me think of the coarse sand on that Turkish beach, and in an instant, I'm there again, with Danny.

I open the henhouse door and release the chickens. My rooster emerges first, head bopping like a disco dancer as he struts down the ramp. "Good morning, ladies," I say as his harem follows, clucking and scrambling toward the feed troughs. I'm glad not to find any dead hens this morning. I have not lost any since the day I killed the fox, but it's only a matter of time before another predator shows up to take its place. They always do.

While the chickens are distracted by food and fresh water, I make quick work of stealing eggs from their nesting boxes. They haven't left me many on this winter's morning, just a few dozen, scarcely worth taking to market. Still, they make a pretty Easter basket jumble of blue and aqua, brown and white. I place the basket of eggs in the RTV and reach for the second water bucket to top off the trough. By afternoon, that trough will be frozen over, and I'll have to return to fill it again.

I grab the handle of the second bucket. As I swing it away from the Kubota, two things happen almost simultaneously. I feel the bucket jerk, and a loud *crack* echoes across the field. Water splashes onto my trouser leg, splatters my boots. Two steady streams are spilling out of holes on opposite sides of the bucket. Time seems to slow down as my brain processes all these details at once. As I realize what they mean.

I fling myself to the ground, and my cheek splats onto the snow just as I hear another rifle crack. I scramble under the bed of the RTV, where I lie, heart hammering. As snowmelt seeps into my jacket, two more shots send bullets pinging into the Kubota. Where the fuck are the shots coming from? Frantically I scan the field and realize the gunman has to be in the woods, to my left.

I roll toward the RTV's passenger side, putting the vehicle between me and the shooter. The windshield shatters, and pelleted glass rains onto the snow. It's obvious now these are not stray bullets fired by some hunter who doesn't know what he's firing at. This shooter is aiming at me.

My rifle is still inside the RTV.

I rise to a crouch, ease open the passenger door.

Bullets slash into one of the tires. Air hisses out and the tire collapses.

I clamber into the cab, grab the rifle from behind the seats, and roll back out again. Scanning the trees through my scope, I glimpse movement. A human figure, dressed in camo.

I squeeze off a shot—just one, because my rifle holds only three more bullets. Whoever's shooting at me almost certainly has me out-gunned, but now he knows I'm armed as well, and I'm not going down without a fight.

I scan the tree line, but the man in camo has melted away into the woods. Is he still there, lurking in the undergrowth, waiting for me to break cover? If I climb into the RTV, I'll expose myself. It's undrivable anyway, with that flat tire. I sweep back and forth with my rifle scope, searching the woods. *Where are you? Where are you?* The wind whips across the field, and my soaked trousers are starting to ice up. I can't crouch out here forever, but I don't dare make a dash across the barren snow.

Faintly I hear the growl of an engine approaching. I turn and see another RTV racing toward me. It's Luther. Even as he pulls up beside me, I still have my rifle aimed at the tree line, and I'm afraid to rise from my crouch.

He steps out of his RTV, wheezing in the cold air. "What's going on here, Maggie? Who's doing all the shooting?"

"I don't know! Get down!"

"Callie's on the phone with the police. They should be on their—"

"Get *down*!"

"What, with these knees? If I get down, I'll never get up." He pauses, staring at my bullet-pocked Kubota. "Jesus fucking Christ. This isn't some idiot hunter."

"No. Whoever he is, he's not hunting deer."

Luther still stands fully exposed as he stares at the trees, a jumbo-size target daring any bullet to bring him down. "Who the hell's trying to kill you, Maggie?"

"I don't know," I say.

But I think I know why.

*

It's unfortunate that Callie called the police, because now I have to deal once again with Acting Chief Thibodeau, who's sitting at my kitchen table, asking a stream of uncomfortable questions. Her blonde hair is again pulled back in a tight ponytail, emphasizing the sharp angles of her face, and the morning light reveals new details I didn't notice before: The scattering of freckles across her cheeks, the hairline scar on her upper lip. Even in February she has a healthy tan, which tells me she's an outdoors girl. I feel as if I'm dealing with a younger version of myself, which makes her a troublesome opponent. When I was her age, I could tell when I was hearing bullshit, and so can she.

"Someone just tried to kill you," she says. "And you really have no idea who it was?"

"I didn't see a face. All I saw was—"

"A figure wearing camo."

"Yes."

"Man or woman? Can you tell me that much?"

"A man."

"How do you know?"

"His build. The way he moved."

"And this man hiked through those woods just to shoot you."

"There are also deer on my property."

"I notice your land is posted."

"Not everyone obeys a 'No Hunting' sign."

"You really think this was just a deer hunter?"

"With bad eyesight."

Her mouth tightens. Jo Thibodeau does not appreciate humor. "I spoke to your neighbor, Mr. Yount. He says there are multiple bullet holes in your RTV, and the windshield is shattered. He and his grand-daughter heard at least ten, maybe more, gunshots. And he found you cowering behind your vehicle."

"I wasn't *cowering*. I took cover and was trying to locate where the shots were coming from."

"That's very levelheaded of you, ma'am."

"I like to think that I am."

"Have you been in a situation like this before?"

The question takes me aback. It's not one I want to answer. "I grew up on a sheep ranch," I finally say. "I'm comfortable around guns. I also know when to keep my head down."

"What does this attack have to do with the dead woman in your driveway?"

"I don't know."

"Who wants *you* dead?"

"I don't know."

"There seems to be an awful lot that you don't know."

"That could be said about anyone."

"I can't help you if you won't help me. Now I need to get some answers, Ms. Bird. Are you hiding from someone? Running from something?"

We're all running away from something. That's what goes through my mind, but she wouldn't appreciate yet another flippant answer, so I merely shake my head.

She looks around at my kitchen. I have not yet washed the morning dishes, and she can see the clutter left over from my breakfast: the greasy frying pan on the stove, the coffee cup, the plate with toast crumbs and yellow specks of scrambled eggs. "The last time I was here, I saw your security system," she says. "All those surveillance cameras, motion sensors. This is a very small town. No one else around here has a system like yours."

"It makes me feel safe."

"Why wouldn't you feel safe here?" She looks straight at me, and I know this woman will never give up. Jo Thibodeau will keep digging and digging, and even though she'll never learn the truth about me, she's going to be a perennial pain in my ass.

The knock on my front door is a welcome interruption. I hear Declan call out "Hello, Mags?" and he walks into the kitchen. "Are you all right?"

"We're in the middle of an interview," says Thibodeau.

"Yes, I heard about the shooting over the police scanner."

"Mr. Rose, if you don't mind—"

"Who was it? Do we have a description? A vehicle?"

"I would like to finish this interview."

Declan looks at me. "Where did it happen?"

"Out in the field. Near my henhouse."

Declan wheels around and heads back toward the door.

Thibodeau yells, *"Mr. Rose!"* but he ignores her and walks outside. There he's joined by Ben Diamond, who's just pulled up in his own car. From my kitchen window, I see the men conferring as they look across the field. Together, they start tramping through the snow.

"Oh Jesus," groans Thibodeau. "They're going to contaminate the scene." She jumps up and yanks her coat off the wall hook. "Who the hell do they think they are?"

You have no idea. I pull on my coat as well and follow her out the door.

Declan and Ben are already crossing the field, well ahead of us. They know enough not to add fresh tracks in the snow, and they follow the same tire tracks left by Luther's RTV when he brought me back to my house.

"Excuse me!" yells Thibodeau, following the trail left by their boot marks. *"Gentlemen!"*

The men just keep walking.

"Are they deaf?" she mutters.

"They're on a mission," I say. "Look, they're not stupid. They won't contaminate your scene."

"They don't know what they're doing!"

"They know more than you might think."

"Who the hell *are* they?"

"You should probably ask them."

By the time we reach my poor RTV, both Ben and Declan are squatting by the fallen water bucket and staring at the twin bullet holes.

Declan looks up at us. "It's a three-oh-eight."

"And how do you know that?" Thibodeau asks.

"Ballistics is a hobby of mine." He rises to his feet. "It would've been a very big hole if it had hit you, Maggie. A good thing it didn't."

"Sheer luck," I say. "He fired just as I was twisting away."

"Did it come from that direction?" Ben asks, looking at the trees.

"Yes. I saw him through my rifle scope. Near those beeches."

Ben and Declan start off toward the trees. Thibodeau has given up trying to stop them. Sighing, she follows the men.

It doesn't take long to locate the shoe prints left behind by the gunman.

"It looks like a size eight, eight and a half. Vibram sole," says Thibodeau. She takes out her phone to snap photos. The shooter has left multiple prints, but this particular impression has the crispest tread mark, unobscured by twigs and protected from the blowing wind. We allow her to do her police thing and stand aside, watching as she collects shell casings. I can't help but glance down at Ben's and Declan's boot prints. Both of theirs are larger than the shooter's, size tens at least. While I know these men and I trust them, there are some habits I can't shake, and one of them is questioning the loyalties of everyone in your life, even those you love.

Especially those you love.

"There's a clear view of your henhouse from here," says Ben, staring through the trees toward the field. "The shooter had to know what he was aiming for."

"And the target wasn't a deer," Thibodeau says, looking at me. "It was you." She's waiting to see my reaction. She must be disappointed when I say nothing, but just stare toward my henhouse. I already knew I was the target, and my mind is leaping ahead to what needs to happen next. I look sadly at my hens, who are scratching around in the snow. I think of all the improvements I was planning to make on the farm: Solar water heaters for the trough. A second mobile henhouse. More heating lamps for the new batch of chicks I've ordered. Here on Blackberry Farm, I've found a measure of peace, even happiness.

Now it's all being wrenched away from me.

Even though we're out of the wind here, standing among the trees, it seems colder. Damper. I see my breath swirl away in a white cloud and feel the chill seep in through my Muck boots. Ben, who's normally immune to the cold, withdraws a knit hat from his pocket and pulls it over his shaved head. The hat has a Harvard logo, which strikes me as a supremely ironic touch, because he did not attend Harvard and has nothing good to say about those who did.

"Let's find out how he got here," says Ben. He heads deeper into the woods.

We follow him as he tracks the boot prints of the retreating shooter. The trail follows the same path both coming and going; the shooter exited the way he came in. No one says a word, but it is a noisy hike anyway, the crunch of our boots through snow, the sharp explosions of snapping twigs and dead leaves. Declan and Ben and I are all in good shape for our ages, but breathing in the frigid air makes my chest tighten, and the old fracture in my ankle is aching. I wonder if Ben and Declan are also feeling old injuries throb back to the surface; even so, they would never admit it. We're three old soldiers, refusing to admit our gears are starting to rust.

At last we emerge from the woods onto the dirt road that divides my property from an abutting neighbor's. Thibodeau crouches down to examine the tire marks, where a vehicle was parked. She takes photos, but I doubt they will help ID the vehicle, because these tread marks could match those of a dozen other SUVs that roll through the village of Purity every day. Out here on the dirt road, there are no handy surveillance cameras, no witnesses to the vehicle's coming and going. I have always felt safe in the woods, but today's attack has shaken my belief that there are any safe places left in the world.

Thibodeau rises back to her feet with a grace that makes me envy the nimbleness of youth. "I'll get right to work on this," she says.

"There's not much to go on."

"It'd help if you gave me more, Ms. Bird."

"I've told you what I know."

She doesn't believe this, but for now she's given up trying to drag the whole truth out of me. Her radio gives a squawk, and she pulls it off her belt. Turns away to talk into it.

"Maggie," says Declan quietly. "This changes things."

I sigh. "I know."

"It's time for you to get out of Dodge."

"And that's what I'm going to do." I turn back toward the woods. Back toward the home I will have to abandon. "But first, there's one more thing I need to do."

*

"I've hauled your henhouse over by our barn," says Luther as he pours me a cup of coffee. "That'll make it easier for Callie to take care of your birds. I'm not sure how we'll be able to keep the flocks separated, though."

"You might as well combine the flocks," I say, and look at Callie. "Since you'll be keeping them."

"I can mark yours with spray paint or something," she suggests.

"No need. They're yours now, Callie."

She frowns. "Don't you want to keep chickens anymore?"

"I do. I love my girls. But I have to leave town, and I want them to have a good home." I smile at her. "Yours is the best."

"I don't mind taking care of them till you get back. We can sort out which ones are yours then."

"The problem is, I don't know when I'll come back." Cradling the cup of Luther's bitter coffee, I go to their kitchen window and see Declan sitting in his Volvo, parked right behind my truck. He refuses to leave me unprotected, and he's keeping watch. He sees me through the window and gives me a reassuring nod. As long as I need him, I know Declan will be there. I look toward my own property, at my farmhouse, beyond the colonnade of maple trees. When I locked my front door only half an hour ago, I knew it might be the last time I'd see my house. Now I linger too long in Luther's kitchen, reluctant to leave behind my farm, to abandon the life I've built over the last two years. A life that's now threatened by ghosts from my past.

"And Blackberry Farm?" Luther asks. "What do you need us to do? If you're gonna be gone awhile, I can drain the pipes, shut off the water."

"I've already done that. Just leave the house alone." I look at Callie, who sits at the kitchen table, watching me with those preternaturally wise eyes. She knows that something is terribly wrong, and even though I haven't told her the reason behind my sudden departure, she understands the gravity of what's happening. I suddenly think of another teenage girl who trusted me, believed in me. I failed that girl, and what happened to her will always haunt me.

I won't let that happen to Callie.

"I want you to stay away from my house, okay?" I tell her. "Don't go inside it; don't even go near it."

"But what about your big ole aloe vera? It'll need watering."

"Leave it."

"Grandpa could haul it over here."

"No, it's too heavy."

"But it'll die."

"That's okay."

She's shocked by my answer. She looks at her grandfather, then back at me, bewildered by the adults in her world.

"Sweetie," I say, sitting down to face her at the table. "I can buy a new plant when I come back."

"You *are* coming back, aren't you?"

"I want that more than anything, Callie. But right now, I need you to promise me you'll stay away from my house, just in case . . ." I stop, not knowing how to finish the sentence. In case of what? Someone booby-traps it? Someone plants a bomb or burns it down? I can't bear the thought of Callie trapped inside. I don't have any children of my own, and she is as close to one as I'll ever know. Like any mother, I'll do whatever it takes to keep her safe.

"Can I call you?" she says.

"I may not be able to answer my phone."

"Where are you going? Can't you just *tell* me?"

"I wish I could. But I don't know. Not yet."

Callie looks at her grandfather, then at me, hungrily searching our faces for answers. I'm surprised when she suddenly swoops in to hug me. Her hair smells like sweet hay and woodsmoke, and as I hold her against me, I feel the prickle of tears in my eyes. This is not what I want to be feeling; it's what I've avoided all these years, and now here is this silly girl, attaching herself to me like a limpet.

It's time to leave. Now.

I peel her off me, but she's holding on so tightly it feels like I'm peeling away my own skin. "Do your homework, Callie," is all I say. It's all I can bring myself to say, or I will start crying. I step out the door.

Luther follows me outside to the porch and shuts the door behind him. "I don't like to ask questions, Maggie, because I don't think it's any of my business. But it might help if you told me what you're running from."

"That's what I need to find out."

"Is it the police? Is it something you've done?"

"No, it's not the police."

"Okay." If he's relieved by that answer, he doesn't show it. Maybe because he knows there are far more frightening possibilities than being pursued by the law. "Then who?"

"Years ago, I was involved with a man," I say.

"You mean romantically?"

"Yes. Then I discovered what kind of people he was associated with."

"Criminals?"

"You could call them that."

"So that's who you're running from? This man?"

It's as good an explanation as any. And in a way it's true; I *am* running away from Danny. Or from the memory of him.

"Well," says Luther. "At least now I know what we're dealing with."

"*You're* not dealing with anything, Luther. This is my problem, and I'm going to handle it."

"How?"

"With the help of a few friends." I go down the steps to my truck. I see Declan, ever my guardian, watching from his car.

Luther calls out: "Aren't *we* your friends? Callie and me?"

I pause by my truck and look back at him. "Yes, you are. Which is why I want you and Callie to stay away from me. I want you to be safe."

"He's that dangerous? This man you're running from?"

I think of Danny smiling at me across the little plastic table in Bangkok. Laughing with me as we lie side by side on a Turkish beach. Singing at the stove as he lovingly grills me a cheese sandwich. "Yes," I say softly. "He is."

CHAPTER 19

London, sixteen years ago

I sit on a bench in Room 17 of the British Museum, where I often come to contemplate the tomb of the Lycian king Arbinas. Once this tomb stood in the city-state of Xanthos, where it must have dazzled with its sculpted friezes and its twenty columns and its statues of Nereid nymphs, who represent all that is good and generous from the sea. Over two and a half centuries, it slowly fell into ruin until it was packed up and shipped to London by an English archaeologist. Now it stands in Room 17, yet another example of the spoils of empire, and a reminder that no kingdom lasts forever. I am homesick for Turkey. This marble monument brings me back to its Lycian coast, to warm beaches and dazzling sunshine and fruits ripened on the tree to perfect sweetness. Here in London, it is a rainy afternoon, and even though it's almost June, the weather's dampness has seeped so deeply into my bones that I cannot seem to get warm. I look up at the podium frieze, at the carved figures of men engaged in battle. So little about humanity has changed since the era of King Arbinas. We are still engaged in a never-ending cycle of conflict and war, and now we have weapons powerful enough to doom us all.

I don't see Diana walk into the room, but I sense her arrival. My antennae pick up a flutter in the air, a shifting thermocline, and there she is, sitting beside me on the stone bench. For a moment we don't speak, don't even look at each other. The Nereids hold my full attention.

"Interesting place to meet," she finally says.

I slide a folded newspaper across the bench to her. The newspaper conceals a flash drive with Hardwicke's medical records, which I downloaded from the Galen clinic computer a few days ago. When she slides the newspaper back to me, the flash drive is gone. She's already slipped it into her pocket.

"And?" she says.

"Along with essential hypertension, he has a seizure disorder that dates back to a serious head injury when he was twenty-six. He had a subdural hematoma requiring surgery."

"How was he hurt?"

"Crashed his parents' Lamborghini into a stone wall."

"Oh, the woes of the rich."

"He has a neurologist who's constantly making adjustments to his meds, but he still has occasional grand mal seizures."

"How often?"

"The last one was three months ago, while he was at his office in Hardwicke Tower. It lasted only a minute or two, but there's always the danger of status epilepticus, when the seizure doesn't stop. It requires urgent medical intervention. That's why he insists on having a doctor travel with him whenever he leaves London. Security blanket. He's also starting to have problems with his short-term memory. It may be related to that same head injury all those years ago."

"How bad is his memory?"

"He has trouble remembering names, numbers. He was concerned enough to mention it to Danny."

Diana falls silent as a bevy of noisy schoolchildren enters Room 17 with their teacher, their voices sharp and magnified by all the marble surfaces. As chaos invades the room, Diana and I stare ahead at the tomb of Arbinas, as if contemplating the hidden meanings carved into the friezes.

"Look, it's a Greek temple!"

"Are those gods fighting on the top, Mrs. Cummings?"

"Can we see the next room?"

"I'm hungry!"

The children are not impressed by statues of nymphs or monuments to a dead king. No, they want to see something more interesting. Where are the Egyptian mummies, Mrs. Cummings? Isn't it time for lunch?

The beleaguered Mrs. Cummings eventually herds her charges out of the room, but their voices continue to echo all the way into the next gallery.

"When will Hardwicke next require your husband's services?" Diana asks.

"In three weeks. Hardwicke is hosting a weekend reception at Manning House, his country home. Danny will be attending as well, in case Hardwicke or any of the guests need medical attention."

"Do you know who these guests are?"

"I'm told it will be Hardwicke's business associates and their wives. He hosts these retreats every few months. English gentry sort of affair, riding horses, shooting clay pigeons. Probably a lot of drinking."

"Maybe a lot of loose tongues."

"If we're lucky."

"You're going as well?"

"I've been invited. I'm not sure why."

Diana considers this for a moment, then reaches into her pocket for a slip of paper. She slides it across the bench to me. "Keep an eye out for this."

I glance at what's written on the slip. *Heme arginate.* "What is it?" I ask.

"A medication. Find out if any Galen patients have received infusions of it lately."

"What is this medication for?"

"Acute intermittent porphyria. It's a rare metabolic disease that causes occasional attacks of severe abdominal pain. The attacks can be prevented by regular prophylactic doses of heme arginate. The drug is stored in vials. See if the clinic keeps any in stock."

I nod and slip the paper in my pocket. For this information, I will have to get back on the clinic computer, which won't be too difficult. The staff knows me now. I'm Dr. Gallagher's wife, who sometimes brings them cake for their tea. Who occasionally helps with the filing, and who now knows their system passcodes.

"Why do you need this information?" I ask. "Who are you trying to find?"

"Cyrano."

I turn and stare at her. I'm well acquainted with the name, because Cyrano is the code name for a Russian sleeper the Agency has been hunting for years. The CIA does not know which name he now uses, but we have gleaned that he was born in Rostov, was recruited and trained by Russia's Directorate S, and was sent abroad to assume a different identity in the West. The first clue he even existed was through an intercepted communication eight years ago, where the code name *Cyrano* first came to our attention. We don't know what he looks like, or what his occupation might be; we know only that the name *Cyrano* repeatedly appears in communications from the Russian Directorate, communications that have also mentioned two current members of Parliament. Like other foreign operatives, he is no doubt tasked with infiltrating and influencing those in power, all to Russia's advantage.

"Is there new intel on him?" I ask.

"An intercepted message from his *kurator*. It referenced a companion. A woman, who requires regular infusions of that drug."

"And you think she's a Galen patient?"

"We don't know. We're just casting a wide net for anyone receiving the drug. With its international clientele, Galen might attract just this sort of client."

Our conversation is again interrupted by visitors to Room 17, this time a couple in their thirties. Americans, judging by the blue jeans and Nikes. The Nereids seem to hold little interest for them, either, and a moment later, they move on.

"That weekend reception at Manning House," says Diana. "Find out more about the guests."

"I will."

"We'll monitor the roads and see who turns up for the weekend. And we'll try to get another pair of ears onto that guest list."

"Another pair?" I frown at her. "What? Who?"

"It's safer if you don't know. For both of you."

"You already have an asset in Hardwicke's circle?"

Diana doesn't answer, instead keeping her gaze on the statuary. I have blown up my old life for her, yet she won't share this vital piece of information. The fact she does not trust me makes me wonder how much I can trust *her*.

Abruptly I rise from the bench. "If you have someone else in there, then you don't really need me."

"We need everyone. We need layers upon layers, because we could lose one of you at any time. You know what kind of people we're dealing with. You know what they're capable of. Or have you forgotten?"

"Forgotten?" I turn to confront her. There is no one else in the room, no other ears to hear me as I fire back in a furious whisper. "You weren't there when Doku bled to death in Istanbul. You weren't there when they lit up his sister and her daughter like human torches. Oh, I know *exactly* what kind of people we're dealing with."

"Then you understand why I can't reveal our asset. It's for his safety. And yours."

Separate boxes so we can't betray each other. We're cut off from each other, each of us forced to work alone. It makes perfect sense, but it also leaves me feeling isolated. Diana said *his* when she referred to the asset, so I know it's a man. What does he know about me? Enough to put me in danger, should he be forced to talk? That is the downside of knowing the ally who's working with you behind enemy lines. Betrayal is always possible.

When I walk out of the museum, I feel painfully exposed, despite all the tourists streaming in around me. Here there are always tourists, Americans with their tennis shoes and fanny packs, Japanese with their selfie sticks. In this crowd, I may be anonymous, but I do not feel safe.

My phone rings. There is no caller identified on my screen, but when I answer it, I recognize the voice. "Mr. Hardwicke would like to see you." It's Keith, from Hardwicke's security team.

I halt at the bottom of the steps and frantically glance around at the crowd. Have I been followed? Do they know I came to meet Diana?

"Did he say why?" I ask, trying to keep my voice steady.

"Just a friendly conversation."

"When does he want to see me?"

"Now. Come to his office in Hardwicke Tower. Twenty-eighth floor."

I consider all the possible reasons for this meeting. Has he found out who I work for? Am I walking into a trap?

"I'm sorry, but I'd really like to know what this is about," I say.

"Mr. Hardwicke will explain when you get here."

*

Hardwicke Tower, in London's Southwark neighborhood, rises thirty stories and overlooks the River Thames. Since my move to London, I have dined inside its restaurant once with Danny, and have walked past it a number of times during my strolls alongside the river, but I have never had occasion to visit the Hardwicke Organization's headquarters on the twenty-eighth floor. Access is via private elevators, and to reach those I must first sign in at the security desk, allow the guard to search my purse, and then walk through a metal detector. This is not merely theater; Hardwicke is genuinely concerned about his security, something that became obvious to me at my wedding dinner, when his men Keith and Victor locked us into the restaurant.

I ride the elevator alone, and as it silently whisks me up to the twenty-eighth floor, I stare at my reflection in the door's polished surface. I see the tension in my face and can feel my heart thrashing in my chest. *Take control. Calm down.* I can't let him see my fear. I'm just Danny's American wife, here to have a conversation about . . . what? My state of mind should be puzzlement. Curiosity. That's what innocent Maggie Gallagher would be feeling now, and that's what he should see in my face.

The floor indicator dings.

I take a breath and step out, to find Keith standing at a desk. He has clearly been waiting for me.

"Your purse," he says. "I need to search it." The man is as charming as ever.

"The guard downstairs already searched it."

"Mr. Hardwicke's rules."

I set my purse on the desk and watch him paw through the contents.

"You need to leave your phone here," he says.

"Excuse me?"

"You'll get it back." He holds out a box. "It's routine."

For a high-security prison, perhaps. I shut off my phone and reluctantly place it in the box. Only then does he press the intercom button.

"She's here," he announces.

A moment later, the door opens and Hardwicke stands, looking at me. "Come in, Maggie."

I step into his office and hear him close and lock the door behind me. This feels more and more like a terrible mistake, but I can't let him see I'm rattled. Instead, I stare at the floor-to-ceiling windows and the impressive view over the Thames.

"Oh my gosh. You get to look at this every day?" I say.

"And the view never gets old." He gestures to the chair facing his rosewood desk. "Please, have a seat."

When he settles into his own chair, he's backlit by the window. It's a disadvantage for me because I can't read the microexpressions on his face, while he can see every detail of mine. "I've been doing a little research on you," he says.

"On me?" I laugh. "I can't imagine why." My pulse quickens under his scrutiny. It occurs to me that only Hardwicke and his men know that I'm here in his office. I think about the locked door. I think about how easy it is for a person to disappear without a trace, even in London.

"I like to know about the people around me. I like to know who they are and how they found their way into my circle."

"Well, that's easy. I married Danny."

"Yes, a chance meeting in Bangkok. You were working at a customs brokerage at the time." He glances at a stack of documents on his desk. "A firm called Europa."

He's done a background check on me. How deeply has he delved? "I was an import analyst, specializing in fashion. Exotic fabrics."

"Sounds like a glamorous job."

"No job seems glamorous when you're in the thick of it." *Including espionage.* "But I did get to travel a lot."

"And you gave up your career to get married." He looks at me with one eyebrow raised. "Really?"

We are moving toward dangerous ground, but I manage to give a laugh. "You know how it is. True love."

"No, I don't know."

"Don't you believe in it?"

"I'm divorced. What do you think?"

"I think Silvia's a beautiful woman."

Now it's his turn to shrug. "Yes, I suppose she is."

He can't deny what's obvious to everyone who lays eyes on Silvia, but his dismissive tone reveals how little it matters to him. Silvia is not his first mistress, and she will probably not be his last.

"It really *was* for love?" he asks.

"Why else would I marry him?"

"Is that the only reason?"

Another flashing red light. Another trap I could fall into if I'm not careful. My heartbeat kicks up another notch. He studies me for what seems like an eternity, and I feel my future balancing on a knife's edge. "I really do love my husband, Mr. Hardwicke. And I happen to like living in London."

"Don't you miss Istanbul? Your job?"

"I miss the paycheck, of course. I admit, it's a little unsettling for me, not having my own source of income, and feeling dependent on someone else. When you grow up poor, as I did, money matters. A lot."

I see a glint of understanding in his eyes. Money is something he understands and appreciates. The gilded lobby of this building, the gold accents, and the marble columns are all shouts for attention and respect. He wants people to know he has money and plenty of it. Oh yes, we understand each other, or so he thinks.

"May I ask what this is all about? It's starting to feel like a job interview," I say.

"It's in my nature to ask questions."

"Are you wondering if your doctor made a mistake and married the wrong woman?"

"No. It's my daughter I'm concerned about."

"Bella?" I frown.

"She's an impressionable girl. Easy to influence, and too naive to know whom to trust." He leans back in his chair, studying me, as if I'm a puzzle box he wants to pry open. "I want to know if you're a good influence on her."

"I like to think I am."

"You have to be, if you're going to be around my daughter. Someday, she's going to control the keys to the kingdom, and before that happens, she needs some sense drilled into her. I'd do it, but I'm just her father. You, however—she's taken a shine to you. She keeps asking me when we'll invite you and your husband out to dinner again. She wants you there for the weekend."

"I have no idea why." But I do know. It's that baggie of blue butterfly pills. I did not betray her secret, and in the eyes of a teenager, that makes me an ally. Danny and I have twice been invited to cocktail parties in Hardwicke Tower, and both times, Bella spent the whole evening at my side. "Maybe it's because I worked in fashion. She seems quite keen on the subject."

"I wouldn't know. I just pay her bills."

"I'd be happy to give her fashion advice. Or I could take her shopping."

"Look, if you could just keep her entertained and out of trouble. Silvia and I are going to be too busy to watch her, and I can't have her sulking or embarrassing us around our guests."

"When am I supposed to do this?"

"The reception at Manning House in three weeks. Your husband will be there for the weekend anyway. I'd appreciate it if you came along as well."

"You mean, to serve as Bella's companion?"

"Ah." He thinks he understands now. "You want to be paid, don't you?"

"No, I just want to be clear exactly what you'd like me to do."

"Keep my daughter amused. Ensure she's well behaved."

"She is a teenager."

"That's the problem. Think you can do it?"

I make a show of considering his proposal. I can't seem too eager, and who would be, having to wrangle a teenager? "Yes, I'll try."

He takes out a checkbook. "How much do you want?"

"You don't need to pay me."

"If you work for me, you'll get paid."

"Not for this. I like Bella. I refuse to be paid just for being her friend."

He looks me up and down, as if searching for some flaw he's missed. For him, this does not make sense, and I wonder if I should have accepted his money. At last, he gives a shrug and puts the checkbook back in his desk.

"Suit yourself. But I did offer."

*

It's almost eight when Danny gets home that evening. I've already eaten dinner and set aside a plate of salmon and new potatoes for him to reheat. I'm sitting on the sofa, sipping my evening glass of whisky, when I hear the door open and shut. He walks into the living room, bringing with him the smell of soap and disinfectant and weariness, and he flops down beside me.

"Hey, sailor," I say.

"God, what an afternoon. There's an outbreak of norovirus, and all our clients are vomiting. I had to make four house calls, which means I'll probably catch it next."

I get up and pour whisky into a glass. "Would you like a drink?"

"Yes. Also a holiday."

I hand him the whisky. "Poor thing. Let me heat up dinner for you. And then I'll book tickets to wherever in the world you want to go."

"Anywhere. As long as it's with you." He pulls me down beside him on the sofa. "And where were you today?"

"Around town."

"I tried calling you."

"When?"

"Noonish. I wanted to tell you not to wait for me for dinner, but I think your phone must have been shut off."

That's because at noon, I was sitting in Room 17 at the British Museum, briefing Diana. Something he cannot know. I scramble for a different explanation and choose one that can be corroborated. "I met with Phillip Hardwicke."

I feel the muscles of his arm tighten against my shoulder. "What? How did that happen?"

"He asked me to come to his office."

"Why?"

"Just to talk."

"About what?"

"His daughter, Bella. Apparently, she's causing typical teenage problems, and he wants me to help rein her in. He asked me to entertain her while we're at Manning House."

Danny takes a sip of whisky. "Is that the only reason he met with you?"

"Yes."

"And you're going to do it?"

"It's just keeping the girl company. He even offered to pay me, but I refused."

"Are you sure you want to be part of that, Maggie?" he says quietly.

"At least I'll be with you. A weekend in a country house sounds like fun. And Bella, she's nothing I can't handle."

He sighs and runs his hand through his hair. "You need to know, these are not easy people. The guests he's inviting, they're from a different universe. To them, we're just the household help."

"You think I won't enjoy it."

"For us, it won't be a party. I'm there to take care of their sniffles and their sprained ankles."

"And I'll be babysitting."

"Yes, that's what it sounds like. The girl's a brat, by the way."

"She's fifteen. They're all brats. I was a brat too."

He laughs. "That, I absolutely believe."

I get up to fetch the whisky bottle for a round of refills. When I return to the sofa, he's staring off into space. I settle down beside him.

"I've been thinking about the day we met," he says. "Remembering how great it was, both of us wandering from country to country."

"We were younger. Poorer."

"Yes, but free."

"I *did* have a job."

"A job you loved. I remember thinking, '*There's* a woman who's at home in the world.' Now here you are, stuck in my apartment, pouring me drinks."

"I'm with you, darling. This is where I want to be."

"Is it, really?" His question is so soft it's more of a thought than a spoken word. As if he did not really mean to say it but could not keep his doubts from spilling out.

"What is it? What's bothering you?"

"I wish we could be the way we used to be. Before I agreed to join Galen. Before the money sucked me in." He takes a breath. "What if we just chucked this all away?" He sets down his whisky and looks at me. "Jumped on a plane and left for South America? Or India? Or wherever the hell we felt like going?"

He's serious, he really is, and I don't know where this is coming from. I only know that I'm being swept into his fantasy, this seductive vision of us out in the world together, where we could forget about Diana and Hardwicke and shadowy men with their bullets and bombs. But those shadowy men are the reason I can't run away. I need to stay and fight.

"Poor darling, you're just tired," I say. "A good night's sleep and everything will look different in the morning."

He doesn't reply, but I see the excitement drain from his eyes. I feel as if I've killed something hopeful, destroyed whatever chance there might be for us, but I have to do it. Duty demands it. Innocent victims demand it.

"Just be careful, all right?" he says. "Watch yourself around Hardwicke. Around his people."

"Why?"

"I don't trust them." He looks me in the eye. "And neither should you."

CHAPTER 20

I have already studied photos and satellite images of Hardwicke's country home, so I know what to expect, but I am still awestruck by my first glimpse of Manning House. Danny and I must first stop at the stone gatehouse, where a guard checks our names off his list before allowing us to drive through, onto a road lined by magnificent plane trees. There, in the distance, is the house, looming beyond an ornamental lake. The photos did not adequately capture the magisterial glow of sunlight on the redbrick facade, or the sweep of the lawn surrounding it, like an emerald-green skirt. As we drive closer, I see stables, a carriage house, a knot garden, and, in the distance, a whimsical folly. I read that the Jacobean mansion, with its seven bays and its balustraded parapet, was originally built for an earl. I wonder how that earl would feel knowing that, centuries later, his country home would be occupied by a man who makes his money by trading with England's enemies.

"My God, Danny," I murmur. "It's a castle."

"It's also cold and drafty in the winter. The windows rattle, and the showers take forever to heat up."

"You're really trying to sell this weekend, aren't you?"

"No matter the lodgings, it's still work for us, Maggie."

He pulls up at the front door and we step out, both of us stiff after the long drive from London. As Danny fetches our bags from the trunk, I look up at the house and see a face staring down at us from a window. Silvia.

The front door opens, and Hardwicke's security man emerges to greet us. "Dr. Gallagher. Mrs. Gallagher."

"Keith," says Danny.

"You'll be staying up in the Mauve Room. It's two flights up, at the east end of—"

"I know where it is."

Danny doesn't usually speak so brusquely to anyone. It's a sign of just how unhappy he is to be here. Carrying our bags, Danny leads the way into the house and up a grand staircase. We climb past portraits of genteel ladies in empire gowns and gentlemen astride steeds, but these are not Hardwicke's ancestors; his family fortune is only two generations old, amassed by a grandfather's canny investments in the arms industry during World War II.

War has been good for the Hardwicke family.

We reach the second floor, and Danny leads me down the carpeted hallway, past bedrooms designated by color, their names engraved on brass plaques. The Amber Room. The Sapphire Room. The Rose Room. Nothing as pedestrian as a simple Red or Blue Room. We walk to the end of the hall, to a doorway that leads to a wing of the house that's clearly meant for the help. Here is a second staircase, a far narrower one, meant for servants. On our way up, we pass a uniformed maid coming down the stairs with an armload of fresh linens. This next flight of stairs takes us up to the third floor, to the room where we will be sleeping.

The Mauve Room really is mauve: the curtains, the bedspread, the wallpaper. I had expected a cramped space, but this room is certainly comfortable enough for the family doctor. Automatically I scan the room for surveillance cameras, but I don't spot any. We are not important enough to monitor.

Our window looks out over the kitchen garden, toward the estate's surrounding parkland. A gravel path winds past stone statues and box hedges and into a mixed woodland where there are multiple footpaths to wander.

And places to hide.

Danny unpacks his suitcase, and out comes his evening jacket, tie, and dress shoes. As he hangs his jacket in the wardrobe, I come up behind him and wrap my arms around his waist.

"At least we're together for the weekend," I murmur.

"You'll get to see how trivial my duties are here."

"You save lives, Danny. That's hardly trivial."

"The only way I'll save a life this weekend is if someone misses the clay pigeon and shoots another guest instead."

"That *would* be exciting."

He turns and wraps his arms around me. "Not as exciting as staying home with you. Instead, here we are, stuck with people with too much bloody money, pretending they're English gentry. They'll shoot at clay pigeons, they'll eat and drink too much, and then they'll demand I treat their hangovers and indigestion."

"Is that why they're all here? To amuse themselves and get drunk?"

"Oh, they and their wives will have a good time, but these weekends are about business. Deals, connections."

"What kind of business?"

"I'd rather not know, so I try not to pay attention." He closes the wardrobe. "You should do the same."

*

According to the chatty cook, thirty-four people are expected for dinner tonight. Like doctors, the kitchen staff always knows intimate details about a client's household, so one of the first places I visit is the kitchen. I tell the cook that I once worked in a restaurant, and I'm curious about tonight's menu. I learn that the guest list includes three vegetarians, one with a shellfish allergy, and two who are on gluten-free diets. I learn that cooking for a full house this weekend meant taking deliveries of multiple cases of wine, wheels of cheese, joints of beef, multiple hams, and trays of guinea fowl and quail. The kitchen staff will start work before dawn to bake the bread and pastries and then continue working until midnight, when the last pot will be washed.

The next morning, it will all start again.

Since she also cooks for Hardwicke's London home, she's able to tell me that Hardwicke is a traditional meat-and-potatoes man, that Silvia, despite being Italian, avoids eating pasta, and that Bella has recently declared that eating meat is intolerably cruel. ("But watch that daft girl change her mind again. Next week she'll be wanting nothing but roast beef.") The cook knows what time the family eats breakfast, that Phillip Hardwicke often snacks on anchovy toast at night, and that he abhors tomatoes. This information doesn't seem particularly useful to me, but it *is* information.

Always talk to the cook.

After my visit to the kitchen, I head into the gardens and wander down a gravel path that winds through lavender and rosemary and box hedges. I settle onto a stone bench, from which I can watch as cars pull up and deliver new guests. From a black limousine, a massively obese man emerges. He looks like a heart attack waiting to happen; Danny's lifesaving skills may be required after all. As I watch the man waddle toward the front door, a voice calls out behind me:

"I know why you're really here, Maggie."

I turn to see Bella approaching along the garden path. Once again, she's wearing pink, an eye-screeching shade that seems almost neon in the subdued grays and violets of the herb garden. She is flushed in the afternoon heat, her cheeks moist and pink, and as she sits down beside me on the bench, I see sweat glistening on the downy hairs of her upper lip.

"I heard them talking about you," she says.

"Who's talking about me?"

"My dad and that jerk-off, Victor. I know your secret." She says this in a perfectly casual way, as if informing me that rain is forecast for tomorrow.

Another limousine pulls up in front of the house, and a middle-aged couple steps out. Once again, Keith comes out the front door to greet them. Keith and Victor, the enforcers. I think about the people around Hardwicke who have met unfortunate ends. Burned alive in a Jaguar. Pushed out a window. Shot in the head. When you cross Phillip Hardwicke, you pay the price.

Stay calm, I think. *Keep things light.*

"Why on earth were they talking about me?" I ask.

"Victor wanted to know more about you. He asked if having you around is a risk."

"A risk?" I laugh. "That's crazy."

"Victor *is* crazy. Silvia hates him. She says he stares at her breasts."

No wonder. Silvia has very nice breasts.

The newly arrived couple has vanished into the house, and the driver pulls away to park the limo with the other cars in the stable courtyard. A dozen vehicles have arrived so far, and all of them would have been captured on the cameras that now monitor the roads leading to Manning House. I wonder if Diana's asset is now on the property as well. I wonder who he is, and whether I can turn to him for help if I need to get out of here in a hurry.

"So what is this big secret I'm supposed to have?" I ask Bella.

"You're here because of me."

"Am I?"

"My dad's paying you to be my minder."

At once, all my tension melts away. This isn't about me at all; it's about Bella. Of course it is. Teenagers always think the world revolves around them.

"I never asked to be paid," I tell her.

"But you *are* my minder. Aren't you?"

I look her in the eye. "Yes, he did ask me to keep an eye on you, but it doesn't mean I agreed to do it."

"What *did* you agree to?"

"I'm here to spend the weekend with my husband. I'm not getting paid, and I'm certainly not here to tell you what you can or can't do." I pause and eye her unflattering dress, which emphasizes all the wrong places. "But I will offer you a little friendly advice. Stop wearing pink, Bella. Seriously, with your red hair, you should banish that color from your closet."

She looks down at her dress, then scowls at me. "No one ever told me that before."

I sigh. "Now I've probably pissed you off."

"At least you told me the truth."

"I always try to." *When I'm not required to lie.*

"Aw, fuck." She rises from the bench.

"Where are you going?"

"To rip this stupid thing off and throw it in the rubbish."

"That looks like an expensive dress. It should go to a charity shop, don't you think? Use it for a good cause."

"Yeah, okay." She starts toward the house, but after a few steps she turns around and comes back. "Would you, um, come up to my room with me?"

"Sure. Why?"

"You're the only one who's ever told me not to wear pink. Maybe you could go through my wardrobe. Tell me what I should keep and what I should give away. If you don't mind, I mean."

I look into those lashless eyes, and I think about what it must be like for her, trapped in this big house with a disinterested father and his mistress, a woman whose glamorous good looks only emphasize Bella's lack of them. I think of what she probably endures in her boarding school, rubbing shoulders with girls who are equally wealthy, but who are blessed with perfect hair and slim hips.

"I'd love to see your wardrobe."

As we walk together to the house, she says: "You never told my dad about those pills, did you?"

"Of course not."

"I hate how everyone's always so quick to rat me out to him. Keith and Victor. Silvia. Even the housemaids."

"I would never do that to you."

"Well, thank you."

We regard each other for a moment, two coconspirators who've forged a bond because we understand the value of silence.

"I know how to keep a secret, Bella," I say.

She gives me a sly smile. "So do I."

*

Bella's lavish bedroom is painted emerald green, the crown molding and pilasters are gold, and rich velvet drapes hang above her canopied bed. It is a room fit for royalty, which is what Hardwicke clearly aspires to, but the girl standing in front of her closet, pink and sweating, looks nothing like a princess.

"It's all crap, isn't it?" she says. She yanks another two dresses off their hangers and tosses them on the bed, onto the growing mound of discarded clothing. "What was I thinking?"

"These are definitely *not* crap, Bella." I pick up one of the dresses she's just discarded. It's from an Italian designer, silk, with exquisite detailing. Clearly expensive, it's meant to be worn skintight. "You just need to find a style that suits you."

"You mean, *hides* me."

"You definitely don't want to hide. You should be *seen*."

"That's not what Mummy says." She tosses a dress with pink-and-orange psychedelic stripes onto the pile. Good riddance, that one. "I think I embarrass her."

"Oh, Bella. I'm sure that's not true."

"You haven't met her. Mummy's perfect. She's *always* been perfect."

She stands with her back to me so I can't see her face, but I heard the catch in her voice, and now I see the slump in her shoulders as she faces a closet filled with clothes that seem designed by the cruel fashion industry to humiliate girls like her. I want to reach out and touch her, comfort her, but that would feel like crossing an emotional line from which I would not be able to retreat. I have to remind myself that I'm not here to be her friend. I'm here to use her, to take advantage of her, and then to walk away. I can't afford to let our attachment go any deeper.

I look out the window, which has a view over the driveway with its stately plane trees, and I see a Range Rover pull up to the front door. Out of the house comes Keith to greet the new arrivals, a young couple who have brought a staggering amount of luggage.

Bella comes to stand beside me at the window. "I hate these weekends," she says, looking down at the guests. "All these people sucking up to Daddy. Pretending they like me."

"Why wouldn't they like you? I do."

"*You're* the only reason it's bearable. Otherwise, I'd rather just spend the weekend at school."

"Have you told your father that?"

"He says I have to be here to meet these people. Learn their names and find out what they do."

"Because he expects you to take over the business someday."

"As if I'd ever want to." She looks at me. "I'd rather do what you did. Work in fashion."

I smile. "You should do whatever *you* want to do. It's not his life, Bella. It's yours."

"No, it isn't." She looks out the window. "He says I'm the only one he can trust to take over. What do I say to that?"

"You could say no."

She snorts. "You don't know Daddy."

But I do know him. I know things about him that she doesn't, things that would horrify her. Things that make me want to tell her: Run, Bella. Run fast, run far, before his poison infects you too. But I can't say these things. I can't save her. All I can do is stand back and observe like the cold-eyed entomologist who watches the spider binding its prey.

I can't bring myself to look at her, this girl who is everyone's pawn. Instead I go to her closet, scan the clothes hanging there, and reach for a black cocktail dress. It's silk, with a low-cut bodice and a flared skirt.

"This one," I say, turning to her. "Wear it tonight."

"Mummy bought that one for me."

"Then your mother has a keen eye."

She takes the dress and frowns. "It's black."

"It will look good on you." I smile. "Trust me."

*

That evening, Bella strolls out onto the back terrace wearing the black cocktail dress, a color that's safe for any figure. I'm standing at the edge of the party, nursing a glass of chilled rosé, when I see her step out the french doors to join the gathering. Before anyone can stop her, she snatches up a glass of white wine from a tray and wanders along the periphery of the crowd, never quite penetrating it, as if magnetically repelled. She peruses the buffet table, where a sumptuous meal is laid out, and she halfheartedly adds carrot sticks and asparagus to her plate before wending her way toward where I'm standing. As she reaches the carving station, she abruptly stops to stare at the rib roast, juicy and glistening under the heat lamp.

"That's like half a baby cow there," she says.

"It's Aberdeen Angus beef, miss," says the server. "The very best. Would you like a slice?"

"God, no! I'm vegetarian." Nose wrinkled, she keeps walking and joins me at the edge of the terrace.

"That dress looks very nice on you," I say.

"How can anyone eat such bloody meat?"

"When did you become vegetarian?"

"Like, forever ago."

Yet I remember her hungrily scarfing down beef Wellington at my wedding dinner last year. So much for the reliability of a teenager's testimony.

"Where's Dr. Gallagher?" she asks, looking around the crowd.

"He's upstairs somewhere. One of the guests got stung by a bee in the garden, and she's gone a bit hysterical about it. I'm glad you're here now, because I don't know anyone at this party."

Bella drags a carrot stick through a puddle of blue cheese dip. "Oh, it's just the same old crowd. Daddy's brought them round before."

"You know who they are?"

"Most of them. Daddy keeps repeating their names, telling me I need to remember them." She crunches down on the carrot stick, then points the end at two men huddled in conversation. "That man's Damien Cawley. He's a loan officer from Deutsche Bank. And the other man is Oleg, from Belarus. He owns hotels all over the world, and he was nice enough to host my birthday party at the Battenberg last year. That's his hotel, in London."

"What's Oleg's last name?"

"Oh, I don't remember. Something Slavic. He's pretty cool. He even let me drink champagne for my birthday."

Which is what a teenager really cares about.

I watch as Oleg and Damien tilt their heads together in quiet conversation. Money, meet laundromat. I'm impressed that Bella knows as much as she does about her father's associates. It's obvious Hardwicke has been coaching her. She may claim she's disinterested in his affairs, but she's clearly been paying attention.

Across the terrace, a woman laughs loudly and drunkenly. "And who is she?" I ask.

"Oh, her." Bella snorts. "The last time she was here, she threw up on the lawn in front of the whole party. It was so gross. I don't know why he stays married to her."

"Who's her husband?"

"Sandy Shoreham. The MP." She points to the bespectacled man who's patting the woman's arm, trying to quiet her down. I know that name. Shoreham is the sort of man who appears so colorless he could easily be overlooked, despite his very recognizable position as a prominent Conservative Party MP.

Silvia glides past us, black hair loose and gleaming, her formfitting dress hugging every curve of her buttocks. Several men turn to eye her as she passes, but she seems adrift in an anesthetized daze, oblivious to their gazes. I have yet to see her eat a thing this evening; a figure as slim as hers requires discipline.

"Oh, crap. Take my glass. Quick!"

"What?"

"It's Daddy." She shoves her wineglass at me, and I take it just as Hardwicke looks in our direction. He frowns at the two of us standing together, and Bella gives him an innocent smile. Yes, the babysitter is here, doing her job. He gives a nod, then turns away to join a circle of his guests.

Bella takes back her glass and gulps down the rest of the wine.

The wife of Sandy Shoreham is laughing more loudly, her head thrown back as she wobbles on high heels. There's one at every cocktail party, the guest who makes everyone shake their heads, the guest who'll wake up the next morning in abject embarrassment. I almost feel sorry for her, being dragged to joyless evenings so her husband can forge alliances with bankers and oligarchs, but this is the way business is conducted, legal and illegal. Hardwicke just brings together all the moving parts.

I watch him circulate among his guests, clapping backs, bending in to listen, smiling intently at the wives. Hovering nearby is Victor, always within a few paces, the man Bella so dislikes. The man who brazenly stares at Silvia's breasts. Victor looks in my direction. I know he's been asking about me, and his gaze makes me uneasy, so I turn away.

That's when I notice the man standing behind me. He has dark hair and owlish glasses and a dinner jacket that sags on his shoulders, as if he has recently lost weight. For a moment our gazes lock; then he walks away. I watch as he descends the terrace steps, to the lawn.

"Who is that man?" I ask Bella. "The one walking on the grass."

She shrugs. "Just one of Daddy's money people. I've only seen him here a few times."

"Do you know his name?"

"Stephen something. I can't keep track of *everyone* Daddy introduces to me. Oh look, they've brought out dessert."

Bella heads back to the buffet table, but I keep my eye on the man as he crosses the lawn. He keeps his head down, his hands in his pockets, as though trying to shrink into invisibility. As he vanishes around the corner of the house, Victor and Hardwicke also descend the terrace steps and follow him.

Something odd is going on.

I set down my drink and circle along the edge of the crowd, keeping my eye on Hardwicke and Victor. At the steps I pause and glance around to see if anyone is watching me, but no one is. No one cares what the doctor's wife is up to.

I step onto the lawn, my high heels sinking into the grass. Victor and Hardwicke don't seem to be in a rush, but they are walking purposefully toward the east wing of the house, clearly with a destination in mind. I trail well behind them, just a guest strolling the grounds. I reach the edge of the east wing and stop in the shadow of a lilac bush.

Hardwicke and Victor are walking across the courtyard, toward the stables.

"Maggie?"

I spin around to see Danny. The lilac bush casts us both in gloom so I can't read his face, and he can't read mine. We are faceless silhouettes, meeting in the shadows. Perhaps we always have been.

"What are you doing out here?" he asks.

"I, um, need to get something out of the car." I nod toward the stable courtyard, where all the vehicles are parked.

"I can get it for you. What do you need?"

"My book. I think I left it on the back seat."

"I'll take a look. How's the party?"

"Lovely."

"Bella behaving herself?"

"Aside from sneaking a glass of wine, yes. How's the beesting patient?"

He sighs and glances up at the bedroom windows. "You'd think the woman needs her arm amputated, the way she was carrying on. I'll go get your book for you. See you back on the terrace."

He walks toward our parked car, but he won't find a book on the back seat because there isn't one. It's yet another lie I've told my husband.

There will be more.

*

It's just after three in the morning when I quietly get dressed in the dark and slip out of our room, leaving Danny asleep in bed. I've lain awake for hours, waiting for the house to quiet down, for the final clatter of dishes, the last whoosh of water in the pipes. Now I make my way down the dimly lit servants' staircase. In a few hours, the kitchen staff will be back at work, prepping for breakfast, but these are the spectral hours between darkness and dawn, when sleep hangs heaviest over a household, and I encounter no one in the stairway.

The lights are off in the kitchen, the stainless steel surfaces only a faint gleam in the darkness. I feel my way through the shadows, past the walk-in refrigerator, past the sinks and prep counters, and emerge outside, into the kitchen garden.

It's time to look inside the stables.

That's where Hardwicke and Victor and the man with the glasses disappeared to last night. Hardwicke and Victor did not return to the party for nearly an hour, and I want to know what kept them away.

I follow the garden path, my passage stirring the scents of lavender and rosemary, and reach the front of the house. The upstairs windows are dark, the guests asleep. Buckets of wine and whisky flowed tonight, and in the morning, there'll be hangovers and desperate calls for tomato juice and aspirin, but now all is silent.

I weave in and out of shadows as I follow the perimeter of the courtyard. Moving behind the cover of parked cars, I make my way to the stables. Inside the lights are off, and when I slip in through the door, I can't see the horses, but I can smell them. And I hear them: The stamping of a hoof. The soft nicker of a greeting.

I turn on my flashlight, and the beam catches the reflection of one bright eye staring back at me from a stall. What were the men doing in here last night? I doubt they came just to admire the horses. My flashlight sweeps back and forth across the straw-littered floor. I don't know what I'm searching for, but I'll recognize it if I see it. A scrap of a document. A cigarette butt with a bonus gift of DNA. I seek a clue, any clue, to what business was being conducted here.

First, I go into the stable manager's office, where I see a desk and two chairs. Photos of handsome horses hang on the walls. I search the desk and rifle through the ledger tucked in one of the drawers, but everything I find seems to be related to horses. There are vet bills, farrier bills, records of feed deliveries. The crazy thought briefly passes through my head that maybe *this* is part of the London laundromat, that Russian money is going to horseflesh, but that would make little sense. Unless it's used as a tax write-off, horse ownership is a poor investment, a bottomless pit into which you pour money you'll never see again.

I shine my flashlight on the chairs and see dust covering the seats. No one has sat in them for quite some time. The men did not come into this office.

I head back out to the stalls and slowly move down the row, past the watchful gazes of half a dozen horses. They are uneasy about my late-night intrusion, and I hear restless stomping, a nervous whinny. What were the men doing here for so long? What brought them into this building?

Then I see, at the far end of the stables, the scrape marks left by something being dragged across the straw-littered floor. The drag marks lead to the last stall.

I unlatch the door to the empty stall and shine my light inside. Something reflects back at me: a pair of eyeglasses, lying in the bedding. But it's not the glasses that make me suck in a gasp. It's what lies beside those glasses: a hand, its fingers frozen in a claw.

My beam follows the hand to the arm, to the shoulder. To the face. I'm too stunned to move, to breathe, as I stare at the dead man lying inside the stall, a man whose face I saw earlier that evening. The man who'd been wearing those glasses, which fell or were kicked away during the fatal struggle. I look at his protruding tongue, note the pinpoint hemorrhages in his eyes, and I know how he died. I crouch down beside him and shine the light on his neck. On the bruise left by the ligature that had been wrapped around his throat. This was the work of a professional.

Who are you? Why did Hardwicke want you dead?

I hear men's voices outside, moving closer.

I jump to my feet, scramble out of the dead man's stall, and latch it shut again. Frantically I look around for a place to hide.

The voices are louder. The men are about to walk into the building, entering through the only way in or out.

I swing open the door to the adjoining stall, dart inside, and latch the door shut again. I'm not alone in here; there's a horse standing right beside me, a horse that's spooked by my invasion. It kicks at the stall and whinnies in distress.

The stable lights come on.

I can't leave the stall now. I'm trapped in here with a jittery horse who's now stamping and snorting. I drop to a crouch in the corner, making myself as small as I can.

The men are walking closer, and I recognize the voices of Keith and Victor.

"What's got that one so spooked?" says Victor.

"What else? He can probably smell him."

Now a third voice speaks, a voice that makes me shrink even deeper into my corner. "Just get him the fuck out of here," Hardwicke orders.

I hear the squeak of wheels. They've brought a cart with them, to move the body. Like me, they've waited until the house was quiet and there'd be no witnesses, no one to see what they're about to do.

The horse snorts again, kicks the wall with a violence that makes me cower in the corner, trying to avoid being slammed by one of those hooves. I hear the squeak of the door opening to the last stall. They're so close that I can hear Victor and Keith grunt as they lift the body and roll it into the cart.

"Glasses," Hardwicke snaps. "Get his glasses."

Heavy breathing. The sound of shoes shuffling in the straw.

The horse gives another kick. His whinny's so loud it sounds like a scream.

"What's wrong with you, eh?" says Victor. I look up as an arm reaches over the stall door to pet the horse. All the man has to do is look down and he'll see me.

"Those teeth can bite straight to bone," says Hardwicke. "Stay away from him."

Victor's arm disappears. "Why do you keep him?"

"He doesn't bite *me*." Hardwicke laughs. "He knows what would happen."

As the cart squeaks away, I stay huddled in the stall corner. I hear the sound of two cars starting outside, then tires crackling across gravel and the growl of car engines fading to silence. Now is the time to slip out, but the stable lights are still on. Have they simply forgotten to turn them off, or are they coming back?

I start to rise to my feet. Freeze.

Someone is whistling a tune. It's Hardwicke. Why has he stayed behind? Why hasn't he left the building? *He must know. Somehow he knows that something is amiss.*

The whistling moves toward me. The melody is "Scotland the Brave," so lilting, so cheerful. So terrifying. Closer and closer it comes as my muscles tense, my legs prepared to spring in a fight to the death, me against Hardwicke. My attack has to be quick. A punch to the throat, a jab into his eye socket. Already my hand is closing into a fist.

The whistling stops.

I hear the clap of his hand against horseflesh and a responding nicker. "There's a good girl," he says. He's paused at one of the stalls to pet his horse. Such a benevolent master he is, doling out affection as casually as he doles out death.

The whistling starts up again, but this time it's in retreat. As "Scotland the Brave" moves away, I release a shaky breath. The stable lights go off. Footsteps crunch across gravel.

In darkness, I wait long enough for Hardwicke to be well away from the stable, long enough for him to make it back to the house. Even then I'm not certain it's safe to come out, but I cannot stay here all night. Soon the kitchen staff will be awake and preparing breakfast; I need to be back in my room before anyone knows I've been out of the house.

My heart is banging in my chest when I slip out of the stall and emerge from the stables. Outside, I see empty spots in the courtyard where the two cars were parked, one of them no doubt belonging to the dead man. In the morning his disappearance will be easy to explain to the household help. *He got a call and had to leave in the middle of the night. One less guest for dinner.*

I slink back into the cover of the trees. The night has turned chilly, but I'm sweating, shaking. Somewhere a car with a dead body is being disposed of, while upstairs, Phillip Hardwicke lies asleep and untroubled in his bed. In a few hours, dawn will brighten the sky, and Manning House will stir awake. Breakfast will be served, and guests will wander outside to walk through the gardens or shoot at clay pigeons. I will join them, because that's what everyone expects me to do. It will be a lovely day.

A perfectly lovely day.

CHAPTER 21

"He was one of ours," says Diana.

We can no longer run the risk of being seen together in public, so we are in a safe house, reserved for meetings like this one, conducted out of sight and impossible for the enemy to monitor. Just getting here required me to exercise multiple evasive maneuvers: doubling back on the tube, then zigzagging on foot through a warren of streets, past shops selling cookware and electronics and cigarettes, to ensure I was not tailed. There'll be no more conversations in the British Museum.

I stand at the window, gazing down at the busy street below. It looks like a normal weekday at noon, with people out and about, shopping or searching for a place to eat lunch. But from our soundproof bubble of a room, what I see are clueless people, unaware of the dark and dangerous currents streaming all around them.

"Who was he?" I ask.

"His name was Stephen Moss. He was a bank compliance officer at UGB. For a year, he'd been flagging suspicious transactions in and out of Hardwicke's accounts, but his superiors did nothing with the information. He was frustrated by their inaction, and when we approached him, he agreed to work with us."

"For a fee?"

"No. That's not why he did it."

So he was a principled asset. They are the best ones, the most reliable ones. And when we lose them, they're also the most tragic ones.

I turn to look at Stephen Moss's photo, which is now displayed on Diana's laptop screen. The man I saw at the Manning House weekend was thinner, but this is definitely the same man. Was it illness that made him lose all that weight, or was it the stress of flying too close to the flames, knowing that at any moment those flames might engulf him?

"His Saab was found abandoned this morning, in the airport parking lot in Leeds," she says.

"And Mr. Moss?"

"His body hasn't been located. I don't need to tell you, this is a major loss. He was feeding us highly valuable financial information on Hardwicke and helping us track which accounts the money was coming from, and where it was going. Now we've gone blind."

I feel hairs prickle on my arms. The tingle of fear. I'm still haunted by the echoes of "Scotland the Brave," whistling in my nightmares. "If they tortured him, he might have told them about me."

"He couldn't have, because he didn't know about you. That's why we kept you both in the dark."

"They knew about *him*."

"But they don't know about you."

"How do you know?"

"Because you're still alive."

"Who exposed him?"

Diana shakes her head. "It might have been someone at UGB. Someone who knew Moss was delving into Hardwicke's accounts."

"Could they have a mole in the National Crime Agency? Or one of their other agencies?"

"That would be a problem," she admits. "There's so much money sloshing around in London, and there's a chance someone, in one of their enforcement agencies, has been bought off. Otherwise, you and I wouldn't have to get involved in this mess."

I sit down at the table. The street below is crowded with traffic, but we don't hear any of it because these insulated windows and soundproof walls shut it all out. We face each other in silence, across a table set with a teapot and teacups. Months of living in London have forced me to succumb to this afternoon tea ritual, even though what I really crave right now is coffee, strong and black.

"I want out of this mission," I say.

"What?" Her chin snaps up. "Why?"

"Because you've already lost one asset and you don't even know how he was exposed."

"Maggie, I understand what you're going through. I know you're scared, but—"

"Yes, I am scared—for Danny. He doesn't know anything about this. If they come after me, they'll go after him as well. I volunteered for this but he didn't, and I won't have him hurt. Plus, it's been fucking hard, living a lie. Sleeping with a man who has no idea who I really am."

"That's the nature of the job. You know that."

"And I've had enough. I've given you what you wanted."

"Not yet. Not everything."

"You have Hardwicke's medical records. You know about every sprain, every mole on his body. That's what you asked me for."

"But now we've lost Stephen Moss. We have no eyes or ears on Hardwicke's financials."

"I'm not his banker. I'm not privy to that."

"You have a relationship with his daughter."

"She's fifteen. She doesn't know a damn thing."

"She likes you. She'll help integrate you into the family."

"Again, she's *just fifteen*."

"Which makes it easier to gain her trust."

I think of Bella in her ridiculous pink outfits, ungainly and starved for attention. I think about needy teenage girls and how easy it is to manipulate them, use them. And how wrong it feels to be doing so. So much about this feels wrong.

"You don't need me anymore," I say. "If you want to nail Hardwicke, you can probably do it now. Alert the police about Moss's murder, and they'll investigate. There's got to be some forensic evidence in the stables."

"There's no body. Hence, no way to prove there *was* a murder."

"If his body does turn up—"

"Even if it does, you're the only witness who can testify where and when he was killed. Are you willing to expose yourself, blow your cover?"

I think about Stephen Moss, and how frantically he must have clawed at the garotte wrapped around his neck. I think of what Hardwicke would do to me if he found out whom I work for. I let out a breath. "No."

"I didn't think so. Anyway, Hardwicke isn't the one we're after now. He's just a cog in a much larger financial machine. We need to know who's actually manipulating that machine on Moscow's behalf. We want Cyrano."

The elusive Russian sleeper. The man's identity is still a mystery, and even after eight years, we have only bits and pieces of information about him, most of it gleaned from intercepted messages from his kurator, or handler. We now know he has a female companion who suffers from acute intermittent porphyria and needs regular infusions of the drug heme arginate. At my last meeting with Diana in the British Museum, she'd asked if such a patient was being treated by Galen doctors, but I haven't found a record of any.

"I gave you the guest list from the Manning House weekend. Maybe Cyrano was one of them. Start there," I suggest.

"He wasn't. SIGINT scooped up a recent communication from Moscow," she says. "We know Cyrano is out of the country right now."

"Then I wish you luck finding him." I stand up to leave. "Because I'll be working on my resignation letter."

"Not yet, Maggie. We still need you."

"I've given you what I can."

"There's one more thing you can deliver. That last SIGINT interception mentioned Malta."

I turn to her. "Malta?"

"There's to be a meeting. A negotiation."

All at once, I understand why I can't resign, not yet. "Hardwicke's going to Malta next week," I say.

"That's why we need you. Your husband will be accompanying him?"

"Yes, but that trip to Malta is nothing. Hardwicke's just going there to pick up Bella and bring her back home to London."

"What is Bella doing on Malta?"

"Her mother, Camilla, is vacationing there. Bella flew out to spend time with her."

"Then I want *you* in Malta too. Talk your way onto Hardwicke's jet, find out if there's another reason he's going there."

"To meet Cyrano, you mean."

She nods. "Both men, on the same island, at the same time. The possibility is tantalizing."

I look at her laptop. The screen has gone dark, but the image of Stephen Moss's face has been burned so indelibly into my memory that I can still see it there, just as I can still see him lying dead in that horse stall, his tongue protruding, his eyes speckled with pinpoint hemorrhages. When you cross Phillip Hardwicke, that's what happens to you.

"I'm not doing this. Find another way."

"This is our best chance. Maybe our only chance."

"Just surveil Hardwicke on Malta. You don't need me for that."

"No one else can get as close to him as Danny can. He's our secret weapon."

"He's my husband."

"Really, Maggie?" Diana laughs. "Sentiment before duty? Have you always been this soft?"

We regard each other across the table. For more than two decades, I have served my country. I've told countless lies, pulled up roots again and again, even risked my life. Now, because I refuse this one assignment, those years of service count for nothing.

"After Malta, I'm out," I finally say. "Permanently."

She nods. "Of course. If that's what you really want."

"I'll tell you what I want. I want an ordinary life with my husband. I want us to *be* ordinary. Have a cat, tend a garden. Take a walk together on the street, without worrying that we're being followed."

"It'll all be yours, Maggie," she says, and then snaps her laptop shut. "But not quite yet."

*

Danny watches me through the frosted glass as I stand under the shower, rinsing shampoo out of my hair. I used to enjoy being the lustful focus of his attention, but tonight, lust is just a distraction. I have hard decisions to make, a future to plan.

Our future. I don't remember when *I* became *we*, when *mine* became *ours*. The melding together of our lives was such a gradual process that I did not notice when the pronouns changed, when I began taking for granted that he would always be standing beside me.

As I step out of the shower, he's waiting with a towel.

"I never get tired of the view," he says, draping the towel around me. He leans me back against the bathroom wall and presses a kiss to my lips. Even as my mind is elsewhere, weighing my choices and considering the possible consequences, my body automatically responds to him. It was never supposed to get this complicated between us. He was just a holiday fling, a warm body on a hot Bangkok night, not someone I should have fallen in love with. Not someone I should have married.

Now I can't bear the thought of losing him. Which means I can't ever tell him the truth about who I work for and how our marriage was part of a larger plan. I can never reveal the lies I told, the deceptions upon deceptions: My fake maid of honor, hired for the role. My clandestine meetings with Diana. The Galen medical records I copied, violating his patients' trust as well as his. The longer I keep up this double life, the more likely the truth will spill out, and when it does, he will doubt our marriage was ever genuine, will assume it was just a convenient fabrication that had nothing to do with love. *If you learned the truth, would you still want me?*

I'm afraid to find out.

That night, lying beside him in the dark, I finally make peace with my decision. I know what I have to do, because nothing matters as much to me as Danny. Not this mission, not my career, not the rest of the turbulent world, just Danny and me. He rolls onto his side and slings his arm around me. I have grown so accustomed to his scent that it is like my own now, as if I have absorbed the very essence of him through my skin.

I stroke his arm and nudge him awake. "Danny?"

"Hmmm."

"Remember when you talked about packing it all in? Leaving London and doing something else, something wild?"

Slowly he opens his eyes. "What is this all about?"

"I've been thinking about the future."

"Oh dear. This sounds serious."

"I am serious. Danny, I think we should do it."

He's fully awake now and looking at me. "You weren't crazy about the idea before."

"I thought about what really matters. You took the job at Galen only because your mother was struggling to pay off her debts, and you wanted to help her. But now she's passed on, and we don't need the money." I pause. "I know you're not happy."

"What do *you* want, Maggie?"

"I don't want you tied to a job you hate, taking care of patients you don't even like."

"Just some of them."

"Galen may pay you well, but it's a velvet trap. The patients, they practically own you. It's how they think about people like us. On a chessboard, we're just the pawns."

He goes silent, but I can feel his body humming with excitement. "If I resign, we'll have to give up this apartment."

"It was never ours, anyway."

"It means moving to something much smaller. Not nearly as nice."

"We could live in a tent, for all I care."

"And we'll need to make a living."

"I have savings. And I can find a job. 'Lady of leisure' never really fit me anyway."

He laughs. A genuinely happy laugh. "Maybe I could be a 'gentleman of leisure.'"

"You could return to charity medicine. You were happy doing that."

"I was, I really was. We could travel again. Go back to Thailand."

"Or South America."

"Or Madagascar!"

Now we're both laughing at our old punch line, just as we laughed at it when we first met. The night feels effervescent with promise. Escape is what we've both longed for, and now we're going to do it together.

"I'll need to give notice," he says. "God, that won't be pleasant. They'll need to reassign my patients, shuffle schedules."

"It can't be the first time a doctor's resigned from Galen. They just have to hire someone else, like any other business."

"I'm scheduled to fly to Malta, with Phillip Hardwicke. It's too late to back out of that trip."

"Don't back out—just make it your final assignment. He may want help wrangling Bella, so I could come along too. And when we're back home, we'll start packing. Jump on a plane and just *go* somewhere. Maybe this time we'll really make it to Madagascar."

"I don't care where we go, Maggie. As long as we're together." He takes a deep breath. "Now. I have to write a resignation letter."

So do I. For two decades, I have faithfully served my country. I've told countless lies, jumped out of airplanes, and taken shrapnel for Uncle Sam. Now I say, fuck it all. Fuck Hardwicke and Cyrano and the eternally bloody state of the world.

Danny and I are running away.

CHAPTER 22
JO

Purity, Maine, now

During the course of her job as a cop, Jo had encountered idiotic hunters here and there, men (and almost all of them were men) who'd tripped and shot themselves in the foot, or thought they were aiming for a deer and instead brought down someone's cow. She'd confronted hunters roaming where they shouldn't, on posted property or within three hundred feet of a residence. Once she'd even taken into custody a man who'd murdered his own father during a hunting trip, except she couldn't *prove* the shooting was intentional. Glen Cooney was chief then, and he'd advised her that a charge of manslaughter was the best they could hope for. To this day she believed a murderer had walked free. Every year, when deer season opened for rifle hunting, she braced herself for the calamities that so often followed when armed men tramped into the woods, eager to blast away at anything with a white tail.

The man who tried to shoot Maggie Bird was not hunting for deer.

That much was obvious to Jo as she stood among the trees where the shooter had fired from. She had already collected all the bullet casings she could find, had retraced the boot prints to the dirt road where he'd left his vehicle, and had sent the state crime lab the images of those prints, as well as the tire-tread impressions. This might not be as exciting as a homicide case, but for Jo it was exhilarating just the same, to be running an investigation without someone like Detective Alfond yanking away the reins. Since no one had been hurt and the only damages were to the RTV, this incident was too minor for a high-and-mighty state of Maine detective. This case was Jo's, and she was thrilled to be in charge.

She tramped back through the woods and climbed in her vehicle, parked on the same dirt road where the shooter's vehicle had been. *Which way did you go next?* she wondered.

Let's try back to town.

She headed down the road that led east toward the village, past snow-covered fields and bare trees, past a farmhouse with a dozen rusting cars in various stages of being cannibalized. The first business she came to was the feedstore. Much more than just a place to buy animal food, it was also the place to buy salt blocks for your horse, spare parts for your lawn mower, and, in the spring, even a box of ducklings, which might or might not survive to fly off into the sunset. She pulled into the parking lot and looked up at the entryway. *There you are. Let's hope you're not just for show.*

"Hey, Jo," said Vern, the feedstore owner, as she walked in the door. "Here for more dog treats?"

"Naw. Lucy's on a diet. I'm not supposed to feed her any more treats."

"She looked slim enough to me."

"You don't have to lift her into the back of a pickup. I'm here on official business."

"That dead woman?"

"No, state police have taken over that case. This is about an incident at Blackberry Farm this morning. Your security camera working? The one out front? I need the footage from this morning. Around eight till nine a.m."

To her surprise, Vern laughed. "I should start charging for pay-per-view."

"What?"

"You're the second person to ask for that video." He went to the store computer. "I'll email the file to you right now . . ."

"Who else asked for it?"

"That nice lady on the library board. She said the library's thinking about installing a security camera, and she wanted to see how sharp my footage is. In case they decide to purchase this model."

"And you showed her the footage?"

"Made a copy for her so the library board can judge the quality." He paused, seeing her scowl. "I didn't see the harm. It's not like anything exciting happened out there."

"What was this woman's name?"

Vern paused, pursing his lips. Senior moment. "You know, it's that fine-looking woman with the pretty scarves. She and her husband bought that house on Chestnut Street."

Jo sighed. "The Slocums."

He slapped himself on the head. "Of course. *That's* their name."

Them again. Why did they keep turning up at the most inappropriate places? Jo was used to dealing with nosy villagers, but the Slocums were out of control.

Her cell phone rang.

"Hey, Mike," she answered as she walked outside to her vehicle.

"The state crime lab called," he said. "They identified the tread marks from the shooter's vehicle."

"Go ahead."

"The tires are Goodyear Wranglers, all season. TrailRunner AT, 235/75R15. Could be installed on any number of SUVs, so it doesn't help us ID the vehicle."

Goodyear. She suddenly remembered the last time she'd clashed with the Slocums, in Maggie Bird's driveway. Remembered they'd been studying a different set of tire tracks in the snow, and Ingrid Slocum had said: *I think these are Goodyears.*

"Call the crime lab," she said to Mike. "I want the tread-mark analysis from Maggie Bird's driveway two nights ago."

"You mean the homicide? That's not our—"

"I *know* it's not our case. Just get me the report."

As she waited in her car, she watched the road in front of the feed-store, counting how many cars passed by. Even though this was one of the roads leading directly to the village, the traffic was light, with a full minute or two between vehicles. Come summer, when the tourists came to town, there'd be plenty more traffic on this road, people driving from their lake cottages to have lobster dinners in town, or to board one of the windjammers for a sunset cruise. But on this winter's day, the road was almost deserted.

Her cell phone rang. Mike again.

"Got it," he said. "The other tires were Goodyear Wranglers, TrailRunner AT, two three . . ." He stopped. "Hey, it's the same vehicle."

"Not necessarily," said Jo. "Just the same type of tire. There's gotta be other SUVs around here with Goodyear TrailRunners."

"But what are the odds?"

She didn't know. That was a question for the mechanic down at the gas station, who'd have a better idea of how many Goodyear TrailRunners were rolling around town. She really *should* alert Detective Alfond, because the shooting could be connected to Bianca's murder. First, though, she wanted to see how far she could chase this. Glen

Cooney once told her that if she insisted on remaining in Purity, she'd never get to stretch herself as a cop. This was her chance to stretch, and it felt good to be working her own case and seeing which way the clues pointed.

At the moment, those clues were all pointing in the same direction: to the mysterious Maggie Bird.

CHAPTER 23
MAGGIE

Declan lives in an old sea captain's house on the water, and even though I have visited it a number of times, I have never been upstairs. Like me, he is a private person who has compartmentalized his life into separate boxes. Downstairs is his public box, where our monthly book group sometimes gathers. We'd sip martinis and trade gossip in his living room, which looks out over Penobscot Bay, and in the summer, we'd take turns peering through his telescope at the schooners returning from their sunset cruises. I have sat down to dinner in his dining room, washed dishes in his kitchen, and paid the occasional visit to his powder room, but not once have I been upstairs, which he reserves for himself. We are both careful to keep those boxes separate: Upstairs/downstairs. Private/public. Before/after.

Today's sniper attack on me, however, has blown up our well-ordered lives—or it's blown up my life, anyway. Now I've taken up temporary residence in his upstairs guest room, a room that is not at all what I imagined it would look like. I expected it to be like Declan himself, coolly understated, with clean lines and a minimum of adornment. Instead I find lace curtains and a quilted bedspread and old black-and-white photos on the dresser, all projecting sentimentality. This is a tender side of him that I did not suspect.

One of the photos shows a smiling woman with a dark-haired toddler on her lap. I turn over the frame and see the year written on the back. This must be Declan and his mother, who died of a ruptured appendix when he was five years old. He scarcely talks about her, but I can imagine what his childhood was like, growing up motherless. I know he was shipped off to boarding school when he was twelve, because his diplomat father was too wrapped up in world affairs to be a proper parent, and I think of my own teenage years, burdened with an alcoholic father I could not wait to escape. It was another variation of being motherless, and neither version was a happy one.

I hear Declan call out to me from the bottom of the stairs: "Maggie, Ben's here! And dinner's ready!"

I leave my half-unpacked suitcase in the room and head downstairs, past framed photos of places where Declan has lived and worked. Budapest. Prague. Warsaw. I pause at an image of him standing on what looks like a university campus, surrounded by a group of students, and I see Polish words on one of the buildings. It's Jagiellonian University in Kraków. His hair is still black and a lot shaggier than it is now, but in his tweed jacket he looks every bit the academic he was supposed to be. How young he appears. Where did the years go, for both of us?

In the kitchen, I find that Ben and Declan have already poured themselves scotch. On the stove, a goulash is simmering, something Declan pulled out of his freezer and made from a recipe that probably dates back to his stint in Budapest.

"Whisky, Mags?" Declan asks, uncorking the bottle.

"Straight to the serious stuff, I see."

"This is a serious development."

I take the glass of whisky. Tonight, I really need it. "Thank you, Declan. For the bed too."

"You can't return home, you know that," says Ben. "Not until we've sorted out who's trying to kill you, and why."

"And thank *you*, Ben, for that uplifting summary of my situation."

"Unfortunately, it's an accurate one," says Declan. He ladles goulash into three bowls and carries them to the kitchen table. I've never seen him wearing an apron before. The one he has tied on is black and embroidered with the stately Cunard logo, which seems perfectly appropriate for a diplomat's son. Declan is the only man I know who can make an apron look dashing. We sit down with our whisky and our bowls of steaming goulash, fragrant with the scent of paprika.

"We have to put our heads together and figure this out, since we can't rely on the local police," says Ben. "Although Ms. Thibodeau seems like a clever enough girl."

"Too clever," I say. "I don't like the tenor of her questions, as if I'm the one under suspicion. She could be a problem."

The doorbell rings. I snap straight in my chair and glance toward the living room.

"That'll be Ingrid and Lloyd," says Declan. He leaves the kitchen to answer the door.

"You told them what happened?" I ask Ben.

"Of course. We're all on the same team here, and we need all hands on deck. It'll be like old times."

"Why do you sound like you're enjoying this?"

"Frankly, retirement hasn't been much fun for any of us. This gives us a chance to see if we've still got what it takes. It's good to feel useful again. Back in the game, so to speak."

"I *am* the game this time."

Declan returns to the kitchen with the new arrivals. Ingrid has brought her laptop computer, and Lloyd is carrying a long cardboard tube. As always, Ingrid is wearing one of her elaborately tied scarves, this one dyed in rich ochers and reds. Autumn colors. I have never mastered the art of scarf-tying, and as she sits down at the kitchen table, I eye the intricate knot, envious of how effortlessly elegant she looks with her silver hair and porcelain skin.

"Is that goulash I smell?" says Lloyd, going straight to the stove as usual.

"Made it with goat meat. Help yourself," says Declan.

Of course, Lloyd does; he's never been shy about digging in. He happily scoops goulash into a bowl and sits down at the table. I did not know that a meeting had been called this evening, but apparently, Declan sent out the Bat-Signal and here we are, five old spies with five lifetimes' worth of experience. Retired does not mean useless. Everyone here has brought their individual tricks of the trade.

Lloyd gulps down a spoonful of goulash, then opens one end of the cardboard tube. Out slides a topographical map, which he unrolls on the table amid our bowls and silverware. I immediately recognize the geography on that map. It includes Blackberry Farm and the area surrounding it, as well as the seaside village of Purity.

"I've highlighted all the access routes to your property," says Lloyd, pointing to the roads he has marked in yellow. "We know where the shooter accessed your land, parking his vehicle on the dirt road that runs between your property and that of your abutting neighbor to the south." Lloyd looks up at me. There's a smear of paprika-red goulash at the edge of his mouth, a souvenir of his unapologetic appetite. It's one of Lloyd's quirky charms, the way he so eagerly devours life. "How well do you know this neighbor? I believe his name is Ronald Farrell?"

"He's an absentee landowner," I say. "I've met him only once, soon after I moved in. He's eighty-two years old, lives in a retirement home in Rockland."

"What else?"

"He has one son, living in Massachusetts. Two granddaughters, neither living in Maine. His property is in conservation, and he's already willed it to the land trust." I look around at my circle of colleagues. "I did backgrounds on all my nearby neighbors before I bought the farm. They all passed muster."

Lloyd nods. "Then let's move on to which route the shooter took to get to your land."

Ben points to the dirt road on the map. "We found his tire tracks here, where he parked."

"The only way to access that dirt road," says Lloyd, "is from West Fork Road, here. Paved, runs north and south."

"We know this, Lloyd."

"Stay with me. West Fork Road has two access routes, Pondside Road to the north, and Village Road, on the south end. Village Road runs straight into Purity. From there, he could have taken any one of four routes out of town, then headed up or down the coast. It's difficult to narrow down where he went from there, so . . ." Lloyd looks at his wife.

"So," says Ingrid, "I did my thing."

Which, because this is Ingrid, could mean anything.

She opens her laptop. "The problem with living in a small town like ours is the relative lack of CCTVs."

"We used to think that was a good thing," says Ben.

"Not when you're tracking down an assassin. So I got in my car and went looking for all the CCTVs in the area. On Pondside Road, there are two houses with security cams, but both are aimed down at their driveways, with no view of the road. On Village Road, however, as you get close to town, we hit pay dirt. There's a CCTV right here." With a pencil, she circles the location on the map. "It's Simonton Feed and Grain. I chatted up the proprietor, and he was happy to share his footage from this morning. And here we are. Eight seventeen a.m., about the time your shooter would have been making his getaway. I think this is the vehicle."

She turns the laptop around to show us her screen. We all lean in and stare at the black Toyota SUV captured in a still shot. It could very well be the same vehicle that dumped Bianca's body in my driveway. Because of its tinted windows, the driver is little more than a dark silhouette.

"I can't be certain this *is* the shooter," says Ingrid. "It's possible he fled north instead, away from the village, where there aren't any CCTVs. But considering the time frame, the type of vehicle, and the fact that a similar vehicle left that woman's body in your driveway a few nights ago, I'm going to go with a ninety-five, maybe ninety-six percent probability that this is our man."

"And *that's* why I married this woman," says Lloyd, who's returned to the stove to get seconds of the goulash.

"I'm not finished yet," says Ingrid. She clicks through images on her laptop until she arrives at an enhanced still shot. It shows the SUV's rear bumper, with a Massachusetts license plate clearly in view.

"It's an Alamo rental car," says Ingrid. "It was picked up four days ago at Logan Airport, by a man with a Florida driver's license, name of Frank Sardini." She glances at me.

"I don't know the name," I say.

"I didn't think so." She pulls up a photo of Frank Sardini's driver's license. "According to the identifying data on his license, he's a forty-two-year-old white male, five foot ten, brown hair, brown eyes. I'll take a wild guess that you don't recognize his face," says Ingrid.

"I've never seen that man before."

"Which is not good," says Declan. "We're dealing with a complete stranger who rolls into town just to kill Maggie?"

"It gets worse," says Ingrid. "*This* Frank Sardini's driver's license and credit card are based on a stolen identity. The real Frank Sardini died forty-one years ago, when he was four months old."

The kitchen goes silent. I can hear the blood hissing in my ears, can feel the ominous drumming of my own heart.

"So he's a dead double," Declan says softly.

Ingrid nods. "I'm afraid so."

This is worse than I thought. This level of craftsmanship tells me I am up against people more formidable than I imagined. I look around the table at my colleagues, and I see from their expressions that they are just as disturbed.

"We need more from you, Maggie," says Ben. "Who the hell wants you dead?"

I shake my head. "I don't know."

"You must know something. You're just not telling us."

What he says is true. There are things I've never told anyone, because what happened is too painful to think about. So painful that for years, I've been running from it.

"Then let's start with what we do know. This all seems to involve Diana Ward, who's gone missing," says Declan. He reaches for the salt-shaker and moves it to the center of the table. "Faction Number One wants to find her. They send the mysterious Bianca to ask you to help locate Diana."

Ben moves the pepper shaker to the center of the table, next to the saltshaker. "And here we have Faction Number Two."

"Yes," says Declan. "These people send Mr. Frank Sardini, or who-ever he really is, to dispose of Bianca. Double tap." He tips over the saltshaker, knocking it onto its side. "Then Mr. Sardini tries to kill *you*. Why?"

As they all watch me, I stare at the fallen saltshaker and think of Bianca's body sprawled in my driveway. "They want both of us dead. Diana *and* me."

"Do you know where she is?" says Declan.

"No. I left the Agency sixteen years ago, and Diana left it a few months later. In all that time, I've had no contact with her."

"So why is this coming up now?" asks Ben.

I look at him. "This has to be blowback, for what happened in Malta. For Operation Cyrano."

They look at each other. Although the details of the operation remain classified, along with the names of the operatives, my friends would have heard about Cyrano, the Russian sleeper who for years was rumored to have penetrated elite circles of British society.

"*You* were part of that takedown?" says Ingrid.

"Yes. So was Diana." I pause. "The operation resulted in . . . unexpected consequences." Consequences so painful that I have never spoken about the mission to anyone. I cannot bear to reopen that wound, but now I have no choice. I look at the saltshaker, which is meant to represent Bianca's body, but it might as well represent mine. Today they tried to kill me, and they'll almost certainly try again. "It's the reason I left the Agency. Because of what happened on Malta."

"Blowback, after all these years?" Ingrid says, frowning. "It took resources to send a dead double and track you down here. They'd have to want you dead pretty badly."

"I assume it's Cyrano's people. Revenge for our capturing him. The Russians don't forget, and they never forgive."

"You *assume*? You mean there could be others?"

"Who want me dead?" I give a weary laugh. "I don't doubt it." I look around the table. "And I'm probably not the only one here who can say that."

No one responds. No one wants to.

An alarm beeps on Declan's phone. We all snap to attention. "Motion sensor," he says, and looks down at his screen.

The doorbell rings. If it's an assassin, he's decided to walk in the front door.

"Are you expecting anyone?" asks Lloyd.

"No." Declan pulls up the camera feed on his phone and sighs. "Relax. It's Jo Thibodeau, our tenacious bird dog. She is rapidly becoming a major annoyance." He stands up, pulls off the apron, and tosses it over his chair. "I'll fend her off."

We listen from the kitchen as Declan answers the front door. He never even gets the chance to speak.

"I'm here to see Maggie Bird," Thibodeau demands.

"Why do you think she's here?" Declan asks.

"Because she's not at Ben Diamond's place, and I see your Volvo is parked on the street, not in your garage. Is that where you hid her pickup?"

"It's not a good time. We're having dinner."

"This won't take long."

Thibodeau strides into the kitchen, clearly unstoppable, and she frowns at the four of us sitting around Declan's table. "Seriously?" she says to me. "After what happened to you today, you're here at a dinner party?"

"These are my friends," I say.

Her attention goes straight to the topo map on the table. To the roads that Lloyd has highlighted in yellow. "What is this?"

"We were looking at access routes," says Lloyd. "On and off Maggie's property. We're just trying to help with the investigation."

Thibodeau sighs. "Okay, folks, I'd like you all to leave. I want to speak with Ms. Bird alone."

"No," I say. "I want them here. As I said, these are my friends, and they might be able to assist you."

"I highly doubt that."

"You don't think we're capable?" says Ingrid, and she fixes Thibodeau with the steely glare that Ingrid manages so well. It's no surprise she was legendary as an interrogator.

Thibodeau flushes. "I didn't say that, ma'am."

Declan pulls out a chair with a gentleman's panache. "Please, Chief Thibodeau, why don't you have a seat and join us? We have no secrets among us."

Thibodeau glowers at the chair, as if his old-fashioned gesture is insulting, but finally she sits down and pulls out her little notebook.

It's already clear to me that she is a persistent woman, and the more we try to push her away, the harder she'll push back. Ben has looked into her background, and we know she's a Purity native, that she's lived all her life in the state of Maine, and that she's been with the local police department for more than a decade. She knows this town and its inhabitants better than we ever will, and now she's trying to fit us into that picture. She may not be trained in the fine art of intelligence gathering, but she's got enough horse sense to know she's outmaneuvered, and she probably wonders how five gray-haired retirees are able to do it.

"So what do you want to ask me?" I say.

Thibodeau flips open her notebook. "We believe we have the shooter's name. Frank Sardini, age forty-two, from Orlando, Florida. Do you know this man, Ms. Bird?"

"No," I say.

She glances up at me, eyebrow raised. "You didn't even stop to think about it."

"I don't need to."

"Or maybe you'd rather not admit you *do* know him?"

"Now why on earth would that be?"

"I don't know! You tell me why a man from Orlando would come all the way up here to shoot a chicken farmer?"

"You should probably ask Frank Sardini."

"We're still trying to locate him. We know that he rented a black Toyota SUV from Alamo in Boston. The car was returned this afternoon at one p.m. The license plate was caught on the feedstore's CCTV, right about the time your assailant would've been fleeing the scene." She looks at Ingrid, an accusatory glare if ever I've seen one. "And *you* shouldn't have been nosing around there, getting Vern's video feed."

"I was there on behalf of the library board."

"Yeah." Jo snorted. "Sure."

I'm actually quite impressed because she's learned these details far more quickly than I expected a small-town cop would be able to. We've underestimated her, which perhaps says more about us than about her. What other surprises will she spring on us?

"His rental SUV was outfitted with Goodyear TrailRunner tires," says Thibodeau. "That's the same brand that was on the vehicle that dumped the body in your driveway." She turns to me. "Interesting coincidence, don't you think, Ms. Bird?"

"Have you tracked down this Mr. Sardini?" Ben asks.

"I'm working on it. I contacted the Orlando police, and so far, I've learned he has no outstanding warrants, no arrests, no convictions. But when I called his listed place of employment, an insurance agency, no one there had ever heard of the man."

"That's because he's dead," says Ingrid.

Thibodeau turns to her. "What?"

"The real Frank Sardini died at age four months, from SIDS. The man who rented that SUV in Boston has simply stolen the name, and I highly doubt you'll be able to find him, much less arrest him."

"How on earth do *you* know all this?"

Ingrid wakes up her laptop and swings the screen around to face Thibodeau. "I did a little digging of my own. Searched birth records, death records, and made a few phone calls to Orlando."

Thibodeau stares at the image of the fake Frank Sardini's Florida driver's license on the laptop screen. She's no doubt feeling humiliatingly upstaged right now, but it's not a fair contest. Ingrid spent a lifetime mastering the art of intelligence gathering. She also has inside sources that a cop in a small Maine town can only dream of.

"Whoever the man really is," says Ben, "he's now long gone from the area."

Thibodeau looks around the table at us. At elegant Ingrid with her silk scarf. At cheerily rotund Lloyd. At Ben, with his thuggishly shaved head, and Declan, with his black-Irish good looks. Then she looks at me, the woman who claims to be just a chicken farmer. The woman who had a dead body dumped in her driveway, and an assassin shooting at her from the woods.

"Who the hell *are* you people?" Thibodeau blurts out.

"Oh, we're just retirees," says Lloyd.

"Retired from *what*?" Thibodeau looks at Ingrid.

"I was an executive secretary, for a multinational firm," says Ingrid.

"And you?" Thibodeau turns to Ben.

"International hospitality supplies. I sold furniture and restaurant equipment to some of the finest hotels around the world."

"I was a history professor," says Declan.

"And I worked for a customs brokerage, as I told you the other night," I say. How easily we all fall back on our nonofficial cover identities. We've been telling lies for so long that it is now second nature for us.

At last Thibodeau looks at Lloyd, the only one of us who did not work under nonofficial cover. The only one who is allowed to reveal which agency actually employed him.

"Oh, I was just an analyst," Lloyd says cheerfully.

"You mean, like a psychoanalyst?" says Thibodeau.

Lloyd laughs. "Lord, no. I sat at a desk all day. Collected information and crunched data for the government. Not very exciting, actually."

"We may be retirees," says Ingrid, "but we're also rabid mystery fans. I mean, who doesn't love a good detective novel? That's what inspired this little crime-solving club of ours. If you read enough murder mysteries, you get quite knowledgeable about police work."

"No kidding," Thibodeau mutters, looking at the topo map. "And what do you call this, uh, club of yours?"

There's a silence. I think of the night we stood around Ingrid's fireplace, sipping drinks as we discussed the mysterious Bianca.

"The Martini Club," I say.

My friends all nod and smile.

"Please, let's not get distracted," says Declan. "We need to keep our focus on this so-called Frank Sardini, whoever he really is."

Thibodeau sighs. "Jesus. This has just gotten way more complicated."

"And we're here to help," says Ingrid. "We may be retired, but we've picked up a few detecting skills over the years."

"By reading mystery novels? Right." Thibodeau looks at me. "*You* must have some answers. Someone just tried to kill you. Do you have any idea who wants you dead?"

I look at the fallen saltshaker, representing Bianca's corpse. She's just one more in a series of deaths, a series that is not yet complete. "I don't know," I answer. *But I may know why.*

*

Declan and I are down to the last two inches of his sixteen-year-old single-grain scotch. I've had more than enough booze for the night, but he says, "We might as well finish this off," and he empties the rest of it into our glasses. Everyone else has gone home. It's just the two of us, sitting in front of his fireplace. The flames have died down and are now barely flickering, but we'll soon be heading upstairs to bed, so he does not feed it any more wood. Instead, we let the fire slowly fade to embers. An inevitable death.

"You remember the first whisky I ever poured for you?" he asks.

"I thought you were trying to poison me."

"It wasn't *that* bad a bottle. Only an eight-year-old cask, but it was a single-malt, if I recall."

"It was my first taste of the stuff. I had an uninitiated palate, so I didn't appreciate it." I sip what he's just poured for me and I sigh, savoring the finish of butterscotch on my tongue. "God, I was such a baby then. In so many ways."

"'Fresh faced' is how Ben described you. Unlike the rest of us, with all these extra miles on our tires."

Yes, Declan does have more miles on his tires than I do. Eight years more, to be precise. When we met as new recruits, he was already thirty, with a PhD in European history under his belt. It was a valuable credential that proved useful when he was operating under nonofficial cover in academics. The passage of time has shot silver through his once-black hair, and webs of laugh lines are etched around his eyes, but the years have only deepened his dark good looks. This son of a distinguished diplomat now looks very much like a diplomat himself.

"Do you ever wonder what you might have done with your life instead?" he asks.

"You mean, instead of the Agency?"

"Yes."

"Maybe I'd work as a *real* import analyst. I actually liked my cover." I look at him. "And I'm guessing you really would have been a history professor."

"Tweed jackets, ivy-covered colleges. A sabbatical every seven years. What's not to like?"

"Plus all those nubile coeds crowding around you."

"That I do not consider a benefit. Robbing cradles has never held any attraction for me." He takes a thoughtful sip of whisky. "If we had taken alternate paths, you and I would never have met. We wouldn't be sitting together right now. It's a sad thing to think about."

"Yet here we are." I smile at him. "I'm grateful for that, at least."

We fall silent, both of us staring at the fireplace. An ash-covered log collapses, sending up a shower of embers.

"What did happen in Malta?" he asks.

"You already know the basics. Operation Cyrano."

"I know that's when he was captured. And I'd heard chatter over the years, that a Russian sleeper may have penetrated Downing Street."

"The first hints came through SIGINT. An intercepted communication from a Russian handler to an operative in the field. The Brits and the Agency had no idea who he was. A member of Parliament?

An official with the Conservative Party? Or maybe he worked in the UK's National Crime Agency, someone high enough to squelch any investigation into Russian money laundering. We weren't even sure if Cyrano was real or just a ghost. A figment of the intelligence community's paranoia."

"Shouldn't the Brits have handled it? Why were we the tip of the spear?"

"Because every move by British intelligence was repeatedly compromised, and more than a few of their assets were assassinated. For eight years, the man was a mystery."

"Until Operation Cyrano?"

I nod. "Diana Ward ran that operation. Rightly or wrongly, she got the credit for taking him down."

"And what was your role?"

"She brought me into the op. I was just a cog in the machine."

"That can't be all you were, Maggie."

"I wasn't present during the actual takedown. Or at the interrogation, after they flew him to Morocco. That was all Diana's work."

"So what was your part in it?"

I shrug. "I just pointed the way. And she took it from there."

"And the last time you heard from her?"

"Not since Malta. She never reached out to me, and I certainly never reached out to her. There was no reason to. The day after they captured Cyrano, I resigned."

"Do you want to tell me why?"

"No, I don't." My answer comes out more brusquely than I intended, and for a moment it silences him. I keep my gaze on the embers in the fireplace, but I can feel him studying me. He is one of my oldest friends, perhaps my dearest friend, but there is a wall between us, built slowly over the years, from a lifetime's accumulation of secrets. And scars.

"Cyrano was captured sixteen years ago," he says. "Do you really think this is payback, after all this time?"

"We dealt the Russians a major blow in the West. We crippled the London laundromat, exposed UK corruption at the highest levels of government. It makes sense that Moscow would retaliate."

"But why wait till now to come after you?"

"Maybe because they only just learned our names. Bianca told me there was a recent security breach at the Agency, and someone accessed the Cyrano file. My name was in that file. It would have taken them time to track me down, because I changed my last name, lived out of a suitcase for years. I was in Costa Rica, Mexico. Bounced around Asia. Then I got your email, that you'd moved to Maine. You made it sound like you'd found nirvana."

"I might have oversold it."

"No. No, you didn't. This village really *does* feel like home. Or it did, until all this happened. I'm just sorry I brought attention to our safe little corner of the world. I feel like I've exposed you all."

"We'll survive it. We always do."

"Not always. This week shattered any superhero delusions I might've had about myself." I gulp down the rest of the whisky and stand up. "It's late. I'll see you in the morning. And thank you, Declan. Not just for tonight, but for . . . everything."

"You'd do the same for me."

I smile at him. *Yes. Yes, I would.* I walk out of the living room and am already at the foot of the stairs when I hear him call out:

"You know you can stay here, Maggie. As long as you need to."

"Be careful what you're offering."

"This is a big house, maybe too big for me. I could use your company." A pause. "I *like* your company."

And I like yours.

Through the living room doorway, I can see him sitting at his fireplace, staring at the ashes. Not looking at me. We have known each other for nearly four decades, but he's always had the detachment of a chilly intellectual. Even though he's opened his home to me, I still feel the distance between us, built into any relationship between two people for whom mistrust is second nature.

"I'll certainly think about it," I say.

I climb the stairs to my bedroom and close the door. I also lock it, just out of habit, even though I feel safe in this house because only my friends and Jo Thibodeau know I'm here. Declan has a state-of-the-art security system, and, like me, he is armed. Earlier this evening, I saw him remove a box of bullets from his gun safe and load up two magazines. On the surface, he appears calm, but he, too, must be on edge.

My phone buzzes with a new message. It's the reply to the encrypted email I sent early this afternoon.

Willing to meet. Bangkok. Details to come.

I know now where I have to go next. I have to track down the woman I despise, the woman who was there with me in Malta. Diana has the answers. She'll know who's trying to kill us.

But that night, when I close my eyes, once again all I can think about is Danny. I remember the way he looked at me that morning as he packed his bags for the last time. As he bent over to kiss me goodbye. How different our lives would have turned out, if only we'd run away as we planned, if only I'd refused that last assignment and never gone to Malta.

That's where everything fell apart. In Malta.

CHAPTER 24

Malta, sixteen years ago

While Bella Hardwicke inherited the same ginger hair and flawless pink complexion as her mother, unfortunately she did not inherit Camilla's swanlike neck or regal posture. It's impossible not to compare the two as I sit across from them at Camilla's breakfast table, the elegant mother with her ugly duckling of a daughter. On this scorching day, the garden terrace of Camilla's rented villa is a cool retreat, shaded by grapevines. A stone fountain splashes nearby, sending a welcome mist drifting our way, and sparrows chirp in the orange tree. On an island sorely lacking in greenery, where too much of the landscape is dominated by stone and concrete, this former monastery is a leafy sanctuary far from the traffic of Valletta.

"I don't know why I can't just fly you back to London on my jet," says Camilla. "It's as if your father doesn't trust me to bring you home."

"Daddy said he had to come here anyway." Bella idly moves strawberries around on her plate with her fork. I gather she doesn't like strawberries, as not a single one has gone into her mouth. Instead, she's arranged them in a defensive line, as if she's under siege.

"He had another reason to come here?" Camilla says.

"He said he has to meet someone. That's why we're not flying out until tomorrow. This trip isn't really about me. It's about work, again."

Bella sighs and puts down the fork. "I'll probably have to hear another business lecture on the way home. He's always on at me about money."

Camilla's expression softens as she looks at her daughter. Oh yes, she understands only too well what her ex-husband's priorities are. "That's because you understand what he's talking about. You have a better head for numbers than I ever will, darling."

"Well, I don't *want* to talk about money. I'd rather talk about what we're going to do today." Bella looks at me. "I'm so glad you came! I wanted my mum to meet you."

"Bella's been talking incessantly about you, Maggie," Camilla says. Her expression is friendly enough, but I sense she's holding back her full approval. I am, after all, part of her ex-husband's entourage and therefore not necessarily trustworthy.

"Maggie works in fashion," says Bella.

"Used to work," I correct her. "In my old job."

"And now you work for Phillip?" Camilla asks.

"Oh no. I'm just here with my husband, Dr. Gallagher. Mr. Hardwicke invited me to come along and keep Bella company on the flight home."

"'Cause he's not interested in anything I have to say," Bella mutters.

"Well, that's just your father," says Camilla. "He behaves like that with everyone. If I'd known what kind of man he was when I . . ." She pauses, suppressing whatever words were on her tongue. Instead, she looks at the garden, where marble statues surround an aqua-blue swimming pool. The villa she's rented is far more charming than the sterile hotel in Valletta where I'm staying with Hardwicke's party, and it's certainly large enough to house everyone, but after their bitter divorce, the ex-spouses continue to keep a wary distance from each other.

"Did he bring that woman with him?" Camilla asks me.

"You mean Silvia?" I shake my head. "No, she stayed in London."

"Keith and Victor?"

"Yes, they're here."

Camilla grimaces. "Tweedledee and Tweedledum. He never goes anywhere without them. How is it going, by the way? Phillip and that woman?"

"Oh, Mum," Bella groans. "Let's not talk about her. Please."

"You're right." Camilla sighs. "Of course, you're right. I just wonder how long *this* one will last."

"Longer than the last one," says Bella. "At least Silvia doesn't act like a bitch to me."

"Bella."

"Well, it's true. The last one was—"

"We'll just have to move on. I need to remind myself of that too. It's only sensible to move on."

Bella slouches back in her chair, arms crossed. For a moment the three of us sit without speaking as sparrows chirp and a housemaid comes down with a tray to collect the breakfast dishes. I wait for the maid to leave again before I ask Bella:

"What business is your father doing on the island?"

"I didn't ask. I just know he's got a meeting tonight."

"With whom?"

She shrugs. "Someone."

Someone. I glance at Camilla, but she's pouring herself another coffee and doesn't seem to be paying attention.

"But that means we have all day today," says Bella, brightening. "So let's go shopping!"

"I can't, darling," says Camilla. "I agreed to meet your father this afternoon. Why don't you two take a taxi into town?"

Bella jumps up. "I'll get my purse!"

Camilla and I are silent as Bella goes up the garden steps and into the villa. Only after her daughter is out of earshot does Camilla ask: "Does he pay you? To be her friend?"

"Not a penny." I look her in the eye. "I *am* her friend."

"Why?"

"I happen to like Bella."

"And that's the only reason Phillip brought you here? Because you *like* Bella?"

"My husband was coming here anyway, and I've never been to Malta. I was happy to tag along."

This, at least, makes sense to her. More sense than my actually being her daughter's friend. As wealthy as her family is, Bella was born into misfortune, with a father who barely tolerates her and a mother who pities her. No wonder she is such a needy girl.

"She doesn't seem to have many friends," I say.

"She won't find any at that horrid school."

"Then why is she there?"

"Phillip says it 'builds character.' He suffered through boarding school, so she has to suffer through it too."

"That doesn't seem very fatherly."

"He's not raising a daughter; he's trying to turn her into a clone of himself, someone to hand the reins to. He's been grooming her for it since she could add two plus two. Everything is about business for him. As I found out too late."

I watch as she stirs more sugar into her coffee, taps her spoon on the chinaware cup with a musical clink. A sparrow in the orange tree chirps a reply.

"How long were you married, may I ask?" I say.

"Eight years. Which was about seven and a half years too long. When we divorced, I wanted custody of Bella, but Phillip never relinquishes ownership of anything, even when it's something he doesn't really want. I was fortunate just to get him to agree to her visits with me." She leans closer and says, quietly: "If you really are her friend, please look out for her."

"Of course."

"And be careful."

I frown. "Careful of what?"

"The people he associates with. They frighten me. They've always frightened me."

"You mean Keith and Victor?"

"Oh, them!" She waves her hand dismissively. "No, they're nothing. It's the others."

"I don't know who you're talking about."

"The people he does business with. Just keep Bella away from them. If something goes wrong, if some deal blows up in Phillip's face, I don't want her anywhere nearby."

"Can't you tell me more?"

"It's better if I don't. For both of us." She regards me for a moment. "Is it true? He *really* doesn't pay you for this?"

"He offered to, but I wouldn't take his money."

"Then you'd be the first person who's ever turned it down."

"Not everything in the world can be bought."

"Phillip would disagree." She glances up as Bella emerges from the house.

"I'm ready, Maggie!" Bella calls out. "Come on, let's go shopping!"

I rise from the table. "Thank you for the coffee."

"And thank you, for being my daughter's friend." She pauses and adds quietly, "If that's what you really are."

*

"I'm so glad Daddy brought you along," says Bella as we walk the narrow alleys of Valletta. "None of my friends from school wanted to hang out with me here, and Mum, well . . ." She shrugs. "She's just Mum."

"Does she come here every summer?"

"No, last year it was Corsica. She just comes to get out of the cold."

"It's not cold in Argentina."

"It's winter there now."

"It's still not that cold."

"It is if you're my mum. The hotter it is, the happier she is. I hate the heat, but she's like some weird kind of lizard."

Bella stops at a street vendor's cart and takes her time perusing the trinket jewelry. She's forgotten her hat, her face is now alarmingly sunburned, and sweat glistens on her swollen cheeks. She looks like a shiny pink beach ball.

"What do you think?" she asks, holding up a pair of tin filigree earrings.

"I think they were cheaper at that other cart up the street."

"They had the exact same ones?"

"Identical."

"Wow, you notice everything, don't you?"

Yes, I do. I noticed Gavin sitting in my hotel lobby this morning, supposedly reading a newspaper. I noticed Diana in the hotel restaurant, sitting a few tables away from where Hardwicke and Keith were eating breakfast. Diana's team is lodged in the same Valletta hotel as Hardwicke's party, luxury digs for a surveillance op, and all courtesy of Uncle Sam.

"Oh, never mind," says Bella, and she places the earrings back on the cart. "I guess I don't like them anyway." She looks up at the glaring sun. "God, it's hot."

"And you're getting burned. You need to wear a hat."

"That's what Mum keeps telling me."

"Do you want to come to the hotel and cool off? Or should I take you back to your mum's villa for lunch?"

Bella makes a face. "Not Mum's place. I hate what her cook serves, nothing but boring salads and grilled fish. You know what I *really* want right now?"

"What?"

"A hamburger and chips. We could get that at your hotel, right?"

"I thought you were a vegetarian."

"I tried. But you know, it's really hard."

I laugh. "Come on, then. A hamburger it is."

We weave our way through the cobblestoned streets, both of us sweating and fanning ourselves in the heat. For a shopping trip, it's been singularly unsuccessful, and Bella carries only one plastic bag containing a silk scarf. I think of her closet at Manning House, filled with a fortune's worth of unflattering dresses. This is definitely progress. She's learning to be selective.

It's that indolent hour of the afternoon, well after lunch but too early for dinner, and when we reach my hotel, we find the inside dining room deserted. The hostess leads us outside instead, to a table on the seaside terrace. Bella immediately snatches up the menu and is so focused on ordering her precious hamburger, bloody rare, with french fries, that she does not notice who else is on the dining terrace. I spot Keith sitting in a far corner, tucked almost out of sight, which means his employer must be nearby as well. I glance around the terrace, and there he is, sitting at a table with Camilla, just beyond a row of potted palms. Neither of them is smiling, and they face each other across the table like chess opponents engaged in a vicious match. While the potted plants partially hide them from view, the foliage doesn't muffle their voices.

". . . a bloody dangerous business! I don't want her dragged into it," Camilla says.

Bella looks up at her mother's voice and she groans. "Oh God. They're here."

"Just pretend they aren't."

"Easy for you to say. Maybe we should leave."

But I don't want to leave. I want to hear what they're saying. "You've already ordered," I tell her. "Just ignore them and eat your lunch."

Hardwicke is speaking now, his voice quieter. All I can make out is: "Not our agreement."

"She's not happy."

"She needs the stability."

"Of a boarding school? She hates it there."

"Sink or swim. She has to find out how the world works. That's how I learned."

"Life is not a boot camp! I want to take her home with me," says Camilla.

"That wasn't our agreement."

"I never agreed to it. You *demanded* it."

"It's not my problem if your lawyers are incompetent."

I look at the couple glaring at each other and think: *No wonder Silvia stayed home in London.* I can't imagine any situation more volatile than a mistress and an ex-wife circling each other on the same island.

Bella drops her head in her hands, as if suffering from a monumental headache. "God, please bring me my hamburger."

"Just pretend you don't know them. That's what I used to do when I was your age."

"With your parents?"

"My father. Whenever he got drunk, if I saw him staggering around town, I'd just keep walking."

"You never told me about him."

"There's not a lot to say."

"You don't like to talk about yourself, do you?"

"I'm not very interesting."

"You see? You're doing it again. Not talking about yourself."

So she's noticed. I forget sometimes how perceptive teenage girls can be. It's time to change the subject. I look at her parents. "They really don't get along, do they?"

"That's why I'm never getting married."

"Never say never."

"Unless I meet someone like Dr. Gallagher."

I smile. "I'm afraid he's spoken for."

"I want a man who looks at me the way he looks at you."

That comment makes me pause. Sometimes it takes a perceptive teenager to drill straight to the truth. I've hidden behind so many lies;

leave it to Bella to recognize the one true thing in my life: that Danny and I love each other. I wonder what else she sees about me. She's already clued in to the fact I avoid her questions, that I share no secrets of my own. She would surely be wounded if she learned the biggest secret I've kept from her: that our friendship is merely fiction.

The food finally arrives, and Bella wastes no time attacking the french fries. She scoops up the hamburger in both hands and is just lifting it to her mouth when she hears her mother say to Hardwicke:

". . . and she's gained four *kilos*. How did you let that happen?"

Bella pauses, hamburger at her lips.

"She seems healthy enough," says Hardwicke. "What difference does it make, what she weighs?"

"Does *anyone* in your household pay attention to her? Does that woman?"

"Silvia has nothing to do with this," says Hardwicke.

"No, of course not. Why would she care? She's got what *she* wants." Camilla shoves back her chair and rises to her feet. "She's your daughter too. At least *try* to show her some affection. If you can't, then she belongs with me." Camilla walks away from Hardwicke and suddenly sees us, sitting a few tables away.

"Hi, Mum," says Bella, sounding cowed.

Camilla frowns at Bella's meal. "A *hamburger*? Oh, Bella."

"I was hungry."

"Try a salad next time." She casts a hostile look back at Hardwicke. "You'll be leaving with your father in the morning. You should come back now and pack."

"I just started eating."

"They can wrap it up for you. Let's go."

Bella looks at her uneaten hamburger and puts it down with a sigh. "I guess I'm not hungry anymore." Defeated, she stands up and says to me, "Thanks for taking me shopping."

"I'll see you at the airport tomorrow, Bella."

As Camilla and her daughter walk out of the restaurant, Hardwicke remains seated at his table, shoulders rigid. It must infuriate him that even with all his money, all his power, he cannot control the women in his life. He sits facing the sea, little more than a black silhouette backlit against the shimmering horizon. I cannot see his face, so I can't pinpoint the instant when it begins, when the spark is struck somewhere in his brain, setting off the electrical storm across his cerebral cortex.

The first clue I have that something is not right is the glass tumbler tipping off his table and shattering. *Careless* is my first reaction. Then I see him topple sideways off his chair, dragging the tablecloth down with him, scattering china and silverware. The crash draws everyone's attention on the terrace. Now they are all watching, stunned, as Hardwicke lies shaking and twitching on the floor.

Keith bolts from his chair. As he kneels beside Hardwicke, he's already barking into his phone: "Dr. Gallagher, he's having a seizure! Restaurant terrace!"

The two servers stand paralyzed as Hardwicke continues to flail. I spot broken glass lying near his head, and I get up to kick away the shards, but he's already cut himself, and fresh blood smears the floor. I hear chairs scrape back, voices gasp as a crowd gathers to watch this humiliating spectacle.

"Get away, all of you! Leave him some room, for fuck's sake!" Keith shouts.

I shove aside chairs, wad up the fallen tablecloth, and slip it under Hardwicke's head to cushion it. The violence of his seizure horrifies me. How long can these convulsions last? How long before bones break or the heart goes into arrest?

Then I hear Danny's voice, commanding everyone to move aside as he pushes through the crowd. He kneels beside me with his medical kit.

"He's bleeding," I say.

"That can wait." He uncaps a plastic cartridge, exposing the delivery nozzle. "Hold his head still!"

With both hands, I grasp Hardwicke's head. Blood mats his hair and smears my fingertips. I look straight down into his eyes. They are half-open, the irises rolled back, showing only the whites. His legs bang the floor, thump thump thump. *How easy it would be to end his life right here and now,* I think. To slice open his throat, or shove a suffocating pillow against his face. It would be one way to deliver justice, to make the world a better place. Instead here I am, helping my husband keep this monster alive.

Danny swiftly inserts the cartridge nozzle into Hardwicke's nostril and presses the plunger.

"What are you giving him?"

"Midazolam. It's not yet officially approved for this, but it's worked for him before." My unflappable husband, just by his steady voice, has managed to calm me down. "What happened out here? What set off the seizure?"

"Nothing. He was just sitting at that table over there, looking at the sea."

Danny glances at the table. "Sunlight. Reflections on the water."

"Can that set it off?"

"The flickering could." He looks down at Hardwicke, whose seizures are already starting to ease. "Okay. I don't think he'll need a second dose. Let's give him a moment, let him wake up. Now let me take a look at that scalp."

I hear an approaching siren.

Keith says, "Who called an ambulance?"

"I did, sir," one of the servers says.

"He doesn't need one! He doesn't want one!"

"I did not know—"

"It's okay, it's okay," says Danny, and he flashes a reassuring smile at the server. "He's had these seizures before, but of course, you didn't know that. Maggie, can you hand me some gauze?"

I rummage inside Danny's medical kit, looking for the sterile gauze, and a label catches my eye. The box itself is unremarkable, just white cardboard with the contents printed in black, but the name of the medication it contains shouts at me from the depths of Danny's medical bag.

I have looked inside his kit multiple times before, so I know which medications he usually stocks, which instruments travel everywhere with him. This is the first time I've seen heme arginate in his bag.

"Maggie?" Danny says.

I hand him the packet of gauze. Watch as he rips it open and presses a square of gauze to Hardwicke's scalp. White cotton blooms red with blood.

Cyrano is on Malta.

The ambulance crew arrives with a stretcher. As they reach Hardwicke, his eyes are already flickering open, and he looks around in confusion.

"Let's move him up to his suite," says Danny.

"Not to the hospital?" a paramedic asks.

"He doesn't need to go to the hospital. Just get him upstairs to his room."

All the focus is on Hardwicke, so no one is watching me. They don't care that I follow them to the elevator and slip inside with them, or that I'm right behind them as they step out on the fourth floor.

They don't notice when I follow them into Hardwicke's private suite.

I have not been in here before. The room where Danny and I are sleeping is one floor below, and there's been no reason for me to come up to this floor. None of Diana's team has been able to access it, because housekeeping has not been allowed in, and either Keith or Victor is always stationed inside the suite. This is our only chance to take a look.

It is a three-bedroom suite, and two of the rooms—presumably Keith's and Victor's—have their doors closed. In the common area are a sofa and chairs, upholstered in lemon-and-cream silk. There's a lavish bowl of fruit on the table, a well-stocked bar with whiskies and champagne, and a big-screen TV on the wall. French doors lead to a balcony with a view of the ocean.

In the corner is a desk with a laptop computer.

I glance through the open doorway, into Hardwicke's bedroom. Everyone is busy transferring him onto his bed; they're not paying attention to me.

I cross to the laptop and tap on the keyboard to wake it up. A sign-in screen appears. It's password protected, of course, but curled up behind the laptop is a USB multiport adapter. Attached to it is a thumb drive.

I hear the squeak of the stretcher wheels. The paramedics are packing up to leave, and there's no time to think about my next move, no time to consider the consequences. All I see is opportunity.

I yank out the thumb drive, slip it in my pocket, and walk out of the suite.

I use the stairwell. When I walk out onto the third floor, I see a housekeeping cart stationed at the far end of the hallway, but the cleaner is busy inside a guest room. She doesn't see me as I go to Room 302, where Diana has set up operations. I tap on the door.

Diana opens it and stares at me in surprise. I slip past her, into her room.

"What are you doing here? You shouldn't be—"

I hand her the thumb drive. "Copy this. *Now.*"

"What is it?"

"It's from Hardwicke's computer."

At once she crosses to her laptop and slips the drive into a USB port. While Hardwicke's laptop was password protected, the thumb drive may not be. I watch, heart pounding, as the contents begin to transfer. File by file, they move onto Diana's laptop.

"What are all these files?" Diana asks, frowning at the screen.

"I don't know. I just pulled it off his computer. I need to get it back before they realize it's missing."

"Is there any chance they saw you—"

"Cyrano's here. On Malta."

Her head whips around, and she stares at me. "What? How do you know?"

"There's a box of heme arginate vials in Danny's medical bag. He must have brought it from London. I've never seen it before."

The files continue to transfer, all of them labeled with cryptic names. I glance at my watch as the seconds tick by. *Hurry. Hurry.* Why the hell is this taking so long? I need to get back upstairs to Hardwicke's suite and return the drive to his computer. Even if I manage that without being noticed, there'll still be another problem to contend with: How can I erase the message on his laptop saying the device was not properly ejected? With all the chaos following his seizure, maybe they'll ignore it. And don't grand mal seizures leave gaps in the memory? That's what I'm counting on—that Hardwicke will assume the error was his.

Transfer complete. At last.

Diana removes the thumb drive and hands it to me. "Did Danny say who those vials are for?"

"No. And there's no reason for him to be carrying the drug. As far as I know, Hardwicke is his only patient on the island."

"Then we put a tail on him. If Cyrano is on Malta—"

"Danny will lead us straight to him."

CHAPTER 25

I feel as if I'm carrying a ticking bomb in my pocket as I climb the stair-well back up to the fourth floor. If Hardwicke's people find the thumb drive on me, it might as well be a bomb, because it will seal my fate. They'll know I'm the one who took it from his computer.

Which means I will have to be eliminated. But first, they'll do everything they can to drag the truth out of me.

I can feel that bomb ticking more loudly as I walk down the hallway to Hardwicke's suite. The door is closed. Locked. My heart is banging and my hand is unsteady as I raise my fist to knock.

Victor opens it. He has never been particularly friendly, and now he eyes me with what looks like suspicion. Or is that just my guilty imagination?

"I wanted to check how Mr. Hardwicke's doing," I say.

"He's asleep."

"May I talk to my husband? I need to tell him—"

"He's gone."

"But he was just here."

"He and Keith had to go meet someone. They'll be back by dinner."

"Where did they go?"

"Look, Mrs. Gallagher," he snaps. "Just go down to the bar and have a drink, why don't you? I've got work to do." He shuts the door.

They've gone to meet someone.

I sprint down four flights and run into the lobby. I don't see Danny.

I dash outside to the porte cochere, where a black Mercedes has just rolled up to the hotel. No Danny here either.

I pull out my phone and alert Diana. He's on the move! I need eyes on . . .

Then I spot them: Danny and Keith, navigating their way across a street clogged with traffic. Danny is carrying his medical bag.

There's no one else nearby to tail them. It has to be me.

The thumb drive is still in my pocket, but I don't have time to worry about how or when I can get it back to Hardwicke's suite; my sole focus is the two men who are now heading down the street. Danny doesn't seem to realize he's being followed, as he never stops to glance behind him. It's Keith who pauses on the corner to survey his surroundings. This is a dangerous game I've been forced into. If he spots me, he'll know I'm following them.

I drop back and give them more of a lead as they continue down the seaside promenade. There's so little cover here, no doorways to huddle in, no nearby shops to duck into. Distance is my only friend, and I hang well behind, my quarry still in sight, but only barely.

They are heading to the marina.

A forest of sailboat masts sway on the water, rocking with the swells left by a motorboat passing through the harbor. As Danny and Keith start down a dock, I'm forced to stop. There's absolutely no cover on that dock, and if I follow them, I will be too easy to spot. In frustration, I watch the men keep walking, toward a waiting skiff. They climb in.

Only as they motor away do I dash onto the dock, my gaze glued to the skiff. It does not have far to motor, but heads straight toward the fleet of megayachts moored in the harbor. It's a whole navy of vessels, devoted solely to the pleasures of the wealthy.

"Is that them?" a voice says.

I turn to see Gavin standing beside me. My attention has been so fixed on Danny and Keith that I did not notice my colleague had swooped in to assist me.

"There," I say, pointing to the yacht where their skiff has just tied up.

Gavin lifts a pair of binoculars to his eyes. "They're going aboard now."

"What's the name of the boat?"

"Take a look." He hands me the binoculars.

I look at the yacht's stern, and through the lenses, the name suddenly comes into sharp focus. *Ravenous.*

"I think we've found Cyrano," says Gavin.

*

I've done what I came to Malta to do. There's nothing to stop me from packing my bags, stepping on a plane, and flying away from it all. That's what I *should* be doing, because my part in Operation Cyrano is over. In two hours, Diana's team will swarm aboard *Ravenous*, a yacht owned by billionaire businessman Sir Alan Holloway, whose minor dealings with Hardwicke have not previously stirred any suspicions. Only now is the Agency focusing on Holloway's murky beginnings and mysteriously rapid climb to the stratosphere of British society. The instant Holloway is whisked onto a rendition flight, bound to a detention site in Morocco for interrogation, the Russians will know their sleeper has been exposed. They will assume the leak came from someone in Hardwicke's circle.

It will not take long for Hardwicke to realize that I am the one who betrayed him.

I should be on a plane now, heading someplace where Hardwicke and the Russians can't find me. My safest course of action is to disappear, but that would mean leaving Danny behind to deal with the repercussions, and that I can't do.

So instead, I wait.

It's almost dark outside when I finally hear his key card unlock the door. He walks into our room and sets his medical bag on the dresser. Just by his silence, I know something is wrong. Something has changed.

"Where have you been?" I ask.

"I had to see a patient."

"Is Hardwicke all right now?"

"Not Hardwicke. Someone else."

"You have another patient on the island?"

"She's living aboard a yacht here, and she needed medical attention. Mr. Hardwicke asked me to make a house call."

"On a yacht? What was it like?"

"Does it really matter?"

"I'm just curious. I've never been on a—"

"Do you have it, Maggie?" he asks quietly.

"Have what?"

"The thumb drive."

For a few heartbeats, I don't know how to answer him. "What are you talking about?" I finally say.

"There's one missing from Hardwicke's computer. It contains highly confidential financial information. Keith and Victor are tearing the suite apart right now, looking for it."

"Why are you asking me?"

"Because you were there, in the room. Because I saw you at his computer."

"How could you—"

"There's a mirror in his bedroom. While we were moving him from the stretcher, I happened to glance up at the mirror, and I saw you in the other room. I saw you at his computer, but I didn't think anything of it at the time. Then I heard they were searching for the drive, and I realized. I realized it might have been you." He sighs, a sound of profound exhaustion. "If you have it, I need to get it back to them, before they start asking questions. Before they come looking for you."

My legs wobble out from under me, and I sink into a chair. "Did you tell them you saw me?" I ask softly.

"I haven't said a word to them. Please, let me take care of this. Before it's too late."

I look into my husband's eyes. I believe that he loves me, that he married me because he wanted to have a life with me. But if I'm wrong, and his true loyalties lie with Phillip Hardwicke, then what I'm about to do could make me a dead woman.

I reach into my pocket for the thumb drive and place it in his hand.

"Thank you," he says, and he turns to leave.

"What are you going to do?"

"I don't know. Slip it in his pocket, or maybe kick it under his bed. His seizures always leave him confused for a while, so maybe they'll believe it's just postictal amnesia. They'll think he removed it himself and forgot he did it."

"Then you won't say anything about me?"

"No." He pauses at the door. "But when I come back, we're going to talk. And you're going to tell me everything."

After he walks out, I don't move from the chair. Now is the time to run, before he returns, before he tells Hardwicke that I am the one who betrayed him, but I cannot seem to stir. I am fixed to my chair, as immobile as a prisoner strapped in for execution. I don't care if someone does put a bullet in my head, because it would mean Danny has betrayed me, and that would feel like a death all its own.

Outside, night falls, but I don't turn on the light. I hear laughter and music from the restaurant below, and I wonder if Danny is ever coming back. I worry that he, too, is in danger because he's married to me. By now, Diana's team have raided *Ravenous* and Sir Alan Holloway is in custody, along with the female companion whose lifelong need for an uncommon drug has led us to him.

Get out. Pack your bags, and get out of Malta now! is what every instinct is shouting at me, yet I am still sitting in my chair when the

253

door opens and Danny walks into the unlit room. He closes the door and stands in the darkness.

"Maggie?" he calls out.

"I'm here," I say.

He does not turn on the light. Perhaps he cannot bear to look at me. "It's taken care of," he says. "I managed to slip it in his pocket. They'll assume he just forgot it was there."

"So it's fine, now. It's all over?"

"As far as that's concerned." He is just a silhouette in the shadows, standing halfway across the room from me, as if he's afraid to come closer. Afraid I'll spring up at him with claws bared. "I took a long walk," he said. "I needed to brace myself, for whatever it is you're going to tell me."

"Are you ready to hear it?"

"Not really. Because I assume it's not going to be good."

"Sit down," I say. "Please, darling."

"It's that bad, is it?"

"I'm afraid it is."

With a sigh, he sits down on the bed. "As long as it's the truth."

*

In darkness, I tell him everything. I can't bear for him to see my face as I reveal all the lies I've told him, lies about who I really am, and who I work for. With every new secret I reveal, I feel myself shedding, little by little, the weight of the deception that's burdened me for so long. I tell him why we needed intel on Phillip Hardwicke and all the reasons why he is dangerous. I tell him about Stephen Moss, whom I found strangled in Hardwicke's stable. I tell him about the other unfortunate people who have worked for Hardwicke, and how he dealt with their disloyalty: with bullets, or a shove out a window, or a living cremation.

I tell him about Cyrano, whose yacht Danny visited just this afternoon.

"These are monsters, Danny. They foment hatreds and arm insurgencies. They profit off the blood of innocent men, women, and children around the world by selling illegal cluster bombs, white phosphorus, nerve gas—whatever the market demands, to whoever has the cash. You're a doctor because you believe in saving lives, and so do I. That's why I do this job, because I believe I'm helping to keep the world safe. I also believe that sometimes, the ends justify the means. That's why I needed to get close to Phillip Hardwicke. It's why I had to forge a bond with Bella, and insinuate my way into the family. It's why I had to steal that thumb drive. We needed to know where his money comes from, and where it's going, because it helps us identify and take down the other monsters in this war machine. I did it for a good cause."

"And that meant using me."

"I had to get into Galen's patient files."

"Is that why you married me? To get to those files?"

"I married you because I love you."

"How do I know if that's the truth?"

"You don't. All I can do is repeat it, every day, for the rest of our lives. I love you."

"The rest of our lives." He says the words as if reciting a foreign language. "Do you really think that's how it will be, you and me together, till death do us part?"

"It's what I want, Danny. That's why I'm sharing all this with you. These are details I'm not supposed to reveal to anyone, but I'm telling you because I love you. I'm choosing to trust you. Please, if you can just find it in your heart to trust *me*."

He takes a deep breath. "I don't know."

We sit in the darkness, not speaking for a moment. After all that's happened between us, all the lies, "I don't know" is the best I can hope for. Uncertainty means there's a chance he'll forgive me, a chance our marriage will survive.

But first it has to make it through this night.

Although we share the same bed that night, we do not touch. We lie side by side, neither of us able to sleep, as the hours drag by. As the sky lightens outside.

At dawn, he climbs out of bed and gets dressed. When I hear him zip up his suitcase, I sit up.

"I should finish packing too," I say.

"No." He sits down on the bed beside me. "You need to stay here, Maggie. I'm going back to London alone."

"What? Why?"

"It's safer if you stay away from Hardwicke. I don't want you anywhere near him."

"What will you tell him? What will you tell Bella?"

"That you wanted to explore the island on your own for a few days."

"What about you?"

"I have to fly back with him. He expects me to, and I can't back out now."

"No, Danny! Let's fly somewhere else, you and me. We can jump on a plane, go someplace he can't find us."

"I have to do this, Maggie."

"Just because he *expects* you to?"

"Because I need time away. From you."

I stare at him. In the morning sunlight, I see with stark clarity all the ways his face has changed since we met in Bangkok years ago. I see more gray hairs, more weariness in his eyes. Even now, as I feel him slipping away, I love him more than I ever thought I could love anyone.

"How long?" I ask softly.

"I don't know. I need time to think. Time to decide how we go forward."

He used the word *we*. It means something, doesn't it, that he chose the plural?

He leans forward and gently kisses me on the forehead. I don't believe this is a goodbye kiss. I refuse to believe it. "I'll call you. I promise," he says. "Maybe not today, but I will call you when I'm ready."

As he walks out of the room, I stay huddled in bed, even though what I really want to do is pack my bag and follow him to the airport, where Hardwicke's jet is waiting for us. What could Danny say if I simply boarded that jet and flew back to London with them?

Or I could do what he asked me to do. I could give him the time and space he needs to decide, and trust that our love will survive this.

I touch my forehead, where he kissed me, savoring the memory of his lips against my skin. He has kissed me so many times before, but this is the memory that lingers. The memory I will have to hold on to, because it's the last kiss he ever gives me.

Three hours later, Phillip Hardwicke's jet explodes over the sea.

CHAPTER 26
JO

Now

The Betty Jones Realty office was located in the same tidy white cottage where it had always been, one of the few businesses on Main Street that had hung on since Jo's childhood. She remembered walking up these same porch steps, remembered the same bell tinkling on the door when it opened, details that never changed. Over the years, Jo and her father had used Betty Jones's services to sell her great-grandfather's house and her great-aunt's farm, to purchase Jo's two-bedroom bungalow and her father's camp on Hobbs Pond. If property changed hands anywhere in the village of Purity during the last forty-five years, the terms had probably been negotiated by Betty Jones, who refused to retire and would probably die with an MLS book clutched in her fist.

At the tinkle of the doorbell, Betty looked up from her desk. Even at seventy-four years old, she still dyed her hair jet black, still wore a blazer and collared white blouse, and still had a saleswoman's eager glint in her eye. "Why hello, Jo!" she said. "Weather warming up out there yet?"

"Not yet."

"People say it'll be an early spring."

"People say a lot of things."

"How's your father's kitchen renovation coming along?"

"You heard about that?"

"Over at the hardware store. Pete says your dad bought one of those newfangled induction stoves. You know, a kitchen remodel usually pays for itself when it comes time to sell, but not everyone's ready to give up on propane. Owen should've considered that."

"Dad's not planning to sell anytime soon, but if he does, I'm sure you'll be ready with the paperwork. Say, Betty, I was wondering about—"

"And your brother? Is Finn still working up in the north country?"

Jo forced herself to slow down and take a breath. *Small talk before big talk* was what her father always told her, trying to rein in Jo's penchant for drilling straight down to business. She had never been one to linger on the street, chatting with neighbors, and she knew this was often misconstrued as unfriendliness when really, compared to everyone else, she just didn't have much to say. On the subject of her brother, Finn, though, she did have news to share.

"It was a tough week for him. The ice is way thinner this year, and a kid on a snowmobile broke through on one of the ponds. Warden Service had to do a search and recovery, so Finn went down to retrieve the body."

Betty shook her head. "Terrible business."

"It's what he's trained to do."

"Well, you tell him Betty says hello. And when he gets ready to buy a house, I have some good prospects for him."

A pause. *That's enough obligatory small talk,* thought Jo. "Betty, I wondered if you could help me with something."

"Oh, are *you* looking for someplace new? That bungalow of yours getting too small?"

"No, I just want to know about some new folks in town. You probably sold them their houses."

"I probably did. Who?"

"Maggie Bird, for one."

"Oh yes. She bought Lillian's old place, Blackberry Farm. That was a real smooth sale."

"What about Declan Rose? Ben Diamond? Ingrid and Lloyd Slocum too."

Betty smiled. "Oh, I was the broker for all of them."

"What can you tell me about them?"

"Well, I sold the house on Maple Street to Mr. and Mrs. Diamond maybe ten years ago. Poor thing, she died a year later. A stroke, I think. Then I sold the house on Chestnut Street to the Slocums. They're friends of Ben Diamond's, and when they came up here to visit him, they liked the town so much they decided to move here too. Then their friend Mr. Rose came here and bought that old sea captain's house, down on the water. It was in rough shape, needed a lot of renovations, but it had all the original woodwork. I hear he's fixed it up real nice."

"So they all knew each other before they moved here?"

"That's what I gathered. Old friends from Virginia."

"May I see their sales contracts?"

Betty frowned. "Wait, is this some kind of police business, Jo? What did they do?"

"Nothing. I'd just like a little background. You know, to get familiar with our new residents."

"Well, they're all retirees. And Mr. Diamond, he's got to be at least seventy years old. I can't imagine they'd get into any trouble."

"They're not in trouble. Trust me."

Betty regarded her for a moment, no doubt weighing client confidentiality against her longtime acquaintance with Jo's family. In a small town, you learn which people you can trust and which you can't, and the Thibodeau family, with its multigenerational roots in the county, had never given her reason to doubt them.

"Let me make you copies," said Betty.

*

That evening, Jo took a brick of leftover meat loaf out of her freezer and scrounged up some limp carrots and a potato that was just starting to sprout. The potato was still safe to eat, right? She should look that up online, or ask her dad about it. Her dad was a retired high school biology teacher, and he'd almost certainly know the answer, but tonight he was up in Greenville visiting Finn, and how poisonous could a green potato be, anyway? She peeled and sliced the potato, and as it simmered in water on the stove, she sat down at the kitchen table to read the photocopied files from Betty's office.

The real estate purchase agreements did not have much in the way of personal information. Most of the details were about the purchased properties themselves: location, when built, how much land, what conveyances were included. There was nothing about the buyers' previous employment, but she did learn that all of their prior addresses were in the same geographical area in Virginia: McLean (the Slocums), Falls Church (Ben Diamond), and Reston (Maggie Bird and Declan Rose). This was probably how they knew each other, having lived in the same community. All of them purchased their Maine homes with cash; none of them required mortgages, which, while unusual, was not surprising. Compared to their neighborhoods in Virginia, real estate in rural Maine was cheap, and the sale of a home in McLean could easily generate enough funds to buy a home, cash, in the village of Purity.

So far, she wasn't gleaning much about this peculiar group of retirees. Neither had she learned much about them on social media, as none of them seemed to be on Facebook or Twitter or Instagram—at least, not under their own names. A Google search, however, did turn up a few hits. Declan Rose really had been a history professor, as he'd claimed, with his name appearing on an old faculty list for a college in Eastern Europe. The only place the others showed up online was in a recent article in the local newspaper, where they were listed as donors to the Purity town library. Prior to moving to Maine, they had been invisible.

Jo looked down again, at the home purchase agreements. What did a history professor, a hotel supply salesman, a secretary, a customs broker, and a government analyst have in common?

An analyst. She remembered what Lloyd Slocum had said about his work as an analyst: *I sat at a desk all day. Collected information and crunched data for the government. Not very exciting, actually.*

A government analyst who lived in McLean, Virginia.

Abruptly, Jo shoved back her chair, almost catching her dog's paw. Lucy gave a startled yelp. "I'm an idiot," she said to the dog. She shut off the stove and grabbed her jacket off the hook. "Come on, Lucy. Let's go for a little drive."

*

Lloyd Slocum answered the door wearing an apron and an oven mitt. From the front porch, Jo could smell meat roasting in the oven. Even Lucy, sitting in Jo's parked car, could smell the savory aroma, and she gave a hungry whine.

"Why hello, Chief Thibodeau," said Lloyd. "How can I help you?"

"May I come in?"

"Of course, of course. Sorry, I'm just distracted by my risotto. It takes constant attention, you know." He waved her into the house, then immediately headed into the kitchen. She followed him and watched as he went straight to the stove to stir a pot of simmering rice. Too bad she didn't have a man at home, cooking for her. She thought of her own dinner tonight, that sorry brick of frozen meat loaf and a green, maybe poisonous potato, and she looked enviously at the freshly minced herbs on the cutting board and the baby lettuces in the salad spinner. She knew she should eat more salads, but she inevitably forgot the lettuce that was in her refrigerator until it had turned into slime.

"So where's your gang tonight?" she asked.

"My gang?"

"Mr. Rose, Mr. Diamond. Maggie Bird. What do you call yourselves? The Martini Club?"

"I'm not the hall monitor. Did you try knocking on their doors?"

"None of them are home. It looks to me like they all skipped town. Do you know where they went?"

Lloyd just kept stirring his risotto, unruffled by her questions. "As I said, I'm not the hall monitor."

"Do you know where your wife is, at least?"

"Ingrid's upstairs, poking around on the computer."

"I'm guessing she's good at that sort of thing."

"Poking around? Oh yes."

"And you must be too, Mr. Analyst. For the CIA, I take it?"

Lloyd just kept stirring his pot, as if he hadn't heard her. She'd hate to have to interrogate this man for a crime, because she'd probably get nowhere.

"Well?" Jo said. "It's true, isn't it?"

"Did I deny it?"

"You never admitted it. Is this, like, some top secret thing? Are you allowed to tell the truth?"

"I'm allowed, but I prefer not to. Since you're an officer of the law, yes, I will admit that I was employed as an analyst for the Central Intelligence Agency. That might sound like I was some sort of James Bond, but really, I just sat at a desk all day. Drank a lot of coffee, went to a lot of meetings."

"And your wife, the 'secretary'?"

That made him pause for a beat. "She was a very good secretary."

"What else was she?"

"You'd have to ask Ingrid."

"If she tells me the truth, will she have to kill me?"

Lloyd gave a weary sigh. "I never did think that joke was very funny."

His kitchen timer dinged. Lloyd opened the oven, releasing the heavenly scent of a pork roast. He removed the pan and set it on the stovetop, and Jo ogled the crisp skin, glistening with fat. Jesus, where could she find a husband who cooked?

"Is that all you wanted to ask, Chief Thibodeau?"

"Your friends. The rest of your gang. Were they also CIA?"

"Why do you ask?"

"I think it's relevant to the attack on Maggie Bird."

He was back to stirring the risotto, not looking at her. A few seconds passed as his wooden spoon traced circles in the pot. "I'll discuss it with, um, the *gang*," he finally said.

"Where are they right now?"

"That I'm not at liberty to reveal."

"So you do know."

"Maybe."

"But you won't tell me."

He put down the spoon and turned to face her. He might have been wearing an apron. He might have been splattered with pork fat and old enough to be her father, but staring at her from behind those owlish glasses were the eyes of a man she did not want to cross. "I will tell you what you need to know, when you need to know it, Chief Thibodeau. There's additional information that my *gang* is still acquiring. It will take time and some amount of excavation, but once we have a better picture, we'll consider sharing it with you."

"Consider?"

"As a courtesy. We do like to be helpful," he said. The smile was back on his face, but he'd made it clear she'd get no more out of him.

Outmaneuvered by a bunch of old folks, she thought as she drove home.

Well, maybe not just *any* old folks. And come to think of it, they weren't that old either. She thought of her grandfather, who at age eighty-eight still chopped his own firewood, and her father, now six-ty-seven, who could still clamber up Tumbledown Mountain without stopping to catch his breath. Ingrid and Lloyd Slocum were only in their seventies and still seemed to be at the top of their game. Hidden inside those heads of silver hair must be a treasure trove of secrets that they were not going to share with her.

Not yet, anyway.

CHAPTER 27
MAGGIE

Bangkok, now

I'm being followed.

I can feel the gaze of my pursuers on my back as I thread my way through the Wang Lang market, stopping every so often to examine the merchants' wares. At a stall selling silk scarves, I peruse the kaleidoscope of colors, each scarf wrapped in crinkly cellophane. The woman selling them looks ancient, with two missing front teeth and skin like tanned leather, but her eyes are bright and alert as she watches me survey her selection. I don't actually want to buy a scarf, as I already have a dozen of them tucked away in a closet at home, ready to give away as gifts for the odd birthday I've forgotten, but I buy one here anyway, choosing one in sedate shades of gray. It really is the color I prefer because it is anonymous. I bargain the price down to six hundred baht and walk away with a plastic bag containing my new purchase swinging from my wrist. I'm in no hurry, just another tourist on vacation, and there are plenty of us strolling the market today in our travelers' garb of sandals and cargo shorts. They're taller than I remember, these young tourists. Or have I shrunk over the years as my hair has gone gray and my joints have stiffened? Certainly, I am not nearly as eye catching as these smooth-skinned youngsters. Once I had to don a disguise to disappear; now it takes no effort at all, because I really *am* invisible.

To everyone except the two men who are now following me.

I don't try to shake them as I stroll through the market. It's always better to appear clueless, because once tails know they've been spotted, the game changes. It becomes much harder to play.

I reach the section of the market where the food carts are located, and I slow down, not because it's part of the cat-and-mouse game, but because here is where I met Danny. Even all these years later, the place is very much the same, as are the smells wafting up from the carts. I inhale the scents of star anise and cinnamon, basil and cilantro, and I can see him standing here again, with his tattered backpack and his T-shirt with the badly translated Thai. And his smile; no one smiled at me the way Danny did, and that was my downfall. I stare at the little plastic tables where we sat together, slurping down our noodles, and grief suddenly sweeps over me, a tidal wave so powerful that I reel back on my heels.

The market turns into a blur of swirling colors flecked with gold leaf. The voices fade into a distant roar. I'm no longer paying attention to the people around me, and I don't care if I'm being followed. I don't even care if someone drags me through a doorway and puts a bullet in my head. If I die now, it will be with Danny's face as my last memory.

I should not have come to this market. I should not have summoned the ghosts.

The air is too close, too dense, a poisonous cloud of steam and sweat and spices. I turn away from the food stalls and blindly head down an alley until I am standing in front of a shop window. I see dresses inside, silk confections displayed on headless mannequins. I take a few deep breaths and swallow back tears as I gaze at the window, as if admiring the dresses inside. I see my own reflection, and it's painful to confront my face as it is now. If the world had no mirrors, we could imagine ourselves frozen in time, our faces decades younger than we really are, but this window shatters that illusion. I am sixty years old, and I can see every one of those years in my reflection. I also see the two men who have been following me ever since I walked out of my hotel. One man stands beside an ice cream cart; the other pretends to examine a selection of animal figurines fashioned from twisted rope. Neither is looking in my direction, but I know their focus is really on me, and I am grateful for that attention.

At last Ben meets y gaze in the window, and he gives a shrug. His face is flushed, and his bald head gleams in the heat. At home in Maine, today's high is twenty-two degrees, and none of us—Ben, Declan, or I—are yet acclimated to the heat of Bangkok. When we were younger, we could bounce from time zone to time zone, walk off a plane, hit the bar, and be ready to rumble the next morning. Those days have passed, and I can see the exhaustion in both Ben's and Declan's faces. There's nothing so sad as three old spies trying to prove they still have what it takes.

I shake my head, indicating it's time to go back. The heat and jet lag have defeated us for now, but at least we've learned something from this little jaunt into the market: no one else is tailing me. With Ben and Declan still trailing behind, I lead the way back to our hotel, so we can all take a nap.

*

When darkness falls, I'm finally able to shake off my tropical sluggishness, and I walk outside, into a velvety Bangkok night. I spot my friends at the edge of the hotel terrace, both of them standing by the railing. Ben has his back turned and is gazing toward the river, his bald head gleaming faintly in the shadows, while Declan faces my direction, his pose disarmingly relaxed even as he monitors the terrace. Years of retirement have not dulled their instincts. They have staked out a 360-degree view, so they know I'm coming, but neither one says a word until I'm standing right beside them.

Declan raises his drink in greeting. I hear the clink of ice cubes in his glass and catch the citrusy whiff of a gin and tonic. "Have a nice nap?" he asks.

"Yes. God, I'd forgotten about this bloody heat. Did you two manage to sleep?"

Declan grunts. "We're getting old, Mags. Naps are now a regular part of our days."

"Which means," says Ben, turning to face our circle, "we've got to pace ourselves."

"A steady crawl should do it." Declan takes a sip of his gin and tonic, and the clatter of ice cubes and the sound of the river splashing against the bank is like a time-travel portal. The sounds whoosh me straight back to the nights when assignments brought me to this city and I would stand beside this same river, inhaling air faintly tinged with diesel exhaust from boats puttering along the Chao Phraya. If only that same portal could transport me back into my younger body as well, to the Maggie who doesn't need afternoon naps, whose ankle doesn't ache when she walks too long. Whose hair is still dark and lustrous.

Ben leans back against the railing, and the lights from a passing tourist boat reflect on his scalp with a multicolored glow. "Well, it seems our trawl net's come up empty."

"It's just the first day," says Declan. "We may spot them tomorrow."

"Or this could be a waste of your time," I say. "Maybe I'm no longer a target. Or they've given up trying to track me. I can carry on from here, so you two should just go home. Or take a beach holiday on Phuket. You can relive your misspent youth."

Ben snorts. "It's not the same when the only women who'll look at us are grannies."

"There's nothing wrong with granny action."

"We're not going to leave you on your own," says Declan. "Not until we understand what's going on."

"This isn't your fight, boys. It's mine."

"Which *makes* it ours."

"We're not the Musketeers anymore. Please. Go home."

"Jesus, Maggie!" says Declan. "What does it take to convince you we're here for the long haul? We've always had each other's backs. Even when we were living at opposite ends of the earth, we knew we could count on each other." Declan looks me in the eye. "That doesn't change now."

"I just don't want you to get hurt."

"Then tell us what we're dealing with," says Ben.

We face off in the darkness, three old friends who really ought to trust each other but are seasoned enough to know better.

"I wish I had the answers," I say.

"You've told us about Malta. About Hardwicke. Is there something you've left out?"

"You know everything I know."

"We know Diana Ward has disappeared," says Ben. "We know someone wants you to find her. And someone else *doesn't* want you to find her, so they sent a dead double to stop you."

"That about sums up the situation."

"What does it all mean? Who are these different factions? Why are they looking for Diana, or are they really after something else?"

"I haven't a clue." I turn to the river and sigh. "It's just like the fucking good old days."

*

It's well after midnight when I slip out of the hotel and take a roundabout route to the Sathorn Pier. This time I'm alone, and I feel both vulnerable and liberated to be walking by myself. At this late hour there are only a few stray tourists on the streets, most of them tipsy. The nearly deserted streets make it far easier for me to spot a tail, but I still take a zigzagging route, up one street and down another. I stop in front of a shop window and study the reflection, to assess who is behind me. I may be rusty, but the skills are still there, burned so permanently into my brain that they're now hardwired reflexes.

No one is following me.

I sidle down to the Sathorn Pier, where one can always find a long-tail boat for hire. There are only half a dozen vessels bobbing on the water, some more decrepit than others. Any boatman trawling for passengers at this hour of the night must be hungry indeed, and the drivers all look up hopefully as I approach. I choose the boat with the most desperate-looking driver, a cadaverous man who belongs in a hospice, not ferrying tourists up and down the river. Tonight, he'll earn enough to equal two weeks of fares.

I step onto his boat, and he's startled when I greet him in Thai. It's another one of my rusty skills, but the vocabulary is still there, bobbing in some dark cavern of my memory. I don't want the other drivers to hear me, so I speak softly as I give him directions. He nods and yanks the two-stroke engine to life. It's a dirty little beast that emits an eye-stinging cloud of exhaust, but it's probably served him for half a century, and I'm sure he's familiar with every screw and piston.

We set off up the river, the water stretching before us like a slick black ribbon. We motor past hotels and shopping centers and high-rises, the modern facade of an ancient city whose bloodstream is this river, along with its tributaries and khlongs. We are bound for one particular waterway, on the Thonburi side of the city. My driver directs his boat down a canal and into a gated lock, where we are the only boat, and as we wait for the water level to drop, I scan both banks, noting that the huts on either side are dark. This is the advantage of traveling at night by water. Anyone following me would also have to travel by boat, and on these tiny canals, there is nowhere for a pursuer to hide.

The lock gates open and we pass through.

It is a different world here on the khlongs. As we drift through the shadows, I see the silhouettes of banana and palm trees, part of the lush tangle of jungle that feeds and shelters those who live in the huts lining the banks. Ours is the only engine I hear, its gentle put-put easing us through the gloom. With every bend, the canal becomes narrower, the banks hugging closer and closer. My driver has only a vague idea of our destination, and I murmur which turns to take and when to slow down. It's been so many years since I've navigated these waterways, and the instructions I received in the email hardly help in this shadowy world. Did we take the correct turn? Did we miss the opening?

Then I see it ahead, on the right: the bright-orange glow of a lantern sitting on a pier. I point it out to the driver.

He guides his boat to the lantern-lit pier and ties up. I hand him a thick wad of cash, then clamber off the boat and up the wooden ladder. I cannot see the driver's face, but I know he must be pleased by what I've just paid him. Pleased enough to be discreet. As he motors away, I see him raise his hand in farewell.

After the sound of his engine fades away, I linger on the pier, scanning the darkness and listening to the chirp of insects and the distant hiss of Bangkok traffic. Even here on the khlongs, that sound is inescapable. I peer through the tangle of underbrush and spot another orange lantern. It's a marker, pointing the way.

The path I follow is curtained by vines that cascade from overhanging tree branches. Only when I reach the second lantern does the house come into view, shrouded by trees. It is a handsome wooden structure on stilts, with a traditional Thai steep roof. Lights glow in the window. He is expecting me.

At the bottom of the steps, I once again stop to glance around. There is so much jungle that it's impossible to know if anyone lurks in those shadows, but I have no choice now; I have already come this far. I climb the steps to an elaborately carved door that's massive enough to guard the home of giants, but when it swings open, the Thai woman standing in the doorway is as small as a child. I see streaks of silver in her hair and realize she's not a child at all, but a woman my age, her regal posture unbowed by the years.

"I'm Maggie," I say.

"He is expecting you. Come in."

I step into the house. She bolts the door and silently leads the way across the polished teak floor. I look down at her bare feet and realize I've committed a Westerner's sin of wearing my shoes inside the house, but she doesn't comment as we continue past a pair of carved wooden elephants, past a vase spilling over with *Dendrobium* orchids. She slides open a panel door and gestures to me to step through.

In the next room I abruptly halt, stunned by what I see. The woman withdraws, closing the door to give us privacy, but for a moment I'm too taken aback to say a word. The man sitting in the wheelchair looks nothing like the friend and colleague I remember. This is a skeletal version of the old Gavin, the muscles of his face so wasted that his veins stand out like blue worms twisting on his temples. He sees my expression of dismay and gives a resigned sigh.

"Getting old is not for wimps," he says. His voice has turned thin and reedy with age. Or is it the illness that has robbed it of its power?

"The years have been hard on both of us," I say.

"At least you're still standing. In fact, you look good, Maggie."

I can hardly respond with the truth: *And you look like death warmed over.* He has clearly been ill for some time. In the corner is a motorized hospital bed, and I see a nebulizer and oxygen tanks nearby. In the far corner is a communications center, equipped with a laptop computer and an array of cell phones. Illness may have physically trapped him in that body, but it hasn't cut him off from the rest of the world.

"I didn't know," I say.

"About my unfortunate circumstances?"

"All I knew was that you'd retired to Bangkok."

"It was a good decision, considering my condition. This country has excellent doctors, a level of medical care I could never afford at home. And if I need any special equipment or medications, I can buy them off the black market." He nods toward the door, which the Thai woman had closed to give us privacy. "She takes excellent care of me. Unlike my wife, Donna, who whipped out the divorce papers as soon as I felt the first twitches in my leg. 'Fasciculations' is what the doctors called them. The clinical term for what was happening to me."

"What did happen to you, Gavin?"

"It's ALS. A slowly progressive form of it, lucky me. Stephen Hawking lived with the disease for decades, so maybe I can too. The body may be falling apart, but at least my brain's still at full throttle."

I look around the room and consider the irony of having one's world shrink down to these four walls after you've spent a lifetime wandering foreign cities, yet Gavin seems to have adapted to his new circumstances. Even in the face of terrible realities, humans are resilient.

And drugs always help.

"I was surprised when I got your message," he says. "After what happened in Malta, I didn't expect you to ever reach out to me."

"Neither did I."

"How is retirement?"

"It's been good. It's been . . . sane. In fact, I wish I was home right now, tending to my chickens."

"Lord, how far we've both fallen."

"I don't consider my new life a comedown at all. I like chickens, which is more than I can say about the people I used to work with."

"Including me?"

"Not to single you out, Gavin. One way or another."

"You have every right to feel that way. We weren't a likable bunch, were we? And unlike chickens, we couldn't even produce eggs." He suddenly starts coughing, and I hear the rattle of mucus in his chest.

"Do you need me to call her for help?" I ask.

He shakes his head. It's painful to watch as he hacks and wheezes, but at last the fit subsides and he slumps back in his wheelchair, exhausted. "This is how it will probably end for me, with pneumonia. But not yet." He looks up at me. "I'm so sorry, Maggie, for what happened. For years, I've wanted to say that to you, but I didn't know how to. The closer one gets to the grave, the clearer everything becomes, and I understand why you cut us all off. I'm glad you finally reached out."

"I didn't have a choice. When they came after me in Maine, I had to."

"Who came after you?"

"I don't know. All I can tell you is, a woman named Bianca showed up at my house, asking if I knew where Diana was. I assumed she was from the Agency. I told her I couldn't help her, and I sent her on her way. That night, her body was dumped in my driveway. She'd been tortured and double-tapped."

"Lovely calling card. Who sent it?"

"Probably the same person who tried to pick me off two days later, while I was out feeding my chickens. If my neighbor hadn't swooped in at the right time, I wouldn't be here. This is what makes it even more worrisome: the man they sent to kill me is a dead double, and he had top-quality documents."

"Jesus. Was he one of ours?"

"I don't know. That's why I contacted you."

"Why do you assume I know anything about it?"

"Because shortly before she vanished, Diana was spotted here in Bangkok. I have to assume she was here because of you."

"Just because I happen to live here?"

"Come on, Gavin!" I snap. "You were there with us, on Malta."

"So were others. It took a whole team of us to yank Cyrano from his yacht."

"But you were the only one who was with us from the beginning. You, me, and Diana. The London laundromat went too far up the food chain, and Diana didn't trust the Brits. That's why she said it had to be just the three of us, in one contained box."

"I blame myself for that."

"For what?"

"Standing by while she dragged you into it. When I saw how she operated, I realized she couldn't be trusted. But by then, it was too late. The operation was like a runaway train, and she didn't care who got flattened by it."

For a moment he's silent as he sits with head drooping, breath rattling. Then he pivots his wheelchair around to his laptop and wakes it up with a nudge on the mouse. "Since you're trying to find her, you'll want to see what she looks like these days."

"You have recent photos?"

"Images from a video call last week. I refused to meet her in person."

"Why?"

"You have strong feelings about her. Well, so do I. I left the Agency two months after you did, because Malta poisoned everything. After the plane went down, it was hard for me to stay on."

"Hard for *you*? I lost my husband on that plane."

"And that will always weigh on me, the innocents who died. Your husband. Hardwicke's daughter. When we scooped up Cyrano, we knew the Russians would retaliate. We *should* have moved to protect people, as soon as we learned . . ." He stops. Looks away.

"Learned what?"

He doesn't answer.

"As soon as you learned *what*, Gavin?"

Reluctantly, he meets my gaze. "The night we captured Alan Holloway, just as we were boarding his yacht, he managed to send out one last message to his kurator. Moscow's reply, minutes later, was intercepted by SIGINT."

"What was their answer?"

"The Motherland is grateful, Comrade. The traitor will pay."

"The traitor," I say softly. *The traitor was me.*

"They assumed Hardwicke, or someone in his circle, betrayed Holloway. The bomb on that plane was their revenge. It was also a message to the rest of the world, that any action against Moscow would have swift and brutal consequences."

"And Danny was just collateral damage. Like Bella. Like the pilots." I pause, suddenly processing what Gavin just said about the message from Moscow. "You said SIGINT intercepted the kurator's reply minutes later."

"Yes."

"When did *our* team hear about that message?"

"I learned about it a few days later, at the debriefing. By then, you were already gone, sent back to Washington."

"And Diana? When did she find out?"

Silence.

"Gavin?"

He sighs. "Diana was told about Moscow's response at midnight. Soon after we seized Cyrano."

"Midnight? That gave the Russians *hours* to plant the bomb on Hardwicke's plane. Diana *knew* there'd be a counterattack. Why didn't she warn me? Why didn't she take action?"

"She *should* have warned you. She *should* have found a way to keep you and Dr. Gallagher off that plane, but she didn't want to tip off Hardwicke that anything was amiss. So she let that plane take off. She figured she'd accomplished her mission. She'd captured Cyrano, and for that, she got a nice pat on the back. But when I found out about the SIGINT intercept, I was disgusted. And soon after that, I resigned."

"I never knew. You never told me."

"You were devastated enough, Maggie. This would only have made it more painful for you, knowing it *could* have been different. That we *could* have kept Dr. Gallagher off that plane."

"But Diana didn't care," I say softly. "She *didn't fucking care.*"

"That's why, when she asked me for help last week, I refused. She wasn't happy about that." He taps on his laptop, and an image appears on-screen. "You can see for yourself."

I stare over his shoulder at the photo. This is not the cool and confident blonde I remember. This Diana Ward looks hungry and haunted, her eyes as hollowed out as a death's-head. Her hair is now brown and cropped in a sloppy haircut that she probably inflicted on herself.

"She's terrified. You can see it in her face," he says.

"The Diana Ward we knew wasn't afraid of anything."

"Things have obviously changed."

I stare at the face of the woman whose ambitions sucked me into an operation that led to Danny's death. I'm no saint, and I can't help feeling righteous satisfaction, seeing how haggard she is. I *want* her to suffer, and I am the last person on earth who will come to her rescue.

Yet here I am.

"She asked me for a place to lie low for a while," says Gavin. "She needed cash, passports."

"She's perfectly capable of scrounging that up herself. She knows how to survive."

"Not with these people after her."

I note the sweat gleaming on his upper lip. "You're scared too."

"As you should be. A few weeks ago, HQS contacted me about Operation Cyrano. They asked me what I remembered about Malta, how Cyrano was captured, how the operation was conducted."

"Why now, after all these years?"

"Because it's back on the Agency's radar. The Cyrano file was recently accessed by an unauthorized party, still unidentified. They want to know who did it, and why."

"The Russians, I assume."

"Yes, that's what you *would* assume, that Moscow is digging into how their sleeper was compromised. That security breach made the Agency take another look at how the operation came together, and that made them take another look at the late Phillip Hardwicke. They discovered a surprise. His overseas accounts—at least, the ones we knew about—have been emptied. Hundreds of millions of dollars, drained over a period of five years."

"They didn't know this before?"

"With Cyrano captured and Hardwicke dead, the file was closed. No one was watching the accounts a year later, when the money started disappearing."

"I never heard about this."

"Because the Agency doesn't trust you. You were so deeply embedded with Hardwicke, they're concerned you've been turned. That your loyalties still lie with him."

"But he's dead."

"That's what everyone thought. That Hardwicke was blown to smithereens over the Mediterranean. We monitored the aftermath, watching for other developments. There was publicity, of course. The UK tabloids had the plane crash all over their front pages. Photos of Lady Camilla in black, sobbing at her daughter's funeral. MPs and aristocrats paying their final respects to Hardwicke. Then the noise died down, as it always does, and the Agency moved on to other concerns.

"Until the Cyrano file was recently accessed, by parties unknown. That security breach forced the Agency to take another look at Hardwicke's death. Since his plane went down in deep water, recovery was difficult, and the only two bodies they found belonged to Victor Martel and one of the pilots. But no one could have survived that crash."

"Then who drained Hardwicke's accounts?"

"That's the question, isn't it? Accessing that money required passwords that only Hardwicke would have. Which raises the possibility he never boarded the plane. And he's alive."

The room suddenly sways under my feet. I stagger back a step. Steady myself. "If we were wrong about him—if Hardwicke's alive . . ."

For a moment I can't speak, can't even focus on Gavin. I'm lost in a time warp, sucked back to a moment I have blocked from my memory. The moment I learned the plane went down.

"If *he* wasn't on the plane, then Danny—he could be—" I don't dare say the word, but we both know what it is: *alive*.

Gavin shakes his head, but I already feel hope blooming inside me, a wild and dangerous flower. I can't let it grow; I can't bear to have it uprooted again.

"Maggie," he says quietly, "my advice is to forget we had this conversation and go home. Back to your chickens or whatever it is you're raising on that farm. Don't bother trying to find Diana. Just leave her in the wilderness."

"What about Danny? What if he—"

"It's been sixteen years. If he's still alive, don't you think you'd have heard from him by now?"

"But I have to know the truth!"

"You already *know* the truth, Maggie. You know it in your heart. Don't you?"

I stare at him, remembering that last day in Malta when Danny said goodbye. Remembering the moment I learned that Hardwicke's plane had gone down, and that Danny was dead. I'd *felt* his death, as powerfully as a physical blow to my chest, and it left me so stunned that I have only hazy memories of what happened afterward. I know I was bundled aboard a jet and evacuated, for my own safety. I remember it was nighttime when I arrived in Washington, that I moved through a grief-stricken fog to a waiting car. Gavin is right. I knew in my heart that Danny was gone, because I felt his absence in the world, like a black void that devoured all light, all joy.

If he *had* survived, he would have come looking for me. I *know* that. And he would have found me.

"Move on with your life," Gavin says quietly. "Go home."

"I can't go home. That's where he'll come looking for me. After what we did to Hardwicke, to Bella, he'd want us dead. He'd want *all* of us dead." I stop, glancing up at the sound of a persistent beeping.

"Something's tripped my perimeter alarm," says Gavin.

The door slides open, and the Thai woman steps into the room. She speaks quietly to Gavin, who nods and looks at me. "There's nothing to be concerned about. My delivery man has arrived."

"A delivery? At this time of night?"

"It's not the sort of exchange you want to make in daylight. My man gets very nervous around strangers, so if you don't mind, I'll ask you to slip out of sight. Just until he leaves."

"Pharmaceuticals."

"The black market provides all, but here, the penalties are quite severe if you're caught. You wouldn't deny a dying man his pain relief, would you? This won't take long. I'll pay him and send him on his way."

The woman crosses the room and opens a panel in the wall, revealing storage space behind it. I step into the closet, and the woman closes the panel. Light glows through the grated transom overhead, enough for me to read the labels on the boxes that are stashed near my feet. Medical supplies. The cartons are stamped with the name of a local hospital, from which they were no doubt liberated. For a Westerner with money, the black market does indeed provide all.

Faintly I hear the woman speaking to the delivery man in Thai. Her voice moves closer as she escorts him toward Gavin's room, and she does not sound at all alarmed. The visitor answers her, also in Thai.

Footsteps creak into the room, and I hear Gavin ask, in English: "Where is Somsak?"

"He cannot come tonight. He asks me to bring this to you."

"He should tell me next time when there's a change in plans. I trust the price is the same as what we agreed to?"

"Of course."

"Let me see what you've brought."

I hear the hiss of a cardboard box being sliced open, then a pause.

"I don't understand," says Gavin, an instant before I hear the thud of a suppressor.

The first bullet punches through the wall of my hiding place, barely missing my right arm. The second bullet angles downward through the wall, whizzes past my ankle. Two points of light now shine in like laser beams through the holes.

I hear the woman cry out. She has no time for a full-throated scream, just a panicked squeak. It's the only sound she manages to make before the third and fourth and fifth bullets are fired into her body.

CHAPTER 28

I stand utterly motionless, scarcely daring to breathe, knowing that one creak, one rustle, will betray my presence. Does the assassin know about this storage closet behind the wall? Is he aware there's a third person, still alive, in the house? And here I am, unarmed and unable to defend myself. Not having the Walther on my hip is like missing a limb, but I came to Bangkok without it, because traveling with a weapon in your luggage is the surest way to blow your cover.

Footsteps move closer, stop. Does he see the crack of the panel door? Does he notice that the bullets have punched through, into a hollow space? If I peered through one of the holes, I might be able to see him, but I don't dare move for fear I'll set off a telltale creak. Through the banging of my own heart, I hear the killer circle the room. Hear the clicking of computer keys as he types on Gavin's laptop. He gives a grunt of frustration. He can't break into it without a passcode.

I hear the laptop clap shut and the hiss of the power cord sliding across the floor. His footsteps move away and recede into silence.

For a long time I hear nothing at all, but I still don't dare make a sound. I stand perfectly still, in gloom pierced by those two laser beams of light. A good hunter is patient; is he somewhere in the house, waiting for his prey to emerge? My back aches and my calves cramp from standing motionless so long. I ease toward the bullet hole near my arm and peer through it.

I see blood, an exploding comet of it, splashed on the opposite wall. Lying on the floor beneath it is the body of the Thai woman, curled into a fetal position as if to protect her vital organs. I can't see Gavin.

I shift sideways, trying to catch a wider view of the room, and I bump up against one of the boxes. Something clatters to the floor, a sound that seems deafening. I glance down at a plastic syringe that's landed beside my foot. Such a small thing. Such a fatal thing. I wait for the killer's returning footsteps, for the panel door to slide open, revealing my hiding place.

All I hear is silence.

With shaking hands, I ease open the panel just a crack, revealing a pool of blood at my feet. As the panel opens wider, I see the source of that blood: Gavin, slumped sideways in his wheelchair. His mouth hangs open, as though in perpetual surprise. His laptop is gone, but nothing else in the room seems to be missing.

"I'm sorry, Gavin," I whisper.

I cannot avoid stepping in blood as I cross the room. My shoes track it across the floor, toward the woman's body. Weapons and surveillance cameras are no protection against someone you trust, and that was their mistake. They thought they knew whom they'd allowed into their home. I step over the woman and move into the hallway. The house is silent. Dead. I make my way past the vase of dendrobiums, past the carved elephants, to the front door.

I step outside into the night and inhale the smell of damp earth and rotting vegetation. The lanterns are still lit, guiding me back to the khlong. I creep down the jungle path toward the water, and my shoe bumps up against what I think at first is a tree root.

I glance down and see it's not a root at all, but a leg, stretched across the path. In the shadowy undergrowth, I can just make out the rest of the man's body, lying among a tangle of vines, like some new growth sprouting from the jungle floor. This must be Somsak, the delivery man Gavin was expecting. Yet another soul, lost in a war he had no part in.

I step over the body and keep moving. It's the story of my life. Leave the bodies behind and move on.

At the landing, there are no boats tied up. If the killer came by water, he is now gone. I wonder how long it will take before the bodies here are discovered and the police are called. Will the boatman who brought me here tell them about his late-night passenger, a generous white woman who paid him in cash? I consider the ways the police could track me down, but it will not be easy for them. I hired the boat at a pier far from my hotel. There are so many other white tourists in Bangkok, and except for the generous tip I gave him, nothing about me is particularly memorable. That is now one of my superpowers; I am easy to forget.

I'll need that superpower tonight, because it is a long walk back to my hotel.

*

"You're an idiot, Maggie," says Declan.

He stands in my hotel room, refusing to leave as I strip off my filthy clothes. I'm too old for modesty and I'm exhausted, so I don't give a fuck that he's getting an eyeful as I peel off my shoes and pants and leave them in a mud-streaked pile on the floor. Declan and I have never been lovers and he's never seen me undressed, but what is there to hide when my body is a road map of battle scars and sun damage? I'm unbuttoning my shirt now, and he still doesn't leave, doesn't turn away, just glowers at me as I shrug off the shirt and add it to the pile, which reeks with the mud of the khlong.

"Ben and I spent hours looking for you," he says.

"You should have slept in."

"Why didn't you answer your phone?"

"I turned it off. I didn't want to be tracked."

"We never would have found your body if—"

"I made it back, didn't I?"

Declan looks me up and down, then turns away, as if suddenly aware there's a half-naked woman standing in front of him. A woman who's definitely the worse for wear after hours of winding my way through alleys and splashing through canals. I did not dare hire a taxi or boatman to bring me back to the hotel because they might remember my face and tell the police. How was I to know my friends were repeatedly calling my phone and searching the neighborhood for me?

Now Declan refuses to leave my room, because I might slip away from them again. We came to Bangkok as a team, and already I've gone rogue, cutting him and Ben out of last night's near-catastrophe. I walk into the bathroom, shut the door, and strip off my underwear. I'm desperate to wash away the stench of sweat and stagnant water. I turn on the shower and make the water almost hot enough to scald.

"Why didn't you tell us you were going out?" Declan yells through the closed door.

I ignore him and step into the shower. Close my eyes under the pounding water, letting the grime wash away down the drain.

"After all the years we've known each other, you still don't trust us?" he says.

Maybe I don't. Maybe I don't know how to.

I shut off the water and wrap a towel around me. When I step out of the bathroom, Declan is still there, still spoiling for an argument.

"I had to do it alone," I say.

"What, so you can die alone?"

"It was a condition of Gavin's. He wouldn't meet with me unless I came alone. Also, I didn't want you and Ben in the line of fire, in case things went south."

"But that's why we're here. So we can take some of that fire."

I pull fresh clothes out of my duffel bag. Declan finally turns around to allow me some privacy as I step into panties, pull on a clean shirt.

"This isn't your fight," I say as I button up. "It's gotten too complicated, too dangerous. Go home, Declan."

"And do what?"

"Sit by the fire. Drink whisky. Enjoy your retirement."

He laughs and turns back to face me. I haven't pulled on clean pants yet, but his gaze stays right on my face. "You mean shrink away into a wheelchair? *That* kind of retirement?"

"You're hardly in need of a wheelchair."

"But that day is coming. It comes for all of us. Right now, I'm still on my feet and still have my wits about me, and I don't want to spend my last good years watching from the sidelines as the battle rages. For people like us, who've been in the thick of it, retirement is like being nailed into your coffin. Now I've got a reason to be back in action, and it's been years since I've felt this useful, this alive."

"So you're here to avoid boredom?"

"No! That's not it at all! I'm here because you're in trouble. Because you're finally back in my life, and if anything happens to you . . ."

"What?"

For a moment he just stares at me. "Oh fuck," he mutters and heads toward the door.

"Declan?"

"Get dressed, for God's sake. And stay out of sight, until we get back."

"Where are you going?"

"Ben and I have work to do." He walks out of my hotel room and slams the door shut behind him.

I stare at the closed door, my damp skin chilling in the blast of the room's air conditioner. Did I imagine what just happened, or was Declan trying to say he had feelings for me? I think back to our long history together, starting as trainees, when we endured the worst that the Farm could throw at us. I think of all the nights we knocked back shots with the other recruits, always as a group, never just the two of us. We were the Four Musketeers, Declan and Ben and Ingrid and me. Not once did he hint he was attracted to me, but then I was the baby of the group, eight years younger than he is, more like a little sister toward whom he was ever the gentleman. I was posted to Asia and he headed to Eastern Europe, and for years it was mostly emails between us, with an occasional meetup when our assignments brought us to the same city, but only as friends and colleagues. Nothing romantic, never romantic.

Then I met Danny, and Declan slipped into the background, temporarily forgotten. I did not tell him about my marriage, because I did not know if it was real, or if it was simply part of the operation. And after Malta, it was too painful to talk about Danny, even to my friends. Desperate to outrun the grief, the regrets, I was a global vagabond, moving from country to country, not wanting to be found.

Until the day Declan reached out to me with an email. Ben and I have landed in a good place. Ingrid and Lloyd have moved here too. This town is quiet and friendly. Lots of trees, lots of room to breathe. You'd like it here. Maybe the band should get back together.

His email came at a moment when I was desperately searching for a safe harbor, a place to rebuild my life and cast off the battered shell of old Maggie, damaged Maggie. It never occurred to me that his message was anything more than just a casual invitation to visit.

Now I think back to all the hints I've overlooked. His frequent glances at me over cocktails. The weekends we spent together on summer hikes, or scouring yard sales for furniture. There were so many clues, but I chose to ignore them all because I wasn't ready to move on from Danny.

Perhaps I never will be.

CHAPTER 29
DIANA

Rome

The world is closing in on me, she thought as she sipped chianti in a bar on Via dei Volsci. She sat at a corner table, her back to the wall, the rear exit only three steps away. This was how she lived her life now, because the Agency wanted her in prison and Phillip Hardwicke wanted her dead.

That was something she'd never even considered, that Hardwicke might be alive, but it was the only explanation for this recent chain of events. Obviously, she had screwed up in Malta, and now she was facing the consequences. She could deal with the threat from the Agency—she just had to stay ahead of them long enough to expunge her financial records—but Hardwicke was a different matter. He must have had assets she knew nothing about, enough wealth to keep his machine running. Now he had every reason to want her dead, and the passage of time would not have cooled his rage. She knew his psychological profile, and she knew the fates of those who'd wronged him. She'd seen the postmortem photos of his victims and read the descriptions of their final agonies. She knew narcissistic sociopaths like Hardwicke were fueled by their hunger for revenge, and he would keep hunting relentlessly for those who'd caused the disaster in Malta. Money could buy anything, including access to top secret Agency files, and if he'd gotten his hands on the Operation Cyrano file, then he knew the names of everyone involved.

It was just a matter of time before he found her.

She raised the wineglass to her lips and froze as two men walked into the bar. They stood inside the doorway, surveying the room. Were they looking for her? She reached under the table, for the gun that was lying on her lap. It was always within reach now, with a bullet in the chamber. If she had to use it in the bar, it would unfortunately be a very public spectacle, unlike the death of Dave the Tourist in Bangkok, whose body she could leave behind in a dark alley. Here there'd be witnesses and the police would soon be on her tail, adding more pursuers that she'd have to elude.

She watched, her finger already on the trigger, as the young men moved deeper into the crowded room. Her heart was throbbing, outpacing the beat of the music that played over the bar's speakers. Time slowed down. Her nerves were sizzling, and every sight, every sound, was amplified. The clatter of the cocktail shaker. The gleam of moisture puddled on the table. You never feel more alive than just before you die. She lifted the gun from her lap and was about to bring it up over the table and take aim.

Then two women called out: *"Qui, Enzo! Siamo qui!"*

The men turned to the women and waved. Grinning, they headed toward the table where the women were sitting and they all embraced, kissed.

Diana released a deep sigh and laid the gun back on her lap.

As she watched the two couples sipping wine together, she envied their relaxed laughter, their normal lives. They would drink and dance and then go home to sleep soundly in their beds, something she might never be able to do again. She thought of the years ahead, of always looking over her shoulder. Years of lying awake at night, listening for an intruder's footsteps. Her death would undoubtedly be brutal, and she wondered where and when it would happen. In a week, a year? In a decade?

As long as Hardwicke was alive, his people would be searching for her, and she saw no way out of this nightmare.

Unless I kill him first.

She paid for her drink and walked out of the bar. It was time to go hunting.

CHAPTER 30
JO

Purity

"Old doesn't mean over the hill, Jo," Owen Thibodeau said as he cooked bacon on his newly installed induction stove. "You young folks, you think you already know everything, but we've got a lifetime of experience under our belts. Don't underestimate us."

"I never said I did."

Her father turned and eyed her over his sagging glasses. "You underestimated those spooks, didn't you?"

"Did *you* know they were spooks?"

Owen laughed and turned back to his sizzling pan. "Not a clue. Maybe that's why they're called spooks."

"All these new people moving to town, and I don't know anything about them. Everything's changing so fast." She watched her father cook his daily five strips of bacon. Despite all that fat and cholesterol in his diet, at sixty-seven, Owen remained lean and wiry, like all Thibodeau men, while the Thibodeau women seemed fated to have the big hips and muscular thighs of farm girls. If only Jo had inherited her father's lean genes. Instead, those genes had gone to her lucky brother, Finn, who ate a steady diet of pizza and cheeseburgers and never gained an ounce.

"Betty Jones thinks it was a mistake, putting in that new induction stove," said Jo. "She says it'll hurt the resale value of your house."

"I'm not planning to sell this house."

"She thinks people still prefer propane."

"I really don't care what Betty Jones thinks." He set a plate of scrambled eggs in front of Jo. "People are never ready to move on from anything. Why do you think your mother stuck it out with me so long?" He said it with a smile, and it was good to once again see a hint of his old humor, which had disappeared after her mother died two years ago. That was the other downside of being a Thibodeau woman: they all seemed to die too young, while the men endured.

"When I pass on, I'm leaving this house to you. Induction stove and all."

She frowned. "What about Finn?"

"Your brother will get the camp on Hobbs Pond. Betty thinks they're worth about the same, so it evens out."

"Stop talking about it, Dad. You're going to live forever."

"I just want to live long enough to see the both of you married with kids." He sat down at the table with his two fried eggs and his five strips of bacon. "When is that gonna happen, Jo?"

"When Prince Charming moves to town."

"Maybe he's already here."

She snorted. "Then he's still disguised as a frog." She started in on her scrambled eggs and fried potatoes, the same meal her father always cooked for her whenever she joined him for breakfast, but this morning he'd added bell peppers to the potatoes, and she had to pick them out and slide them to the side of the plate.

"Don't like those?" he asked.

"It's just, um, different."

He laughed. "You never did like things to change. I remember when you were four years old and you screamed your head off when your mother bought a new bedspread."

"There was nothing wrong with the old bedspread."

Her cell phone rang. She picked it up and saw Mike's name on caller ID.

"It's your day off. Do you really have to answer it?" Owen said.

"Mike wouldn't call me today unless he had to." She answered the call. "Hey, what's up?"

"I think we need you over here, Jo," said her officer.

"Why? Where are you?"

"Luther Yount's place. His granddaughter's gone missing."

*

When she pulled up in the driveway, both of Purity's patrol cars were already there. Mike had called in the next shift as well, and four officers stood in the front yard, trying to calm down Luther Yount. As Jo climbed out of her car, Mike flashed a look of profound relief that someone else was now here to deal with Yount, who was sobbing and shouting for them to *fucking do something!* Mike stepped away from the other officers and pulled Jo aside.

"He last saw his granddaughter around seven this morning, when she left the house and went to the barn to take care of the animals. When she didn't come back to the house, he went out to check on her, and he found—"

"You're all wasting *time!*" Yount shouted. He focused on Jo. "You! You're supposed to be the new chief of police. What the fuck are you doing about my Callie?"

Jo approached him with hands extended, palms pointed down, as if trying to calm a dangerous animal. "Sir, we need to find out what happened first. Is it possible she's just wandered off and—"

297

"No. No, that is *not* what happened. They took her!"

"How do you know someone took her?"

"Jo," Mike said quietly. "You need to see the barn."

"Excuse me, Mr. Yount," she said, and followed Mike away from the house. Even before she reached the barn, she saw that things were not right. The cow was wandering loose in the yard, its rope lead dragging on the ground. Although it was free to escape the property, it had remained nearby, wary and watching them. Last night had been clear and cold, and the ground had frozen to a polished glaze, so there were no footprints in the snow, no way to discern who had recently walked this path between barn and cabin. The barn door was wide open, and she heard the noisy squawks of chickens, the bleating of goats. Not the sounds of contentment, but alarm.

"It's inside," said Mike.

The ominous tone of his voice made her hesitate at the barn doorway. She stepped inside and saw free-roaming chickens scurrying across the straw, flapping their wings. In a corner pen, a dozen goats crowded together in a defensive huddle, wild eyed and agitated.

She stared at the wall and saw why they were afraid.

The butchered goat lay in a heap of gray and white fur, one dead eye staring directly at her. Its throat had been slashed, and blood from its severed artery was splattered across the pine boards. Slowly she walked toward it, her boots rustling through straw, her throat dry, but her attention was not on the goat. Nailed to the wall above the dead animal was a sheet of paper with a message written in block letters:

MALTA

A LIFE FOR A LIFE.

"What does it mean?" Mike said softly.

She swallowed. "I have no idea."

"A life for a life." Mike looked at her. "Are they asking for something in exchange?"

"Or maybe it's about revenge," said Jo. "Payback for something Luther Yount did? 'You took mine, now I'm taking yours.'"

They heard a commotion outside. The slamming of car doors, and one of her officers yelling: "You people can't be here! This is a crime scene!"

Jo walked out of the barn and saw Lloyd and Ingrid Slocum standing by the house, arguing with her officers.

"What is going on here?" Jo demanded, striding toward the couple.

"These people just showed up," her officer said. "They insist on talking to you."

"We heard it over the police radio," said Ingrid. "There's been a possible kidnapping?"

"Why are you here?" Jo asked.

"We can help. This might be connected."

"Connected to what?" said Mike.

"Chief Thibodeau knows what I'm talking about."

Everyone looked at Jo.

"I just want my Callie back!" said Luther. "I don't care how you do it. If they can help, let them!"

Jo looked across the field at Blackberry Farm. That was where this had all started, with a dead body in the driveway, followed by the attempt on Maggie Bird's life. Now a fourteen-year-old neighbor was missing, and Jo had little doubt the abduction was part of the same puzzle. The Slocums, with their connections and their unique set of skills, might help her put the pieces together.

"Come with me," she said.

She led them into the barn, where the surviving goats were still huddled in the corner of their pen, traumatized. For a moment, neither Ingrid nor Lloyd said a word. They just stared in silence at the note nailed to the blood-spattered wall.

Tess Gerritsen

"Certainly not subtle," Ingrid said.

"Something the SVR might do?" said Lloyd.

"No. I don't think the Russians left this message."

"What's the SVR?" asked Jo. They ignored her.

"It's a call to action," said Ingrid. "That's how I read it."

"Whose life are they asking for, in exchange?" Lloyd asked.

"I could make a guess. But Maggie would know."

"Will you two tell me what the hell is going on?" Jo blurted out.

"Later," said Ingrid, and she pulled a phone from her pocket. "First, I need to make a call."

CHAPTER 31
MAGGIE

Bangkok

It's nearly sunset when Declan phones my hotel room and tells me to meet them downstairs on the terrace. I find him and Ben sitting at a table by the river, both of them already sipping gin and tonics. It's too warm an evening for anything but a gin and tonic, so I order one too. As the waiter sets down my drink, as well as refills for the men, we sit without speaking, the silence broken only by the clink of ice cubes in our glasses. Declan is once again wearing his coolly unreadable mask. Unlike Danny, whose face I could read at a glance, Declan has mastered the art of hiding his feelings. All this time, I'd simply assumed there'd been women in his life, and why wouldn't there be? But discretion is second nature to him, and he has never revealed that part of himself to me.

Even now, his defenses are up, and I feel I'm looking at Declan through layers of frosted glass, deflecting and distorting. Surely Ben is aware of the tense currents swirling around us, but he pretends to focus instead on digging into the bowl of nuts on the table. Only after the waiter walks away does Ben finally say anything.

"So the rumors are true. You're alive after all," he observes.

"By the skin of my teeth."

"You do know we spent hours trying to track you down? Not cool, Mags. Leaving us in the dark. Not answering your phone."

"I'm sorry."

"We thought we'd have to fish your body out of the river. It put Declan here in a real panic."

I look at Declan. He doesn't look panicked, but is staring off in another direction.

"What have you two been doing all day?" I ask.

"We hired a longboat and took a tour of the khlongs this morning," says Ben. "We saw at least a dozen police officers swarming Gavin's property. The housekeeper found the bodies this morning. Since Gavin used to be a NOC, the Agency's keeping close tabs on the investigation, just in case this murder is related to his intelligence work. According to their contacts in law enforcement, no official alerts have been sent out for any suspect fitting your description. I don't think they know you were there, in the house."

Which means my boat driver has not talked to the police. Either he hasn't heard about the murders yet, or the thick bundle of cash I gave him last night has bought his silence. "What *do* the police know?" I ask.

"The killer took Gavin's computer, so the surveillance footage is gone, which means there's no video evidence. The police think this is tied into the black market. They found the body of a known supplier on the property, plus a stash of illegal drugs in the house."

"The drugs were for his personal use. He was sick, dying."

"But the black market theory does turn attention away from you. Contract killings are cheap here. Piss off a black market kingpin, and a hit man gets dispatched from Chonburi Province. All it takes is ten thousand dollars to make your competitor go away. If that's what the police want to believe, then you're home free."

I sigh. "Well, that's some good news, anyway."

"Is there any possibility *you* led the killer to him?"

"No, I took every precaution. I'm sure I wasn't followed. And Gavin was already on edge, before I got there."

"Why?" Declan asks.

I look at him, but I still feel a distance between us. He has withdrawn back into his self-protective shell, where I can't reach him. Can't hurt him. "Diana Ward recently contacted him, asking for his help. She said someone's trying to kill her, and she wanted a safe place to hide. He turned her away."

"Rather harsh."

"Bad history. You'd understand if you ever had to work with her."

"Who's trying to kill her?" Ben asks.

"Probably the same person who wants me dead. Phillip Hardwicke."

Ben and Declan stare at me. We fall silent as a tourist boat rumbles past with music blaring, its deck crammed with dancing bodies. I pick up my drink, but the ice cubes have melted and my gin and tonic has gone watery and weak. I feel as if I'm melting as well, my brain dulled by heat and exhaustion.

"Alive?" Ben says. "He wasn't on the plane?"

"Which means this could all be about revenge. If Hardwicke got his hands on the file to Operation Cyrano, then he knows every detail of how it was planned, who was involved. That's why Gavin's dead, why Diana's on the run. She's so paranoid, she doesn't even trust the Agency."

"Then you probably shouldn't either," Declan says quietly. He's finally looking at me, *really* looking at me. "You can't go home, Maggie. Not now."

Maybe not ever.

I think about Blackberry Farm, and suddenly I feel so homesick that it's a physical pain, an ache as real as hunger pangs. I miss looking out at the fields from my kitchen window. I miss the noisy plumbing in my house and the frost on the windows and the sound of my boots crunching through the snow. I miss my chickens.

"I need to figure out what to do next," I say.

"Here's what you do: you stay out of sight, while we find a way to track him down and neutralize the threat," says Declan.

"What if we can't?" I look at Ben. "Do you *really* think three old spies can go up against someone with Hardwicke's resources? If he has a mole in the Agency—"

"I agree with Declan," says Ben. "You need to disappear."

"I've already been in contact with an old friend in Singapore," Declan says. "Someone I'd trust with my own life. He has a safe house, a place where no one will find you."

"That's what my farm was supposed to be. My safe place." I look across the Chao Phraya, across floating mats of vegetation that drift by like a lush green carpet, a view so different from my beloved fields and woodlands in Maine. "It took me years to find a place I could call home. I've finally put down roots, and I don't want to pull them up again."

"This is only temporary, Maggie."

"Is it?" I look at Declan. "Or am I never going home?"

He doesn't reply, but in his silence lies the answer. I am once again adrift and homeless, as I was in the years after Malta.

Another riverboat motors past, its engine so noisy that at first, I don't hear the ringing cell phone. The sound is coming from my backpack. There are only a few people in the world who know the number to my burner phone, and two of those people are sitting with me right now, at this table. The number is reserved for matters of urgency, and both Ben and Declan have snapped to attention. They watch as I pull the cell phone out of my backpack, as I look at the caller's name.

It's Ingrid.

*

The advantage of having no family ties, no children, no husband or lover, is that it makes you invulnerable. Every person you love is a weakness in your armor. When you care about no one, you can be fearless because the world cannot destroy you, the way it almost destroyed me. That's the lesson I learned from Danny, and for years I have avoided attachments, grown accustomed to a life unfettered by affections.

But relationships have a way of creeping up on you. You may not register the little jolt of oxytocin released into your bloodstream whenever your neighbor waves at you, or when his granddaughter beams at you as you step into their kitchen. Through countless mornings spent together sipping Luther's terrible burned coffee, or boiling down maple syrup with Callie, through a blizzard when they towed my truck out of a snowbank, through a summer afternoon when Callie and I chased after her wayward goats, the threads of a relationship slowly bound us together. Now I'm ensnared, and I cannot walk away from Luther or his granddaughter.

Callie is only fourteen years old.

I think of Bella, long dead now, her remains lying somewhere in the Mediterranean Sea with Danny's. I could have saved her. I could have warned her about her father and helped her escape the dangerous world he lived in, but I didn't, because she was too useful. Too exploitable. Bella is dead because of my inaction.

I won't let that happen to Callie.

As I stuff clothes into a duffel bag, I remember myself at her age: independent and already working shifts at the diner to pay the bills that my father left piling up on the kitchen counter. At fourteen, I was already an adult, but Callie isn't. She's still just a girl.

Malta. A life for a life. That was the note nailed to the barn wall above the slaughtered goat, and the message couldn't be clearer. It's addressed to me. This is a tiger kidnapping, meant to force me to do their bidding. They are not new at this, and they know I'll cooperate only if I believe they will keep their end of the bargain.

"You can't go home," says Declan.

"If Callie needs me, I have to go home." I roll up another T-shirt, stuff it into the duffel bag.

"Ben and I will go back and deal with this. You need to stay away."

"And sit uselessly by the phone?"

"Go to Singapore and keep your head down. We'll do everything we can to find the girl, but you can't be part of this. Not when you're the real target."

My cell phone buzzes with a text message from Ingrid. It's the answer I've been waiting for these last nine hours. I read it and, without a word, I turn and go to the window. The sun has just come up here in Bangkok, but at home in Maine it's 7:00 p.m. on a dark winter's night, and Luther Yount would be frantic. He'd wonder if his granddaughter is cold and hungry or, God forbid, already dead. I desperately want to be with him in Purity, helping with the search, but Declan is right. I can't go home. I have a job to do, and somewhere else I need to be. It's the only way the girl will live.

I turn to face Declan. "All right," I say. "I'll go to Singapore."

"Good." Declan heaves out a sigh. He thinks he's won the argument. "Ben's waiting downstairs in the taxi. There's a flight for Singapore leaving at ten fifteen. Let's get you on it."

It's a silent drive to the airport. Ben sits in the front, and I sit in back with Declan. We don't look at each other, don't say all the things two old friends should be saying when they're about to part for maybe the last time. I am already resigned to the likelihood that these might well be our final moments together. He and Ben will return to Maine and search for Callie, while I'm bound for a different destination, one I will probably not survive.

But that is the deal I've agreed to. *A life for a life.*

All these years, I've considered Declan merely a friend, a good and loyal colleague. Only now, in the winter of our lives, am I realizing how many clues I've missed as the years slipped by. It's yet another item to add to my lifelong tally of regrets: *I never gave Declan a chance.*

At the airport, Ben and Declan stand beside me at the Singapore Airlines desk as I buy my ticket, flash my fake passport, get my boarding pass.

"My friend will be waiting for your call," says Declan as he walks me to the security gates. "You'll be safe with him, Mags."

"Just find Callie for me, okay?"

"We will." He smiles. "Looks like the band is back in business."

We don't kiss, don't hug. I just walk away and join the security line. Only when I'm on the other side do I glance back. Both men have vanished, headed to a different terminal for their flight to Boston. I wait a few minutes to be certain they are really gone. Only then do I exit the secure area and head back to the ticketing desks, because I am not going to Singapore.

Once again, I pull out my passport and wallet, and I buy a different one-way ticket.

To Milan.

CHAPTER 32

Lake Como, Italy

Perched on a sloping hillside above Lake Como, the villa's ocher walls glow like gold in the afternoon sunlight. Manicured gardens surround it, a fairyland of topiary and hedges and a lawn that sweeps down to the shore. Through binoculars, I peer through the villa's open gate at the half dozen vehicles parked in the driveway, two of them large delivery trucks. Men are unloading tables and chairs from one of the trucks and carrying them down to the gardens. Now another vehicle pulls in through the gates. It's the catering van, and I watch as trays of food and cases of wine are carried into the house. Judging by the number of chairs being set up, at least a hundred guests will be attending the party here tonight.

I scan the road leading to and from the villa gates. There are no security guards anywhere in sight, no one to stop an uninvited woman from simply strolling onto the grounds and mingling with the crowd, but the threat of assassination is probably not a concern for Mr. Giacomo Lazio, who owns this villa. Mr. Lazio made his fortune manufacturing ladies' luxury undergarments, a business that doesn't usually require bodyguards, although a villa this impressive really ought to have a security guard or two.

I know this is where Silvia Moretti now lives, thanks to the text I received from Ingrid while I was in Bangkok. Ingrid knows how to track down anyone in the world, and it took her less than a day to find out that Phillip Hardwicke's former mistress now shares the bed of a man twenty-two years her senior. Silvia would be in her late forties now, and she is no doubt still stunning, but the shelf life of a mistress is limited. The clock is always ticking.

Judging by this lakeside villa, she has done well for herself. She's bounced back from the tragedy of losing Phillip Hardwicke and landed nicely on her feet with Giacomo Lazio. When you lose one rich lover, you simply find another.

The last of the tables have been unloaded, and the men slam the truck's rear gate shut. Another delivery van pulls through the gates. The florists, who haul out vases and vases of lavish floral arrangements.

I put down my binoculars and look up at a cloudless sky. It's an unseasonably warm day for the end of February, but Lake Como can be chilly at night. Still, one cannot show up at an elegant party dressed in flannels, like a lumberjack.

I start my rental car. It's time to go shopping for a dress.

*

By nine that night, the narrow road leading to Giacomo Lazio's villa is lined with parked cars. I leave mine at the bottom of the road and walk uphill, past the parked Ferraris and Maseratis and Mercedes, to reach the villa's wrought iron gate. It is wide open and manned only by two uniformed valets, who smile and tip their heads at me as I approach. I see no armed guards, no weapons anywhere, just these two dark-haired charmers who call out *Buona sera* as I walk through the gate. The ladies' lingerie business is far more amiable than the world I'm accustomed to.

My high heels wobble on the paving stones as I walk up the driveway. It has been a long time since I had to wear heels, and already I feel a blister forming after the trudge up the hill from my parked car. I miss my farm boots and jeans and flannel shirt, but tonight, this evening dress is my battle uniform, and green silk swishes against my legs as I follow the stone path toward the sounds of live music and laughter. I may not be a hot babe anymore, but my hips are still slim, my arms are toned, and I still know how to work a dress.

The path takes me to the villa's back terrace, which tonight is aglow from hanging paper lanterns that sway in the breezes off the lake. I snag a glass of champagne from a passing waiter and move along the edge of the terrace, surveying the faces. It is a different crowd from the circles I'm accustomed to surveilling. These people are younger and hipper and far more attractive. Instead of silver-haired diplomats and bankers and politicians, I see men with swooping black hair and women who are stunning enough to be strutting on fashion catwalks. No one pays attention to me, and why should they? I'm just an anonymous figure drifting past, with nothing to distinguish myself.

I cruise past the live band, which plays the thumping electronic noise that passes for music these days, and help myself to the canapé trays, with their tempting array of smoked fish and bruschetta, cheeses and Parma ham. My Italian is rusty, but it's still good enough for me to understand a few snatches of overheard conversations.

Which hotel did you stay in?

Did you hear Paolo moved out? She's devastated.

I'm on this horrible new diet. I'm going insane for a glass of wine.

At last, I spot the person I've been searching for, and she's surrounded by a circle of her guests. Silvia's hair is clipped shorter these days, but it is still jet black, and her figure is every bit as stunning. Her red knit dress is unforgiving, a skintight sheath that clings to every curve and provides no disguise for any bulge, any excess flesh. Either the years have been exceptionally kind to her or she has worked hard to maintain that toned body.

I pivot away before she notices that I am here.

The sliding glass doors to the villa are wide open, allowing the catering staff to freely circulate between kitchen and terrace. I use those open doors to slip into the house.

Inside, the decor is sleek and white, with only a few artistic pops of color designed to draw attention to a burnt orange glass sculpture and a painting in turquoise and gold. My heels click noisily across white marble. I pull off my shoes, relieved to walk barefoot. In seconds I'm down the hall and out of sight of the other guests. If anyone confronts me here, I'm just an old lady with a small bladder, desperate to find the toilet. None of the doors leading from the hallway are locked, and I peek into them, finding a bathroom (white marble, of course), a guest bedroom, and a linen closet. In this household, it seems there are no secret spaces.

At the end of the hall, I finally reach the main bedroom. I slip inside and shut the door. The same white marble reigns in here as well, a decor that some might call sophisticated, but it strikes me instead as cold and passionless. Is this a reflection of Silvia's taste, or did this come with the new man she acquired?

A pair of aquamarine reading glasses on the nightstand tells me the far side of the bed is Silvia's. I circle around the bed and open her nightstand drawer. Inside is her passport, plus the usual array of feminine necessities: hand cream, a sleeping mask, sanitary pads.

I reach in deeper, and at the back of the drawer, I find a tattered address book. The pages are bent, and some of the entries have faded to mere ghosts of themselves. While most of us now keep our contact information in digital files, few of us are ready to toss out our old handwritten address books. I flip to the *H*'s and find the name I knew would be there: Hardwicke. There are phone numbers for Phillip as well as for his daughter, Bella, but these are old entries, numbers that date back to when Silvia was still his mistress. No new contact information is written here, no updated phone numbers or addresses. It's a document frozen in time.

I place the address book back into the nightstand and am about to slide the drawer shut when I hear the bedroom door suddenly creak open.

There's no time to dash for the closet, no time to even shut the drawer. Instantly I drop to the floor and lie there, face pressed to cold marble, as footsteps tread into the room. Peering under the bed, I see a pair of men's shoes pacing back and forth. He is talking on the phone in rapid Italian, and he sounds agitated. Something about a mistake. He wants to know who is responsible.

Now the shoes move toward the bed, and the mattress gives a sigh as he sits down. I see his shoes are brown leather, no doubt expensive, and one of the soles taps incessantly against the floor. He's too engaged in his phone call to notice that anything is amiss in his bedroom. I look up at Silvia's nightstand and see the drawer still hanging open. The space under the bed is too narrow for me to wedge myself into. If he comes around to close the drawer, he'll find me here.

The bedroom door swings open again. This time I see a pair of high heels walk in. It's Silvia.

Don't look at the nightstand. Don't look this way.

Silvia wants to know why Giacomo's left the party. Even here, on the other side of the bed, I can feel the tension crackling between them.

He barks at her in Italian: "A minute!"

"It's *your* party," she snaps back.

"I have a problem. In the factory."

"These people are your friends, not mine."

"All right, all right." The mattress hisses as he stands up. "I'm coming."

I watch their shoes exit the room, and the bedroom door thuds shut.

My heart is hammering as I clamber back to my feet. I close the nightstand drawer, then pad barefoot to the bedroom door and press my ear against it. I hear no voices, nothing except the distant thump of the band. I crack open the door and peek out at the hallway.

There's no one in sight.

By the time I make it back outside to the terrace, my pulse has steadied. I slip my shoes back on, pick up another glass of champagne, and weave my way into the crowd, back into the sea of beautiful people with their perfect skin and tailored suits. But even here, in this little slice of paradise on Lake Como, life is not perfect for Silvia and her lover. That much I gathered from overhearing their conversation in the bedroom. I see the silver-maned Giacomo, holding court with a half dozen guests, but Silvia is nowhere in sight. Scanning the crowd, I finally spot her. She is heading down the terrace steps, toward the lake, and she is alone.

I follow her.

The stone steps descend to a manicured lawn that rolls down to the water's edge. That's where I find Silvia, standing by the lapping water. Her back is turned to me, and her silhouette is framed by the silvery reflection from the lake. She stares across Como like a woman trapped on the wrong side, yearning to be on the opposite shore.

She does not hear me walking toward her, and when I say, "Hello, Silvia," she gives a start and spins around to face me. "Who—do I know you?"

"You don't remember me, do you?" It's hardly surprising that she wouldn't. Too many years have passed, and I was merely a bit player in her life, someone so unimportant that she would barely have registered my existence.

"I'm sorry. I don't," she says.

"My husband was Dr. Danny Gallagher, Phillip's doctor. Danny was on that plane. We both lost someone that day. At least, that's what I was led to believe."

She shakes her head. "I don't understand. Why are you here? After all these years, why do you come to my house and—"

"Phillip Hardwicke is alive, isn't he?"

She goes dead silent. Here at the water's edge, we are standing in shadow and I cannot read her expression, but I see her silhouette standing utterly still.

"No," she whispers.

"Do you know where he is?"

"It's not possible. He's dead."

"That's what they *want* us to believe."

"There was a bomb on the plane. They all died, all seven of them."

"But they found only two bodies in the sea. We don't know who else was aboard, who might have stepped off the plane at the very last minute."

She hugs herself. Even in the gloom I can see she's shaking. "If he was alive, I would *know*. I would *feel* it. And why wouldn't he call me? Why would he make me think he's dead?"

"It's how he's stayed alive, by making everyone believe he's dead. He's still out there, Silvia. Probably living under a different name, with a different identity."

"No. No, this is not true! He wouldn't leave me to suffer like this!"

I hear real anguish in her voice, and I realize, to my astonishment, that this is not a performance. She really doesn't know that Hardwicke is alive.

"You loved him," I say in wonder.

She turns back to the water and says softly: "Of course I did."

"Did he love you?"

"I thought . . ." Her head droops. "I believed he did. I believed so many things."

"Yet he never contacted you? After the plane went down, you never heard from him?"

"No."

"Do you have any idea where he is now?"

315

"At the bottom of the sea. That's what I believed then. It's what I believe now." She looks at me. "Why do you ask all these questions? Who are you, really?"

For a moment we just stare at each other, two women whose lives intersected in ways that left us both damaged, both forever in mourning.

"I'm Danny Gallagher's wife," I say. "That's all you need to know."

I turn and walk back up the stone steps to the terrace, back through the crowd of beautiful people in their beautiful clothes. My visit here has revealed this much: Silvia really does not know where Hardwicke is. She really does believe he is dead.

I don't know where to look next.

Most people on the run can't help but seek out familiar places, but Hardwicke is too clever to return to his old haunts. The only way he could stay hidden all these years was by *not* doing what is expected of him. What he could not avoid, though, was dipping into his multiple offshore accounts over the years. Perhaps he actually needed those funds, or he's back to brokering new deals, but those shifts of capital did not go unnoticed by the Agency. That was his big mistake. It was the clue that he's still alive.

I consider my next moves. I can't go home, and perhaps I'll never be able to. For the moment I'm adrift, as I was in the years after Danny's death, moving from place to place, searching for a landing spot where I could leave behind the old Maggie and become someone new, someone who wasn't haunted by thoughts of what *might* have been. If only I had refused that last assignment in Malta. If only Danny and I had run away. We would be together now, our hair gray, our faces etched more deeply with laugh lines. I imagine us someplace warm, maybe in South America, in a village where chickens and goats and barefoot children run free.

Instead, I am alone as I walk out the villa gates. I leave behind the music, the laughter, the could-have-beens, and head down the hill to my car. The high heels pinch, and I'm tempted to hurl them away and continue barefoot across the sharp gravel. I want the pain. I need the pain, as penance for my sins. I round the bend and reach my rental car, parked behind a black Ferrari. I fish the key fob out of my purse and click open the lock.

That's when I hear the clatter of gravel on the pavement. Someone is right behind me.

I turn and stare at Diana. At the gun she's pointing at my chest.

"Hello, Maggie. What a surprise, you turning up here."

"Put the gun down, Diana. We're on the same side."

"Are we?" She nods at my parked car. "Get in. You're driving."

CHAPTER 33

A church is the last place I expected Diana Ward to use as a bolt-hole, but that's where she has brought me, up a bumpy road to this dilapidated stone building on a hill. In the glow of our headlights, I see boarded-up windows and a tangle of aggressive vines that have clambered up the walls. I turn off the engine, and the night goes black. On this hill there are no nearby houses, no lights. No witnesses.

Instead of entering through the front door, Diana leads me through a side entrance. It's clear she's been hiding out here long enough to become familiar with the layout. When she lights a kerosene lantern, I see that this church has not been used as a place for worship in a very long time. The pews are scattered and broken, some of the unboarded stained glass windows above are shattered, and cobwebs hang like silken drapes from the rafters. Near where the altar once stood, there's a small table with a backpack, the remains of a sandwich, and a half-empty bottle of wine. It's a convenient shelter, clearly long abandoned and private, yet close enough to the villa to monitor Silvia and her visitors. Of course, that's why Diana is here in Como; she came for the same reason I did. She knows Hardwicke is alive, and she believes that Silvia knows where he is.

It is chilly in this stone church. While Diana's wearing black jeans and a fleece jacket, I'm dressed only in the silk evening dress and a thin wrap, which I hug to my shoulders as I face her across the flickering lamp. She has not lowered her gun, and the barrel is like an accusing third eye, staring at me.

"Why are you in Como?" she asks.

"For the same reason you're here. I thought Silvia could tell me where Hardwicke is."

"Who sent you?"

"You did. In a way."

"Don't be ridiculous."

"Someone from the Agency showed up at my house in Maine. She said you'd vanished and you might be in need of help."

"You're here to *help* me?" Her laughter echoes in the vast stone church, the sound shattering into the voices of a dozen semihysterical Dianas. "Maggie to the rescue!"

"I don't give a shit what happens to you. But Gavin's dead. He was assassinated in Bangkok a few nights ago. I was there when it happened. You and I are probably next on the hit list."

Her hand remains perfectly steady, her weapon still fixed on my chest. "Did Gavin tell you why this is happening?"

"Hardwicke's alive," I say. "This is revenge for Malta."

She doesn't seem surprised by this revelation. "Do you know that for a fact? He's alive?"

"The Agency thinks so."

"What's their proof?"

"Money has vanished from his accounts. A lot of it. Accessing those accounts requires passcodes, which only he would know."

At last, she lowers her gun. Her hair is uncombed, her cheeks sunken. In her face I see the paranoia that comes from too little sleep and too much fear. She begins to pace, moving back and forth past the kerosene lamp. In her agitation, she doesn't seem to care that I'm standing there, and I'm just relieved I no longer have a gun pointed at me.

"We have to neutralize Hardwicke," she says. "We have to work together."

"The way we did in Malta?" I give a bitter laugh. "As if I'd trust you."

"We brought down Cyrano together, didn't we?"

"And you killed my husband."

She halts and looks at me. Just as quickly, she looks away. "That was unfortunate. I wish we could have stopped it," she says, but I glimpsed the truth in her eyes. The flash of guilt just before she turned away.

"You *could* have stopped it."

"There was no way to know a bomb would be—"

"Gavin told me the truth. You knew, hours before, that the Russians were going to strike back, and you didn't think to warn me. You just let the plane take off, with Danny on board."

"The threat in the message was nonspecific."

"It was clear enough to take action."

"I couldn't be sure."

"No. You just didn't *care!*" My voice echoes back at me in a repeating shriek of anguish, a shriek I've held in all these years. The last echoes fade away, and for a moment we stare at each other without speaking.

A rumble breaks the silence of the church. It's the growl of an approaching engine.

Diana's chin snaps up in alarm. "They followed us. Fuck, they followed *you*." She blows out the lantern and snatches up her backpack. The only light is through the broken windows, the faint glow from the village a mile away.

"Give me a gun," I whisper as we crouch in the darkness.

"Shut up."

"If they're here to kill us, you're going to need me to help hold them off. Give me a gun."

It takes her only a few seconds to weigh her options and realize I'm right. She does need me. I hear her rustle around in her pack, and she presses a pistol in my hand. A nine-millimeter. It's not my trusty Walther, but it will do.

Someone rattles the front door, but it's locked. Maybe it's just a church caretaker? God, let it be just some harmless old man, here to see who is squatting in his building. Then I hear the spit of a suppressor and the splintering of wood. Three kicks and the door flies open. I glimpse the shadowy silhouettes of two men stepping inside. No, there are three.

Diana doesn't hesitate. In rapid fire, she squeezes off four shots. I hear a grunt of pain, then there's a burst of return fire. A bullet whistles past my face and shatters the wine bottle on the table.

Diana fires two more shots and retreats, moving deeper into the shadows. Leaving me behind to face the invaders alone, of course. That's how she operates. She knows the layout of this church, knows every possible hiding place, and all I can do is follow her lead and hope she's heading toward a defensible position. My high heels clatter too loudly, so I kick them off. I can just make out her retreating shadow in the gloom.

Bullets ricochet against the wall. Stone fragments sting my cheek. The men are advancing; I hear the thump of someone bumping against a pew, and I blindly fire off three shots at the sound before scrambling after Diana.

She's taken the only route of retreat: up a circular staircase that must lead up to the bell tower. I start up the steps and feel the bite of a loose nail in the sole of my foot. Wincing at the pain, I hobble up the steps. The winding staircase is too narrow and twisting for a clear shot in any direction; my only hope is to make it to the top, where we can hold off the attackers and pick them off as they emerge from the stairway. I scramble up the last steps into the belfry. There is Diana, crouched off to the side. The glow from the village is just bright enough to illuminate her tense face and the gleam of the gun in her hands.

I don't say a word, just drop down beside her. Together we wait to face our attackers. I have no choice now; I have to fight alongside this woman I despise.

Through the banging of my heart, I hear footfalls in the stairwell. A shadow eases into view.

Both Diana and I open fire, our bullets pinging into stone. This is our last stand, but we have the advantage. Here, we can hold them off.

And then I run out of ammo.

A bullet slashes past me. I dive sideways, and my shoulder slams onto ancient floorboards. I roll back to a crouch and frantically scan the tower for an alternate escape route, but the only other way off the belfry is to dive over the edge in a fatal plunge to the parking lot.

So this is how it ends, barefoot and cornered with the woman who destroyed my life, the woman whose decisions a decade and a half ago sent us both down the path to this final moment.

I drop my empty gun. I don't believe in an afterlife, don't believe that dying heroically earns you a seat in Valhalla. I know only that a senseless struggle will prolong the agony, and I choose acceptance over panic. But Diana is not prepared to die. She moves beside me, and her voice is low and panicked.

"What the fuck? Your gun—"

"I'm out of bullets. It's over, Diana."

"No. No, it's not."

She strikes with the speed of a cobra, slinging her arm around my throat. I'm thrown off balance as she wrenches me backward against her chest. I'm her shield, a sacrificial mass of flesh and bone against bullets. Till the end, Diana is all about Diana, even though it makes no difference now, because she, too, will soon be out of bullets.

A man's silhouette appears, then a second. Diana backs away, dragging me with her, until she's up against the belfry railing and we can retreat no further.

"A deal!" she calls out. *"Voglio fare un patto!"*

The men say nothing, but they do not lower their weapons.

"There's money," she says. "I can give you twenty million dollars! It's all yours, but you have to let me go!"

She has twenty million dollars?

Even now, as I stand on the edge of death, that revelation sends my mind spinning. I juggle the puzzle pieces, feel them start to click into place. I think about the millions of dollars drained from Hardwicke's offshore accounts, by someone who had to know his passcodes. I think about Hardwicke's failing memory, his difficulty keeping track of numbers and names and dates. In an instant, it all comes together. Where did he store his passcodes? They would have to be easily accessible to him, in a notebook or a phone.

Or a thumb drive. Like the one I gave Diana to copy in Malta.

Another puzzle piece clicks into place.

Diana had the passcodes, but she couldn't use them while Hardwicke was alive. He would notice if money vanished from his accounts, so she needed him out of the picture. She needed him dead, and the easiest way to make that happen was to let the Russians exact their revenge. So she let his plane take off, let him fly to his death, and she didn't care who died with him.

More footsteps echo in the stairwell. They climb at a steady, unhurried pace, the grim rhythm of our approaching executioner.

"Twenty million dollars!" Diana says again. In her desperation to make a deal, she loses her grip on me. I wrench out of her grasp and scramble away, out of reach. She now stands exposed, without my body to shield her.

"That's more money than you'll ever see," she says. "You can have *her*. Kill *her*. Just let me go, and I'll—"

The pop of a suppressor freezes her in midsentence. Her head jerks back, and then her body sways against the edge of the belfry. For a few heartbeats she seems to balance there, her spine arched over the iron railing. Then gravity asserts itself, and she tips backward over the barrier and plummets into shadow.

I do not see her land, but I hear the impact. The thud of flesh and bone slamming onto the concrete below.

CHAPTER 34

From the gloom of the belfry staircase, a figure slowly emerges. I expect to see Phillip Hardwicke walk into view, but this is a woman. The men stand aside to let her pass. She moves to the edge of the belfry and stares down at the ground. Although sixteen years have passed since I last laid eyes on her, I recognize the generous hips, the rounded slope of her shoulders. In the moonlight, I catch the gleam of ginger hair ruffling in the breeze.

"It wasn't her money to offer," she says and turns to look at me. In her hand is the gun she just used to kill Diana, and the barrel is now pointed at me. "My question's finally been answered. It was her."

"Bella," I murmur. "How is this possible?"

"My mother," she says. "I wouldn't be alive if not for her."

"You weren't on the plane."

"She wouldn't let me go to the airport, not after she heard about the raid on Alan Holloway's yacht. Oh, Mummy knew about my father's deals with the Russians. She knew what they were capable of. When his plane went down, she thought they might come after me too. Make me an example of what happens to your family if you cross them. So she took me home on her own jet. To Argentina."

"I had no idea you were alive. There was a funeral—your mother was there."

"There had to be a funeral. It was part of the game, and she knew how to play it."

"All this time. I had no idea you were with her."

"Until the day she died." Bella's voice wavers, and the barrel of her gun dips toward the floor.

"God, I'm sorry, Bella," I murmur. "She loved you. She only ever wanted the best for you."

"Unlike *you*." Her gun snaps up and is once again pointed at my chest. "When I finally got my hands on that file, I learned the truth about you." Her voice cuts like glass. "And what you did."

"I really *was* your friend."

"Friend?" Her laugh is loud and bitter. "You *used* me. You would have sent me to my death."

"I was supposed to be on that plane too! I would have gone down with all of you."

"But you weren't aboard, were you?"

"My *husband* was! The man I *loved*. Do you think I'd have let him go if I knew what would happen?"

There's a long silence. "No," she finally murmurs. She turns to the railing and stares down at the parking lot. "God, I was such a *stupid* girl."

"You were only fifteen. You didn't know what your father really was."

"I'm not talking about my father. I'm talking about *you*. What *you* were. All this time, I had no idea who you worked for. Then I discovered that someone raided my father's accounts, even though I'm the only one who knew his passcodes. 'The keys to the kingdom,' he called them. He made me memorize them, because he was having trouble with his memory. Someone else moved that money, and I had no idea who could have done it. Until I learned about Operation Cyrano."

"How?"

She shrugs. "Everything can be bought, Maggie. Loyalty. Access. There's always someone willing to sell secrets, even in your precious CIA." She turns to face me. "You're the last one alive. Do you have any final words?"

"How did it come to this, Bella? How did *you* come to this?"

"Necessity. I know names. I know how to use them. My father taught me that much."

"This isn't who you really are. I *knew* that Bella, and I was happy to be her friend. Whether you believe it or not, I really was."

"Well, say hello to the new Bella. I am my father's daughter, after all."

I don't believe that. When I look at her, it's not Phillip Hardwicke I see, but that innocent fifteen-year-old girl. And I think of another girl, another innocent, whose life now depends on me.

"When this is over, when you're finished with me, you'll let Callie go?"

"The girl?"

"She's only fourteen."

"Does it really matter, what happens to her?"

"'A life for a life.' If I die, the girl lives. Isn't that what you were asking me to do? That's why I came, to make the trade. My life for hers."

For a moment she just studies me, and I remember the girl she once was. Lonely and awkward and unsure of her place in the world. It seems she has found that place, now. Her father's death has forged her into this self-assured but bitter creature, an avenging Medea for whom one murder demands another in return. Who am I to disabuse her of that notion? I was part of the machine that brought down her father and took the lives of six people, one of them my husband. That same machine destroyed Bella's life, as well. The girl I once knew is gone, and I am partly to blame. I've been trying to run from the guilt, but I cannot escape it. I will carry it to my grave.

I stand up straight. I am prepared. "I'm sorry for everything, Bella. I know it won't make a difference, hearing that now, but I truly am."

She raises the gun to my head.

I look her in the eyes and wait for the bullet. *I'm coming, Danny. I'm almost there.* The seconds pass, yet I am still standing, still looking at her. I want her to see who I am, the friend who never wished her harm. The friend who suffered a loss as deep and devastating as her own.

She turns to her men. "Go. Leave us."

After a hesitation, they retreat back down into the gloom of the stairwell.

Slowly Bella lowers the gun. She moves to the railing and looks down at Diana's body lying below. "She was ready to kill you."

"*She* was never my friend."

A moment passes. Now, while she's not looking at me, is the time for me to attack and wrestle away her gun, but I find I cannot do it. I don't have the heart to betray her yet again.

"A life for a life," she says softly. She turns to face me. "You brought me Diana Ward. Let's call it good."

"Bella . . ."

"Goodbye, Maggie. May we never meet again." She turns and disappears into the stairwell. I hear the echo of her footsteps as she descends the tower.

My legs suddenly wobble. I sink to the floor, where I huddle, shaking, not from the cold, but from the shock of everything that has happened tonight. Death came so close that I could feel its breath in my ear, and I'm stunned that I am still here. I should not be, and every breath I take from this moment on is a gift I will never take for granted, one I do not deserve. The chill seeps through my thin dress and my bones ache from the hard floor, but these discomforts are blessings in disguise, because to feel them means I am alive.

I haul myself back to my feet and look down over the railing. Far below, I see Bella and her men emerging from the church. They walk past Diana's body and head toward their car.

"What about Callie?" I call out.

Bella pauses and looks up, but she doesn't answer.

"You promised. A life for a life!" I shout. "What about the girl?"

Bella climbs into the back seat of the car, and it drives away.

Still unsteady, I slowly make my way down the tower staircase. I have no idea where my shoes are, or my purse with the car key fob, and I dread the long and uncomfortable walk on bare feet to the village.

But I have endured worse.

The church's front door hangs open. I hobble my way to the moon-lit doorway, and there, on the stoop, are my shoes and my purse, placed conveniently where I would be sure to find them. One final gesture of mercy from Bella. I pick up my purse and immediately detect the difference in weight. I reach inside and find a phone that was not there before. Bella has kept open a line of communication between us. I can only hope it's for the purpose I think it is.

I step out into the parking lot and confront Diana's body, which lies face up on gravel that is now stained black with her blood. The bullet hole punched in her forehead will tell the police this was no suicidal leap from the tower.

I need to be miles away from here when they find her.

I climb into the rental car and drive away, leaving Diana where she lies. Once again, I leave behind the dead.

*

Dawn is just breaking when I reach Milan. I don't check into a hotel but head straight to Malpensa Airport, change clothes, and settle in at a café to wait the four hours until I fly to Boston, connecting through London. The adrenaline has faded, and my limbs feel rubbery with exhaustion. When I was a young woman, I could work for forty-eight hours straight without sleep, but I am not that woman anymore. I order espresso after espresso, trying to stay awake, checking and rechecking the burner phone that was left in my purse, searching for the message I'm waiting for.

There is nothing.

I wonder if Diana's body has been found yet, and what the local police will make of it. A mob killing? A robbery? A jealous lover? All the usual motives will be explored, but I doubt the true reason will ever occur to them. I pity the police; they lack the imagination to understand half of what they see.

A life for a life. I delivered my end of the bargain. Now Bella has to deliver hers.

I drain my espresso and stand up. My first flight takes off in two hours. It's time to go home and rescue Callie.

*

From Logan Airport, it's a four-hour drive north to Purity, and it is 11:00 p.m. when I finally reach the outskirts of town. Just as I cross the town line, my phone dings with the text message I've been waiting for. Somehow, she knows that I am close to home, and it is unsettling to realize I'm being tracked, that Bella has followed my progress as I flew from Milan to London to Boston, as I drove north into Maine. Unsettling, yes, but not frightening. If she wanted to kill me, she would have done it in Como.

I glance at the burner phone, and my exhaustion instantly evaporates. I have been awake for almost forty-eight hours, but the text I see on my screen sends a jolt of adrenaline through my bone-weary body.

I hit the gas pedal.

Fifteen minutes later, I am standing in front of an abandoned house on Connor Road. I have driven past this property several times before, but it is so overgrown with weeds and briars that I have never before glimpsed the building itself. My flashlight reveals peeling paint and a rotting porch, and I know that no one has lived here in a very long time, yet in the driveway, I see fresh tire tracks in the snow.

I catch the scent of smoke in the air. Someone has lit a fire.

My heart is hammering as I climb the steps to the sagging porch. I am not afraid for myself, but I fear what I will find inside. The door is unlocked. I give it a push, and it swings open, hinges squealing, to reveal only darkness inside.

"Callie?" I call out.

I step into the house, and it immediately strikes me that, while it is twenty degrees outside, inside the house it's warm, almost comfortable. I sweep my flashlight around the living room, which is devoid of furniture and is just an empty space with pine floors and cobwebs drooping from the ceiling. My beam stops at the brick hearth, where I see only unswept ashes. I cross the room and touch the bricks. They are cool.

Yet the house is warm. Where is the heat coming from?

The floor creaks as I walk out of the living room, into the kitchen. My flashlight beam moves across battered pine countertops, cabinets with doors sagging open, a porcelain sink stained brown. I spot the woodstove, and as I move closer, I can already feel the heat emanating from it, and I see a rack of firewood in the corner. Someone has been keeping the house warm.

"Callie?"

The sound is so faint I almost miss it. A whimper, coming from somewhere nearby. I turn, and my flashlight beam lands on the pantry door. It hangs ajar.

Even before I pull it open, I know she is in there. I know she is safe. I shine my flashlight into the space, and there she is, tied to a chair, a strip of duct tape over her mouth.

In seconds I have her freed, and instantly she's on me like an octo-pus, her arms wrapped in a strangling hug around my neck. She has wet her pants and she smells like sweat and urine and smoke, but she is alive. Wildly, tremblingly alive.

"You're here!" she cries. "I knew you'd come. I just knew!"

"Of course I'm here. I'm right here, darling." I pull her tight against me, and as she sobs in my arms, I begin to cry too. I have not cried in a long, long time, and now that I've started, I cannot stop. I cry for Callie, and for everyone else who has suffered because of me. For Doku and his family, for Gavin and Bella and Danny.

Most of all, for Danny.

"I want to see my grandpa," she says. "I want to go home."

"You will." I wrap my arm around her waist and haul her to her feet. "But not yet."

CHAPTER 35
JO

Jo banged through the stairwell door, strode into the second-floor hospital ward, and headed straight to the unit desk. "Where's Callie Yount?" she asked the nurse.

"She's in Room 201, but let me call the doctor first. Hey, you can't just go in there. Wait!"

Jo was already headed down the hall, to Room 201. She gave two brisk knocks and pushed into the room, only to stop just inside the threshold.

The girl was sound asleep in bed.

The room was lit by only one dim nightstand lamp, and in the gloom, Jo saw Luther Yount hunched in a chair at the bedside. He was wearing a flannel pajama top, and his white hair was an uncombed swirl on his head. Like Jo, he must have come straight from his bed, but he was wide awake now and glaring at Jo.

"Not now. She needs to rest," he said. "Don't wake her."

"Where was she found? How did she get here?"

"Later. All you need to know is that she's fine. They didn't hurt her."

"*Who* didn't hurt her?"

"Maggie can tell you the rest. Talk to her."

"Where is she?"

"She just left. You might still be able to catch her."

Damn straight I'm going to catch her.

Jo ran down the stairwell to the lobby and dashed out of the hospital entrance, into the parking lot. There she spotted her quarry a few rows away, unlocking her pickup truck.

"Maggie!" Jo called out. "Maggie Bird!"

The woman turned, and the sigh she released sent a cloud of steam into the air. "Please. Not now."

"Yes, *now*. You should have called me the instant you knew."

"I did call you. Isn't that why you're here?"

"It was *our* job to rescue the girl."

"And you would have shown up with your sirens screaming. I didn't know what the situation would be. It had to be a quiet extraction."

"Now we've lost any chance of an arrest."

Maggie shook her head. "You never had a chance. Trust me, the people who took her are long gone from here."

"Are you going to tell me who they are?"

"If I knew their names, I would."

They faced each other in the silence of a winter's night, and the condensation from their breaths swirled and snarled together into a single entwined cloud. They might be living in the same town and breathing the same air, but there would always be a gulf between them because Maggie was the outsider, an alien creature from a world far beyond the familiar confines of Purity, Maine. One day they might become friends, they might even learn to trust each other, but this was not that day. For now, they faced each other as opponents, in a game whose rules Jo was still trying to understand.

"What was this kidnapping all about?" said Jo. "You need to tell me."

"What I *need* right now is my bed." Maggie opened the door to her pickup and climbed into the driver's seat. "Come see me tomorrow, Jo. I'll tell you what I can." She started the engine and drove away.

"What does that mean, 'what I can'?" Jo yelled.

Of course, there was no answer. With Maggie Bird, there almost never was.

Jo stood alone in the parking lot, watching the taillights fade into the darkness. A snowflake fluttered down, and then another, like wounded butterflies tumbling from the sky. It was 2:00 a.m., she was cold, and there was nothing she wanted to do more than to go home and crawl back into bed, but this falling snow would soon cover any tire marks at the house where Callie Yount had been held. With every minute that passed, vital clues about the kidnapping were vanishing beneath a blanket of white. She had a crime scene to process, the evidence team to muster, and questions—so many questions—to answer. Her bed, as tempting as it was, would have to wait, because the citizens of Purity counted on her. She might not be brilliant, but she knew that what really mattered to the people in her town was the day-to-day certainty that they could depend on her to do her job. So, with a sigh, she climbed into her car and did what she always did.

Jo Thibodeau got to work.

CHAPTER 36
BELLA

She stood at the window, looking out at her garden. It was raining again, the cold, spitting rain that was so common in this remote corner of Scotland, but she could see the signs that spring would come early this year. It was only February, and the daffodils had already sent up their green shoots; by March, the garden would be awash in drifts of golden blooms. The earth was changing fast. The great rivers of Europe and Asia were drying to trickles, the rain forests of South America were burning, and in the Pacific, coral atolls were vanishing under the rising seas. Everywhere, new turmoil simmered, and that meant there was money to be made, money with which one could tilt foreign elections, inflame hatreds old and new, and ignite revolutions.

When Bella was a girl, she did not appreciate gardens, but now that she nurtured one of her own, she realized she was looking at a microcosm of the larger world, where survival was never guaranteed, where competitors lurked unnoticed in the shade, waiting for the chance to overtake and smother you. That was a fundamental principle she'd learned from her father: someone was always waiting to take your place, so one must do whatever was necessary to grasp the advantage.

Even if it meant abducting a fourteen-year-old girl.

She knew her mother would not have approved of the tactic, but Camilla was no longer here. Six years ago, she succumbed to a brain tumor that all the money in the world could not have cured. Now Bella was on her own, no longer held back by her mother's benevolent counsel, and she'd done what was needed to ensure her own place at the table. When it came to surviving, she'd already had the best possible teacher. She'd made use of the foundation her father laid down and built a network all her own.

She heard a knock on the door and turned to look at her assistant. "And?" she asked him.

"The girl's been released from the hospital. She's back at home with her grandfather."

"And our team?"

"Already on the plane home."

"Then you can release their payment."

"Of course."

Her assistant left the room, and she turned back to the window, back to the view of her garden. The rain had picked up, the drops now mixed with sleet that clattered on the brick walkway. She wondered if it was snowing where Maggie lived. She'd looked up the town of Purity on the map and seen that the state of Maine was tucked up next to Canada. It was an odd place to retire to, there in the frozen north. She imagined a landscape of blizzards and snowdrifts and biting winds, a hard place to live in the winter.

Maggie should not be alive at all. She should have died in Como, with a bullet in her brain, and Bella had had every intention of carrying out that execution. But at that moment in the tower, when she'd held the gun to Maggie's head and looked into her eyes, she could not pull the trigger. She'd realized that Maggie was a victim as well, that her life, too, had disintegrated in an explosion of flames and ash over the Mediterranean. Phillip Hardwicke would not have hesitated to pull the trigger, but Bella chose not to.

Perhaps she was more like her mother than she realized.

I spared you that time, Maggie. If we ever meet again, I can't guarantee I will be as generous.

She did not think they would ever meet again, although they would certainly be aware of each other's existence, even as they maintained their wary distance, Maggie in her obscure village on the coast of Maine, and Bella in her world of shadows and anonymity. Her father's world. At fifteen, she may have been an awkward teenager, but she was never clueless. She'd listened and learned and absorbed the lessons Phillip taught her. She knew what it took to survive, and those lessons would serve her well in the years to come as she clawed back the money that Diana Ward stole, as she spread out her tentacles and consolidated her power.

Was it a mistake to let Maggie live? She didn't know. If her father were alive, he'd be berating her for letting Maggie walk away, and one day, she might well regret that moment of weakness and sentimentality. If it was a mistake, it was one that could be remedied.

I know where you live, Maggie. I can always change my mind.

CHAPTER 37
MAGGIE

With the five of us sitting around my dining table, it seems as if life has returned to normal. At 5:00 p.m., Ingrid and Lloyd were the first to show up unannounced at my door, bearing a Pyrex dish with moussaka, still warm from the oven. Ten minutes later, Ben arrived with his offering of Persian rice and lamb, and then Declan walked in with green beans and slivered almonds. A bounty of casseroles is what friends bring you in a crisis, if you've just lost your spouse or broken your leg, and here they are, my four closest friends, their visit unexpected but welcome. It seems the band really is back together, once again sharing recipes and gossip, a head-spinning return to normalcy. Bangkok and Lake Como now seem as distant to me as a bad dream.

But those things did happen, and now Diana is dead. According to Declan's sources, the Como police are saying that the body of an American woman, found at an abandoned church with a bullet hole in her head, was probably murdered by local gangsters after she unwittingly stumbled into their lair. That's the theory they'll probably hold to, because digging for the truth requires too much effort. It usually does.

"And now we have a new problem to deal with," Ben says.

"Which one?" Ingrid says.

"What to do about Bella Hardwicke."

They all look at me, because I am the one who actually knows Bella—or knew her in a different lifetime, before she was tempered by loss and grief into the woman who held a gun to my head. She could have killed me there, in the bell tower, and she had every reason to want me dead. Instead, she chose to walk away. I have to believe that deep inside her, buried within all the scar tissue, is the fifteen-year-old girl I once knew and liked.

"Bella is not our problem," I say.

"She's Phillip Hardwicke's successor," says Ingrid.

"But she isn't Phillip Hardwicke."

"Then what is she?"

I don't know the answer. All I know is, she could have killed me, and she didn't. Her father would not have been so merciful.

"It's not up to us," I say. "After all, we *are* retired."

"Maggie's right," says Declan. "We've informed the Agency about Bella, so the ball's now in their court. Let them deal with her."

"We could help," says Ingrid. "If only they'd ask."

And that's what we must learn to deal with: Our place in a world that sees us as used up and irrelevant. This new generation looks only to the future, with little regard for the past and what it could teach them. What *we* could teach them.

I bring out five glasses and the just-opened bottle of thirty-year-old Longmorn whisky, a gift from Ingrid, who managed to ferret out a source in Leith, Scotland. This bottle is the signal that our conversation is about to get serious. I hand the Longmorn first to Declan, who has said very little all evening. He's also avoiding my gaze, because he's still feeling wounded that I went rogue and took that detour to Italy without telling him, even though he knows the reason why I did it. This was my battle to fight, and I did not want him hurt in the cross fire.

But here is the consequence: It will take time for Declan to forgive me, time for us to rebuild the trust between us. Add it to the long list of issues that Declan and I will need to settle between us.

Lloyd raises his whisky glass in a toast. *"Cin cin! Alla vostre salute!"*

"Cin cin!" we chant, and take our first sips.

My perimeter alarm goes off.

"Who are you expecting?" Ben asks.

I rise from the table. "I think we all know who this is."

I open the front door, and there she stands, her hand poised to knock. Jo Thibodeau looks like she has not slept in days. Dark circles ring her eyes, her ponytail has fallen apart, and limp strands of blonde hair have escaped and hang loose around her face. I can almost smell the exhaustion wafting off her.

"Ms. Bird," she says. "I have questions."

"Of course you do. Come in."

She follows me into the dining room and looks around the table at my guests. "Why am I not surprised to find another meeting of the Martini Club?"

Declan, ever the gentleman, pulls out a chair. "Please, Chief Thibodeau. Have a seat and join us."

"And a glass of whisky?" offers Lloyd.

"I'm still on duty," she says.

"Do you ever go *off* duty?" I ask.

"Ms. Bird, can we step into another room to talk?"

"These are my friends. I'd like them to hear whatever it is we say."

Thibodeau sighs. She's too weary to argue with me tonight, and she knows she would not prevail, so she drops into the chair that Declan has pulled out for her. Under the dining room lights, her face looks washed out and older than her thirty-two years. In the short time I've known her, I've come to appreciate her doggedness. She's not a sprinter but a marathon runner who just keeps moving forward, one foot in front of the other, always focused on her objective. She can't outsmart us but she can outlast us, and she would be a problem if we were on opposing sides. For the moment, we are not, and I think we both know this.

"The state police have looked into that text message you received, about where to find the girl," she says. "They're unable to trace who sent it to you."

"I told you they wouldn't be able to," I say.

"Do *you* know who sent the text?"

"The kidnappers, I presume."

"Why would they suddenly reveal Callie's location? Did someone pay a ransom?"

"Not that I'm aware of."

She looks around the table. "Does *anyone* here know?"

"How would we?" Lloyd says innocently.

"Will I ever get a straight answer from you people?"

"You look like you could use this," Declan says, and with almost magical sleight of hand, he slides a glass of whisky in front of her.

Thibodeau looks down at the glass of caramel-colored temptation, and we all watch, wondering if she'll succumb. "What the hell," she mutters. She takes a gulp and immediately bursts out coughing. Clearly she's not a seasoned whisky drinker, but with a little encouragement, she'll learn.

"How is Callie doing?" Declan asks.

Thibodeau wipes her mouth. "She's fine, considering. They didn't hurt her."

"What does she recall?"

"They kept her blindfolded, so she never saw their faces. Based on their voices, it was a man and a woman. They fed her, kept her warm, never threatened her. We have no idea why they did it." She looks at me. "Maybe you know?"

I do know. Callie was never meant to be harmed; she was merely a means to an end, a way for Bella to force me into the open. But that information will be of little use to the police, because the people who kidnapped Callie are now beyond Jo Thibodeau's reach. So is the woman who ordered the abduction. How could a small-town cop, working in a quiet corner of Maine, ever tackle the Phillip Hardwickes of the world? This is why I choose to live here, and why my friends live here. For most of our lives, we served our country fighting on the covert battlefields of the world, bringing down monsters like Hardwicke. Now we want a quiet life. We deserve a quiet life.

"I'm sorry," I say. "There's really nothing more I can tell you."

"Yeah. That's what I thought you'd say."

Her radio crackles to life, and we hear the dispatcher's voice: *All units, ten-thirty-one, ten-thirty-one. Location two-four-two Birch Road . . .*

Thibodeau doesn't pause to say goodbye. In an instant she's on her feet and headed out the door. Seconds later, we hear her vehicle roar away down my driveway.

"Ten-thirty-one," says Ingrid. "That's their radio code for a crime in progress. Perhaps we could be of assistance. It would be our civic duty, don't you think?"

We consider that question as we once again pass around the bottle of Longmorn and refill our whisky glasses. *Crime in progress.* Is there any village, any town, where these words do not apply? We have learned that even our small town is not protected from the woes of the world. If a nuclear bomb falls on Washington, the prevailing winds will bring radioactive dust straight to our safe little corner. If countries collapse in Europe, or war erupts in East Asia, the ripples of devastation will eventually wash up in Purity, Maine. We are not immune. No one is.

"Whatever it is, I'm sure Jo Thibodeau can handle it," I say. "And if she needs our help, she knows where to find us."

AUTHOR'S NOTE

The Spy Coast was inspired by an odd little secret I discovered years ago about my small Maine town. Soon after we moved here, my physician husband opened a medical practice, and when he asked his new patients about their prior occupations, this was how the conversation sometimes went:

Doctor: "What did you do for a living?"

Patient: "I used to work for the government."

Doctor: "And what did you do for the government?"

Patient: "I can't talk about it."

After about the third or fourth time this happened, my husband realized there was something very peculiar about the retirees who live here. A local Realtor finally revealed the secret: "Oh, they were all CIA." We discovered that, just on our short street, we had two retired spies as neighbors. Why have so many of them congregated in this town of only five thousand inhabitants? Is it because they feel safely anonymous here in the woodsy north, far from any nuclear targets? Is it because our town was featured prominently (or so our Realtor told us) in a retirement magazine for spies? Or because Maine has been used so often as a location for safe houses in the past? These are among the theories I've heard, but I've never managed to get a straight answer because the people who actually know that answer can't—or won't—talk about it.

Because of their age and their silver hair, we may not give these retirees a second glance. They are simply our neighbors who rub shoulders with us in the local coffee shop, push their carts down the grocery store aisles as we do, and wish us good morning at the post office. They blend in so well that we never stop to wonder about who they *used* to be, or what secrets they'll guard till the grave.

Unassuming retirees with secret past lives make fascinating characters to explore, and that's how *The Spy Coast* was born. I wanted to write about spies who *don't* look like James Bond but instead are like my neighbors, quietly living as utterly ordinary retirees . . . until the past comes back to haunt them, and they're forced to call on old skills they thought they'd never have to use again.

ACKNOWLEDGMENTS

It's always daunting to breathe life into a new cast of characters, and I'm grateful to everyone who helped me introduce Maggie Bird and the Martini Club to the world. Meg Ruley, Rebecca Scherer, and the incomparable team at the Jane Rotrosen literary agency have been there for me from the start, when *The Spy Coast* was merely a flicker of an idea. Through the ups and downs of my decades-long writing career, the Rotrosen team has cheered me on, offering advice, sympathy, and the occasional martini, and they have never discouraged me from pursuing even my most outlandish book ideas. That freedom to stretch my wings is why, all these years later, I'm still happily writing.

My US editor, Grace Doyle, helped me deepen the story with her wise and sensitive guidance, and I thank her, Allyson Cullinan, Megan Beattie, and the entire team at Thomas & Mercer for their embrace of *The Spy Coast*. Thanks also to my superb UK editor, Sarah Adams, and to Alison Barrow, Larry Finlay, Jen Porter, Richard Ogle, and the always-enthusiastic team at Transworld.

Closer to home, I owe a big thanks to Dana Strout, who introduced me to the pleasures of sipping a truly fine whisky, to the ever-supportive ladies of my breakfast club, to my son Adam for his ready expertise in firearms, and to my son Josh for his magic with a camera. And as always, I thank my husband, Jacob, who's stood by me through thick and thin. Thirty-three years ago, we took a leap together into the unknown, and we moved to Maine. How lucky we are to call this place home.

ABOUT THE AUTHOR

Photo © 2023 Josh Gerritsen

International bestselling author **Tess Gerritsen** began to write fiction whilst on maternity leave as a physician. She published her first novel in 1987 and has since sold over forty million copies of her books in forty countries. Her series featuring homicide detective Jane Rizzoli and medical examiner Maura Isles inspired the television series *Rizzoli and Isles*, starring Angie Harmon and Sasha Alexander. Now retired from medicine, she lives in Maine and writes full time.